Books by J. A. Jance

Joanna Brady Mysteries

DESERT HEAT • TOMBSTONE COURAGE
SHOOT/DON'T SHOOT • DEAD TO RIGHTS
SKELETON CANYON • RATTLESNAKE CROSSING
OUTLAW MOUNTAIN • DEVIL'S CLAW
PARADISE LOST • PARTNER IN CRIME • EXIT WOUNDS
DEAD WRONG • DAMAGE CONTROL • FIRE AND ICE

J.P. Beaumont Mysteries

UNTIL PROVEN GUILTY • INJUSTICE FOR ALL
TRIAL BY FURY • TAKING THE FIFTH
IMPROBABLE CAUSE • A MORE PERFECT UNION
DISMISSED WITH PREJUDICE • MINOR IN POSSESSION
PAYMENT IN KIND • WITHOUT DUE PROCESS
FAILURE TO APPEAR • LYING IN WAIT
NAME WITHHELD • BREACH OF DUTY • BIRDS OF PREY
PARTNER IN CRIME • LONG TIME GONE
JUSTICE DENIED • FIRE AND ICE • BETRAYAL OF TRUST

and

HOUR OF THE HUNTER
KISS OF THE BEES
DAY OF THE DEAD
EDGE OF EVIL
QUEEN OF THE NIGHT

SHOOT
DON'T
SHOOT

J. A. JANCE

HARPER

An Imprint of HarperCollinsPublishers

This is a work of fiction. Names, characters, places, and incidents are drawn from the author's imagination or are used fictitiously and are not to be construed as real. Any resemblance to actual events, locales, organizations, or persons, living or dead, is entirely coincidental.

HARPER

An Imprint of HarperCollins*Publishers*
10 East 53rd Street
New York, New York 10022-5299

Copyright © 1995 by J. A. Jance
Excerpt from *Fire and Ice* copyright © 2009 by J. A. Jance
ISBN 978-0-06-177480-5

First Harper Premium paperback printing: July 2009
First Avon Books paperback printing: October 1996
First William Morrow hardcover printing: July 1995

HarperCollins® and Harper® are registered trademarks of Harper-Collins Publishers.

Printed in the United States of America

Visit Harper paperbacks on the World Wide Web at
www.harpercollins.com

10   9   8   7   6   5

SHOOT
DON'T
SHOOT

PROLOGUE

LYING HOT and sleepless in the narrow upper bunk, nine-year-old Ceci Grijalva knew her mother was leaving long before she left, long before the outside door opened and closed. When it did, Ceci pulled back a corner of the sheet that served as a curtain and peered out at the weed-infested yard that separated their dingy duplex from the one next door. Moments later, Serena Grijalva's pilfered grocery cart, stacked high with dirty laundry, rattled past the window toward the potholed gravel track that passed for a street inside the dreary complex known as Esperanza Village.

Hope Village. Even a little kid could tell that the name was a bad joke. Hopeless was more like it.

Ceci dropped back on her thin mattress and lay there hot and miserable. Back home in Bisbee where they used to live or down in Douglas with Grandma Grijalva, the weather would be cooler

1

now. But not here in Phoenix. Peoria, really. The way her mother had talked about it, Phoenix was one huge, magical city—a wonderful place. Ceci had discovered that it was actually a bunch of places—Phoenix, Glendale, Peoria, Sun City. She could never tell where one stopped and another began, although the kids who had always lived there seemed to know—and they made fun of Ceci when she didn't.

Phoenix was hot. And the cooler didn't work. Even when it was running, it didn't do much good, and it smelled awful—like something green and moldy. Ceci hated that smell.

She lay on the bed, tossing restlessly. The knowledge that her mother was gone kept Ceci awake while her little brother, Pablo, snored peacefully in the bottom bunk. Out in the living room she heard the steady drone of the un-watched television set. Just before she left, Serena had turned on the TV.

She always did that. Ceci knew the blaring television set was a trick. Her mother thought if the kids woke up in the night and heard a mumble of voices from the other room, they'd think Serena was out there watching a program when in reality she'd probably been gone for hours, leaving the two children alone. Again.

Finally, careful not to disturb her brother, the sleepless child pulled her rosary beads out from under her pillow and climbed down from the top bunk. Clutching the beads close to her chest, she tiptoed out into the living room and turned off the TV.

There was no lamp in the sparsely furnished room, and Ceci didn't bother to switch on the overhead light. With the room illuminated by the streetlight on the corner outside, she made her way to the sweat-stained armchair one of Serena's pickup-driving boyfriends had dragged home from a pile of unsold refuse after a Sun City estate sale. Moving the chair close enough to the window to see out, Cecelia curled up inside it. This was where she sat and waited when her mother went out late at night. This was where she sat and worried. And even though she tried to stay awake, she sometimes fell into a fitful sleep. Once Serena had come in and found her there, but usually Ceci managed to rouse herself. Serena's cart clattering back through the yard would give the child enough warning to turn the TV set back on and scurry into her bed.

Ceci sniffed the air. Serena had been gone for some time, but the heavy scent of her perfume and hair spray still lingered in the room. Ceci shook her head. Even though the grocery cart had been full of dirty clothes when Serena left the house, Ceci wasn't fooled. The laundry was only an excuse—almost as much of a trick as the blaring television set. If washing clothes was all her mother had in mind, she could have used the laundry room right there in the complex. For that one—the one next to the manager's apartment—she wouldn't have needed hair spray or perfume.

Serena always said that the machines in the Esperanza Village laundry room weren't any good. She refused to use them, claiming that the clothes never came clean enough, and that the dryers were too slow. That's why she always took the laundry four blocks down the street to the WE-DO-YU-DO Washateria. Ceci may have been only nine, but she understood that that story wasn't the truth, either. Not the whole truth. The real answer lay in the business next door to the laundry—a place called the Roundhouse Bar and Grill.

Sometimes, on weekends, Ceci and Pablo would go along with Serena to do the wash. Usually the two children would be left on their own in the laundry while their mother went next door to get some change. That's what she always told them—that she was going for change—even though Pablo had pointed out the change machine right there beside the soap machine. Once Serena disappeared into the bar, she'd be gone for a long time—for hours. When she came back, her hair would smell of cigarette smoke, and her breath would smell like beer. By then Ceci and Pablo would already have removed the clothes from the dryers, folded them, and loaded them back into the waiting cart.

Often it would be late afternoon or even early evening by the time they started the four-block walk home. Ceci and Pablo would be hungry—grateful to munch on whatever treats Serena happened to bring out to them from the bar—potato chips or peanuts or even hunks of tough beef jerky. Sometimes a nice man from the bar would come find them and bring them hamburgers with real french fries.

Chances were, as Serena pushed the cart along, she would be singing or giggling or both. She never really walked straight after she'd been inside the Roundhouse for an hour or so. Ceci would spend the whole trip home praying to the Holy Mother that they wouldn't meet any of her friends from school along the way.

Sitting in the stifling living room, waiting for her mother to return, Ceci Grijalva felt incredibly lonely. She missed her father. Even though her mother and father used to fight a lot, she still missed him. And she missed her grandmother, too. The happiest hours of Ceci's life had been spent at the rickety table in her Grandmother Grijalva's tiny house watching the old woman make tortillas. Grandma was blind, from something Ceci could never remember, something that started with a *g*. But even blind, the old woman's practiced hands still remembered how to make tortillas—how much flour and water to put into the bowl, how to pat the soft, white dough into perfect circles, how long to leave them on the hot griddle, and how to pluck them off with her thumb and finger without ever getting burned.

Waiting for her mother to return, Ceci ached for the comfort of her grandmother's ample breast and wondered if and when she and Pablo would ever see their father's mother again. Serena had said they might go down to Douglas at Christmastime, but Ceci didn't see how that was possible. Douglas was more than two hundred miles away. They didn't have a car. Two hundred miles was too far to push a grocery cart.

Blinking back tears of loneliness, Ceci fingered the beads that lay in her lap, the ones she usually kept hidden under her pillow. Grandmother Grijalva had given her the string of black beads last year when she made her first communion. Nana had told Ceci that saying Hail Marys would help her feel better, no matter what was wrong. In the months since Ceci's mother had left her father and brought the children to Phoenix, Ceci had often used the hidden beads to put herself to sleep, slipping them out from under the pillow only after the lights were off and her mother had left the room.

Ceci didn't really need to hide them from her mother. Serena was sort of a Catholic, even though she hadn't been to mass since they moved. The real problem was Serena's mother, Ernestina Duffy. Nana Duffy, as she liked the children to call her. Nana Duffy was a Baptist, Ceci could never remember what kind, and she was always telling Ceci and Pablo that the pope was evil. Ceci didn't believe it.

"Holy Mary, mother of God . . ." she whispered. As the beads slipped through her fingers, Ceci's eyes grew heavy. Gradually she drifted off into a troubled sleep. Only this time the return of her mother's clattering grocery cart didn't wake her. Pablo did. He was standing in front of her in his underwear, frowning, both hands on his hips.

"How come you're sleeping there?" he demanded.

Ceci's eyes popped open. It was morning. Where the streetlight had glowed hours before, now bright late-summer sunshine filled the window. She shifted stiffly in the chair. The foot that had been curled under her was sound asleep. As soon as she moved it, needles and pins shot up her leg.

"Where's Mom?" she asked.

Pablo turned on the TV set and squatted in front of it. "I dunno," he said. "Maybe she already went to work. I'm hungry."

"She isn't here?" Ceci asked.

Pablo didn't answer. When the needles and pins went away enough so Ceci could walk, she limped into Serena's bedroom. There was no sign of the laundry basket. Hurrying to the back door, she looked outside. The grocery cart wasn't where it belonged, either. Dismayed, Ceci realized her mother had never come home from the WE-DO-YU-DO Washateria.

Ceci felt sick, but there was no phone in the house; no way for her to call someone and ask for help. She did the only thing that seemed reasonable at the time.

"Turn off the cartoons, Pepe," she said. "Get dressed. We've got to get ready for school."

ONE

You never should have gone out with him in the first place," Lael Weaver Gastone told her thirty-year-old daughter, Rhonda. "You should have figured out from the very beginning that a guy like that would be trouble, and you certainly shouldn't have married him."

Holding her hands in her lap, Rhonda Norton examined her tender fingertips. She was so on edge that she had chewed the nails off all the way down to the quick. "How was I supposed to know that?" she asked, trying her best not to cry.

Lael looked up from the thumbnail sketch she was working on. The bar of pastel stopped scratching on the rough surface of the Sabertooth paper.

"Oh, for God's sake, Rhonda. How dumb can you be?" Lael demanded. "If a married professor starts dating an unmarried undergraduate, you can pretty well figure the man's a jackass. And so's the girl for that matter."

Rhonda Weaver Norton's cheeks reddened with anger. The tears retreated. "Thanks, Mom," she said. "I always know I can count on you for sympathy."

"You can always count on me for a straight answer," Lael corrected. "Now tell me, why exactly are you here?"

Rhonda looked around the spacious, well-lit studio her stepfather, Jean Paul Gastone, had built as a place for his lovely new wife to pursue her artistic endeavors. Rhonda interpreted that cluttered but isolated work space as an act of self-serving generosity on Jean Paul's part. Lael had always been messy. If nothing else, the physical separation of the studio from the main house would help keep most of that mess localized. That way the main house—a breathtakingly canti-levered mountaintop mansion—could continue to look picture-perfect, as if the photographers from *House Beautiful* or *Architectural Digest* were due at any moment.

The place where Lael and Jean Paul lived now was a far cry from the way Rhonda and her mother had lived when Rhonda was a child. She and the free-spirited, starving artist Lael Weaver had lived a nomadic existence that took them from place to place, from drafty furnished rooms to countless roach-infested apartments. This million-dollar-plus architectural wonder was perched on a steep hillside overlooking one of Sedona, Arizona's, most photographed red-rocked cliffs. The fourteen-foot floor-to-ceiling windows offered a clear and unobstructed view.

All the furnishings in both the house and studio had been tastefully chosen by someone with an eye for beauty. Rhonda didn't have to look at any of the labels to know that all the assembled pieces were name brand, as were the clothes on her mother's back. That was far different from the past as well. Rhonda had spent her school years living with the daily humiliation of wearing the secondhand clothing her mother had bought at thrift stores and rummage sales. She had endured the steady taunts from other children who somehow knew she ate the free lunches offered at school. And she recalled all too well how embarrassed she had been every time her mother sent her to the grocery store with a fistful of food stamps instead of money.

Lael's life had taken a definite turn for the better. In the last few years, her oddball pastels had finally started to sell. She had met Jean Paul Gastone at a gallery opening when he had stopped by to say how much he admired her work. Now they were married—seemingly happily—and living a gracious and beautiful life together. Rhonda couldn't help envying the idea of her mother living happily ever after. Too bad things hadn't worked out nearly that well for Lael's daughter.

In the course of a long, lingering silence, Lael returned to her sketch. With nothing more to say, Rhonda once more examined the room. She realized with a start that her mother's studio—that one room, not counting either the private bath or the convenient kitchenette that had been built off to one side—was larger than her entire studio apartment.

She had moved into that god-awful, low-life complex only two days earlier. Already she hated it. But she had come face-to-face with stark economic reality. Rhonda Norton was a newly separated, unemployed woman, with no recent work history and only marginally salable skills. Her university work was sixteen credits shy of a bachelor's degree with a major in American history, a curriculum that didn't have much going for it in the world of business. As a consequence, that tiny upstairs apartment facing directly into the afternoon sun was all she could afford. In fact, it was more than she could afford.

Confronted with the obvious dichotomy between her mother's newfound wealth and her own newfound poverty, Rhonda Norton felt doubly impoverished. And defeated. It would have been easy to give up, to make like Chief Joseph, leader of the Nez Percé, and say to all the world, "I will fight no more forever."

"Well?" Lael prompted impatiently, dragging Rhonda back to the present and to the real issue at hand.

She dropped her eyes once more. "I'm afraid," she said softly.

"Afraid of what?"

Rhonda dreaded saying the words aloud, especially since she didn't think her mother had ever been afraid of anything in her whole life. As far as Rhonda was concerned, Lael had always seemed as brave and daring as the brilliant greens, blues, and reds she was swiftly daubing onto the paper.

"Afraid of what?" Lael asked again.

"Of him," Rhonda answered. "Of Dean. He threatened me. He told me that if I went through with the divorce, he'd see me in hell before he'd pay me a single dime of alimony or give me a property settlement."

"Oh, hell," Lael said. "The man's just pissed because he got passed over for department head and then they shipped him off to that other campus, wherever that is."

"The ASU West campus is on Thunderbird, Mom," Rhonda returned quietly. "But he's not bluffing. He means it. He won't give me a dime."

Lael Weaver Gastone was incensed. "If it's the money, don't worry about it. He's bluffing. Jean Paul and I could always help out if it came to that, but it won't. You'll see. The courts will make him pay."

But Rhonda was no longer looking at her mother. She had dropped her gaze once more. "It's not just the money, Mom. I don't care about that." She took a deep breath. "I'm afraid he'll kill me, Mom." She paused and bit her lip. "He hits me sometimes," she added almost in a whisper.

"He what?" Lael asked. "I can't hear you if you don't speak up."

"He hits me," Rhonda repeated raggedly. "Hard." A single tear leaked from her eye and slipped down her cheek. "And he told me the other day when I was packing that he'd kill me if I go through with it—with getting a divorce."

Slowly, without looking directly at her mother's face, Rhonda Weaver Norton unbuttoned the top three buttons of her cardigan sweater; then she slipped the soft knit material down over her shoulder. Under the sweater her bare shoulder and back were discolored by a mass of green-and-purple bruises. Lael gasped when she saw them.

"You let him do this to you?" she demanded. "Why didn't you say so in the first place?"

Blushing furiously, Rhonda pulled her sweater back up. "The first two times he promised he'd never do it again, so I dropped the charges. This time I haven't . . . not yet."

Lael tossed the piece of blue pastel in the general direction of her box, then slammed the lid shut. "And you're not going to, either. Come on. We'll go talk to Jean Paul. He'll know what to do."

HE WAITED until midnight. Not that midnight had any special significance, other than the fact that it was the time of day he liked best—the time when he felt most at home.

He thought about what he was doing as a bridge—a ritual bridge—between the past and the future, between the women who had already died and the ones who soon would. Although he didn't think of himself as particularly superstitious, he always performed the midnight ceremony in exactly the same way, starting with closing all the blinds. Only when they were all safely closed did he light the candle.

Once upon a time, he had used incense, but his damn fool of a landlady in Sacramento had reported him to the cops. She had turned him in because she thought he was smoking dope in her precious downstairs apartment. That was right after Lois Hart, and he was nervous as hell. When the young cop showed up on the doorstep and knocked on his door, he'd been so scared that he almost peed his pants. He'd managed to talk his way out of that one—barely—but he'd also learned his lesson. No more incense. From that day on, he'd used only candles.

As the wick of the scented candle caught fire, he breathed in the sweet, cinnamon scent. He preferred cinnamon over all the others because they always reminded him of his grandmother's freshly baked pumpkin pies. Cinnamon candles were easy to come by during the holidays, and he usually stocked up so he wouldn't run out during the rest of the year.

After setting the burning candle in the center of his kitchen table, he went around the whole house and switched off all the other lights. Turning off the lights slowly, one by one, always added to his sense of anticipation. He liked finishing his preparations in darkened rooms with the only light coming from the flickering glow of a single candle. Everybody always said candlelight made things more romantic. No argument there.

Next came the music. That was always the same, too—Mantovani. In her later years, his mother had kept only one Mantovani album, and she had played it over and over until he thought he would lose his mind. The record had worn out eventually, thank God. So had the record player, for that matter, but when he had wanted to play the familiar music once again, he'd had no trouble finding it.

Now he used a cassette player and cheap cassettes that he picked up for a buck or two apiece at used-record stores. He himself didn't care all that much for Mantovani, certainly not enough to pay full retail.

By the time he turned on the music, his eyes had adjusted to the dim light. With the soft strains of violins playing soothingly in the background, and with his whole body burning with anticipation, he would finally allow himself to go to the bottom right-hand corner of his closet to retrieve his precious faux alabaster jewelry box.

The box wasn't inherently valuable. What gave it worth was where it came from, what it meant. Like that single scratched Mantovani album, the jewelry box had been one of his mother's prized possessions. When he was twelve, he had bought it for her as a Mother's Day present. He had paid for it with money he earned delivering newspapers.

His mother had loved the box, treasured it. When she died, though, the gift had reverted to the giver. He remembered how, on the day she unwrapped it, his mother had run her finger over the smooth, cool stonelike stuff, how she had admired the figure of the young Grecian woman

whose delicate image had been carved in trans-
luscent relief on the hinged top.

He looked down now at the graceful young
woman in the revealing, loosely flowing gown.
His mother had thought her very beautiful. As a
matter of fact, so did he. In a lifetime of quarrel-
ing with his mother, the Greek maiden's virginal
beauty was one of the few things the two of them
had ever agreed upon. The girl's obvious innocence was one of the reasons he used the box as
an integral part of his midnight ritual. He liked
the symbolism. The other reason for using it was
equally satisfying in the same way Mantovani
was—the box had belonged to his mother. Had
she known the use he made of it, the knowledge
would have made her crazy, if she hadn't been
already. That aspect of the ceremony always added
a whole other dimension to his amusement. He
had never loved his mother, never even liked her.

As he carried the box to the kitchen table, his
hands shook with anticipation. His whole body
quivered. But he held back. Instead of giving in
to his growing physical need, he forced himself
to sit down and wait. He calmed himself by staring into the flickering glow of the lighted candle,
by watching its muted, soothing light reflected in
the satiny finish of the jewelry box.

He liked knowing that he could control the
urge, that he could turn it off and on at will. He
prided himself on being able to go all the way to
the edge and then pull himself back if he had to,
although sometimes, like tonight, waiting was

almost more than he could bear. It reminded him of the game he used to play with his mother's old dog, Prudence. He'd dish up the food and put it on the floor, but instead of letting the dog eat it, he'd put her on a down stay and make her wait for it, sometimes for hours. And if she tried to sneak over to it without permission, he'd beat the crap out of her. It had been great training for Prudence. It had taught her the meaning of self-control. It had taught him the same valuable lesson.

So he sat at the table, in front of the flickering candle, and waited for however long it took for his breathing to slow, for his heart to stop pounding, and for the painful bulge in his pants to disappear. Only after he was totally under control did he allow himself to lift the hinged lid and look inside at the folded treasures waiting there—six pairs of panties.

Each pair had its own size, shape, and color. He could have sorted through the box blindfolded and still known which was which because he knew them intimately, more by feel than looks.

Except for the beige ones, which he quickly laid aside, he always stored the underwear according to a LIFO (last in/first out) style of inventory—a system he had learned about way back in college. That was when he was so naive that he had wanted to be an accountant just like his daddy, when he was still growing up and all gung ho on following in his father's footsteps. Screw that!

Even though the box was open, still he delayed, postponing for a few minutes longer the moment of gratification. It struck him as interesting that each pair was so different from all the others. But then, since the women were so different, that was only to be expected. Every time he sorted through his collection, he felt like a decorated veteran examining his medals. Each trophy brought to mind a name, a place, and a time. The sounds, the feelings, replayed themselves as vividly as if it were happening all over again. He was sure his memory did a better job at replaying the details than any of that virtual reality stuff he kept reading about in the newspaper.

Finally, satisfied that he had waited long enough, he picked up the first pair—white cotton briefs so worn that the material was see-through thin. Holding it to his face, he closed his eyes and breathed in and out through the soft folds of material. With each breath he remembered everything about that Mexican girl with long, dark hair and big tits. Serena was her name. She had been anything *but* serene out there on the mountain. He smiled again remembering her good looks and those soft, voluptuous breasts.

He didn't usually target women he knew. He often had no idea what any of the women looked like when he first chose them. At the time he selected them, they were only names on paper. Due to the luck of the draw, some of them turned out to be a whole lot better looking than others. In fact, one had been a real dog. In Serena's case he had created the opportunity rather than waiting for it to present itself. It had worked like a charm. Not only that, other than Rochelle, Serena Grijalva had been the best looking of the bunch.

Laying Serena's underwear aside, he picked up the next pair. Jockey, the label said. Whoever heard of Jockey for women? What a queer idea! And then he giggled because the thought itself was so funny. It figured. These had belonged to Constance Fredricks, and she was queer all right— as a three-dollar bill. He had suspected her of being a lesbian just from the paperwork, and of course she was. When he followed her to ground down in Miami, Florida, she and her partying friends had verified all his worst suspicions. It didn't bother him that Constance liked women. What she liked or didn't like had no bearing on him. As a matter of fact, he had enjoyed watching the way Constance and the others carried on. They did things to one another that, up to that time, he'd only read about in books, things that his uptight mother never would have believed possible.

He put down the Jockeys and picked up the next pair. Black lace. Control top. These had belonged to Maddy Piper, an aging showgirl-turned-stripper from Las Vegas whose figure was starting to go to seed. She would have been far better off if she hadn't ended up getting into a big fight with her agent, an ex-middleweight boxer.

Next came the pink satin bikini briefs with the Frederick's of Hollywood label. They had belonged to Lois Hart, a barmaid at the Lucky Strike bowling alley in Stockton, California. Lois had sold drinks during the day and dealt in other kinds of chemical mood enhancers by night. When she was found bludgeoned to death and tied to a snag on the banks of the Sacramento River, nobody had gone out of their way looking for her killer. The cops had written Lois off as a drug deal gone bad and let it go at that.

That brought him to the bright red pair at the very bottom of the box, the ones that had once belonged to Rochelle Newton. Lovely, tall, and slender Rochelle from Tacoma, Washington. Years earlier, when he was up in Seattle, training to be an eager-beaver CPA, Rochelle had been the not-too-savvy hooker who had laughed at him when he couldn't perform. She had been his very first victim—an accident almost. He hadn't really intended to kill her. It had just happened. But once he started hitting her, he had found he couldn't stop himself. Afterward, when he knew she was dead and after he had carefully disposed of her body, he took the key to her apartment on Pacific Highway South, let himself in, and helped himself to a single pair of panties from her dresser drawer.

At that point, all he had wanted was a token—something that belonged to her, something to remember her by. The moment he had found the red panties in a drawer, a tradition was born.

Over the years, he had figured out how stupid he had been. It was a miracle nobody had seen him going to or coming from Rochelle's apartment. Now he either took the panties at the time of the killing—if he thought he could take them without investigators seeing it as a signature M.O.—or he did without.

For years after killing Rochelle, he had lived in terror—waiting for the knock on the door that would mean the cops had finally caught up with him. The knock never came. And then one day Rochelle's name had turned up on the list of missing persons who were thought to be possible victims of one of the Northwest's most notorious serial killers. The very night Rochelle's killer read her name in the paper, he went to bed and slept like a baby, safe in the knowledge that the cops were no longer looking for him. They were looking for someone else, someone they called a serial killer.

He had quit his father's firm the next day and gone off on his own, working at two-bit jobs, but savoring the freedom. And knowing that his mother would always slip him a little something if he got caught short.

Once on the road, he realized there was a world of difference between serial killers and recreational ones. The first kind kill because some evil compulsion forces them to. The second ones do it for the fun of it—because they want to.

Breathing deeply, he fondled the swatch of bright red silk. Rochelle. She was the one who had shown him the rules and taught him how to play the game. Once he knew how simple it was to fake the cops out and trick them into looking the other way, everything else was easy.

All six pairs of panties were out on the table now, laying there in full view. Allowing himself to become excited again, he studied them under the glow of the candle's flickering light, stroking each one in turn. One at a time, he held five of the six up to his face once more, trying to make up his mind.

As he did so, his heartbeat quickened. Which would it be tonight? Which one should he choose?

Other than Rochelle, he had never raped his victims, not at the time. He knew better than that. DNA tests were far too reliable these days, and some cops were a whole lot smarter than they looked. Besides, he didn't want to pick up some kind of sexually transmitted disease. One way or another, all women were whores. When it came to that, he believed in the old adage, Better safe than sorry.

At the time he was doing it, he enjoyed killing them. That was satisfying in a way, but he took his real pleasure from them later on, over and over, in the privacy of his own home. There—with the doors carefully closed and locked, with the blinds pulled, and with a scented candle burning on the table—they offered him the relief he craved. No questions asked.

By then his breath was coming in short, sharp gasps. His pants were bulging so badly that it hurt. He breathed a sigh of relief when he finally opened the zipper and allowed the caged prisoner to roam free. A moment later his other hand settled on the newest prize in his collection— Serena Grijalva's thin white cotton briefs.

It didn't take long. He grasped himself and masturbated into the soft material, groaning with pleasure when he came. Afterward, he hurried to the bathroom and washed out the panties with soap and water before hanging them on the towel bar to dry. Then he went back to the kitchen table, turned on the overhead light, and blew out the candle.

Sitting down once more, he picked up a single piece of paper that had slipped out of sight temporarily under Maddy Piper's black lace panties. The paper was a fragment hastily torn from the corner of a yellow legal pad. A few words had been noted on it in painstakingly careful printing.

"Rhonda Weaver Norton," it said. "Fourteen twenty-five Apache Boulevard, number six, Tempe, Arizona."

Using a strip of tape, he fastened the piece of paper to the bottom of the box and then sat there for a moment, admiring his handiwork.

"Rhonda," the man whispered aloud. "Rhonda, Rhonda, Rhonda. You'd better watch out, little girl. The big bad wolf is coming to get you."

🌵 TWO

JOANNA BRADY zipped the last suitcase shut and then sat down on the edge of the bed. "Off you go," she said to her daughter, who was sprawled crosswise on the bed, thumbing through a stack of family photos.

"I like this one best," Jenny said, plucking one out of the stack and handing it to her mother. The picture had been taken by Joanna's father, Big Hank Lathrop, with his Brownie Hawkeye camera. The irregularly sized, old-fashioned, black-and-white snapshot showed an eight-year-old Joanna Lathrop, dressed in her Brownie uniform. She stood at attention in front of her mother's old Maverick. In the foreground cartons of Girl Scout cookies were stacked into a Radio Flyer wagon.

Joanna was almost thirty years old now. Big Hank Lathrop had been dead for fifteen years, but as Joanna held the photo in her hand she missed her father more than she could have thought possible. She missed him almost as much as she missed her deputy sheriff husband, Andy, who had died, a victim of the country's continuing war on drugs, only two months earlier.

It took real effort for her to speak around the word-trapping lump that mysteriously filled her throat. "I always liked that one, too," she managed.

Joanna usually thought of Jenny as resembling Andy far more than she did her mother's side of the family, but studying the photo closely, she could see that Jenny and the little girl in the twenty-two-year-old picture might have been sisters.

"How come none of these are in color?" Jenny asked. "They look funny. Like pictures in a museum."

"Because Grandpa Lathrop developed them himself," Joanna answered. "In that room below the stairs in Grandma Lathrop's basement. That was his darkroom. He always said he liked working in black and white better than he did in color."

Carefully, Joanna began gathering the scattered photos, returning them to the familiar shoe box that had been their storage place for as many years as she could remember. "Come on now," she urged. "It's time to go to bed in your own room."

Jenny pouted. "Oh, Mom, do I have to? Can't I stay up just a little longer?"

Joanna shook her head. "No way. I don't know

about you, but I have a big day ahead of me tomorrow. After church and as soon as dinner is
over, I have to drive all the way to Phoenix—
that's a good four-hour trip. I'd better get some
sleep tonight, or I'll doze off at the wheel."

Folding down the covers on what she still considered to be her side of the bed, Joanna crawled
in and pulled the comforter up around her chin.
Climbing into the double bed was when the now
familiar ache of Andy's absence hit her anew
with soul-wrenching reality.

Instead of taking the hint and heading for her
own bed, Jenny simply snuggled closer. "Do you
have to go to Phoenix?" she asked.

"Peoria," Joanna corrected, fighting her way
through her pain and back into the conversation.
"It's north of Phoenix, remember?" Jenny said
nothing and Joanna shook her head in exaspera-
tion. "Jennifer Ann Brady, you know I have to
go. We've been over this a million times."

"But since you're already elected sheriff, how
come you have to take classes? If you didn't go to
the academy, they wouldn't diselect you, would
they?"

"Diselect isn't a word," Joanna pointed out.
"But you're right. Even if I flunked this course—
which I won't—no one is going to take my badge
away."

"Then why go? Why couldn't you just stay
home instead of going all the way up there? I
want you here."

Joanna tried to be patient. "I may have been
elected sheriff," she explained, "but I've never

been a real police officer—a trained police officer—
before. I know something about it because of
Grandpa Lathrop and Daddy, but the bottom line
is I know a whole lot more about selling insurance
than I do about being a cop. The most important
job the sheriff does is to be the department's leader.
You know what a leader is, don't you?"

Jenny considered for a moment before she
nodded. "Mrs. Mosley's my Brownie leader."

"Right. And what does she do?"

"She takes us on camp-outs. She shows us how
to make things, like sit-upons and buddy-burners
and stuff. Last week she started teaching us how
to tie knots."

"But she couldn't teach you how to do any of
those things if she didn't already know them herself, could she?"

Jennifer shrugged. "I guess not," she said.

"Being sheriff is just like being a troop leader,"
Joanna explained. "In order to lead the department, I have to be able to show the people who
work under me that I know what's going on—that
I know what I'm doing. I have to know what to
do and how to do it before I can tell my officers
what I expect of them. And the only way to learn
all those things in a hurry is to take a crash
course like the one they offer at the Arizona Police Officers Academy."

"But why does it have to start the week before
Thanksgiving?" Jenny objected. "Couldn't it start
afterward? You won't even be back home until
two days before Christmas. When will we go
Christmas shopping?"

Andrew Roy Brady, Joanna's husband and Jenny's father, had been gunned down in mid-September and had died a day later. After ten years of marriage, this was the first holiday season Joanna would spend without him. She couldn't very well tell Jenny how much she dreaded what was coming, starting with Thanksgiving later that week.

After all, with Andy dead, what did Joanna have to be thankful for? How could she explain to her daughter that the little house the family had lived in on High Lonesome Ranch—the only home Jenny had ever known—was the very last place Joanna Brady wanted to be when it came time for Thanksgiving or Christmas dinner? How would she be able to eat a celebratory dinner with an empty place in Andy's spot at the head of the table? How could she make Jenny understand how much Joanna dreaded the prospect of hauling the holiday decorations down from the tiny attic or of putting up a tree? Some words simply couldn't be spoken.

"Thanksgiving is already under control," Joanna said firmly. "Grandma and Grandpa Brady will bring you up to see me right after school on Wednesday afternoon. We'll have a nice Thanksgiving dinner in the restaurant at the hotel. I won't have to be in class again until Monday. We'll have the whole weekend together up until Sunday afternoon. Maybe we can do some of our Christmas shopping then. We might even try visiting the Phoenix Zoo. Would you like that?"

"I guess," Jenny answered without enthusiasm. "Why isn't Grandma Lathrop coming along? Didn't you ask her?"

Good question, Joanna thought. Why isn't my mother coming along? Eleanor Lathrop had been invited to join the Thanksgiving expedition not just once, but three separate times—by Joanna and by both Jim Bob and Eva Lou Brady. Eleanor had turned down each separate invitation. She claimed she had some pressing social engagement that would keep her from spending even one night away from home, to say nothing of three. Joanna had no doubt that Eleanor would have been more enthusiastic about the trip had the idea been hers originally rather than Jim Bob and Eva Lou's. That was something else Joanna couldn't explain to Jenny.

"I asked her, but I guess she's just too busy," Joanna answered lamely. With a firm but loving shove, Joanna finally booted her daughter out of bed. "Go on, now. It's time to get in your own bed."

Reluctantly, Jenny made her way across the room. She stopped beside the three packed and zippered suitcases. She glowered at them as if they were cause rather than result. "I liked it better when Daddy was here," she said.

Joanna knew part of the reason Jenny didn't want to go to her own room—part of the reason she didn't want her mother to be away from home—stemmed from a totally understandable sense of loss. The child was still grieving, and rightfully so. And although Jenny's blurted words weren't meant to be hurtful to her mother, they hurt nonetheless.

Joanna winced. "So did I," she answered.

Jenny made it as far as the bedroom door before she paused again. "Come on, you dogs," she ordered. "Time for bed."

Slowly Sadie and Tigger, Jenny's two dogs, rose from their sprawled sleeping positions on the bedside rug. They both stretched languorously, then followed Jenny out of the room. When the door closed, Joanna switched off her light and then lay there in the dark, wrestling with her own feelings of loneliness and grief.

She had been agonizingly honest when she told Jenny that she too had liked things better the way they were before Andy's death. It was two months now since Joanna had found Andy lying wounded and bleeding in the sand beside his pickup. There were still times when she couldn't believe he was gone, when she wanted to call him up at work to tell him about something Jenny had said or done. Times Joanna longed to have him sitting across from her in the breakfast nook, drinking coffee and talking over the day's scheduling logistics. Times she wanted desperately to have him back beside her in the bed so she could cuddle up next to his back and draw Andy's radiating warmth into her own body. Even now her feet were so distressingly cold that she wondered if she'd ever be able to get to sleep.

Minutes later, despite her cold feet, Joanna

was starting to drift off when the telephone rang. She snapped on the light before picking up the receiver. It was almost eleven. "Hello?"

"Damn," Chief Deputy for Administration Frank Montoya said, hearing her sleep-fogged voice. "It's late, isn't it? I just got home a few minutes ago, but I should have checked the time before I called. I woke you up, didn't I?"

"It's okay, Frank," Joanna mumbled as graciously as she could manage. "I wasn't really asleep. What's up?"

Frank Montoya, the former Willcox city marshal, had been one of Joanna's two opponents in her race for the office of sheriff. In joint appearances on the campaign trail, they had each confronted the loudmouthed third candidate, Al Freeman. Those appearances had resulted in the formation of an unlikely friendship. Once elected and trying to handle the department's entrenched and none-too-subtle opposition to her new administration, Joanna had drafted fellow outsider Frank Montoya to serve as her chief deputy for administration.

"I had dinner with my folks tonight," Frank said. "My cousin's getting married two weeks from now, so my mother had one of her command performance dinners in honor of the soon-to-be newlyweds. I was on my way out the door when she pulled me aside and asked me what are we going to do about Jorge Grijalva. 'Who the hell is Jorge Grijalva?' I asked." Frank paused for a moment. "Ever heard of him?"

"Who, me?" Joanna returned.

"Yes, you."

Joanna closed her eyes in concentration. She had been so caught up in her own troubles that it was hard to remember someone else's, but it came to her a moment later. "Ceci's father," she breathed.

"Ceci?" Frank asked.

"Ceci Grijalva. She was in school and Brownies with Jenny last year. I believe her parents must have gotten a divorce. The mother and the two kids moved to Phoenix right after school got out. The father worked at the lime plant down by Paul Spur until the mother turned up dead somewhere outside Phoenix. It happened about the same time Andy was killed, so I didn't pay that much attention. As I understand it, Jorge is the prime suspect."

"Only suspect," Frank Montoya corrected.

Joanna sat up in bed so she could think better. "Didn't the detectives on the case pick him up at work down in Paul Spur? A day or so after I was sworn in, I remember seeing a letter from the chief of police up in Peoria. He sent a note to the department, thanking us for our cooperation. Since it happened on Dick Voland's watch, I passed the letter along to him. That's all I know about it."

"You know a lot more than I did, then," Frank Montoya returned. "You're right. The family had been living in Bisbee for a while, but Jorge is originally from Douglas. Pirtleville, actually. And it turns out that Jorge's mother, Juanita, is an old friend of my mother's. They used to work together years ago, picking peaches at the orchards out in Elfrida. According to Mom, Juanita thinks Jorge is being sold down the river on account of something he didn't do. She asked me if I . . . I mean, if *we* . . . could do anything to help."

"Like what?" Joanna asked.

"I don't know. All I can tell you is his mother swears he didn't do it."

"Mothers *always* swear their darlings didn't do it," Joanna countered. "Didn't you know that?"

"I suppose I did," Frank agreed, "but if we could just . . ."

"Just what?"

"Listen to her," Frank said. "That's all Mom wanted us to do—listen."

Joanna shook her head. "Look, Frank," she said. "Be reasonable. What good will listening do? This case doesn't have anything at all to do with Cochise County. In case you haven't noticed, Peoria, Arizona, happens to be in Maricopa County, a good hundred and forty miles outside our jurisdiction."

"But you're going up there tomorrow," Frank argued. "Couldn't you talk to her for a few minutes before you go?"

"It was a domestic, Frank," Joanna said. "You know the statistics as well as I do. What could I say to Juanita Grijalva other than to tell her that the cops who arrested her precious Jorge are most likely on the right track?"

"Probably nothing," Frank Montoya agreed somberly. "But if you talk to her, it might help. If nothing else, maybe she'll feel better. Jorge is her only son. No matter what happens afterward, if she's actually spoken to someone in authority, she'll at least have the comfort of knowing she did everything in her power to help."

Frank Montoya's arguments were tough to turn aside. Knowing she was losing, Joanna shook her head. "You should have been in sales, Frank," she said with a short laugh. "You sure as hell know how to close a deal. But here's the next problem—scheduling. I go to church in the morning. We finish up with that around eleven-thirty or so, then we come rushing home because my mother-in-law is cooking up a big Sunday dinner. We'll probably eat around two, and I'll need to light out of here for Phoenix no later than three. When in all that do you think I'll be able to squeeze in an appointment with Juanita Grijalva?"

"How about if I bring her by the High Lonesome right around one?" Frank asked. "Would that be all right?"

"All right, all right," Joanna agreed at last. "But why do you have to bring her? Tell her how to find the place, and she can come by herself."

"No, she can't," Frank said. "Not very well. For one thing, Juanita Grijalva doesn't have a car. For another, she can't drive. She's legally blind."

Joanna assimilated what he had said. "There's nothing like playing on a person's sympathy, is there?"

Now it was Frank Montoya's turn to laugh. "I had to," he said sheepishly. "I'm sorry, Joanna, but if you hadn't agreed to talk to Juanita, I never would have heard the end of it. Once my mother gets going on something like this, she can be hell on wheels."

Joanna stopped him in mid-apology. "Don't worry about it, Frank. It'll be fine. I've never met your mother, but I have one just like her."

"So you know how it is?"

"In spades," Joanna answered. "So get off the phone and let me get some sleep. I'll see you to-morrow. Around one."

Joanna put down the phone. Once again she switched off the lamp on her bedside table. In the long weeks following Andy's murder, sleeping properly was one of the most difficult things Joanna Brady had to do. Loneliness usually de-scended like a smothering cloud every time she crawled into the bed she and Andy had shared for so many years. Usually she tossed and turned through the endless nighttime hours, rather than falling asleep.

This time, Joanna surprised herself by falling asleep almost instantly—as soon as she put her head back down on the pillow. It was a much-needed and welcome change.

"LAST CALL," the bartender said. "Motel time."

At ten to one on a Sunday morning, only the last few Saturday night regulars were still hang-ing out in Peoria's Roundhouse Bar and Grill.

"Hit me again, Butch," Dave Thompson said,

sagging over the bar, resting his beefy arms along the rounded edge. "The last crop of students for this year shows up this afternoon. Classes this session don't end until a couple of days before Christmas. With the holidays messing things up, this one is always a bitch. You can't get 'em to concentrate on what they're supposed to be doing. Can't keep 'em focused. Naturally, the women are worse than the men."

"Naturally," Butch Dixon agreed mildly, putting a draft Coors on the bar in front of Dave Thompson, the superintendent of the Arizona Police Officers Academy three quarters of a mile away. "By the way, you've had several, Dave," Butch observed. "Want me to call you a cab?"

"Naw," Thompson replied. "Thanks but no thanks. Before I decided to get snockered on my last night out, I asked Larry here if he'd mind giving me a ride home. Shit. Last thing I need is a damned DWI. Right, Larry?"

Larry Dysart was also a Roundhouse regular. These days his drink of choice was limited to coffee or tonic with lime. He came to the bar almost every night and spent long congenial evenings discussing literature with the bartender, arguing politics with everybody else, and scribbling in a series of battered spiral notebooks.

He looked up now from pen and paper. "Right, Dave," Larry said. "No problem. I'll be glad to give you a lift home."

THREE

EVEN THOUGH Joanna was only going through the motions, she went to church the next morning. She sat there in the pew, seemingly attentive, while her best friend and pastor, the Reverend Marianne Maculyea, gave a stirring pre-Thanksgiving sermon. Instead of listening, though, Joanna's mind was focused on the fact that she would be gone—completely out of town—for more than a month. She was scheduled to spend five and a half weeks taking a basic training class at the Arizona Police Officers Academy in Peoria.

There was plenty to worry about. For instance, what about clothes? Yes, her suitcases were all zipped shut, but had she packed enough of the right things? This would be the longest time she had ever been away from home. She wasn't terrifically happy about the idea of staying in a dorm. As much trouble as she'd had lately sleeping in her own bed, how well would she fare in a strange one?

But the bottom line—the real focus of her worry—was always Jenny. How would a protracted absence from her mother affect this child whose sense of well-being had already been shattered by her father's murder? Had it not been for the generosity of her in-laws, Joanna might well have had to bag the whole idea and stay home. Putting their own lives on hold, Jim Bob and Eva Lou Brady had agreed to come out and stay on High Lonesome Ranch for the duration of Joanna's absence. Not only would they care for Jenny, getting her to and from school each day, they would also look after the livestock and do any other chores that needed doing.

Professionally, Joanna's attendance at the academy was a thorny issue. Of course she needed to go. That was self-evident, even to Joanna. Her close call during an armed showdown on a copper-mine tailings dump a few days earlier had shown her in life-and-death, up-close-and-personal terms exactly how much she didn't know about the world of law enforcement.

Joanna's connections to law enforcement were peripheral rather than professional. Years earlier, her father, D. H. "Big Hank" Lathrop, had served as sheriff of Cochise County. And Andy, her husband, had been a deputy sheriff as well as a candidate for the office of sheriff when he was gunned down by a drug lord's hired hit man. Joanna's work résumé as office manager of an insurance agency contained no items of legal background or law enforcement training. Some of those educational gaps could be made up by reading and studying on her own, but an organized course of study taught by professional instructors would provide a more thorough and efficient way of getting the job done.

As the word *job* surfaced in Joanna's head, so did a whole other line of concern—work. If a five-and-a-half-week absence could wreak havoc in her personal life, what would it do to her two-week-old administration at the Cochise County Sheriff's Department? While she was gone, her two chief deputies—Frank Montoya for administration and Dick Voland for operations—would be running the show. That arrangement—the possibly volatile combination of two former antagonists—would either function as a form of checks and balances or else it would blow up in Joanna's face. Sitting there in church, not listening to the sermon, Joanna could worry about what might happen, but she couldn't predict which way things would go.

Almost without warning, the people in surrounding pews rose to their feet and opened their hymnals as the organist pounded through the first few bars of "Faith of Our Fathers." As Joanna fumbled hurriedly to find the proper page of the final hymn, she realized Reverend Maculyea's sermon was over. Joanna hadn't listened to a word of it. No doubt Marianne had figured that out as well. When she and her husband, Jeff Daniels, followed the choir down the center aisle to the door of the church, the pastor caught Joanna's eye as they passed by. Marianne smiled and winked. Weakly, Joanna smiled back.

She had planned to skip coffee hour after church, but Jenny headed her off at the front door. "Can't we stay for just a few minutes?" she begged.

Joanna shook her head. "I have so much to do. . . ."

"But, Mom," Jenny countered. "It's Birthday Sunday. When I was coming upstairs from Sunday school, I saw Mrs. Sawyer carrying two cakes into the kitchen. Both of 'em are pecan praline—my favorite. Please? Just for a little while?"

"Well, I suppose," Joanna relented. "But remember, only one piece. Grandma Brady's cooking dinner at home. It's supposed to be ready to eat by two o'clock. If you spoil your appetite, it'll hurt her feelings."

Waiting barely long enough for her mother to finish speaking, Jenny slipped her hand out of Joanna's grasp and skipped off happily toward the social hall. As Jenny thundered down the stairway, Joanna bit back the urge to call after her, "Don't run." The first caution, the one about Jenny not spoiling her appetite, sounded as though it had come directly from the lips of Joanna's own mother, Eleanor Lathrop. And as Joanna stood in line, awaiting her turn to greet and be greeted by Jeff and Marianne, she told herself to cut it out.

As the line moved forward, Joanna found herself standing directly behind Marliss Shackleford. "I was surprised to find someone had chosen

'Faith of Our Fathers' as the recessional," Marliss announced when she reached Marianne's husband. "Isn't that a little, you know, passé?" she asked with a slight shudder. "It's sexist to say the least."

Jeff Daniels cocked his head to one side, regarding the woman with a puzzled frown. "Really," he said, pumping Marliss Shackleford's outstretched hand. "But it doesn't seem to me that 'Faith of Our Parents' has quite the same ring to it."

Jeff's comment was made with such disarming ingenuousness that Marliss was left with no possible comeback. Behind her in line, Joanna choked back a potentially noisy chuckle as Marliss moved on to tackle Marianne. When Joanna stepped forward to greet Jeff, they were both grinning.

"How's it going, Joanna?" he asked, diplomatically removing the grin from his face. "Are you all packed for your six-week excursion?"

As far as Bisbee "clergy couples" went, Jeff Daniels and Marianne Maculyea weren't at all typical. For one thing, although they were officially, and legally, "man and wife," they didn't share the same last name. Marianne was the minister while Jeff served in the capacity of minister's spouse. She was the one with the full-time career, while he was a stay-at-home husband with no paid employment "outside the home."

In southeastern Arizona, this newfangled and seemingly odd arrangement had raised more than a few eyebrows when the young couple had first come to town to assume Marianne's clerical duties at Canyon Methodist Church. Now, though, several years later, they had worked their way so far into the fabric of the community that no one was surprised to learn that the newly elected treasurer of the local Kiwanis Club listed his job on his membership application as "house-husband."

"Almost," Joanna answered. "And not a moment too soon. I'm supposed to leave the house at three. You and Marianne are still coming out to the ranch for Grandma Brady's farewell dinner, aren't you? She's acting as though I'm off on a worldwide tour."

Jeff shook his head. "Wouldn't miss one of Eva Lou's dinners for the world. What time are we due?"

"Between one-thirty and two."

Finished with Marliss, Marianne stepped back to greet Joanna with a heartfelt hug. "We're all going to miss you," she said. "But everything's going to be fine here at home. Don't worry."

Not surprisingly, Marianne's intuitive comment went straight to the heart of Joanna's problem. "Thank you," she gulped, blinking back tears.

Marianne smiled. "See you downstairs," she said.

Joanna glanced at her watch as she headed for the stairway. There wasn't much time. She hurried into the social hall, scanning the tables for a glimpse of Jennifer. Initially seeing no sign of her daughter, Joanna made a single swift pass through the refreshment line and picked up a cup of coffee. With cup in hand, she finally spotted Jenny and one of her friends. The two girls were already seated at a table and scarfing down cake.

Not wanting to crab at her daughter in public, Joanna deliberately moved in the opposite direction. Too late she realized she was walking directly into the arms of Marliss Shackleford.

Joanna Brady had never liked Marliss Shackleford and for more than one reason. The woman had a real propensity for minding other people's business. She thrived on gossip, and she had managed to find a way to turn that hobby into a job. Once a week Marliss held forth in a written gossip column called "Bisbee Buzzings" that appeared in the local paper, *The Bisbee Bee*.

To a private citizen, columnist Marliss Shackleford could be a bothersome annoyance. Now that Joanna was in the public eye, however, annoyance had escalated into something else. From the moment Joanna Brady began making her bid for the office of sheriff, Marliss had chosen to regard everything related to Joanna and Jennifer Brady as possibly newsworthy material for her weekly column.

At first, Joanna hadn't tumbled to her changed circumstances. Then one day, she was shocked to see her own words quoted verbatim in Marliss Shackleford's column—words taken from a conversation with a third party in what Joanna had mistakenly assumed to be the relative privacy of an after-church coffee hour. Only in retrospect did she recall the reporter hovering in the background in the social hall during the conversation.

Since then, Joanna had gone out of her way to avoid Marliss Shackleford.

Veering to one side, Joanna dodged the Marliss pitfall only to stumble into another one that proved almost equally troubling.

"Why, Joanna Brady!" Esther Brockner exclaimed, clasping the younger woman by the hand. "How are you and that poor little girl of yours doing these days?"

Two weeks after Andy's death, Esther Brockner had been the first elderly widow who had felt free to advise Joanna that since she was so young and attractive, she wouldn't have any trouble at all marrying again. That well-intentioned but tactless comment had left Joanna fuming. She had forced herself to bite back the angry retort that she didn't *want* any other husband. Now, after being told much the same thing by several other thoughtless acquaintances, Joanna's hide had toughened considerably.

Facing Esther now over a cup of coffee, Joanna had little difficulty maintaining her composure. "We're doing fine, Esther," she returned civilly. "How about you?"

"Every day gets a little better, doesn't it?" Esther continued.

Not exactly, Joanna thought. It was more like one step forward and two back, but she nodded in reply. Nodding a lie didn't seem quite as bad as telling one outright.

"Why, Sheriff Brady," Marliss said, using her cup and saucer to wedge her way into the two-way conversation. "I guess you're off to school in Phoenix this week."

"Peoria," Joanna corrected. "The Arizona Police Officers Academy is based in Peoria, outside of Phoenix."

Marliss waved her hand in disgust. "What's the difference? Peoria. Glendale. Tempe. Mesa. If you ask me, those places are all alike. From the outlet stores in Casa Grande on, there's way too much traffic. I hear it's almost as bad as L.A. All those people!" She clicked her tongue in disapproval. "It's not like a small town. In a place like that, nobody cares if you live or die. In fact, I've heard it isn't safe for a woman alone to drive around Phoenix. I wouldn't go there if you paid me."

Joanna felt a sudden urge to smile because she was, in fact, being paid to go to the Phoenix area. Not only that, some of Marliss Shackleford's hard-earned tax dollars were partially footing the bill.

"I'm sure most people in metropolitan Phoenix are just fine," Joanna said.

Marliss drew herself up to her full five foot three. "I understand the course work at that school is pretty tough," she said. "Aren't you worried about that?"

"Why should I be?"

Marliss shrugged, in a vain attempt to look innocent. "If you didn't pass for some reason, it might be a bad reflection on your ability to do the job, wouldn't it?"

"I expect to pass all right," Joanna replied.

"Speaking of doing the job, I need a picture of you."

"What for," Joanna asked, "the paper?"

"No. For the display in the Sheriff's Department lobby. I'm on the Women's Club facilities committee, and I'm supposed to get a glossy eleven-by-fourteen of you to put up along with those of all the previous sheriffs. I don't need it this minute, but I will need it soon. I'll have to have it framed in time for an official presentation at our annual luncheon in January."

Looking around the room for Jenny, Joanna nodded. "I'll take care of it as soon as I can."

From across the room she succeeded in catching Jenny's eye. Joanna motioned toward the door. In response, Jenny pointed toward her empty plate, then folded her hands prayerfully under her chin. The gestured message came through loud and clear. Jenny wanted a second piece of Mrs. Sawyer's cake.

Shaking her head, Joanna walked up to her daughter. "No," she said firmly. "Come on. We've got to go."

Scowling, Jenny got up to follow, but as they started toward the stairway, Cynthia Sawyer abandoned her spot behind the refreshment table and came hurrying after them. She was carrying a paper plate laden with several pieces of her rich, dark-brown pecan praline cake.

"I know this is Jenny's favorite," Cynthia said, smiling and carefully placing the loaded plate in Jenny's outstretched hand. "She mentioned that you folks were having a little going-away party this afternoon. We have more than enough for the people who are here. I thought you might want a piece or two for dessert."

Joanna knew she'd been suckered. There was no way to turn down Mrs. Sawyer's generous offer without making a public fool of herself.

"Why, thank you, Cynthia," Joanna said. "That's very thoughtful."

Clutching the plate, Jenny scampered triumphantly up the stairway to safety while her mother stalked after her.

"Jennifer Ann Brady, you're a brat," Joanna muttered when she knew they were both safely out of Cynthia's hearing.

"But, Mom," Jenny protested. "I didn't *ask* for it. Mrs. Sawyer *offered*. And not just because it's my favorite. She asked me if you liked it, too. I said you did. You do, don't you?"

Joanna laughed in spite of herself. "Oh, all right," she said. "I suppose I do like it. Praline cake is one of those things that grows on you . . . in more ways than one."

JUANITA GRIJALVA sat at her wobbly Formica-topped kitchen table wearing only a bra and slip, waiting for Lucy, her brother's wife, to finish ironing her best dress. The starched cotton was so well worn it had taken on a satiny sheen. Juanita knew the dress was getting old. She could tell that from the gradually changing texture of the aging material, but glaucoma kept her from being able to see it.

The navy-blue dress—brand-new then and with all the stickers still pinned to the sleeve— had been a final, extravagant gift from the lady whose house Juanita had cleaned and whose washing and ironing she had done for twenty years before failing vision had forced her to stop working altogether. If Juanita had worked as a maid in the hotel or as a cook in the county hospital, she might have had a pension and some retirement income instead of just a blue dress. But it was too late to worry about that now.

Juanita had lain awake in her bed all night long, worrying about the coming interview. She had finally fallen asleep just before dawn when her brother's rooster next door started his early-morning serenade. Now, as noon approached and with it time for Frank Montoya to come pick her up, Juanita found herself so weary that she could barely stay awake. Her sightless eyes burned. Her shoulders ached from the heavy weight of her sagging breasts. To relieve the burden, she heaved them up and rested them on the edge of the table.

"Who's coming for you?" Lucy asked.

"Maria Montoya's son. Frank. He used to be city marshal over in Willcox, but he works for the Sheriff's Department now. He told me last night that he'd drive me up to Bisbee to see that new woman sheriff."

Lucy plucked the dress off the ironing board, then held it up, examining the garment critically under the light of the room's single ceiling fixture. Finding a crease over one pocket, she put the dress back on the board.

Lucy was quiet for some time, seemingly concentrating on eradicating the stubborn crease in Juanita's dress. She and her husband, Reuben, had long since decided that their no-good nephew, Jorge, was a lost cause. He drank too much—at least he always used to. For years he had bounced from job to job, frittering away whatever money he made. Not only that; anyone his age who would mess around with a girl as young as Serena Duffy had been wasn't worth the trouble.

Finally, Lucy set the steaming iron back down on the cloth-covered board. "I don't know why you bother about him," she said. "It's not going to do any good."

"I bother because I have to," Juanita replied reproachfully, staring with unblinking and unseeing eyes in the direction of her sister-in-law's voice. "Because Jorge's my son. If I don't stick up for him, who will?"

Nobody, Lucy thought, but she didn't say it. She had already said far too much.

"Besides," Juanita added a moment later, "if Jorge goes to prison, I'll never see Ceci and Pablo again."

Lucy nodded. "I suppose that's true," she said.

Lucy Gomez understood about grandchildren. She loved her own to distraction and spoiled them as much as she was able. Living next door, she had seen how it grieved Juanita when her daughter-in-law took Ceci and Pablo and moved to Phoenix. But then there had still been the possibility of seeing them occasionally. With Jorge accused of Serena's murder, things were much worse than that now.

Lucy plucked the carefully ironed but threadbare dress off the ironing board and handed it to Juanita. "You're right," Lucy said, shaking her head. "I feel sorry for the kids. They're the only reason I'm here."

FOUR

Eva Lou Brady shooed her daughter-in-law out of the kitchen at High Lonesome Ranch. "Get out of here, Joanna," she ordered. "Either go load your things into the car or sit down and take it easy, but get out from under hand and foot. I've certainly spent enough time in this kitchen to know how to put a Sunday dinner together."

No doubt Eva Lou Brady knew Joanna's kitchen backward and forward. Joanna and Andy had lived in the house on High Lonesome Ranch for years now, but there were still times when Joanna felt like an outsider—as though the kitchen continued to belong to her mother-in-law rather than to the new generation of owners. It was the house where she and Jim Bob had raised their son, Andrew.

A country girl born and bred, Eva Lou had loved the cozy Sears Craftsman bungalow, but the whole time she had lived there, she had harbored the secret dream of one day living in town. When Andy and Joanna were ready to start looking for a place of their own, Eva Lou was the one who had broached the radical idea of selling the ranch to the younger couple so she and Jim Bob could move into Bisbee proper.

Right that minute, though, with her face red and with a steaming pot on every burner of the stove, Eva Lou Brady was clearly in her element and back on her home turf.

Joanna lingered in the doorway for a moment, watching her mother-in-law's efficient movements. Eva Lou cooked without ever wasting a single motion. She never seemed hurried or rushed. Her skillful gestures and businesslike approach to meal preparation always left Joanna feeling like an inept home ec washout.

"At least I could set the table," Joanna offered lamely.

"Jenny will help with that, won't you?" Eva Lou asked, pausing with the rolling pin poised over the biscuit dough and raising a flour-dusted eyebrow in Jenny's direction.

"How many places?" Jenny asked.

"Seven," Eva Lou answered. "Grandma Lathrop phoned after church to say that she's coming, too."

"That's a switch," Joanna said. "If she changed her mind about coming to dinner, maybe she'll change her mind about Phoenix as well."

Eva Lou shook her head. "I doubt it. I asked her again, but she said no—that she's meeting someone here in Bisbee over the weekend, but she wouldn't say who." Eva Lou shot Joanna an inquiring glance. "You don't suppose Eleanor Lathrop has a boyfriend after all these years, do you?"

"Boyfriend?" Joanna echoed. "My mother? You've got to be kidding. Whatever makes you say that?"

Eva Lou shrugged. "I don't know," she said. "Eleanor hasn't been at all herself the last few weeks. She's been acting funny—funnier than usual, I mean. It's like she's carrying around some secret that she can barely keep from spilling."

"Spilling secrets is my mother's specialty," Joanna said shortly. "I don't think she's ever kept one in her life, certainly not anybody else's. And a boyfriend? No way. It couldn't be."

"Your mother's an attractive woman," Eva Lou returned. "And stranger things than that have happened, you know."

Joanna considered for a moment, then shook her head. "I agree," she said. "It would be strange, all right."

With that, banished from the kitchen, Joanna did as she'd been told. She retreated to her bedroom for one last check of her luggage to make sure she had packed everything she would need. When it came time to open the closet door, she hesitated, knowing that the sight of it would leave her with a quick clutch of emptiness in her stomach that had nothing at all to do with hunger.

At her mother's insistence, Joanna had finally found the strength to take Andy's clothing to a church-run used-clothing bank down in Naco, Sonora. Although half of the closet was now totally empty, Joanna's clothing was still jammed together at one end of a clothes rod while the other end held nothing but a few discarded hangers. Two months had passed, but Joanna could not yet bring herself to hang her own clothes on the other side of that invisible line that divided her part of the closet from what she still thought of as Andy's. The time for claiming and rearranging the whole closet would come eventually—at least, she hoped it would—but for now, she still wasn't ready.

As she turned away from the closet, there was a gentle tap on the bedroom door. "Joanna, Eva Lou says you may need some help packing your stuff out to the car," Jim Bob Brady said. "Are you ready, or do you want to do it later?"

"Why not now?" Joanna returned. "Things are pretty well gathered up."

Her father-in-law carried two suitcases while Joanna took one. She also lugged along a briefcase crammed full of paperwork in need of her perusal. "I've never been away from home this long before. I'm probably bringing too much," she said, as they loaded the luggage into her county-owned Blazer.

"Better to take too much than too little," Jim Bob replied.

When all of the suitcases were stowed in the back, Jim Bob Brady closed the cargo gate, then looked at Joanna quizzically. "Seems to me like Peoria's pretty much flat. And last time I was up in those parts, I do believe all the streets were paved. So how come you're going up there in a Blazer, for Pete's sake? You'd get a whole lot better gas mileage from that little Eagle of yours than you will from this gas-guzzling outfit."

"It's a requirement," Joanna explained. "The academy suggests that, wherever possible, students bring along the vehicle they'll actually be using once they're out patrolling on their own. That way, when it comes time to practicing pursuit driving, not only will we be learning pursuit-driving techniques, we'll also be learning the real capabilities of our own vehicles."

"Oh," Jim Bob said, scratching his almost bald head. "Guess it does make sense, after all. Need anything else hauled out?"

Joanna shook her head. "That's it."

"I'm gonna go on back inside, if you don't mind," he said. "Maybe I can watch a few minutes of pro football before Eva Lou makes me turn off the set to come eat dinner. She's real stubborn that way. Fussy. To hear her tell it, you'd think food eaten in front of a television set is plumb wasted."

"It does seem like a waste of good cooking to me," Joanna said.

Jim Bob Brady squinted at her and then grinned. "You women are all alike, aren't you?" he muttered. "Not a hair of difference."

As he marched off toward the house, Joanna stayed behind, enjoying the warmth of the early-afternoon sunshine and the crystal-clear blue of the sky overhead. It had been a strange fall with unseasonably cold and wet weather in October. Now, the week before Thanksgiving, warm, shirt-sleeve temperatures had returned, even in the high desert country of southeastern Arizona.

Joanna stood near the Blazer and gazed off across the broad, flat stretches of the Sulphur Springs Valley toward the broken blue lines of mountain that surrounded it—the Chiricahuas and the Swisshelms to the north and east, the Dragoons directly to the north, and behind her, to the west, the steeply rising foothills of the Mules.

As clearly as if it were yesterday, she remembered the first time she had stood in almost that same spot with Andy while he had pointed out those same mountain ranges. Andy had loved High Lonesome Ranch when he had lived there as a boy with his parents. Because he had cared about the place so much and because it had been so much a part of him, Joanna had loved it, too—at least she had when she was sharing it with Andy. Now, though, she wasn't so sure. Trying to run the place by herself seemed overwhelming at times. Maybe . . .

The half-formed thought was interrupted when the two dogs—Tigger and Sadie—scrambled out from under the empty swing, leaped off the porch, and came bounding through the gate, barking wildly. Ranch dogs traditionally earn their keep by functioning as noisy early-warning systems. Over the chorus of barking, Joanna couldn't tell what kind of vehicle was making its way up the road, but she knew for sure that someone was coming. Moments later Frank Montoya's blue Chevy pickup rounded the corner, followed by the two noisy dogs.

"Quiet, you two," Joanna ordered. "It's okay."

The dogs headed for the porch while Frank stopped the truck a few feet away from Joanna. "Some watchdogs you've got there," he observed through a partially opened window. "Do they actually chase bad guys or just break their eardrums?"

"Maybe a little of both," she answered. "How's it going, Frank?"

Chief Deputy Frank Montoya climbed down out of the truck. He was a tall, spare, easygoing Hispanic. The youngest son in a family of no-longer-migrant workers, he was the first person on either side of his family tree ever to attend college. Working full-time and taking mostly night courses, Frank had completed his associate of arts degree at Cochise College. Now, commuting back and forth to Tucson and taking only one or two classes a semester, he was slowly working away at attaining a B.A. in law enforcement.

Well into his mid-thirties, Frank's neatly trimmed crew-cut hairline was showing definite signs of receding. Friends, including Joanna Brady, teased him, telling him that when he was finally ready to graduate, he wouldn't have any hair left to wear under his mortarboard.

Frank hurried around his truck to the rider's side. He opened the door to reveal a short but massive Mexican woman whose iron-gray hair had been plaited into a long, thin braid. It was wrapped into a dinner-plate-sized halo and pinned to her head. Her features were stolid, impassive. When Frank opened the door to help her out, she stepped down heavily and stood, splay-footed and unsmiling, with her hands folded across her broad waist as Joanna moved forward to greet her. An oversized black purse dangled from the crook of one elbow. The other hand gripped a large manila envelope.

"You must be Mrs. Grijalva," Joanna said, holding out her hand.

The older woman responded by turning toward the sound of Joanna's voice, but she made no move to return the handshake. Cataracts leave visible signs of their damage. The glaucoma that had robbed Juanita Grijalva of her vision had left no apparent blemish on her eyes themselves. She looked past Joanna with a disconcerting, unblinking stare.

After a moment, Joanna reached out and grasped Juanita's free hand. "I'm Sheriff Brady," she said.

Juanita Grijalva frowned briefly in Frank's direction. "She sounds very young to be sheriff," she said.

"Young, yes," Frank put in hurriedly, "but she's also very smart. After all, she hired me, didn't she?"

"Your mother seems to think that was smart," Juanita observed.

Frank's face reddened slightly, and Joanna laughed aloud at his discomfort. The awkward moment passed, and Joanna took the woman's arm. "Won't you come into the house?" she asked.

A few steps into the yard, Juanita Grijalva stopped short, sniffing the air. "I smell cooking," she said. "I think we are disturbing you. We should go and come back another time."

"No," Joanna insisted. "It's all right. My mother-in-law is cooking dinner, but it isn't quite ready yet. There's time for us to talk. Come on inside."

Unwilling to usher the newcomers into the house through the laundry room and kitchen, Joanna led Juanita Grijalva and Frank Montoya around to the seldom-used front door, which happened to be locked. Joanna rang the bell. Moments later, Jenny threw open the door.

"What are you doing out here?" the child asked.

"We have company, Jenny," Joanna answered smoothly. "You know Mr. Montoya, and this is Mrs. Grijalva."

As they came into the room, Jim Bob switched off the television set and retreated to the kitchen. Nodding to Frank, Jenny moved away from the door, but her piercing blue eyes remained focused on the older woman.

"I know you, too," she said. "You're Ceci's grandmother. Last year you came to our Brownie meeting and taught us how to make tortillas."

Juanita nodded. "One of the boys at school said that Ceci's mother got killed up in Phoenix," Jenny continued. "Is that true?"

"Yes," Juanita said. "My daughter-in-law is dead."

"Is Ceci going to come back to Bisbee, then? We both had Mrs. Sampson in second grade. Maybe we'd be in the same class again."

Juanita shook her head. "I don't think so," she said. "Ceci and her brother are staying in Phoenix right now. With her other grandparents."

"Jenny," Eva Lou called from the kitchen. "You haven't finished setting the table."

Jenny started toward the kitchen, then turned back to Juanita Grijalva. "When you see Ceci, tell her hi for me, would you?"

Juanita nodded again. "I'll be sure to tell her."

Jenny left the living room without seeing the stray tear Juanita Grijalva brushed from her weathered cheek as Joanna eased the older woman down onto the couch. "I may not, you know."

"May not what?" Joanna asked.

"Ever see Ceci again. Or Pablo, either. And that's why I'm here," she said. "Because I don't want to lose them, too."

Joanna had settled herself on the hassock. Jolted by Juanita's last comment, Joanna leaned forward, her face alive with concern. "Has someone threatened your grandchildren?" she asked.

"If my son is convicted of killing Serena," Juanita said, "I'll never see them again. The Duffys—Serena's parents—will see to it. Even now, they won't allow me to talk to them on the telephone. I got a ride all the way to Phoenix and back, but they wouldn't even let me go to Serena's funeral. Ernestina's brother was there, and he told me to go away. They didn't let me see the kids then, either."

"Mrs. Grijalva," Joanna began, but Juanita hurried on, ignoring the interruption.

"Do you know anything about my son's case?" she asked.

Joanna shook her head. "Not very much. It was all happening right around the time my own husband died, and I'm afraid I wasn't paying attention to much of anything else."

"That's all right." Juanita picked up the bulging envelope she had dropped on the couch beside her and handed it to Joanna. "Here are all the articles from the papers. The ones we could find. Lucy, my sister-in-law, read them to me. And she made copies. You can keep those."

"But, Mrs. Grijalva," Joanna objected, "I don't know what you expect me to do with them. You have to understand, this isn't my case. It happened up in Phoenix, didn't it?"

"Peoria."

"Peoria, then. My department only has jurisdiction over things that happen in Cochise County. We have no business meddling in a case that happened that far away from here."

"You don't want to help me, then?"

"Mrs. Grijalva, please believe me. It's not a matter of not wanting to," Joanna said. "I can't."

"His lawyer wants him to plea-bargain," Juanita Grijalva said.

Joanna nodded. "That probably makes sense. If he can plead guilty to a lesser charge, sometimes that's better than taking chances with a judge and jury."

"But he didn't do it," Juanita insisted firmly. "No matter what they say, I know my Jorge didn't kill Serena. She may have given him plenty of cause, but he didn't do it."

"Even so, there's nothing I can do about it," Joanna responded. "It's not my case. I'm sorry."

Juanita Grijalva rose abruptly to her feet. "We could just as well go, then, Frank. This isn't doing any good."

Frank hurriedly took Juanita's arm and led her back out of the house. Still holding the unopened envelope, Joanna watched as Chief Deputy Montoya guided the grieving woman out the door, across the porch, and down the steps. Following behind them, Joanna resisted the temptation to say something more, to make an empty promise she had no power to keep. Even though her heart ached with sympathy, there was nothing she could do to help Jorge Grijalva. To claim otherwise would have been dishonest.

Frank was busy maneuvering his pickup out of the yard when Eleanor Lathrop's elderly Plymouth Volare came coughing up the road. Seeing her daughter standing just inside the front door, Eleanor parked in an unaccustomed spot nearer the front door than the back.

"Who was that?" she asked, bustling up onto the porch. "Frank Montoya?"

"Yes," Joanna answered. "Frank and a friend

of his mother's. Her name's Juanita Grijalva. Her son has been accused of murdering his ex-wife up in Phoenix. Juanita thought I might be able to help him, but I had to tell her I can't."

"If it happened up in Phoenix, of course you can't do anything about it," Eleanor said huffily. "What a stupid idea! I can't imagine why they'd even bother to ask. Frank certainly knows better than that."

"Frank wasn't the one doing the asking, Mother," Joanna said.

"But he brought her here, didn't he?" Eleanor returned. "And on your day off, too. I don't know about him, Joanna. He just doesn't seem all that sharp to me. And why you'd want to go out on a limb and make one of the men who ran against you your chief deputy . . ."

This was ground Joanna and Eleanor had already covered. Several times over. "Never mind, Mother," Joanna said, opening the door and herding Eleanor into the house. "Let's go on out to the kitchen and see if Eva Lou needs any help."

Just then, Marianne and Jeff's sea-foam-green VW pulled into the yard and stopped at the back gate. When Joanna went out through the laundry room to open the door, she was still holding Juanita Grijalva's envelope.

Joanna stood by the dryer for a moment, examining the still-sealed package. The best course of action would probably be to throw it away without ever knowing what was inside. Still, Jorge Grijalva's mother had gone to a lot of trouble to bring her that material. Didn't Joanna owe the woman at least the courtesy of reading it?

True, the case was 140 miles outside Joanna's jurisdiction. And no, she couldn't possibly do anything about it, but there was no law against her reading about it. What could that hurt?

Making up her mind, Joanna dropped the envelope onto the dryer next to her car keys and purse; then she hurried outside to greet the last of Eva Lou's invited guests.

FIVE

THE DINNER went off surprisingly well, from the moment they sat down at the dining room table until the last morsel of Cynthia Sawyer's praline cake had been scraped off the dessert plates.

All through the meal, Joanna couldn't help noticing that Eva Lou was right. Eleanor Lathrop wasn't at all herself. After the initial wrangle about Frank Montoya, she had curbed her critical tongue. She was so uncommonly cheerful— so uncharacteristically free of complaint—that Joanna found herself wondering if it was the same woman. Once, when Eleanor was laughing gaily—almost flirtatiously—at one of Jim Bob's folksy, time-worn quips, Joanna found herself speculating for just the smallest fraction of a moment if there was a chance Eva Lou was right after all. Maybe there was a new man in Eleanor Lathrop's life.

In the end, though, Joanna attributed her mother's lighthearted mood to the fact that there were nonfamily guests at dinner. She reasoned that Jeff and Marianne's presence must have been enough to force Eleanor Lathrop to don her company manners. Whatever the cause of her mother's sudden transformation, Joanna welcomed it.

The festive dinner with its good food and untroubled conversation helped ease Joanna past her earlier misapprehensions about being away at school. Jenny and the ranch would be in good hands while Joanna was gone. There was no need for her to worry. She said her flurry of good-byes to everyone else in the house; then Jenny alone walked Joanna out to the loaded Blazer.

"Ceci and I are almost alike, aren't we," Jenny said thoughtfully.

"What do you mean?"

"Well, my daddy's dead, and her mom is. She's staying with her grandparents. While you're away, I'll be staying with mine."

The situations of the two girls weren't exactly mirror images. Joanna was on her way to take a course that would help her be a better police officer. Jorge Grijalva was in jail, charged with murdering his former wife. Jenny's surviving grandparents had just enjoyed a companionable meal with one another. Ceci Grijalva's maternal grandparents had refused to allow Juanita Grijalva to attend her own daughter-in-law's funeral. But Joanna didn't mention any of that to Jenny.

"You're right," she said simply. "You have a lot in common."

"Could we go see her?"

"Who?"

"Ceci. Next weekend when I come up for Thanksgiving?"

Joanna was carrying her purse and keys. Jenny was carrying Juanita Grijalva's envelope. As far as Joanna could see, it hadn't been opened. Joanna found herself wondering if Jenny had been hanging around the living room eavesdropping while Joanna had been talking to Juanita.

"Why would you want to do that?" Joanna asked guardedly.

Jenny shrugged. "Almost everyone else in Mrs. Lassiter's class has two parents. There are two kids whose parents are divorced. I'm the only one whose dad is dead."

"So?"

"At Daddy's funeral, everybody said how sorry they were and that they knew how I felt. But they didn't, not really. They weren't nine years old when their fathers died. If I tell Ceci I know how she feels, it'll be for real, 'cause she's nine years old and so am I. Maybe if I tell her that, it'll make her feel better."

They had reached the truck by then. Joanna wrenched open the door and tossed both her purse and Juanita's envelope into the car. Now she leaned down and pulled Jenny toward her, grasping her in a tight hug while a sudden gust of wind blew a wisp of Jenny's long, smooth hair across Joanna's cheek.

"Did anyone ever tell you that you're one special kid?" Joanna asked, holding Jenny at arm's length so she could look the child in the eye.

"Daddy did sometimes," Jenny answered wistfully.

"He was right," Joanna said. "You're right to be concerned about Ceci. And I'll see what I can do. If I can find out where she's staying, maybe we could take her out to do something with us while you're there."

"Like going to Baskin-Robbins?" Jenny asked.

"Just like," Joanna said with a fond smile.

Joanna had spent days and nights agonizing in advance about this leave-taking. Now the moment came and went with unexpected ease and without a single tear. "I'll miss you, Mommy," Jenny said, hugging Joanna one last time. "I'll miss you, but I'll be good. I promise. Girl Scout's honor."

"I'll be good, too," Joanna replied.

"Promise?"

"I promise. I'll see you Wednesday night."

Jenny stepped away from Joanna's grasp. "What's the name of the place we're staying again?"

"The Hohokam Resort Hotel."

"Does it have a swimming pool?"

"It's supposed to."

"Come on, Sadie and Tigger," Jenny said to the dogs. Then she looked innocently back up at her mother. "Me and the dogs'll race you to the corner of the fence."

Joanna's grammar-correcting reflex was automatic. "The dogs and *I* will race *you*," Joanna countered.

Jenny grinned up at her impishly. "Does that mean I get to drive?" she asked.

The nine-year-old humor was subtle. It took a moment for Joanna to realize she'd been had, that for the first time in months, Jennifer Ann Brady had actually cracked a joke. And then Joanna was grinning, too.

"Last one to the corner is a rotten egg," she said, bounding into the Blazer and turning the key in the ignition. Jenny and the dogs took off running. Joanna let them win, but only just barely.

After passing them, Joanna glanced in the mirror. The last thing she saw as she drove away from High Lonesome Ranch was Jenny, standing on tiptoe by the corner of the fence and waving her heart out. Her long hair blew in blond streamers behind her, while the two dogs danced around her in crazy circles.

"She's going to be all right," Joanna marveled to herself as the Blazer jounced across the rutted track that led out to High Lonesome Road.

A couple of stray tears leaked out the corners of her eyes as she drove, but they were welcome tears—not at all the kind she had expected.

MAYBE IT was trying to drive two hundred miles on a full stomach. Maybe it was the warm autumn sun slanting in on her through

the driver's window. By the time Joanna had
driven as far as Eloy, she could barely stay awake.
She stopped at a truck stop for a coffee break.
Reaching for her purse, she caught sight of Juanita Grijalva's envelope and carried it along into
the coffee shop. As she slipped into a booth, she
tore open the flap.

Sipping coffee, she shuffled through the stack
of copied newspaper articles. Even though most
of the articles were undated, as soon as she
started reading them, the chronology of events
was clear enough.

The first article was little more than three
inches long. It reported that the partially clad,
badly beaten body of an unidentified woman had
been found in the desert a few miles south of
Lake Pleasant. The grisly remains had been discovered by a group of high school students ditch-
ing school for an afternoon keg party. Officers
from the Peoria Police Department were investigating.

The next article identified the murdered
woman as Serena Maria Grijalva, formerly of Bisbee. At age twenty-four, she was the divorced
mother of two small children.

Joanna stopped short when she read Serena's
age. Twenty-four was very young to have a nine-
year-old daughter. Joanna herself had been eigh-
teen years old when she got pregnant and
nineteen when Jenny was born. Serena had been
four whole years—four critical years—younger
than that.

The article noted that Peoria Police Detective

Carol Strong, primary investigator in the case, indicated that detectives were following up on several leads and that they expected a break soon.

The third article was longer—more of a feature story. Because it was situated at the top of the page, the date showed, and Joanna's eye stopped there. September 20. The day of Andy's funeral. No wonder that two months later, most of this was news to Joanna. That nightmare week in September she had been far too preoccupied with the tragedy in her own life to be aware of anyone else's. Still, the realization that Serena and Andy had died within days of each other put a whole new perspective on the words she was reading.

When Serena Maria Grijalva left her children home alone last Wednesday night to go four blocks down the street to the WE-DO-YU-DO Washateria, she had every intention of coming right back with a grocery cart loaded with clean laundry. Instead, the twenty-four-year-old single mother was bludgeoned to death in a desert area a few miles north of Sun City.

The mother's absence did not initially alarm the Grijalva children, nine-year-old Cecelia and six-year-old Pablo. Ever since moving to Phoenix from Bisbee several months earlier, they had been latchkey kids. That morning, when they awoke and discovered their mother wasn't home, they dressed themselves, fixed breakfast, packed lunches, and went to school. And when they came home that afternoon and their mother

still hadn't returned, they helped themselves to a simple dinner of microwaved hot dogs and refried beans.

Almost twenty hours after she left home, Serena Grijalva's supervisor from the Desert View Nursing Home stopped by the house, checking to see why Serena hadn't reported for work. Only then did the resourceful Grijalva children realize something was wrong.

A call from the nursing home brought the children's maternal grandmother into the case. A missing person report from her filed with the Peoria Police Department resulted in authorities making the connection between the two abandoned children and an unidentified dead woman found earlier that afternoon in the desert north of Peoria.

Joanna found herself blinking back tears as she read. She was appalled at the idea of those two little kids being left on their own for such a long time. They had coped with an independence and resourcefulness that went far beyond their tender years, but they shouldn't have had to, Joanna thought, turning back to the article.

The tragedy of the Grijalva children is only one shocking example of an increasingly widespread problem of the nineties—that of latchkey kids. Cute movies notwithstanding, children in this country are routinely being left alone in shockingly large numbers.

Most children who are left to their own devices don't go to luxury hotels and order room service. The houses they live in are often squalid and cold. There is little or no food available. They play with matches and die in fires. They play with guns and die of bullet wounds. They become involved in the gang scene because gang membership offers a sense of belonging that they don't find at home.

Sometimes the parents are simply bad parents. In some cases the neglect is caused or made worse by parental addiction to drugs or alcohol. Increasingly, however, these children live in single-parent households where the family budget will simply not stretch far enough to include suitable day care arrangements. Divorce is often a contributing factor.

Although Serena Grijalva's divorce from her forty-three-year-old husband was not yet final, Cecelia and Pablo Grijalva fall into that last category.

"Serena was determined to make it on her own," says Madeline Bellerman, the attorney who helped Serena Grijalva obtain a restraining order against her estranged husband. "She had taken two jobs—one full-time and one part-time. She made enough so she didn't have to take her kids and go home to her parents, but beyond food and rent there wasn't room for much else. Regular day care was obviously well outside her budget."

Serena's two minor children have now been placed in the custody of their maternal grandparents, but what happened to them has forced the community to examine what options are available to parents who find themselves caught in similar circumstances. This is the first in a series of three articles that will address the issue of childcare for underemployed women in the Phoenix area. Where can they turn for help? What options are available to them?

"You want a refill?"

Joanna looked up. A waitress stood beside the booth, a steaming coffeepot poised over Joanna's cup.

"Please."

The waitress glanced curiously at the article on the table as she poured. "That was awful, waddn't it, what happened to those two little kids? Whatever became of them anyway? Their father's the one who did it, isn't he?"

Joanna lifted the one page and glanced at the next one. EX-HUSBAND ARRESTED IN WIFE'S SLAYING, the headline blared.

"See there?" the waitress said. "I told you." She marched away from the table, and Joanna picked up the article.

Antonio Jorge Grijalva, age 43, was arrested today and booked into the Maricopa County Jail on an open charge of murder in connection with the bludgeon slaying of his estranged wife two weeks ago. He surrendered without incident outside his place of employment in southeastern Arizona. Sources close to the investigation say Mr. Grijalva has been a person of interest in the case since the beginning.

Two City of Peoria police officers, Detectives Carol Strong and Mark Hansen, traveled over four hundred miles from Peoria to Paul Spur to make the arrest. The Cochise County Sheriff's Department assisted in collaring the suspect, who was placed under arrest in the parking lot of a lime plant as he was leaving work.

Court records reveal that the slain woman had sworn out a no-contact order against her estranged husband four days before her disappearance and death. The fact that the suspect was not at work on the night in question and could not account for his whereabouts caused investigators to focus in on him very early in the investigation.

Mr. Jefferson Duffy, father of the slain victim, when contacted at his home in Wittmann, expressed relief. "We're glad to know he's under lock and key. The wife and I have Serena's two kids here with us. With Jorge on the loose like that, there was no telling what might happen next."

"Hey, good-looking, you're working too hard. I'd be glad to buy you a piece of pie to go with that coffee."

Joanna heard the voice and looked up, not sure the words were intended for her. An overall-clad, cigarette-smoke-shrouded man was leering at her from the booth next to hers in a section reserved for professional truck drivers.

"You look kind of lonesome sitting there all by yourself."

"I was reading," Joanna said.

"I noticed. So what are you, some kind of student?"

Joanna looked down at her left hand. She still wore her wedding ring and the diamond engagement ring she had received as a gift only after Andy was already in the hospital dying. Seeing them made the pain of Andy's loss burn anew. She looked from her hand back to the man in the booth. If he had noticed either the gesture or the pain engendered by his unwanted intrusion, it made no difference.

"I'm not a student, I'm a cop," she answered evenly.

"Sure you are." He nodded. "And I'm a monkey's uncle. I've got me a nice little double bed in my truck out there. I'll bet the two of us could make beautiful music together."

For a moment, Joanna was too stunned by his rude proposition to even think of a comeback. Instead, she shuffled the stack of papers back into the envelope. "Which truck is that?" she asked.

"That big red, white, and blue Peterbilt out there in the parking lot." He grinned; then he tipped the bill of his San Diego Padres baseball cap in her direction. "Peewee Wright Hauling at your service, ma'am."

"Where are you headed?"

Peewee Wright beamed with unwarranted confidence. "El Paso," he said. "After I sleep awhile, that is. It'd be a real shame to have to sleep alone, don't you think?"

"I see you're wearing a ring, Mr. Wright," Joanna observed. "What would Mrs. Wright have to say about that?"

Peewee waved his cigarette and shook his head. "She wouldn't mind none. Me and her have one of them open marriages."

"Do you really?" Joanna stood up, gathering her belongings and her check. "The problem is, I don't believe in open marriages." She reached into her pocket and pulled out one of her newly printed business cards. She paused beside his table, fingering the card, looking at the words that were printed there: JOANNA BRADY, SHERIFF, COCHISE COUNTY, BISBEE, ARIZONA.

"And how will you be going to El Paso?" she asked.

"Interstate Ten from Tucson," he said.

Joanna nodded. "That's about what I figured," she said, dropping the card on his table. "If I were you, I'd check my equipment for any violations before I left here. I'd also be very careful not to speed once I got inside Cochise County."

She waited while he reached out one meaty paw to pick up the card and read it.

Because the Arizona Highway Patrol, not the Sheriff's Department, patrols the segment of I-10 that slices through Cochise County from the Pima County line to the New Mexico border, Joanna knew her words to be nothing more than an empty threat. Still, when the man read the text on her business card, he blanched.

He was still holding the card as Joanna walked away. If nothing else, the experience would give him something to think about the next time he tried to pick up a lone woman minding her own business in a truck stop.

SIX

HAD JOANNA been going to the Hohokam Resort Hotel that evening instead of later on during the week, it would have been easy to find. The only high-rise for miles around, the twelve-story newly finished hotel towered over its low-rise Old Peoria neighbors, its layers of lighted windows glowing like beacons as Joanna made her way north on Grand Avenue.

The Arizona Police Officers Academy turned out to be directly across the street. It was also across the railroad tracks, however, and the only way to get there was to cross the railroad at Olive and then turn in off Hatcher.

The triangular site was located in an area that seemed to be zoned commercial. Along both Seventy-fifth and Hatcher, a high brick wall marked two sides of the property. Entry was gained through an ornate portal. Two cast-concrete angels stood guard on either side of the drive. An arched lintel rose up and over behind them. One of the angels had lost part of a wing—probably to vandals—while the other was still intact. The words GOD IS LOVE were carved into the lintel itself.

The verse wasn't exactly in keeping with the mission of a police academy, but Joanna knew where it came from—a man named Tommy Tompkins. The Reverend Tommy Tompkins.

For years the APOA had limped along in the deteriorating classrooms of a decommissioned high school in central Phoenix. Only recently had the academy moved to its new home in Peoria. The APOA's good fortune came as a result of Tommy's fall from grace. He and his two top lieutenants had been shipped off to federal prison on income tax evasion convictions. As his religious and financial empire collapsed, the property he had envisioned as world headquarters of Tommy Tompkins International had fallen into the hands of the Resolution Trust Corporation.

On fifteen acres of donated cotton field, Tommy had planned to build not only a glass-walled cathedral, but also the dorms and classrooms that would have allowed him to indoctrinate a cadre of handpicked missionaries. By the time Tommy Tompkins International fell victim to the RTC, the planned complex was only partially completed. The classroom wing along with dormitories, a temporary residence for Tommy himself, as well as a few outbuildings were all that were or ever would be finished.

When the place went up for grabs, the state of Arizona had jumped at the chance to buy the property at a bargain-basement price since the site lay directly in the path of a proposed freeway extension. While awaiting voter approval of road-building monies, the state had leased the complex to the multijurisdictional consortium running the APOA. The transaction was accomplished with the strict understanding that little or no money would be spent on remodeling. As a result, angels continued to guard the entrance of the place where police officers from all over the state of Arizona received their basic law enforcement training.

Maybe guardian angels aren't such a bad idea, Joanna thought as she drove across the vast, patchily lit parking lot to the place where two dozen or so cars were grouped together near two buildings connected by breezeways and laid out in a long L.

The two-story structure built along one leg had the regularly spaced windows, doors, and lights that indicated living quarters. That was probably the dorm. Although lights were on in some of the rooms, there was no sign of life. The other building was only one story high. From the spacing of the rooms, Joanna surmised that one contained classrooms. She parked the car and walked to the end of the dorm nearest the classroom building. There, she found a wall-mounted plaque that said OFFICE along with an arrow that pointed toward the other building.

Past a closed wrought-iron gate, Joanna discovered that the last door on the classroom building was equipped with a bell. Even though no lights were visible inside, she rang the doorbell anyway.

"I'm out here on the patio. Who is it?" a male voice called from somewhere outside, somewhere beyond that iron gate.

"Joanna Brady. Cochise County," she answered. When she tried the gate, it fell open under her hand. Across a small patio between the two buildings, she could see a cigarette glowing in the dark.

"It's about time you got here," the man growled in return. "You're the last of the Mohicans, you know. You're late."

Nothing like getting off on the right foot, Joanna thought. "Sorry," she said. "My paperwork said suggested arrival times were between four and six. If whoever wrote that meant required, they should have said so."

The man ground out his cigarette and stood up. In the dim light, she couldn't make out his features, but he was tall—six four or so—and well over two hundred pounds. He smelled of beer and cigarettes, and he swayed slightly as he looked down at her.

"I wrote it," he said. "In my vocabulary, suggested and required mean the same thing. Suggested maybe sounds nicer, but I wanted you all checked in by six."

"I see," Joanna replied. "I'll certainly know better next time, won't I?"

"Maybe," he said. "We'll see. Come on, then," he added. "Your key's inside. Let's get this over with so I can go back to enjoying the rest of my evening off."

Instead of heading back through the gate, he stomped across the patio to a sliding door that opened into the office unit. Before entering, he paused long enough to drop his empty beer can into an almost full recycling box that sat just outside the door. Shaking her head, Joanna followed. This was a man who could afford to take some civility lessons from Welcome Wagon.

Joanna had expected to step inside a modest motel office/apartment. Instead, she found herself in a huge but sparsely furnished living room that looked more like a semiabandoned hotel lobby than it did either an office or an apartment.

Leaving Joanna standing there, the man headed off toward what turned out to be the kitchen. "I'll be right back," he said, over his shoulder, but he was gone for some time, giving Joanna a chance to examine the room in detail.

It seemed oddly disjointed. On the one hand, the ornate details—polished granite floors, high ceilings, gilt cove moldings, floor-to-ceiling mirrors, and lush chintz drapes—seemed almost palatial, while the furnishings were Danish-modern thrift store rejects. Between the living room and kitchen was a huge formal dining room with a crystal chandelier. Instead of a polished dining table and chairs, the room contained nothing but a desk and chair. And not a fancy one, at that. The battered, gunmetal-gray affair, its surface covered with a scatter of papers, was almost as ugly as it was old.

The man emerged from the kitchen carrying a bottle of Coors beer. He paused by the desk long enough to pick up a set of keys. When he was barely within range, he tossed them in the general direction of where Joanna was standing. Despite his poor throw, she managed to snag them out of midair.

"Good reflexes." He nodded appreciatively. "You're in room one oh nine," he said. "It's in the next building two doors down, just on the other side of the student lounge. The gold key is to your room. The silver one next to it opens the lounge door in case you need to go in after I lock it up for the night. The little one is for the laundry. It's way down at the far end of the first floor, last door on the left. There's a phone in your room, but it's only for local calls. For long distance, there's a pay phone in the lounge."

"Thank you . . ." Joanna paused. "I don't believe I caught your name."

"Thompson," he said. "Dave Thompson. I run this place."

"And you live here?"

He took a sip of beer and gave Joanna an appraising look that stopped just short of saying, "You want to make something of it?" Aloud he said, "Comes with the job. They actually hired a dorm manager once, but she got sick. They asked me to handle the dorm arrangements on a temporary basis, and I've been doing it ever since. It's not that much work, once everybody finally gets checked in, that is."

Another little zinger. This guy isn't easy to like, Joanna thought. Stuffing the keys in her pocket, she started toward the door.

"Class starts at eight-thirty sharp in the morning," Dave Thompson said to her back. "Not eight-thirty-five or eight-thirty-one, but eight-thirty. There's coffee and a pickup breakfast in the student lounge. It's not fancy—cereal, toast, and juice is all—but it'll hold you."

Joanna turned back to him. "You'll be in class?"

He raised the bottle to his lips, took a swallow, and then grinned at her. "You bet," he said. "I teach the morning class. We've got a real good-looking crop of officers this time around."

Joanna started to ask exactly what he meant by that, but she thought better of it. Her little go-round with Peewee Wright at the truck stop earlier that afternoon had left her feeling overly sensitive. Thompson probably meant nothing more or less than the fact that the students looked as though they'd make fine police officers.

"Any questions?" Thompson asked.

Joanna shook her head. "I'd better go drag my stuff in from the car and unpack. I want to put everything away, shower, and get a decent night's rest."

"That's right," he said. "Wouldn't do at all for you to fall asleep in class. Might miss something important."

As Joanna hurried out the door and headed for her car, she was suddenly filled with misgivings. If Dave Thompson was indicative of the caliber of people running APOA, maybe she had let herself in for a five-and-a-half-week waste of time.

After lugging the last of her suitcases into the room and looking around, she felt somewhat better. Although the room wasn't as large or as nice as Dave Thompson's, it was done in much the same style with floor-to-ceiling mirrors covering one wall of both the room and the adjacent bath. The ceilings weren't nearly as high as they were in the office unit, and the floor was covered with a commercial-grade medium-gray carpet. The bathroom, however, was luxury itself. The floor and counter tops were polished granite. The room came complete with both a king-sized Jacuzzi and glass-doored shower. All the fixtures boasted solid brass fittings.

Looking back from the bathroom door to the modest pressboard dresser, desk, headboard, and nightstand, Joanna found herself giggling, struck by the idea that she was standing in a cross between a castle and Motel 6.

Joanna spent the next half hour emptying her suitcases and putting things away. Her threadbare bath towels looked especially shabby in the upscale bathroom. When she was totally unpacked, she treated herself to a long, hot bath with the Jacuzzi heads bubbling full blast. Lying there in the steaming tub, supposedly relaxing, she couldn't get the Grijalva kids out of her mind.

Ceci and Pablo. They were orphans, all right. Twice over. Their mother was dead, and their father might just as well be.

Sighing, Joanna clambered out of the tub into the steam-filled room and turned on the exhaust fan, hoping to clear the fogged mirrors. The first whirl of the blades brought a whiff of cigarette smoke into her nostrils. A moment later it was gone. Obviously, her next door neighbor was a smoker.

After toweling herself dry, Joanna pulled on a robe. By then it was only nine o'clock. Instead of getting into bed, she walked over to the desk and picked up Juanita Grijalva's envelope, which she had dropped there in the course of unpacking. Settling at the desk, she emptied the envelope and read through all the contents, including re-reading the articles she had read earlier that afternoon in the truck stop.

This time, she took pen and paper and jotted notes as she read, writing down names and addresses as they appeared in the various articles. The Grijalvas—Antonio Jorge, Ceci, and Pablo; Jefferson Davis and Ernestina Duffy of Wittmann; City of Peoria Detectives Carol Strong and Mark Hansen; Butch Dixon, bartender of the Roundhouse Bar and Grill; Anna-Ray Melton, manager of the WE-DO-YU-DO Washateria; Madeline Bellerman, Serena's attorney.

Those were the players in the Serena Grijalva case—the ones whose names had made it into the papers. If Joanna was going to do any questioning on her own, those were the people she'd need to contact.

It was after eleven when she finally put the contents back in the envelope, climbed into bed, and turned off the light. As she lay there waiting for sleep to come and trying to decide what, if anything, she was going to do about Jorge Grijalva, another faint whiff of cigarette smoke wafted into her room.

Her last thought before she fell asleep was that whoever lived in the room next door had to be a chain smoker.

Joanna woke early the next morning, dressed, and hurried down to the lounge, hoping to call Jenny before she left for school. Unfortunately, there was a long line at the single pay phone. All her classmates seemed to have the same need to call home.

While she waited, Joanna helped herself to coffee, juice, and a piece of toast. A newspaper had been left on the table. She picked up the paper and read one of the articles. A power-line installation crew, working on a project southwest of Carefree, had stumbled across the decomposing body of a partially clad woman. Officers from the Maricopa County Sheriff's Department were investigating the death of the so-far unidentified woman as an apparent homicide.

Joanna's stomach turned leaden. Some other as yet unnamed family was about to have its heart torn out. Unfortunately, Joanna Brady knew exactly how that felt.

"You can use the phone now," someone said.

Joanna glanced at her watch. Ten after eight. "That's all right," she said. "My daughter's already left for school. I don't need it anymore."

SEVEN

WITHIN MINUTES of the beginning of Dave Thompson's opening classroom lecture, Joanna was ready to pack her bags and go back home to Bisbee. Her first encounter with the bull-necked Thompson hadn't left a very good impression. The lecture made his stock go down even further.

Listening to him talk, Joanna could close her eyes and imagine that she was listening to her chief deputy for operations, Dick Voland. The words used, the opinions voiced, were almost the same. Why had she bothered to travel four hundred miles round-trip and spend the better part of six weeks locked up in a classroom when she could have the same kind of aggravation for free at home just by going into the office? The only difference between listening to Dave Thompson and being lectured to by Dick Voland lay in the fact that after a day of wrangling with Dick

Voland, Joanna could at least go home to her own bed at night. As far as beds were concerned, the ones in the APOA dormitory weren't worth a damn.

The man droned on and on. Joanna had to fight to stay awake while Dave Thompson paced back and forth in front of the class. Joanna had spent years listening to Jim Bob Brady's warm southern drawl. Thompson's strained down-home manner of speech sounded put on and gratingly phony. Waving an old-fashioned pointer for emphasis, he delivered a drill-instructor-style diatribe meant to scare off all but the most serious-minded of the assembled students.

"Look around you," he urged, waggling the pointer until it encompassed all the people in the room. "There'll be some faces missing by the time we get to the end of this course. We generally expect a washout rate of between forty and fifty percent, and that's in a good class."

Joanna raised her eyebrows at that. The night before, Dave Thompson had said this was a good class. This morning, it evidently wasn't. What had changed his mind?

"You may have noticed that there aren't any television sets in those rooms of yours," Thompson continued. "No swimming pool or tennis courts, either. This ain't no paid vacation, my friends. You're here to work, plain and simple. You'd by God better get that straight from the get-go.

"There may be a few party animals in the crowd. If you think you can party all night long and then drag ass in here the next morning and sleep through the lectures, think again. Days are for classwork, and nights are for hitting the books. Do I make myself clear?"

Careful not to move her head in any direction, Joanna kept her eyes focused full on Thompson's beefy face. Peripheral vision allowed her a glimpse of movement in the front row where a young blond-haired man nodded his head in earnest agreement. The gesture of unquestioning approval was so pronounced it was a wonder the guy's teeth didn't rattle.

"Over the next few weeks, you'll be working with a staff made up from outstanding officers who have been selected from jurisdictions all over the state," Thompson was saying. "These are the guys who, along with yours truly, will be conducting most of the classroom instruction. We'll be overseeing some of the hands-on training as well as evaluating each student's individual progress. All told, the instructors here have a combined total of more than a hundred twenty years of law enforcement experience. Try that on for size."

He paused and grinned. "You know what they say about experience and treachery, don't you? Wins out over youth and enthusiasm every time. Count on it."

The room was quiet. No doubt the comment had been meant as a joke, but no one laughed. While Thompson consulted his notes, Joanna noticed that the young guy in the front row was busily nodding once again.

"That brings us to the subject of ride-alongs," Thompson resumed. "When it comes time for those, you'll be doing them with experienced on-duty officers from one or more of the participating agencies here in the Valley. By the way, be sure to sign the ride-along waivers in your packet and return them to me by the end of the day.

"This particular class—procedures—is my baby. It's also the backbone of what we do here. As you all know, the academy is being funded partially by state and federal grants and partially by the tuition paid by each participating agency. Tuition doesn't come cheap. The state maybe picked up this fine facility for a song from the folks at the RTC, but we've gotta pay our way. Here's how it works, folks. Listen up.

"Each person's whole tuition and room rent is due and payable on the first day of class. In other words, today. The minute you all walked through our door this morning, that money was gone. The academy doesn't do refunds. You quit tonight? Too bad. The guy who hired you—the one who sent you here in the first place—doesn't get to put that money back in his departmental budget. That means anybody who drops out turns into a regular pain in the bottom line.

"In other words, boys and girls, if you blow this chance, you end up outta here and outta law enforcement, too. Nobody in his right mind's gonna give a quitter another opportunity.

"For those of you who don't blow it, for those of you who make the grade, when you go back to your various departments, you're more than welcome to do things the way they do them there. Here at the academy, we have our own procedures, and we do things our way. The APOA way. In other words, as that great American hero, A. J. Foyt, has been quoted as saying, 'my way or the highway.'

"It's like you and your ex-wife own this little dog, and the doggie spends part of the time at her house and part of the time at yours. Maybe your ex doesn't mind if the dog climbs all over her damn furniture, but you do. When the dog goes to her house, he does whatever the hell he damn well pleases, but when he's at your house, he lives by your rules. Got it?"

Joanna didn't even have to look to know that the guy in the front row was nodding once again. Disgusted by what she'd heard, and convinced the whole training experience was destined to be nothing more than five weeks of hot air, Joanna folded her arms across her chest, sighed, and sank down in her seat. Next to her at the table sat a tall, slender young woman with hair almost as red as Joanna's.

Using one hand to shield her face from the speaker's view, the other woman grinned in Joanna's direction then crossed both eyes. Wary that Thompson might have spotted the derogatory gesture, Joanna glanced in the speaker's direction, but he was far too busy pontificating to notice the humorous byplay. Relieved, Joanna smiled back. Somehow that bit of schoolgirlish high-jinks made Joanna feel better. If nothing else, it convinced her that she wasn't the only person in the room who regarded Dave Thompson as a loudmouthed, overbearing jerk.

"Our mission here is to turn you people into police officers," Thompson continued. "It's not easy, and it's gonna get down and dirty at times. If you two ladies think you're going to come through this course looking like one of the sexy babe lawyers that used to be on *L.A. Law,* you'd better think again."

The redhead at the table next to Joanna scribbled a hasty note on a yellow notepad and then pushed it close enough so Joanna could read it. "Who has time to watch TV?" the note asked.

This time Joanna had to cough in order to suppress an involuntary giggle. She had never watched the show herself, but according to Eva Lou, *L.A. Law* had once been a favorite with Jim Bob Brady. Eva Lou said she thought it had something to do with the length of the women's skirts.

Thompson glowered once in Joanna's direction, but he didn't pause for breath. "Out on the streets it's gonna be a matter of life and death— your life or your partner's, or the life of some innocent bystander. Every department in the state has a mandate to bring more women and minorities on board. Cultural diversity is okay, I guess," he added, sounding unconvinced.

"It's probably even a good thing, up to a point—as long as those new hires are all fully qualified people. And that's where the APOA comes in. The buck stops here. The training we offer is supposed to help separate the men from the boys, if you will. The wheat from the chaff. The people who can handle this job from the wimps who can't. We're going to start that process here and now. Could I have a volunteer?"

Pausing momentarily, Thompson's gray eyes scanned the room. Naturally the guy in the front row, the head-bobber, raised his hand and waved it in the air. Thompson ignored him. Tapping the end of the pointer with one hand, he allowed his gaze to come to rest on Joanna. A half smile tweaked the corners of his mouth.

"My mother always taught me that it was ladies before gentlemen. Tell the class your name."

"Joanna," she answered. "Joanna Brady."

"And where are you from?"

"Cochise County," Joanna answered.

"And how long have you been a police officer now?" he asked.

"Less than two weeks."

Thompson nodded. "That's good. We like to get our recruits in here early—before they have time to learn too many bad habits. And why, exactly, do you want to be a cop?"

Joanna wasn't sure what to say. Each student in the class wore a plastic badge that listed his or her name and home jurisdiction. The badges gave no indication of rank. Hoping to blend in with her classmates, Joanna wasn't eager to reveal that, although she was as much of a rookie as any of the others, she was also a newly elected county sheriff.

"Well?" Thompson urged impatiently.

"My father was a police officer," she said flatly. "So was my husband."

Thompson frowned. "That's right," he said. "I remember your daddy, old D. H. Lathrop. Good man. And your husband's the one who got shot in the line of duty, isn't he?"

Joanna bit her lip and nodded. Andy's death as well as its violent aftermath had been big news back in September. Both their pictures and names had been plastered in newspapers and on television broadcasts all over Arizona.

"And unless I'm mistaken, you had something to do with the end of that case, didn't you, Mrs. Brady? Wasn't there some kind of shoot-out?"

"Yes," Joanna answered, recalling the charred edges of the single bullet hole that still branded the pocket of her sheepskin-lined jacket.

"So it would be safe to assume that you've used a handgun before—that you have some experience?" The rising inflection in Dave Thompson's voice made it sound as if he were asking a question, but Joanna understood that he already knew the answer.

A vivid flush crept up her neck and face. The last thing Joanna wanted was to be singled out from her classmates, the other academy attendees. Dave Thompson seemed to have other ideas. He focused on her in a way that caused all the other people in the room to recede into the background.

"Yes," she answered softly, keeping her voice level, fending off the natural urge to blink. "I suppose it would."

Thompson smiled and nodded. "Good," he said. "You come on up here then. We'll have you take the first shot, if you'll excuse the pun." Visibly appreciative of his own joke, he grinned and seemed only vaguely disappointed when Joanna didn't respond in kind.

Unsure what the joke was, Joanna rose resolutely from her chair and walked to the front of the classroom. Her hands shook, more from suppressed anger at being singled out than with any kind of nervousness or stage fright. Weeks of public speaking on the campaign trail had cured her of all fear of appearing in front of a group of strangers.

The room was arranged as a formal classroom with half a dozen rows of tables facing a front podium. Behind the podium stood several carts loaded with an assortment of audiovisual equipment. As he spoke, Thompson moved one cart holding a video console and VCR to a spot beside the podium. He knelt for a few moments in front of the cart and selected a video from a locked storage cabinet underneath. After inserting the video in the VCR, Thompson reached into another locked storage cabinet and withdrew a holstered service revolver and belt.

"Ever seen one of these before?"

The way he was holding the weapon, Joanna wasn't able to see anything about it. "I'm not sure," she said.

"For your information," Thompson returned haughtily, "it happens to be a revolver."

His contemptuous tone implied that he had

misread her inability to see the weapon as total ignorance as far as guns were concerned. "It's a thirty-eight," he continued. "A Smith and Wesson Model Ten military and police revolver with a four-inch barrel."

He handed the belt and holstered weapon to Joanna. "Here," he said. "Take this and put it on. Don't be afraid," he added. "It's loaded with blanks."

Removing the gun from its holster, Joanna swung open the cylinder. One by one, she checked each of the rounds, ascertaining for herself that they were indeed blanks, loaded with paper wadding, rather than metal bullets. Only after reinserting the rounds did she look back at Dave Thompson, who was watching her with rapt interest.

"So you do know something about guns."

"A little," she returned with a grim smile. "And you're right. They are all blanks. I hope you don't mind my checking for myself. My father always taught me that when it comes to loaded weapons, I shouldn't take anybody else's word for it."

There was a rustle of appreciative chuckles from a few of Joanna's fellow classmates. Dave Thompson was not amused. "What else did your daddy teach you?" he asked.

"One or two things," Joanna answered. "Now what do you want me to do with this pistol?"

"Put it back in the holster and strap on the belt."

The belt—designed to be used on adult male bodies—was cumbersome and several sizes too large for Joanna's slender waist. Even fastened in the smallest hole, the heavy belt slipped down until it rested on the curve of her hips rather than staying where it belonged. Convinced the low-slung gun made her look like a comic parody of some old-time gunfighter, Joanna felt ridiculous. As she struggled with the awkward belt, she barely heard what Thompson was saying.

"You ever hear of a shoot/don't shoot scenario?"

"I don't think so."

"You're about to. Here's what we're gonna do. Once you get that belt on properly, I want you to spend a few minutes practicing removing the weapon from and returning it to the holster. No matter what you see on TV, cops don't spend all their time walking around holding drawn side-arms in their hands. But when you need a gun, you've gotta be able to get it out in a hell of a hurry."

Joanna attempted to do as she was told. By then the belt had slipped so far down her body, she was afraid it was going to fall off altogether. Each time she tried to draw the weapon, the belt jerked up right along with the gun. With the belt sliding loosely around her waist, she couldn't get enough leverage to pull the gun free of the holster. It took several bumbling tries before she finally succeeded in freeing the gun from the leather.

"Very good," Dave Thompson said at last. "Now, here's the next step. I want you to stand right here beside this VCR. The tape I just loaded is one of about a hundred or so that we use here at the academy. In each one, the camera is the cop. The lens of the camera is situated at the cop's eye level. You'll be seeing the incident unfold through the cop's eyes, through his point of view. You'll see what he sees, hear what he hears.

"Each scenario is based on a real case," he added. "You'll have the same information available to you as the cop did in the real case. At some point in the film—some critical juncture in the action—you will have to decide whether or not to draw your weapon, whether or not to fire. It's up to you. Ready?"

Joanna nodded. Aware that all eyes in the room were turned on her, she waited while Thompson checked to be sure the plug was in and then switched on the video.

For a moment the screen was covered with snow, then the room was filled with the sound of a mumbled police radio transmission. When the picture came on, Joanna was seeing the world through the front windshield of a moving patrol car, one that was following another vehicle—a Ford Taurus—down a broad city street. Moments after the tape started, the lead vehicle, carrying two visible occupants, signaled for a right-hand turn and then pulled off onto a tree-lined residential side street. Seconds later the patrol car turned as well. After it followed the lead vehicle for a block or two, there was the brief squawk from a siren as the officer signaled for the other car to pull over.

In what seemed like slow motion, the door of

the patrol car opened and the officer stepped out into the seemingly peaceful street. The camera, positioned at shoulder height, moved jerkily toward the stopped car. In the background came a steady murmur of continuing radio transmissions. Standing just to the rear of the driver's door, the camera bent down and peered inside. Two young men were seated in front.

"Step out of the car please," the officer said, speaking over the sound of loud music blaring from the radio in the Taurus.

The driver hesitated for a moment, then moved to comply. As he did so, his passenger suddenly slammed open the rider's door. He leaped from the car and went racing up the toy-littered sidewalk of a nearby home. For a moment, the point of view stayed beside the door of the stopped Taurus, but the scene on-screen swung back and forth several times, darting between the passenger fleeing up the sidewalk and the driver who was already raising his hands in the air and leaning over the hood of his vehicle.

"How come you stopped us?" the driver whined. "We wasn't doin' nothin'."

By then Joanna had lost track of everything but what was happening on the screen. A sudden knot tightened in her stomach as she was sucked into the scene's unfolding drama. She felt the responding officer's momentary but agonizing indecision. His hesitation was hers as well. Should he stay with the one suspect or go pounding up the sidewalk after the other one?

Joanna's mind raced as she tried to sort things

out. As the fleeing suspect ran toward the house, she caught a glimpse of something in his right hand. Was it a stick or a tire iron? Or was it a gun? From the little she had seen, there was no way to know for sure, but if one suspect carried a gun, chances were the other one did, too.

The kid with his hands in the air couldn't have been more than sixteen or seventeen. He wasn't a total innocent. No doubt he'd been involved in previous run-ins with the law. He knew the drill. Without being ordered to do so, he had automatically raised his hands, spread his legs, and bent over the hood of the car. Most law-abiding folks don't react quite that way when stopped for a routine traffic violation. They are far more likely to start rummaging shakily through glove compartments, searching frantically for elusive insurance papers and vehicle registrations.

As the camera's focus switched once more from the driver back to the fleeing suspect, Joanna again glimpsed something in his hand. Again she couldn't identify what it was, not for certain.

"Stop, police!" the invisible officer bellowed. "Drop it!"

The shouted order came too late. Even as the voice thundered out through speakers, the fleeing suspect vaulted up the steps, bounded across the porch, flung open the screen door, and shouldered his way into the house.

At once the camera started moving forward, jerking awkwardly up and down as the cop, too, raced up the sidewalk and onto the porch.

Taking a hint from what was happening on-screen, Joanna began trying to wrest the Smith & Wesson out of the holster. Once again, the gun hung up on the balky leather while the belt and holster twisted loosely around her waist. Only after three separate tries did she manage to draw the weapon.

When she was once more able to glance back at the screen, the cop/camera had taken up a defensive position on the porch, crouching next to the wall of the house just to the right of the screen door. "Come out," the cop yelled. "Come out with your hands up!"

Just then Joanna heard the sound of a woman's voice coming from inside the house. "Who are you?" the rising female voice demanded. "What are you doing in my house? What do you want? What . . ."

Suddenly the voice changed. Angry outrage changed in pitch and became a shriek of terror. "No. Don't do that. Don't please! No! Oh, no! Noooooooooo!"

"Come out," the officer ordered again. "Now!"

By then Joanna had the gun firmly in hand. She spread her feet into the proper stance and raised the revolver. The Smith & Wesson seemed far heavier than the brand-new Colt 2000 she owned personally, the one she was accustomed to using in daily target practice. Even holding the gun with both hands, it wasn't easy to keep her aim steady.

Suddenly the screen door crashed open. The

first thing that appeared beyond the edge of the door was an arm holding the unmistakable silhouette of a drawn gun followed by the dark figure of the man who was carrying it.

As the suspect burst out through the open doorway, Joanna bit her lip. Aiming high enough for a chest shot, Joanna eased back on the trigger. At once the classroom reverberated with the roar of the blank cartridge. Immediately the room filled with the smell of burned cordite, and the video screen went blank.

Holding the VCR's remote control, smiling and nodding, Dave Thompson stood up and looked around the room. "The lady seems to know how to shoot," he said. "But the question is, did she do the right thing?"

The guy in the front row was already waving his hand in the air. "The officer never should have left the vehicle," he announced triumphantly. "He should have stayed where he was and radioed for backup."

That same sentiment was echoed in so many words by most of the rest of the class. While debate over Joanna's handling of the incident swirled around her, she resumed her seat.

The main focus of the discussion was what the officer should have done to take better control of the situation. "He for sure should have called for backup," someone else offered. "What if the other guy was armed, too? While the officer was chasing after the one guy, the other one could have turned on him as well."

The consensus seemed to be that, in the heat of the moment, the officer may not have done everything in his power to avert a possible tragedy. The same held true for Joanna.

Finally Dave Thompson called a halt to any further discussion. "All right, boys and girls," he said. "That's enough. Now we're going to see whether or not Officer Brady's response was right or wrong."

With a flick of the remote, the video came back to life. The man in the video image stepped out from behind the screen door. His right hand was fully extended, and the gun was now completely visible. He let the door slam shut behind him and then turned directly into the lens of the camera. As soon as he did so, there was a collective gasp from the entire room.

To her horror Joanna saw that he was holding something in his left hand, something else in addition to the gun in his right—a baby. A screaming, diaper-clad baby was clutched in the crook of his left elbow. As he moved toward the camera, the suspect held the frightened child chest high, using the baby as a human shield.

A wave of goose bumps swept down Joanna's body. Sickened, she realized she had deliberately aimed for the suspect's chest when she fired off her round. Had this been a real incident—had that been a real bullet—it would have sliced through the child. The baby would have died.

From the front of the classroom Dave Thompson looked squarely at Joanna. A superior, knowing grin played around the corners of his mouth.

"I guess you lose, little lady," he said, tapping the pointer in his right hand into the palm of his left. "Better luck next time."

EIGHT

THAT WHOLE first day was spent on lectures. By the time class was out for the evening, Joanna was more than ready. On the way back to her room, Joanna stopped by the lounge long enough to buy a diet Coke from the vending machine and to make a few phone calls from the pay phone.

The soda was more rewarding than the phone calling was. No one was available to talk to her, not at home and not at the office, either. Both Frank Montoya and Dick Voland were out of the office, and the answering machine out at the High Lonesome clicked on after the fourth ring. Joanna hung up without leaving a message.

Back in her room, Joanna settled herself at the desk and tried to wade into the seventy-six pages of text Dave Thompson had assigned to be read prior to class the following day. It didn't work. Chilling flashbacks from the shoot/don't shoot scenario kept getting in the way of her concentration. Finally, exasperated, she tossed the book aside, picked up her notebook, and began scribbling a hasty letter:

Dear Jenny,

I'm supposed to be studying, but I can't seem to concentrate. Claustrophobia, I think. You do know what that is, don't you? If not, ask Grandpa Brady to explain it.

The only windows in this place are right up almost at the ceiling. They're called clerestory windows—the kind they have in church. They let light in, but they're too high for someone inside to see out. It reminds me of a jail. . . .

As soon as Joanna wrote the word "jail," she remembered Jorge Grijalva. And his two children.

Turning away from the letter, Joanna paged back through her notebook beyond the day's lecture notes until she found the page of notations she had written down based on the articles in Juanita Grijalva's envelope. For several moments, she sat staring at the names that were written there. Then, making up her mind, she opened the nightstand drawer and pulled out the phone book. After all, since this was Peoria, a call to the Peoria Police Department ought to be a local call.

But when she dialed the number, Carol Strong wasn't available, and Joanna didn't have nerve enough to leave a message. Instead, she looked up the other two businesses that were mentioned there. At the WE-DO-YU-DO Washateria, Anna-Ray Melton wasn't expected in until seven the following morning, and none of the white page listings for Melton gave the name Anna-Ray. Next, Joanna tried asking for Butch Dixon at the Round-house Bar and Grill. Raucous country/western music wailed in the background.

"Who do you want? Butch?" the person who answered the phone shouted into the receiver. "Sure, he's here, but he's busy. It's Happy Hour, you know. Can I take a message?"

"No, thanks," Joanna said. "I'll call back later."

She put the phone down. Then, while she was still looking at it, it rang, startling her. "Joanna?" a woman's voice said. "I'll bet you're cracking the books, aren't you."

"Not exactly. Who is this?"

"Leann Jessup," she said. "Your tablemate in class. And unless I'm mistaken, we're next-door neighbors here in the dorm, too. Do you have plans for dinner? Most of the guys are going out for Italian, but I'm not wild about pasta. Or the men in the class, either, for that matter. How about you?"

The unexpected invitation of going off to din-ner with Leann Jessup was tempting. Maybe Jo-anna should take the call as a hint and drop the whole idea of stopping by the Roundhouse. Maybe Joanna's tentative plan of questioning Butch Dixon, the bartender there, was a fruitcake no-tion that ought to be dropped like a hot potato.

For only a moment Joanna considered inviting Leann to come along with her, but the words never made it out of her mouth. If she went to the bar, talked to Butch, and ended up making a botch of things, why bring along a relative stranger to witness her falling flat on her face?

"Sorry," Joanna said. "I wish you had called ten minutes ago."

Leann seemed to take the rejection in stride. "No problem," she said. "I'll figure out some alternative. See you tomorrow."

Joanna put down the phone and pulled on jeans and a sweater. Armed with an address from the phone book and her notes, she headed for downtown Peoria and the Roundhouse Bar and Grill. Based on the name, she expected the address would take her somewhere close to the railroad track. Instead, Roundhouse derived from the shape of the building itself, which was, in fact, round. The railroad part had been grafted on as an afterthought in the form of an almost life-size train outlined in orange neon tubes along the outside of the building.

This must be the place, Joanna thought to herself, pulling into the potholed and vehicle-crowded parking lot. As she parked the Blazer, she could almost hear Eleanor Lathrop's sniff of disapproval. Women in general and her daughter in particular weren't supposed to visit bars to begin with. And they certainly weren't supposed to venture into those kinds of places alone. "A woman who goes into bars without an escort is asking for trouble," Eleanor would have said.

So are women who run for the office of sheriff, Joanna thought with a rueful smile. Squaring her shoulders, she climbed out of the truck and headed for the entrance. Just inside the door, she paused to get her bearings, allowing her ears to adjust to the noisy din and her eyes to become accustomed to the dim light.

The joint was divided almost evenly between dining area and bar. The smoke-filled bar was jammed nearly full while the restaurant was largely empty. In both sections, railroad memorabilia—from fading pictures and travel posters to crossing signs—decorated every inch of available wall space. A platform, dropped from the ceiling, ran around the outside of the room and supported the tracks for several running electric trains that hummed overhead at odd intervals. One wall was devoted to a big-screen television where a raucous group of sports-minded drinkers were jockeying for tables in advance of a Monday-night football game. Above the din of the pregame announcements, a blaring jukebox wailed out Roger Miller's plaintive version of "Engine, Engine Nine."

The semicircular bar in the dead center of the room was jammed with people. Seeing the crowd, Joanna's heart fell. She had hoped that by now the Happy Hour crowd would have gone home and the Roundhouse would be reasonably quiet. A slow evening would give her a chance to talk to the bartender. Under these busy circumstances, that wouldn't be easy.

With a sigh Joanna made for the single unoccupied stool she had spotted at the bar. If she sat there, she might manage to monopolize the bartender long enough for a word or two. He was a short, round-shouldered man with a shaved head, heavy black eyebrows, and a neatly trimmed, pencil-thin mustache. The name tag pinned to his shirt said BUTCH.

Butch Dixon appeared in front of Joanna almost before she finished hoisting herself onto the seat, shoving a wooden salad bowl overflowing with popcorn in her direction. "What'll it be?" he asked.

"Diet Coke," she said.

"Diet Pepsi okay?"

"Sure."

He went several steps down the bar, filled two glasses with ice, and then added liquid using a push-button dispenser. When he returned, he set both glasses in front of Joanna. "That'll be a buck," he said.

Joanna dug in her purse for money. "I only asked for one," she said.

Butch Dixon grinned. "Hey, don't fight it, lady," he said. "It's Happy Hour and Ladies' Night both. You get two drinks for the price of one. You new around here?"

Joanna nodded.

"Well, welcome to the neighborhood."

A cocktail waitress with a tray laden with empty glasses showed up at her station several seats away. While Butch Dixon hurried to take the used glasses and fill the waitress's new orders, Joanna sipped her Diet Pepsi and surveyed the room. On first glance the Roundhouse appeared to be respectable enough, and, unlike the truck stop, no one tried to proposition her. She had finished one drink and was started on the other before Butch paused in front of her again.

"How're you doing?" he asked.

"Fine. Is the food here any good?"

"Are you kidding? We were voted Best Bar Hamburgers in the Valley of the Sun two years in a row. Want one? I can bring it to you here, or you could move to the dining room."

"Here," she said.

"Fries? The works?"

After fighting sleep all morning, Joanna had skipped lunch at noontime in favor of grabbing a nap. Hungry now, she nodded.

"Have the Roundhouse Special then," Butch said, writing her order down on a ticket. "It's the best buy. How do you want it?"

"Medium."

He nodded. "And seeing as how you're new, I'll throw in the Caboose for free."

"What's a Caboose?" Joanna asked.

"A dish of vanilla ice cream with Spanish peanuts and chocolate syrup. Not very imaginative, but little kids love it."

He came back a few moments later and dropped a napkin-wrapped bundle of silverware in front of her. "Just move here?" he asked.

There seemed to be a slight lull among the customers at the bar right then, and Joanna decided it was time to make her move. For an answer, Joanna shook her head and then pulled one of her business cards from her jeans pocket. She handed it to him.

"I'll only be here for a few weeks. I'm attending police academy classes at the APOA just down the road," she said.

"Oh, yeah?" he said, shoving the card into his pocket without bothering to look at it. "Some of those folks show up here now and then. For dinner," he added quickly. "Most of 'em hang out in the dining room rather than in the bar, if you know what I mean. I guess they're all afraid of what people will think."

Joanna took a breath. "Actually, I came here today to talk to you."

"To me?" Butch Dixon echoed with a frown. "How come?"

"It's about Serena Grijalva," Joanna said quietly.

Butch Dixon's eyes hardened and the engaging grin disappeared. From the expression on his face, Joanna expected him to tell her to get lost and forget the Roundhouse Special. Just then someone a few stools down the bar tapped his empty beer glass on the counter.

"Hey, barkeep," the impatient customer muttered. "A guy could thirst to death around here."

Dixon hurried away. Thinking she had blown her chances of gaining any useful information, Joanna sat forlornly at the bar with her half-empty glass in front of her and wondered if there would have been a better way to approach him. Eventually, he came back with a platter laden with food.

"How come the sheriff of Cochise County is interested in Serena Grijalva?" he asked. "And why bother talking to me instead of Carol Strong, the detective on the case? Besides, you won't want to hear what I have to say any more than she did."

"This isn't exactly an official inquiry," Joanna answered. "I just wanted to check some things out."

"Like what?"

"According to what it said in the paper, you were one of the last people to see Serena alive."

"That's right," Butch Dixon answered. "Me and Serena's ex-husband and a whole roomful of other people. Serena and her ex were having themselves a little heart-to-heart. We all heard them. You can see how private it is in here."

Once again Butch was called down the bar while Joanna bit into her hamburger. That one bite told her that the Roundhouse Special lived up to its glowing advance billing.

Butch came back to stand opposite Joanna's stool "How's the burger?"

"It's great. But tell me about Serena and Jorge Grijalva. They were having a fight?"

"Do you ever read Ogden Nash?" Butch asked.

Joanna was taken aback. "No. Why?"

"If you'd ever read 'I Never Even Suggested It,' you'd know it only takes one person to make a quarrel."

"Only one of them was fighting? Which one?"

"Serena was screaming like a banshee. I guess she had a restraining order on him or something, but he acted like a gentleman. Didn't threaten her or anything. Didn't even raise his voice. I felt sorry for the poor guy. All he was asking was for her to let the kids come to his mother's for Thanksgiving dinner. It didn't seem all that out of line to me."

Again Butch was summoned away, this time by the cocktail waitress again. When he finally returned, Joanna was done with her hamburger. He picked up the empty platter and stood holding it, eyeing Joanna.

"I don't care what the detectives and prosecutors say, I still don't think he did it. After she stomped out the door, he sat here for a long time, all hunched over. He had himself a couple more drinks and both of those were straight coffee. He said he had to drive all the way back to Douglas to be there in time to work in the morning. Does that sound like someone who's about to go knock off his ex-wife?"

Thoughtfully, Butch Dixon shook his head. "I'll go get your ice cream," he added. "You want coffee or something to go with it?"

"No. I'm fine."

He walked away, carrying the dirty dishes. Joanna watched him go. That made two different people who were convinced of Antonio Jorge Grijalva's innocence—a poetry-quoting bartender and the accused's own mother.

Butch Dixon returned with the dish of ice cream. "Did the prosecutor's office talk to you about any of this?" Joanna asked.

Dixon shook his head. "Naw. Like I said, the

detective just brushed me off. She claimed that she had enough physical evidence to get a conviction."

"Like what?"

"She didn't say. Not at the time. Later I heard about a possible plea bargain, and it pissed me off. I wanted to see him fight it. I even called up his public defender and offered to testify. He wasn't buying. I hate plea bargains."

Thoughtfully, Joanna carved off a spoonful of ice cream. "There are two primary reasons for so many plea bargains these days. Are you aware of what they are?"

Butch rolled his eyes. "I have a feeling you're going to tell me."

"The first one is to keep the system moving. If the case is reasonably solid, the prosecutors may decide to go for a lesser sentence just to spare themselves the time and aggravation of going to trial."

"And the second reason?"

"If the case is so weak they don't think they'll be able to get a conviction, they may go for a plea bargain as the best alternative to letting the guy walk. Maybe that's what's happened here."

"Wait a minute," Butch said. "Do you think that's possible? Maybe the case is weak and that's why they're going for a plea bargain?"

"It isn't really my case, but that's what I'm trying to find out," Joanna said. "If it's a strong case or if it isn't."

"Well, I'll be damned!" Butch Dixon exclaimed, beaming at her. "I figured you were just like all the others. You let me know if there's anything I can do to help, you hear?"

Joanna nodded. "Sure thing."

He had paused long enough that now he was behind in his duties. Joanna finished her ice cream and waited for some time, hoping he'd drop off her check. Finally, she waved him down. "Could I have my bill, please?"

"Forget it," he said. "It's taken care of."

"What do you mean?"

"You ever been divorced?"

Joanna shook her head.

"I have," Butch Dixon said. "Twice. Believe me, no matter what, the man is always the bad guy. I get sick and tired of men always getting walked on, know what I mean?"

"What does that have to do with my not paying for my hamburger?"

"Any friend of Jorge Grijalva's is a friend of mine."

NINE

WALKING FROM the bar into the parking lot, Joanna was surprised by how warm it was. Bisbee, two hundred miles to the south and east, was also four thousand feet higher in elevation. November nights in Cochise County had a crisp, wintery bite to them. By comparison, the evening air in Phoenix seemed quite balmy.

Once in the Blazer, Joanna sat for some time, not only considering what she had heard from Butch Dixon, but also wondering about her next move. Obviously, Butch was no more a disinterested observer than Juanita Grijalva was. Something in the bartender's own marital past had caused him to be uncommonly sympathetic to Jorge Grijalva's plight. Had he, in fact, called the man's public defender with an offer to testify on Jorge's behalf? That's what Dixon claimed. In an era when most people don't want to get involved, that in itself was remarkable.

So, in addition to his mother, Jorge Grijalva has at least one other partisan, Joanna thought. Despite Butch Dixon's professed willingness to do so, however, he would never be called to a witness stand to testify. Plea bargain arrangements don't call for either witnesses or testimony. There would be no defense, and that seemed wrong. Somehow, without Joanna quite being able to put her finger on the way he had done it, Butch Dixon had caused the smallest hairline crack to appear in her previous conviction that Juanita Grijalva was wrong. Maybe her son was about to plead guilty to a crime he hadn't committed.

It was only seven o'clock. The sensible thing to do would have been to head straight back to the dorm and put in a couple of hours reading the next day's assignment. Instead, Joanna reached into the glove compartment and pulled out the detailed Phoenix *Thomas Guide* Jim Bob Brady had insisted she bring along. Even as she did it, Joanna knew what was happening. She was wading deeper and deeper into the muck. Inevitably. One little step at a time. Just like the stupid dire wolves at the La Brea tar pits, she thought.

Switching on the overhead light, she studied the map until she located the Maricopa County Jail complex at First and Madison. Then, she turned on the Blazer's engine and pulled out of the parking lot, headed for downtown Phoenix.

Accustomed to Cochise County's almost non-existent traffic, Joanna was appalled by what awaited her once she turned onto what was euphemistically referred to as the Black Canyon Freeway. Even that late in the evening, both north and southbound traffic was amazingly heavy. And once she crossed under Camelback, southbound traffic stopped altogether. From there on, cars moved at a snail's pace due to what the radio traffic reports said was a rollover semi, injury accident at the junction of I-10 and I-17. That wreck, along with related fender-benders, had created massive tie-ups all around the I-17 corridor, the exact area Joanna had to traverse in order to reach downtown.

Continuing to try to decode the traffic reports, Joanna was frustrated by the way the information was delivered. The various freeways were all referred to by name rather than number, and most of them seemed to be named after mountains— Superstition, Red Mountain, Squaw Peak. If an out-of-town driver didn't know which mountains were which and where they were located, the traffic reports could just as well have been issued in code.

Most of Joanna's experience with Phoenix came from an earlier, less complicated, nonfreeway era. At Indian School she left the freeway, resorting to surface streets for the remainder of the trip. She navigated the straightforward east-west/north-south grids with little difficulty once she had escaped the freeway-related gridlock.

She reached the jail late enough that there was plenty of on-street parking. After locking her Colt 2000 in the glove compartment, she stepped out of the Blazer and looked up at the lit facade of an imposing building.

Had Joanna not been a police officer, she might have liked it better. The Maricopa County Jail had received numerous architectural accolades, but for cops the complex's beauty was only skin deep. The portico and mezzanine above the lighted entrance were eminently attractive from an aesthetic point of view. Unfortunately, they were also popular with a number of enterprising inmates, several of whom had used those selfsame architectural details as a launching pad for well-planned escapes. Using rock climbing equipment that had been smuggled into the jail, they had rappelled down the side of the building to freedom.

Joanna stood on the street, eyeing the building critically and knowing that her own jail shared some of the same escape-prone defects. Old-fashioned jails—the kind with bars on the windows—may not have been all that aesthetically pleasing, but at least they did the job.

Shaking her head, she walked into the building. Immediately upon entering, she was stopped by a uniformed guard seated behind a chest-high counter. "What can I do for you?" he asked, shoving his reading glasses up on top of his head and lowering his newspaper.

"I'm here to see a prisoner," Joanna said.

The guard shook his head, pulled the glasses back down on his nose, raised the paper, and resumed reading. "Too late," he said without looking at her. "No more visitors tonight. Come back tomorrow."

Joanna removed both her I.D. and badge from her purse. She laid them on the counter and waited for the guard to examine them. He didn't bother. He spoke from behind the paper without even looking at them. "Like I said. It's too late to see anybody tonight."

"What about the jail commander?" Joanna said quietly. "You do have one of those, don't you?"

The guard lowered the paper and glanced furtively down at the counter. When his eyes focused on the badge lying in front of him, he frowned. "The commander went home already."

"Then I'll speak to whoever's in charge."

When he spoke again, the guard sounded exasperated. "Lady, I don't know what's the matter with you, but—"

"The matter," Joanna interrupted, keeping her voice firm but even, "is that I want to see a prisoner, and I want to see him tonight."

With a glower, the guard folded his newspaper and tossed it into a cabinet under the counter. "What did you say your name was?"

"I didn't say," she said, "because you didn't ask. But it's Brady. Joanna Brady. *Sheriff* Joanna Brady, from Cochise County."

The word *sheriff* did seem to carry a certain amount of weight, even with a surly, antagonistic guard. "And who is it you want to see?" he asked grudgingly.

"Antonio Jorge Grijalva," she answered. "He's charged with murdering his wife."

"Even if you get in, the guy won't see you," the guard said. "Not without his attorney present."

"I believe he will," Joanna answered. "All you have to do is tell him his mother sent me."

Shaking his head and muttering under his breath, the guard reached for the phone and dialed a number. Less than ten minutes later, with the help of the jail's night watch commander, Joanna was seated in a small prisoner interview room. Peering through the scratched Plexiglas barrier, she watched as Jorge Grijalva, dressed in orange inmate coveralls and soft slippers, was led into the adjoining room.

Joanna had studied all the articles in Juanita's envelope. She knew that Serena had been twenty-four when she died and that her husband was almost twenty years older. At first glimpse, the man in the next room seemed far older than forty-three. His face was careworn. He was small, bowlegged, and slightly stooped, with the spareness that comes from years of hard labor and too much drinking. Dark, questioning eyes sought Joanna's as he edged his way into the plastic chair.

"Who are you?" he demanded, picking up the phone on his side of the barrier. "What do you want?"

Joanna didn't hear the questions. He had asked them before she had a chance to pick up the receiver on her phone, but she knew what he wanted to know.

"I'm Joanna Brady," she answered. "I'm the new sheriff down in Cochise County."

"What's this about my mother? Is something wrong with her?"

"No. Your mother's fine."

"Why are you here, then?"

"She wanted me to talk to you."

Jorge leaned back in his chair. For a moment Joanna thought he might simply hang up and ask to be returned to his cell. "Why?" he said finally.

"Your mother says you didn't do it," Joanna answered. "She says you're innocent, but that you're going to plead guilty anyway. Is that true?"

Jorge Grijalva's face contorted into a scowl. "Go away," he said. "I don't want to talk to you. My mother's a foolish old woman. She doesn't know anything."

"She knows about losing her grandchildren," Joanna answered quietly. "If you go to prison for killing Serena, the Duffys will never let your mother see Ceci and Pablo again."

In the garish fluorescent light, even through the scarred and yellowed Plexiglas window, Joanna could see the knuckles of his olive-skinned fingers turn stark white. For a long time, Jorge stared at the table, gripping the phone and saying nothing. Then, after a time, he raised his gaze until his troubled eyes were staring directly into Joanna's.

"My wife was a whore," he said simply. "She sold herself for money and for other things as well. When I found out about it, I was afraid the same thing would happen to Ceci, to my daughter. I was afraid she'd turn Ceci into a whore, too.

So I got drunk once and beat Serena up. The cops put me in jail." He paused for a moment and studied Joanna before adding, "It only happened once."

"And when was that?"

"Last year in Bisbee. Before she and the kids moved to Phoenix. Before she filed for a divorce."

"What about now? What about this time?"

"I wanted the kids to come to Douglas for Thanksgiving. My mother hasn't seen them since last spring. She misses them."

"That doesn't seem all that unreasonable. Why was Serena so angry then that night in the bar?"

Jorge looked surprised. "You know about that?"

Joanna nodded.

He shrugged. "She saw my truck."

"Your truck?"

"I bought a new truck. A Jimmy. Not brand-new, but new to me. Serena said it wasn't fair for me to have a new truck when she didn't have any transportation at all, when she was having to walk to work. I tried to tell her that the other truck needed a new engine and that if I couldn't get to work, I couldn't pay any child support. It didn't make any difference."

"Speaking of kids. Did you see Ceci and Pablo that night?"

"No."

"Why not?"

Jorge Grijalva hung his head and didn't answer.

"Why not?" Joanna repeated.

"Because I didn't want them to know I was in town," he said huskily. "Because Serena didn't," he added. "She said if the kids saw me there, they'd think we were getting back together, but we weren't."

"So you and Serena met at the bar to discuss arrangements for Thanksgiving?"

Jorge Grijalva shook his head. "Not exactly."

"What then?"

"Serena was very beautiful," he answered. "And she was much younger. . . . But you knew that, didn't you?"

He paused and looked at Joanna, his features screwed into an unreadable grimace.

"Yes," she said.

"I used to be good-looking, too," Jorge said. "Back when I was younger."

Again he stopped speaking. Joanna was having difficulty following his train of thought. "What difference does that make?" she prompted.

He looked at her then. The silent, soul-deep pain in his dark eyes cut through the cloudy plastic between them and seared into Joanna's own heart. Slowly both his eyes filled with tears. "So very beautiful," he murmured. "And me? Compared to her, I was nothing but an old man. But sometimes . . ."

He stopped yet again. Despite the plastic barrier between them, an unlikely intimacy had sprouted between Joanna Brady and Jorge Grijalva as they sat facing each other in the harsh glare of fluorescent light in those two equally grim rooms.

"Sometimes what?" Joanna whispered urgently.

Jorge Grijalva's head stayed bowed. "Sometimes she would go with me. If I brought her something extra along with the child support. Sometimes she would . . ." His voice faded away.

"Would what?" Joanna asked. "Go to bed with you? Is that what you mean?"

Jorge nodded but didn't speak. His silence now gave Joanna some inkling of the depth of Jorge Grijalva's shame, and also of his pride. Serena Duffy Grijalva had been a whore, all right. Even with him. Even with her husband.

"So you came to see her," Joanna said, after a long pause. "Did you bring both the child support and . . . the extra?"

He nodded again.

"But after she found out about the truck—about your new truck—then she refused to go with you and you killed her. Is that what happened?"

"That's what the *bruja* thinks," Jorge answered sullenly. For the first time, there was something else in his voice, something besides hurt.

"What witch?" Joanna asked.

"The black-haired one. The detective."

"The detective from Peoria? Carol Strong?"

"Yes. That's the one, but it didn't happen the way she thinks. I didn't kill Serena. She left the bar first. After a while, so did I."

Joanna leaned back in her chair and regarded Jorge speculatively. "Your mother is right then, isn't she, Jorge? You're going to plead guilty to a crime you didn't commit."

With effort, Jorge Grijalva pulled himself

together. He sat up straighter in his chair. His gaze met and held Joanna's. "I told you my wife was a whore," he said quietly, "but I will not go to court to prove it. Serena's dead. Ceci and Pablo don't need worse than that."

"But you're their father. If you go to prison for murdering the children's mother, isn't that worse?"

"Pablo is mine," he said softly. "But I'm not Ceci's father. She doesn't know that. Serena was already pregnant when I met her."

That soft-spoken, self-effacing revelation came like a bolt out of the blue and stunned Joanna into her own momentary silence. "Still," she said finally, "you're the only father she's ever known. Think what it will be like for her with you in prison."

"Think what it would be like for her with me dead," Jorge countered. He shrugged his shoulders. "Manslaughter isn't murder. You're an Anglo. Why would you understand?"

"Understand what?"

"Supposing I go to court, say all those things about Serena to a judge and jury and then they find me guilty anyway. Of murder. They've got themselves one more dirty Mexican to send to the gas chamber. This way, if I take the plea bargain, maybe I'll still be alive long enough to see my kids grow up. By the time they're grown, maybe I'll be out. Maybe then Ceci will be old enough so I can tell her the truth and she'll be able to understand."

"But . . ." Joanna began.

Jorge shook his head, squelching her objection. "If you see my mother, tell her what I told you. That way, maybe she'll understand, too. Tell her for me that I'm sorry."

With that, Jorge Grijalva put down his phone and signaled to the guard that he was ready to go. He got up and walked away, leaving Joanna sitting on her side of the Plexiglas barrier, sputtering to herself.

As he walked out of the room, Joanna was filled with the terrible knowledge that she had heard the truth. Juanita Grijalva was right. Her son, Jorge, hadn't killed Serena, but he would accept the blame. In order to protect his children from hearing an awful truth about their mother, he would willingly go to prison for a crime he hadn't committed. Meanwhile, the real killer—whoever that was—would go free.

Sitting there by herself, all those separate realizations came to Joanna almost simultaneously. They were followed immediately by a thought that was even worse: There wasn't a damn thing she could do about any of them.

Drained, Joanna pressed the buzzer for a guard to come let her out. As she was led back to the jail's guarded entrance, through a maze of electronically locked gates that clanged shut behind her, Joanna realized something else as well.

Mr. Bailey, her high school social studies teacher, had done his best to drum the words into the heads of each Bisbee High School senior who came through his civics class. "We hold these truths to be self-evident," he had read reverently from the textbook, "that all men are created equal. . . ."

For the first time, as clearly as if she'd heard a pane of glass shatter into a thousand pieces, Joanna Brady understood with absolute clarity that those words weren't necessarily true, not for everyone. Certainly not for Jorge Grijalva.

And not for his mother, either.

TEN

JOANNA LEFT the jail complex and headed north
with her mind in a complete turmoil. What
should she do? Drop it? Forget everything she had
heard in that grim interview room and go on
about business as usual as if nothing had happened? What then? That would mean Jorge would
most likely go to prison on a manslaughter charge
while Serena's killer would be on the loose, carrying on with his own life, free as a bird. Those two
separate outcomes went against everything Joanna Brady stood for and believed in, against her
sense of justice and fair play.

Joanna Lathrop Brady had grown up under
her mother's critical eye with Eleanor telling her
constantly, day after day, how headstrong and
hard to handle she was, how she never had sense
enough to mind her own business or leave well
enough alone. Maybe what was about to happen
to Jorge Grijalva's already shattered life wasn't

any of her business, but if she didn't do something to prevent a terrible miscarriage of justice, who would? Carol Strong, the local homicide detective on the case, the one Jorge had called the *bruja*? No, if the prosecutors and defense attorneys were negotiating a plea bargain, that meant the case was officially closed and out of the hands of police investigators.

If it is to be, it is up to me, Joanna thought with grim humor as she drove north through much lighter traffic. It would give her one more opportunity to live up to her mother's worst expectations.

She made it back to Peoria in twenty minutes, which seemed like record time. When she came to the turnoff that would have taken her home to the APOA campus, she kept right on going across the railroad tracks and right on Grand, returning once more to the Roundhouse Bar and Grill. Instead of going back to the dorm and her reading assignment, she was going back to see Butch Dixon, her one and only slender lead in this oddball investigation. Even Joanna was forced to acknowledge the irony. She would be enlisting the bartender in a possibly ill-fated and harebrained crusade to save someone who wasn't the least bit interested in being saved. Who was, in fact, dead set against it.

By ten o'clock, *Monday Night Football* was over. With only local news on TV, the bar was nearly deserted when she stepped inside. Butch waved to her as she threaded her way across the floor through a scatter of empty tables. There was only one other customer seated at the bar. Even though she could have taken any one of a number of empty seats, she made directly for the same spot she had abandoned several hours earlier.

"The usual?" Butch Dixon asked with a pleasant grin as she hoisted herself up onto the stool. Joanna nodded. Moments later, he set a Diet Pepsi on the counter in front of her. While she took a tentative sip from her drink, he began diligently polishing the nearby surface of the bar even though it didn't look particularly in need of polishing.

"I suppose you get asked this question all the time," he said.

"What question?"

"What's a nice girl like you doing in this line of work? I mean, how come you're sheriff?"

"The usual way," she answered. "I got elected."

"I figured that out, but what did you do before the election? Is being a cop something you always wanted to be, or is it like me and bartending? I sort of fell into it by accident, but it turns out it's something I'm pretty good at."

Joanna considered before she answered. Butch must be one of the few people in Arizona who had somehow missed the media blitz about Andy's death and about his widow being the first-ever elected female sheriff in the state. If he had seen some of the news reports or read the newspaper articles, he had long since forgotten. It was all far enough in the past that for him there was no connection between those events back in September and Joanna's name and title on the business card she had given him.

So what should she do? Tell Butch Dixon the painful story about what had happened to Andy? Or should she just gloss over it? After a moment's hesitation, she decided on the latter. If she was going to try to enlist Butch Dixon's help, it would be better to approach him as a professional rather than play on his sympathies as some kind of damsel in distress.

"Fell into it by accident, I'd say," she replied. "I used to sell insurance."

"And what are you doing over at the academy, teaching classes?"

"I wish," she answered. "No, I'm taking them. I'm there as a student, not as an instructor."

When Butch stopped polishing the counter, his towel was only inches from Joanna's hand. For a moment he seemed to be staring at it. Then he looked up at her face. "What does your husband do?"

Joanna's gaze had followed his to where the diamond on her engagement ring reflected back one of the lights over the bar. No matter how hard she tried, there didn't seem to be any way to avoid telling this inquisitive man about Andy.

"He's dead," Joanna said at last, feeling both relieved that she had told him and surprised by how easy it was right then to say the words that placed Andrew Roy Brady's life and death totally in the past tense.

"Andy was a police officer," she added. "He

died in the line of duty." She told the story briefly and dispassionately, without giving way to tears.

Hearing what had happened, Butch Dixon was instantly contrite. "I'm sorry," he apologized. "I didn't mean to pry. It's just that—"

Joanna held her hand up. "I know. The rings. I suppose I ought to take them off and put them away, but I'm not ready to do that yet. I'm used to wearing them. I may not be married anymore, but I still *feel* married."

Butch nodded. "When did it happen?" he asked.

"Two months ago, back in the middle of September."

"So it wasn't all that long ago. Do you have kids?"

Joanna nodded. "Only one, a girl. Her name's Jennifer. Jenny. She's nine."

"That's got to be tough."

"It's no picnic."

"Who's taking care of her while you're here going to school?"

"Her grandparents. My in-laws. They're from Bisbee, too. They're staying out at the ranch and looking after things while I'm away."

"Ranch?" Butch asked.

Joanna laughed. "Not a big ranch. A little one. It's only forty acres, but it does have a name. The High Lonesome. It's been in Andy's family for years. Right now it belongs to me, but it'll belong to Jenny someday."

"Hey, Butch, my margarita's long gone. I know

the broad's good-looking, but how about paying a little attention to this part of the bar?"

A look of annoyance washed over Butch Dixon's face as he turned toward the complaining customer. "Keep your shirt on, Mike," he growled. "And keep a civil damn tongue in your mouth or go on down the road."

Joanna watched as Butch mixed Mike's drink. It was difficult to estimate how old he was. He looked forty but that could have been the lack of hair. He was probably somewhat younger than that. Butch wasn't particularly tall—only about five ten or so—but what there was of him was powerfully and compactly built. As soon as he dropped off the margarita and rang the sale into the cash register, Butch came back to where Joanna was sitting. Resting his forearms on the counter, he leaned in front of her.

"Sorry about that," he said. "Mike's one of those guys who gets a little out of line on occasion."

"Compared to some of the things I've been called lately, broad's not all that bad," Joanna reassured him with a smile. "And I can see why you make a good bartender. You're very easy to talk to."

Butch didn't seem entirely comfortable with the compliment. In reply he picked up her empty glass. "Want another?"

"No. Too much caffeine. When I go home to bed, I'm going to need to sleep. But I did want to discuss something with you. I'm just now on my way home from the Maricopa County Jail. I went down there to talk to Jorge Grijalva."

"Really? Did you manage to talk him out of that plea bargain crap?"

"No. He's still hell-bent for election to go through with it. Even so, talking to him has convinced me that you may be right. Some of the things he said made me think maybe he didn't kill her after all."

"What are you going to do, go to the cops?"

Joanna shook her head. "I am a cop, remember?" she said. "But since this happened in Peoria PD's jurisdiction, I wouldn't be able to do anything about it, not officially. And even if I tried, that case is closed as far as homicide cops are concerned because they've already turned it over to the prosecutor."

"What's the point, then?"

"The point is I'm going to do a little nosing around on my own. Unofficial nosing around. Do you still have my card?"

Butch reached into his shirt pocket and pulled out Joanna's business card. She jotted a number on the back and returned it to him. "That's the number of my room over at the academy. There's no answering machine, so either you'll get me or you won't. You won't be able to leave a message."

"What do you want me to do?"

"I want you to write down everything you can remember about the night Serena Grijalva died. I'm sure you've already given this information to the investigating officers, but since mine isn't an official inquiry, I most likely won't have access to those reports. There's no real rush. I'll come by tomorrow or the next day and pick it up."

"Wednesday's the day before Thanksgiving," Butch said, pocketing the card once more. "I suppose you'll be going home for the holiday?"

Joanna shook her head. "No, Jenny and the Gs are coming up here for the weekend. We've got a super-duper holiday weekend package at that brand-new hotel just down the street."

"The Hohokam?" Butch asked. "It's only been open a couple of months. I've never been inside. It's supposed to be very nice."

"I hope so," Joanna said.

"And who all did you say is coming, Jenny and the Gs? Sounds like some kind of rock band."

Joanna laughed. "That's my daughter and her grandparents, my in-laws. Ever since she was able to spell, Jenny's called them the Gs." She paused for a moment. "Speaking of names, where did Butch come from?"

Running one hand over the bare skin on his shiny, bald skull, Butch Dixon grinned. "My real name was Frederick. People called me Freddy for short. I hated it; thought it sounded sissy. So when I was six, my uncle started teasing me about my new haircut, calling me Butch. The name stuck. I've been Butch ever since, and I wore my hair that way for years, back when I still had hair, that is. When it started to disappear, I gave Mother Nature a little shove in the right direction. What do you think?"

Joanna smiled. "It looks fine to me. I'd better

be heading back," she said, standing up. "I'm taking you away from your other customers. . . ."

"Customer," Butch corrected, holding up his hand.

"And I've got a reading assignment to do before class in the morning."

"And I've got a writing assignment," he said, patting his shirt pocket. "I'll start on it first thing tomorrow morning. Do you want me to call you when it's finished?"

"Please. And in the meantime, if anything comes up that you think is too important to wait, give me a call."

"Sure thing," Butch Dixon said. "You can count on it."

By the time Joanna drove back into the APOA parking lot, it was past eleven. Checking the clerestory windows on both the upper and lower breezeways, she saw that some were lit and some weren't. It was possible some of her classmates were still out. Others might already be in bed and asleep.

Stopping off at the lower-floor student lounge, Joanna found the place deserted. She made straight for the telephone. It was far too late to phone the High Lonesome, but Frank Montoya had told her that he never went to bed without watching *The Tonight Show.*

"How are things going?" she asked, when he answered. "I tried calling earlier, but neither you nor Dick Voland could be found."

"Well," Frank said slowly, "we did have our hands full today."

"How's that?"

"For one thing," he replied, "somebody sent me a petition signed by sixty-three prisoners asking that you fire the cook in the jail."

"Fire him? How come?"

"They say the food's bad, that they can't eat it, and that he cooks the same thing week after week."

"Is that true?" Joanna asked. "Is the jail food really as bad as all that?"

"Beats me."

"Have you tried it?"

"No, but . . ."

"These guys are prisoners," Joanna said. "We're supposed to house and feed them, but nobody said it has to be gourmet cuisine. You taste the food, Frank, and then you decide. If the food's fit to eat, tell the prisoners to go piss up a rope. If the food's as bad as they say, get rid of the cook and find somebody else."

"You really did hire me to do the dirty work, didn't you?" Frank complained, but Joanna heard the unspoken humor in his voice and knew he was teasing.

"What else is going on down there today?"

"The big news is the fracas at the Sunset Inn out over the Divide."

The Mule Mountains, north of Bisbee, effectively cut the town off from the remainder of the state. In the old days, the Divide, as locals called it, was a formidable barrier. Now, although modern highway engineering and a tunnel had tamed the worst of the steep grades, the name—the Divide—still remained.

The Sunset Inn, an outpost supper club on the far side of the Divide, had changed ownership and identities many times over the years. It had reopened under the name of Sunset Inn only two months earlier.

"What happened?" Joanna asked.

"From what we can piece together this is a pair of relative newlyweds, been married less than a year. It turns out the husband's something of a slob who tends to leave his clothes lying wherever they fall. His wife got tired of picking up after him, so she took a hammer and nailed them all to the floor wherever they happened to fall. He tore hell out of his favorite western shirt when he tried to pick it up. Made him pretty mad. He went outside and sliced up the tires on his wife's Chevette."

"Thank God it was only the tires," Joanna breathed. "I guess it could have been worse."

Frank laughed. "Wait'll you hear the rest. One of our patrol cars happened to drive by in time to see her taking a sledgehammer to the windshield of his pickup truck—unfortunately with him still inside. She's in jail tonight on a charge of assault with intent, drunk and disorderly, and resisting arrest. The last I heard of the husband, he took his dog and what was left of his truck and was heading back home to his mother's place in Silver City, New Mexico."

The way Frank told the story, it might have

sounded almost comical, but Joanna was living too close to what had happened in the aftermath of similar violence between Serena and Jorge Grijalva. Right that minute, she couldn't see any humor in the situation.

"I'm sorry to hear it," Joanna said. "Especially with a young couple like that. It's too bad they didn't go for counseling."

"Did I say young?" Frank echoed. "They're not young. He's sixty-eight. She's sixty-three or so, but hell on wheels with a sledgehammer. The whole time the deputy was driving her to jail, she was yelling her head off about how she should have known better than to marry a bachelor who was also a mama's boy. Mama, by the way—the one he's going home to—must be pushing ninety if she's a day."

Joanna did laugh then. She couldn't help it. "I thought people were supposed to get wise when they got that old."

"I wouldn't count on it," Frank advised. "So that's what's happening on the home front. What about you? How's class?"

"B-O-R-I-N-G," Joanna answered. "It's like being thrown all the way back into elementary school. I can't wait for Thanksgiving vacation."

"And is Dave Thompson still the same sexist son of a bitch he was when I was there a couple of years ago?" Frank asked.

"Indications are," Joanna answered, "but I probably shouldn't talk about that now. You never can tell when somebody might walk in."

"Right," Frank said. "Well, hang in there. It's

bound to get better. What about Jorge Grijalva?" he asked, changing the subject. "Did you have time to check on him?"

"I just came home from seeing him a few minutes ago."

"What do you think?" Frank asked.

"I don't know what to think. I'm doing some checking. I'll let you know."

"Fair enough. Should I tell Juanita you're looking into it?"

"For right now, don't tell anybody anything."

"Sure thing, Joanna," Frank Montoya answered. "You're the boss."

There was no hint of teasing in Frank Montoya's voice now. Joanna knew that he really meant what he said.

"Thanks," Joanna said. "And thanks for keeping an eye on things while I'm gone."

Once off the telephone, Joanna headed for her room. In the breezeway outside, she almost collided head-on with Leann Jessup. The other woman was dressed in tennies, shorts, and a glow-in-the-dark T-shirt. "I'm going for a run," she said. "Care to join me?"

The idea of going for a jog carried no appeal. "No, thanks," Joanna replied. "I'm saving myself for that first session of physical training tomorrow afternoon. I'm going to shower, hit the books, and then try to get some sleep."

For a moment Joanna watched Leann's stretching exercises, then she glanced at her watch. It was almost eleven-thirty. "Isn't this a little late to go jogging?"

Leann grinned. "Not in Phoenix it isn't. Most of the year it's too hot to go out any earlier. Besides, I'm a night owl—one of those midnight joggers. Actually, this is early for me."

Joanna laughed. "Where I come from, coyotes are the only ones who go jogging this time of night."

Back in her dormitory room, Joanna quickly stripped out of her clothing and headed for the shower.

Standing under the torrent of pulsing hot water, Joanna marveled at the unaccustomed force of the water. Back on the High Lonesome, a private well, temperamental pump, and aging pipes all combined to create perpetual low pressure. Reveling in the steamy warmth, she stayed in the shower far longer than she would have at home.

When she finally emerged from the shower, she once again found her bathroom tinged with cigarette smoke. The bath towel she used to dry her face, the one she had brought from home, stank to high heaven.

Her nose wrinkled in distaste. Ever since she'd been forced to use high school rest rooms that had reeked of smoke, she had been bugged by the people who hid out in bathrooms to smoke. Why the hell couldn't they be honest enough to smoke in public, in front of God and everybody? she thought. Why did so many of them have to be so damned sneaky about it?

With the exhaust fan going full blast, the mirror cleared gradually. As the steam dissipated,

Joanna's body slowly came into focus. Back home, with Jenny bouncing in and out of rooms, standing naked in front of a full-length mirror wasn't something Joanna Brady did very often. Now she subjected her body to a critical self-appraisal—something she hadn't done for years. In fact, the last time she had looked at herself in that fashion had been nine years earlier, just after Jenny's birth. She had been concerned about whether or not she'd get her pre-pregnancy figure back.

She had, of course, within months, thanks more to genetics than to dietary diligence on Joanna's part. Even in her sixties, Eleanor Lathrop remained pencil thin, and Joanna had inherited that tendency. Now, except for two faded stretch marks—one on each breast—there were no other physical indications that she had ever borne a child. Her breasts were still firm. Her small waist curved out into fuller hips. Her figure suffered some in comparison with that of someone as elegantly tall as Leann Jessup. For one thing, Joanna was somewhat heavier. So be it. Joanna wasn't a daily—or nightly—jogger. Her muscle tone came from real work on the ranch—from wrestling bales of hay and long-legged calves—rather than from a prescribed program of gym-bound weight lifting.

Moving closer to the mirror, Joanna examined her face. She still wasn't sleeping through the night. She hadn't done that regularly since Andy died, but she was getting more rest. Her skin was clear. The dark circles under her eyes were fading. The new hairdo Eleanor had badgered her into on the day of the election was an improvement over her old one. Even though she still wasn't quite accustomed to the shorter length, Joanna had to admit it was easier to care for. She found herself using far less shampoo, and the time she was forced to waste waving her hairdryer around in the bathroom had been reduced from ten minutes to five.

Standing there naked, Joanna Brady finally saw herself for the first time as someone else might see her, the way some man who wasn't Andy might see her. A man who . . .

With a start, she remembered Butch Dixon staring at the rings on her fingers. She saw him standing there talking to her, leaning against the bar, obviously enjoying her company. She saw again the pleased look on his face when she had walked back into the Roundhouse after her trip down to the Maricopa County Jail. She remembered how quickly he had apologized when he'd inadvertently stumbled onto Andy's death, and how he'd jumped down the throat of the poor guy he thought might have insulted her.

Certainly Butch Dixon wasn't interested in her, was he?

Joanna barely allowed her mind time enough to frame the question.

"Nah!" she said aloud to the naked image staring back at her from the mirror. "No way! Couldn't be!"

With that, pulling on her nightgown, Joanna

headed for bed. She fell asleep much later with the light on and with the heavy textbook open on her chest—only thirty pages into Dave Thompson's seventy-six-page reading assignment.

☙ ELEVEN

Because Jim Bob and Eva Lou were both early risers, Joanna had read another twenty pages and was down in the student lounge with the telephone receiver in hand by ten after six the next morning. Her mother-in-law answered the phone.

"Is Jenny out of bed yet?" Joanna asked.

"Oh, my," Eva Lou replied. "She isn't here. Your mother invited her to sleep over in town last night. I didn't think it would be a problem. I know Jenny will be sorry to miss you. If you want, you might try calling over to your mother's."

"Except you know how Eleanor is if she doesn't get her beauty sleep," Joanna returned. "And by the time she's up and around, this phone will be too busy to use. I'll call back later this evening. Tell Jenny I'll talk to her then."

"Sure thing," Eva Lou replied. "As far as I know, she plans on coming straight home from school."

Relinquishing the phone to another student,

Joanna poured herself juice and coffee and toasted a couple of pieces of whole wheat bread. Then she settled down at one of the small, round tables, flipped open *Historical Guide to Police Science*, and went back to her reading assignment of which she still had another twenty-six pages to go.

"Mind if I sit here?"

Joanna looked up to find Leann Jessup standing beside the table. She was carrying a loaded breakfast tray. "Sure," Joanna said, moving her notebook and purse out of the way. "Be my guest. There's plenty of room."

Leann began unloading her tray. Toast, coffee, orange juice, corn flakes, milk. She set a still-folded newspaper on the table beside her food.

"Not much variety," Leann commented. "By Christmas, the food in that buffet line could become pretty old. But I shouldn't complain," she added. "It's food I don't have to pay for out of my own pocket.

"How close are you to done with that stupid reading assignment?" Leann asked, nodding in the direction of Joanna's textbook as she sat down.

Joanna sighed. "Twenty pages to go is all. History never was my best subject, and this stuff is dry as dust." While she returned to the book, Leann Jessup picked up the newspaper and unfolded it. Moments later she groaned.

"Damn!" Leann Jessup exclaimed, slamming the palm of her hand into the table, rattling everything on its surface. "I knew it. As soon as she turned up missing, I knew he was behind it."

Joanna glanced up to find Leann Jessup shaking her head in dismay over something she had read in the paper.

"Who was behind what?" Joanna asked. "Is something wrong?"

Tight-lipped, Leann didn't answer. Instead, she flipped the opened newspaper across the table. "It's the lead story," she said. "Page one."

Joanna picked up the paper. The story at the top of the page was datelined Tempe.

The battered and partially clad body of a woman found in the desert outside Carefree last week has been identified as that of Rhonda Weaver Norton, the estranged and missing wife of Arizona State University economics professor, Dr. Dean R. Norton.

According to the Maricopa County Medical Examiner's Office, Ms. Norton died as a result of homicidal violence. The victim was reported missing last week by her attorney, Abigail Weismann, when she failed to show up for an appointment. When Ms. Weismann was unable to locate her client at her apartment, the attorney called the Tempe police saying she was concerned for Ms. Norton's safety.

Two weeks ago Ms. Weismann obtained a no-contact order on Ms. Norton's behalf. The court document ordered her estranged husband to have no further dealings with his wife, either in person or by telephone.

Reached at his Tempe residence, Professor Norton refused comment other than saying he

was deeply shocked and saddened by news of
his wife's death.

The investigation is continuing, but according to usually reliable sources inside the Tempe
Police Department, Professor Norton is being
considered a person of interest. . . . see Missing,
pg. B-4.

Instead of finishing the article, Joanna looked
up at Leann Jessup's pained face.

"I took the missing person call," Leann explained. "Afterward, I checked the professor's
address for priors. Bingo. Guess what? Three do-
mestics reported within the last three months. The
son of a bitch killed her. He probably figures since
he's a middle-aged white guy with a nice home
and a good job, that the cops'll let him off. And
the thing that pisses the hell out of me is that he's
probably right."

"Three separate priors?" Joanna asked. "When
the officers responded each of those other times,
was he ever arrested?"

"Not once."

"Why not?" Joanna asked.

Leann Jessup's attractive lips curled into a dis-
dainful and decidedly unattractive sneer. "Are
you kidding? You read what he does for a living."

Joanna consulted the article to be sure. "He's a
professor at ASU," she returned. "What difference does that make?"

"The university is Tempe's bread and butter.
The professors who work and live there can do
no wrong."

"Surely that doesn't include getting away with murder."

"I wouldn't bet on it if I were you," Leann answered bitterly. As she spoke, she thumbed through the pages until she located the continuation of the article. "Do you want me to read it aloud?" she asked.

Joanna nodded. "Sure," she said.

Lael Weaver Gastone, mother of the slain woman, was in seclusion at her home in Sedona, but her husband, Jean Paul Gastone, told reporters that women like his stepdaughter—women married to violent men—need more than court documents to protect them.

"Our daughter would have been better off if she had ignored the lawyers and judges in the court system and spent the same amount of money on a .357 Magnum," he said from the porch of his mountaintop home.

Much the same sentiment was echoed hours later by Matilda Hirales-Steinowitz, spokeswoman for a group called MAVEN, the Maricopa Anti-Violence Empowerment Network, an umbrella organization comprising several different battered women's advocacy groups.

"Handing a woman something called a protective order and telling her that will fix things is a bad joke, almost as bad as giving the emperor his nonexistent new clothes and telling him to wear them in public. If a man doesn't respect his wife—a living, breathing human being—why would he respect a piece of paper?"

Ms. Hirales-Steinowitz stated that crimes against women, particularly domestic-partner homicides, have increased dramatically in Arizona in recent years. According to her, MAVEN has scheduled a candlelight vigil to be held starting at eight tonight on the steps of the Arizona State Capitol building in downtown Phoenix.

MAVEN hopes the vigil will draw public attention not only to what happened to Rhonda Norton but also to the other sixteen women who have died as a result of suspected domestic violence in the Phoenix metropolitan area in the course of this year.

Michelle Greer Dobson, a friend and former classmate of the slain woman, attended Wickenburg High School with Rhonda Weaver Norton. According to Dobson, the victim, class valedictorian in 1983, was exceptionally bright during her teenage years.

"Rhonda was always the smartest girl—the smartest person—in our class when it came to cracking the books. She went to Arizona State University on a full-ride scholarship. As soon as she ran into that professor down there at the university, she was hooked. I don't think she ever looked at another boy our age."

According to Ms. Dobson, Rhonda Weaver met Professor Norton when she took his class in microeconomics as an ASU undergraduate student nine years ago. Norton divorced his first

wife the following summer. He married Rhonda Weaver a short time later. It was his third marriage and her first. They have no children.

Leann Jessup finished reading and put the paper down on the table. "This crap makes me sick. We should have been able to do more. I agree with what the man in the article said. The system let her down, although I guess it's not fair to second-guess the guys who took those other calls. After all, we weren't there. If I had been, maybe I would have done something differently."

"Maybe," Joanna said. "And maybe not. In that shoot/don't shoot scenario yesterday, I evidently pulled the same boner the responding officer did. If that had been a real life situation, I would have plugged that poor little kid, sure as hell."

Folding the paper, Leann shoved it into her purse and then stood up. "It's almost time for class," she said. "We'd better get going."

Joanna glanced around the room and was surprised to find it nearly empty. Only one student remained in the room, a guy from Flagstaff who was still talking on the telephone. He and his wife were having a heated argument over what she should do about a broken washing machine while he was away at school. The public nature of the lounge telephone made no allowances for domestic privacy.

Joanna and Leann cleared their table and headed for class. Determinedly, Leann Jessup changed the subject. "It's going to be a long day," she said. "I've been up since four. The train woke me."

"What train?" Joanna asked. "I didn't hear any train."

"You must have been sleeping the sleep of the dead," Leann said. "It was so loud that I thought we were having an earthquake."

Outside the classroom a small group of smokers clustered around a single, stand-alone ashtray. Grinding out his own cigarette butt, Dave Thompson began urging the others to come inside. Other than the guy from Flagstaff, Joanna and Leann were the last people to enter.

Something about the searching look Dave gave her made Joanna feel distinctly uneasy. Leann evidently noticed it as well.

"Oops," she whispered, as they ducked between other students' chairs and tables to reach their own. "The head honcho looks a little surly today. We'd better be on our best behavior."

Moments later, Dave Thompson closed the door behind the last straggler and marched forward to the podium. "I hope you've all read last night's assignment, boys and girls," he said. "We're going to spend the morning discussing some of the material on the worldwide history of law enforcement as well as some additional material on law enforcement here in the great state of Arizona. I'm a great believer in the idea that you can't tell where you're going if you don't know where you've been."

During the course of Dave Thompson's long lecture, Joanna almost succeeded in staying awake by forcing herself to take detailed notes. As the mid-morning break neared, she once again found herself counting down the minutes like a restless school kid longing for recess.

When the break finally came, Joanna raced out of the classroom and managed to beat everyone to the student lounge. She poured herself a cup of terrible coffee from the communal urn and then made for the pay phone and dialed her own office number first. Kristin Marsten, her nubile young secretary, answered the phone sounding perky and cheerful. "Sheriff Brady's office."

"Hello, Kristin," Joanna said. "How are things?"

Kristin's tone of voice changed abruptly as the cheeriness disappeared. "All right, I guess," she answered.

Kristin's tenure as secretary to the Cochise County sheriff preceded Joanna's arrival on the scene by only a matter of months. Kristin had started out the previous summer in the lowly position of temporary clerk/intern. Through a series of unlikely promotions, she had somehow landed the secretarial job. Joanna credited Kristin's swift rise far more to good looks than ability. No doubt, in the pervasively all-male atmosphere that had existed under the previous administrations, blond good looks and blatant sex appeal had worked wonders.

By the time Joanna arrived on the scene, Kristin had carved out some fairly cushy working conditions. Because Joanna's reforms threatened the status quo, the new sheriff understood why Kristin might view her new female boss with undisguised resentment. Given time, Joanna thought she might actually effect a beneficial change in the young woman's troublesome attitude. The problem was, between the election and now there had been no time—at least not enough. Kristin's brusque, stilted replies bordered on rudeness, but Joanna waded into her questions as though nothing was out of line.

"Is anything happening?" she asked.

"Nothing much," Kristin returned.

"No messages?"

Nothing happening. No messages. Joanna recognized the symptoms at once. Kristin was enjoying the fact that her boss was temporarily out of the loop. The secretary no doubt planned to keep Joanna that way for as long as possible.

"Something must be happening," Joanna pressed. "It is a county sheriff's office."

"Not really," Kristin responded easily. "I've been passing things along to Dick . . . I mean, to Chief Deputy Voland, or else to Chief Deputy for Administration Montoya."

"What kind of things?"

"Just routine," Kristin answered.

Joanna had to work at keeping the growing annoyance out of her own voice. She knew there was no possibility of effecting a miraculous adjustment in Kristin's attitude over long-distance telephone lines. But if Kristin wanted to play the old I-know-and-you-don't game, it was certainly possible to call her bluff.

"Oh," Joanna offered casually. "You mean like the prisoner petitions asking me to fire the cook or the domestic assault out at the Sunset Inn?"

"Well . . . yes," Kristin stammered. "I guess so. How did you know about those?"

Hearing the surprise in Kristin's voice, Joanna allowed herself a smile of grim satisfaction. She resented being drawn into playing useless power-trip games, but it was nice to know she could deliver a telling blow when called upon to do so. After all, Joanna had been schooled at her mother's knee, and Eleanor Lathrop was an expert manipulator. The sooner Kristin Marsten figured that out, the better it would be for all concerned.

"A little bird told me," Joanna answered, "but I shouldn't have to check with him. Calling you ought to be enough."

Bristling at the reprimand, Kristin did at last cough up some useful information. "Adam York called," she said curtly.

Adam York was the agent in charge of the Tucson office of the Drug Enforcement Agency. Joanna had met him months earlier when, at the time of Andy's death, she herself had come under suspicion as a possible drug smuggler. It was due to Adam York's firm suggestion that she had enrolled in the APOA program in the first place.

"Did he say what he wanted?" Joanna asked. "Did he want me to call him back?"

"Yes."

"Where was he calling from?" Joanna asked. "Did he leave a number?"

"He said you had it," Kristin replied. "He said

for you to call his home number. He has some
fancy kind of thingamajig on his phone that tracks
him down automatically."

Not taking down telephone numbers was another part of Kristin's game. Joanna had Adam
York's number back in the room, but not with
her. Not here at the phone where and when she
needed it. Her level of annoyance rose another
notch, but she held it inside.

"What else?" Joanna asked.

"Well, there was a call from someone named
Grijalva."

"Someone who?" Joanna asked impatiently.
"A man? Woman?"

"A woman," Kristin said. "Juanita was her
name. She wouldn't tell me what it was all about.
She just said to tell you thank you."

Joanna drew a long breath. There was very little
point in lighting into Kristin over the telephone.
What was needed was a way to make things work
for the time being.

"I'll tell you what, Kristin," Joanna said. "From
now on I'd like you to bag up all my correspondence and copies of all phone calls that come into
my office. My in-laws are coming up here tomorrow for Thanksgiving. Bundle the stuff up in a
single envelope. I'll have my father-in-law stop
by the office to pick it up tomorrow the last thing
before they leave town."

"You want everything?"

"That's right. Even if you've passed a call along
to someone else to handle, I still want to see a
copy of the original message. That way I'll know

who called and why and where the problem went from there."

"But that's a lot of trouble—"

Pushed beyond bearing, Joanna cut off Kristin's objection. "No buts," she said. "You're being paid to be *my* secretary, remember? To do *my* work. For as long as I'm gone, this is the way we're going to handle things. After tomorrow's batch, you can FedEx me the next one Monday morning. After that, I want packets from you twice a week for as long as I'm here. Is that clear?"

"Yes."

"Good. Now, is Frank Montoya around?"

"He's not in his office. He's over in the jail talking to the cook. Want me to see if I can put you through to the kitchen?"

"No, thanks. What about Dick Voland?"

"Yes." Joanna could almost see Kristin's tight-lipped acquiescence in the single word of her answer. Moments later, Dick Voland came on the phone.

"Hello," he said. "How are you, Sheriff Brady, and what's the matter with Kristin?"

"I'm fine," Joanna answered. "Kristin, on the other hand, doesn't seem to be having a very good day."

"I'll say," Dick returned. "I thought she was going to bite my head off when she buzzed me about your call. What can I do for you?"

Joanna listened between the words, trying to tell if anything was wrong, but Voland sounded cordial enough. "How are things?" she asked.

"Everything's fine. Let's say pretty much everything. The prisoners are all pissed off about the quality of their grub, but Frank tells me he's working on that. We've had a few things happening, but nothing out of the ordinary. How are your classes going?"

"All right so far," Joanna answered.

"Is my ol' buddy, Dave Thompson, still doing the bulk of the teaching up there?"

"You know him?"

"Sure. Dave and I go way back. I'm talking years, now. We've been to a couple national conferences together, served on a few statewide committees. He fell on a little bit of hard times after his wife divorced him. Ended up getting himself remoted."

"Remoted?" Joanna repeated, wondering if she'd heard the strange word correctly. "What's that?"

Voland chuckled. "You never heard of a remotion? Well, Dave Thompson was always a good cop. Spent almost his whole adult life working for the city of Chandler. But about the time he got divorced, while he was all screwed up from that, he worked himself into a situation where he was a problem. Or at least he was perceived as a problem. So they got rid of him."

"You mean the city fired him?"

"Not exactly," Dick answered. "The way it works is this. If the brass reaches a point where they can't promote a guy, and if they don't want to demote him, they find a way to get him out of their hair. They send him somewhere else. The more remote, the better."

"The gutless approach," Joanna said, and Dick Voland laughed.

"Most people would call it taking the line of least resistance."

Once she understood the process, Joanna's first thought was whether or not remoting would work with Kristin Marsten. Where could she possibly send her? Out to the little town of Elfrida, maybe? Or up to the Wonderland of Rocks?

Dick Voland went right on talking. "Believe me, you can't go wrong listening to Thompson. He knows what it's all about. Of all the instructors the APOA has up there, I think he's probably tops. You say your classes are going all right?"

Joanna took a deep breath. No wonder listening to Dave was just like listening to Dick Voland. They were two peas in a pod and old buddies besides. Bearing that in mind, it didn't seem wise to mention that she was bored out of her tree, especially not now when the lounge was filled with most of her fellow students.

"The classes are great," she answered after a pause. "As a matter of fact, they couldn't be better."

For the next few moments and in a very businesslike fashion, Dick Voland briefed the sheriff on all the latest Cochise County law-and-order issues, including the Sunset Inn domestic assault. Try as she might, Joanna couldn't hear any ominous subtext in what Chief Deputy Voland was telling her. He seemed surprisingly upbeat and positive.

Joanna waited until he was finished before

broaching the question she'd been toying with off and on since leaving Jorge Grijalva and the Maricopa County Jail the night before. And when she did it, she tried to be as offhand as possible.

"By the way," she said, "I've been meaning to ask. I can't remember exactly when it was, back in early to mid-October, you helped a couple of out-of-town officers make an arrest down at the Paul Spur lime plant. Remember that?"

"Sure. That guy from Pirtleville—I believe his name was Grijalva. Killed his ex-wife somewhere up around Phoenix. What about it?"

"What can you tell me about the detectives who were working the case?"

"I only remember one of them," Dick Voland answered. "The woman. Her name was Carol Strong."

"What about her?"

"I can only remember one thing."

"What's that?"

"I'm not sure you want to know."

"Tell me."

"Legs," Dick Voland answered. "That woman had great legs."

TWELVE

WHEN JOANNA hung up the phone, she saw Leann Jessup heading for the door on her way back to class.

"Wait up," Joanna called after her. "I'll walk with you."

As they started down the breezeway toward the classroom wing, Joanna studied her tablemate. Since breakfast, Leann had said almost nothing. During class that day, there had been no hint of the previous day's lighthearted banter or note passing. Leann had spent the morning, her face set in an unsmiling mask, staring intently at their instructor, seemingly intent on every word. Even now a deep frown creased Leann Jessup's forehead.

"Are you getting a lot out of this?" Joanna asked.

"Out of what?" Leann returned.

"Out of the class. It looked to me as though

you were devouring every word Dave Thompson said this morning."

Leann shook her head ruefully. "Appearances can be deceiving. I hope you've taken good notes, because I barely heard a word he said. I was too busy thinking about Rhonda Norton and what happened to her. Her husband may have landed the fatal blow, but we're all responsible."

"We?" Joanna said.

Leann nodded. "You and me. We're cops, part of the system—a system that left her vulnerable to a man who had already beaten the crap out of her three different times."

"You shouldn't take it personally," Joanna counseled.

Even as she said the words, Joanna recognized the irony behind them. It took a hell of a lot of nerve for her to pass that timeworn advice along to someone else. After all, who had spent most of the previous evening tracking down leads in a case that was literally none of her business?

Leann shot Joanna a bleak look. "You're right, I suppose," she said. "After all, domestic violence is hardly a brand-new problem. It's why my mother divorced my father."

"He beat her?"

"Evidently," Leann answered. "He knocked her around and my older brother, too. I was just a baby, so I don't remember any of it. Still, it affected all of us from then on. And maybe that's why it bothers me so when I see or hear about it happening to others. In fact, preventing that kind of damage is one of the reasons I wanted to become a cop in the first place. And then, the first case I have any connection to ends like this—with the woman dead." She shrugged her shoulders dejectedly.

They were standing outside the classroom, just beyond the cluster of smokers. "I've been thinking about that candlelight vigil down at the capitol tonight," Leann continued. "The one they mentioned in the paper. I think I'm going to go. Want to go along?"

The subject of the vigil had crossed Joanna's own mind several times in the course of the morning. Obviously, Serena Grijalva would be one of the remembered victims. Joanna, too, had considered going.

"Maybe," she said. "But before we decide one way or the other, we'd better see how much homework we have."

Leann gave her a wan smile. "You're almost too focused for your own good," she said. "Has anybody ever told you that?"

"Maybe once or twice. Come on."

Once again, the two women were among the last stragglers to find their seats. Dave Thompson was at the podium. "Why, I'm so glad you two ladies could join us," he said. "I hope class isn't interfering too much with your socializing."

In the uncomfortable silence that followed Thompson's cutting remark, Leann ducked into her chair and appeared to be engrossed in studying her notes, all the while flushing furiously. Joanna, on the other hand, met and held the

instructor's gaze. Of all the people in the room—
the two women and their twenty-three male
classmates—Joanna was the only one whose entire future in law enforcement didn't depend in
great measure on the opinion of that overbearing
jerk.

With Dick Voland's tale of Dave Thompson's
"remotion" still ringing in her ears, Joanna
couldn't manage to keep her mouth shut. "That's
all right," she returned with a tight smile. "We
were finished anyway."

The rest of the morning lecture didn't drag
nearly as much. At lunchtime two carloads of students headed for the nearest Pizza Hut. Joanna
had already taken a seat at one of the three APOA-
occupied tables when the perpetual head-nodder
from the front row paused beside her. "Is this seat
taken?" he asked.

Joanna didn't much want to sit beside someone
she had pegged as a natural-born brown noser.
Still, since the seat was clearly empty, there was
no graceful way for Joanna to tell the guy to
move on. His badge said his name was Rod Bascom and that he hailed from Casa Grande.

"Help yourself," Joanna said.

Watching as he put down his plate and drink,
Joanna was surprised to note that although he
was naturally handsome, he was also surprisingly
ungainly. While the conversation hummed around
the table, Rod attacked his food with a peculiar
intensity. When he glanced up and caught Joanna
observing him, he blushed furiously, from the top

of his collar to the roots of his fine blond hair. For the first time, Joanna wondered if Rod Bascom wasn't an inveterate head-nodder in class because he was actually painfully shy? The very possibility made him seem less annoying. At twenty-five or -six, Rod was close to Joanna's age. In terms of life experience, there seemed to be a world of difference between them.

"Are you enjoying the classes?" Joanna asked, trying to break the ice.

Once again Rod Bascom nodded his head. Joanna had to conceal a smile. Even in private conversation he couldn't seem to stop doing it.

"There's a lot to learn," he said. "I never was very good at taking notes. I'm having a hard time keeping up. I suppose this is all old hat to you."

"Old hat? Why would you say that?" Joanna returned.

"You're not like the rest of us," he said, shrugging uncomfortably. "I mean, you're already a sheriff. By comparison, the rest of us are just a bunch of rookies."

Joanna flushed slightly herself. No matter how earnestly she wanted to fit in with the rest of her classmates, it wasn't really working. She smiled at Rod Bascom then, hoping to put him at ease.

"I'm here for the same reason you are," she said. "Some of this stuff may be boring as hell, but we all need to learn it just the same."

He nodded, chewing thoughtfully for a moment before he spoke again. "I'm sorry about your husband," he said. "It took me a while to figure out why your face is so familiar. I finally realized I saw you on TV back when all that was going on. It must have been awful."

Rod's kind and totally unexpected words of condolence caught Joanna off guard, touching her in a way that surprised them both. Tears sprang to her eyes, momentarily blurring her vision.

"It's still awful," she murmured, impatiently brushing the tears away. "But thanks for mentioning it."

"You have a little girl, don't you?" Rod asked. "How's she doing?"

Joanna smiled ruefully. "Jenny's fine, although she does have her days," she said. "We both know it's going to take time."

"Are you going home for Thanksgiving?"

"No, Jenny and her grandparents are coming up here."

Rod Bascom nodded. "That's probably a good idea," he said. "That first Thanksgiving at home after my father died was awful."

He got up then and hurried away, as though worried that he had said too much. Touched by his sharing comment and aware that she'd somehow misjudged the man, Joanna watched him go.

What was it Marliss Shackleford had said about people in the big city? She had implied that most of the people Joanna would meet in Phoenix were a savage, uncaring, and untrustworthy lot.

So far during her stay in Phoenix, Joanna had met several people. Four in particular stood out from the rest. Leann Jessup—her red-haired note-writing tablemate; Dave Thompson, her loud-mouthed jerk of an instructor; Butch Dixon, the poetry-quoting bartender from the Roundhouse Bar and Grill; and now Rod Bascom, who despite his propensity for head nodding, gave every indication of being a decent, caring human being.

There you go, Marliss, Joanna thought to herself, as she stood up to clear her place. Three out of four ain't bad.

THE MORNING lectures may have dragged, but the afternoon lab sessions flew by. They started with the most fundamental part of police work—paper—and the how and why of filling it out properly. Joanna didn't expect to be fascinated, but she was—right up until time for the end-of-day session of heavy-duty physical training.

Once the PT class was over, Joanna could barely walk. There was no part of her that didn't hurt. It was four-thirty when she finished her last painful lap on the running track and dragged her protesting body back to the gym.

The PT instructor, Brad Mason, was a disgustingly fit fifty-something. His skin was bronze and leatherlike. His lean frame carried not an ounce of extra subcutaneous fat. Brad stood waiting by the door to the gym with his arms folded casually across his chest, watching as the last of the trainees finished up on the field. Running laps was something Joanna hadn't done since high school. She was among the last stragglers to limp into the gym.

"No pain, no gain," Mason said with a grin as Joanna hobbled past.

Her first instinct was to deck him. Instead, Joanna straightened her shoulders. "Thanks," she said. "I'll try to remember that."

After lunch Joanna had told Leann she'd be happy to go to the candlelight vigil, but by the time she finished showering and drying her hair, she was beginning to regret that decision. She was tired. Her body hurt. She had homework to do, including a new hundred-page reading assignment from Dave Thompson. But it was hard to pull herself together and turn to the task at hand when she was feeling so lost and lonely. She missed Jenny, and she missed being home. The partially completed letter she had started writing to Jenny the night before remained in her notebook, incomplete and unmailed.

Joanna went to her room only long enough to change clothes; then she took her reading assignment and hurried back to the student lounge. Naturally, one of the guys from class was already on the phone, and there were three more people waiting in line behind him. After putting her name on the list, Joanna bought herself a caffeine-laden diet Coke from the coin-operated vending machine and sat down to read and wait.

The reading assignment was in a book called *The Interrogation Handbook*. It should have been interesting material. Had Joanna been in a spot more conducive to concentration, she might have found it fascinating. As it was, people wandered in and out of the lounge, chatting and laughing along the way while collecting sodas or snacks or ice. Finally, Joanna gave up all pretense of studying and simply sat and watched. She tried to sort out her various classmates. Some of them she already knew by name and jurisdiction. With most of them, though, she had to resort to checking the name tag before she could remember.

Eventually it was Joanna's turn to use the phone. Jenny answered after only one ring.

"Hullo?"

At the sound of her daughter's voice, Joanna felt her heart constrict. "Hi, Jenny," she said. "How are things?"

"Okay."

Joanna blinked at that. After two whole days, Jenny sounded distant and lethargic and not at all thrilled to hear her mother's voice. "Are you all packed for tomorrow?" Joanna asked.

"I guess so," Jenny answered woodenly. "Grandpa says we're going to leave in the afternoon as soon as school is out."

"Aren't you going to ask how I'm doing?" Joanna asked.

"How are you doing?"

"I'm tired," Joanna answered. "How about you? Are you all right? You sound upset."

"How come you're tired?"

"It may have something to do with running laps and doing push-ups."

"You have to do push-ups? Really?" Jenny asked dubiously. "How many?"

"Too many," Joanna answered. "And I have a mountain of homework to do as well, but Jenny, you didn't answer my question. Is something wrong?"

"No," Jenny said finally, but the slight pause before she answered was enough to shift Joanna's maternal warning light to a low orange glow.

"Jennifer Ann . . ." Joanna began.

"It was supposed to be a surprise." Jenny's blurted answer sounded on the verge of tears. "Grandma said you'd like it. I thought you would, too."

"Like what?"

"My hair," Jenny wailed.

"What about your hair?" Joanna demanded.

"I got it cut," Jenny sobbed. "Grandma Lathrop took me to see Helen Barco last night, and she cut it all off."

A wave of resentment boiled up inside Joanna. How like her mother to pull a stunt like that! She had to go and drag Jenny off to Helene's Salon of Hair and Beauty the moment Joanna's back was turned. Just because Eleanor Lathrop lived for weekly visits to the beauty shop Vincent Barco had built for his wife in their former two-car garage didn't mean everybody else did. In Eleanor Lathrop's skewed view of the world, there was no crisis so terrible that a quick trip to a beautician wouldn't fix.

Joanna, on the other hand, held beauty shops and beauticians at a wary arm's length. Her distrust had its origins in the first time her mother had taken Joanna into a beauty shop for her own first haircut. Eleanor had been going to old Mrs. Boxer back then, in a now long-closed shop that had been next door to the post office. Joanna had walked into the place wearing beautiful, foot-long braids. She had emerged carrying her chopped-off braids in a little metal box and wearing her hair in what Mrs. Boxer had called an "adorable pixie." Joanna had hated her pixie with an abiding passion. All these years later, she still couldn't understand how a place that had nerve enough to call itself a beauty shop could produce something that ugly.

"It'll grow out, you know," Joanna said, hoping to offer Jenny some consolation. "It'll take six months or so, but it will grow out."

"But it's so frizzy," Jenny was saying. "The kids at school all made fun of me, especially the boys."

"Frizzy?" Joanna asked. "Don't tell me. You mean Grandma Lathrop had Helen Barco give you a permanent?"

"It was just supposed to be wavy," Jenny wailed. She really was crying now, as though her heart was broken. "But it's awful. You should see it!"

Joanna had always loved the straight, smooth texture of her daughter's hair, which was so like Andy's. Had Eleanor been available right then, Joanna would have ripped into her mother and told her to mind her own damn business. As it was, though, there was only a heartbroken Jenny sobbing on the phone.

"That'll grow out, too," Joanna said patiently. "Ask Grandma Brady to try putting some of her crème rinse on it. That should help. And remember, Helen Barco and Grandma Lathrop may call it a permanent, but it's not. It's only temporary."

"Will it be better by Monday?" Jenny sniffed.

"Probably not by Monday," Joanna answered. "But by Christmas it will be." She decided to change the subject. "Are you looking forward to coming up tomorrow?"

"I am now," Jenny answered. "I was afraid you'd be mad at me. Because of my hair."

If there's anyone to be mad at, Joanna seethed silently, it's your grandmother, but she couldn't say that out loud.

"Jenny," she replied instead, "you're my daughter. You could shave your hair off completely, for all I care. It wouldn't make any difference. I'd still love you."

"Should I? Shave it off, I mean? Maybe Grandpa Brady would do it with his razor."

Joanna laughed. "Don't do that," she said. "I was just teasing. Most likely your hair doesn't look nearly as bad as you think it does. Now," she added, "is Grandma Brady there? I'd like to talk to her."

Moments later Eva Lou Brady came on the phone. "Is Jenny right there?" Joanna asked.

"No. She went outside to play with the dogs."

"How bad is her hair, really?"

"Pretty bad," Eva Lou allowed. "Jim Bob says he could have gotten the same look by holding her finger in an electrical socket. Don't be upset about it, Joanna," Eva Lou added. "Your mother didn't mean any harm. She and Jenny just wanted to surprise you."

"I'm surprised, all right," Joanna answered stiffly. "Now, is everything set for tomorrow?"

"As far as I can tell," Eva Lou replied. "Kristin called and said you need us to bring along some papers from your office. We'll pick them up on our way to get Jenny from school. We'll leave right after that, between three-thirty and four."

"Good," Joanna said. "If you drive straight through, that should put you here right around eight o'clock."

"That's the only way Jim Bob Brady drives," his wife said with a laugh. "Straight through."

"How about directions to the hotel?"

"Jimmy already has it all mapped out. Do you want us to come by the school to pick you up? Jenny wants to see where you're staying."

"No, I'll meet you at the hotel. It's so close you can see it from here on campus. Jenny and I can walk over here Thursday morning so I can give her the grand tour."

"Speaking of dinner, do we have reservations for Thanksgiving dinner yet?" Eva Lou asked.

"Yes. Right there in the hotel dining room," Joanna answered.

"Jim Bob needs to know if he should bring along a tie."

"Probably," Joanna answered. "From the outside, it looks like a pretty nice place."

"I'll tell him," Eva Lou said. "I don't suppose it'll make his day, but since you're the one asking, he'll probably do it."

Joanna put down the phone and left the lounge. Back in her own room, she realized she still hadn't returned Adam York's call, but she didn't bother to go back down to the lounge. Instead, she lay on the bed in her room and thought about strangling her infuriatingly meddlesome mother.

Jenny's long blond hair had been perfectly fine the way it was. Joanna remembered it floating in the wind as Jenny had waved good-bye.

Where the hell did Eleanor Lathrop get off?

THIRTEEN

JOANNA BRADY and Leann Jessup ate dinner at
La Piñata, a Mexican restaurant near the capitol
mall. Over orders of *machaca tacos,* the two women
talked. In the course of a few minutes' worth of
conversation, they shared their life stories, giving
one another the necessary background in the
shorthand way women use to establish quick but
lasting friendships.

"My mother divorced my dad when my brother
was five and I was three," Leann told Joanna.
"The last time I saw my father was twenty years
ago. He showed up at my sixth birthday party so
drunk he could barely walk. Mom threw him out
of the house and called the cops. He never came
back."

"You haven't talked to him since?" Joanna
asked.

Leann shook her head. "Not once."

"Is he still alive?"

Leann shrugged. "Maybe, but who cares? He never called, never sent any money. My mother had to do it all. Most of the time, while Rick and I were little, she worked two jobs—one full-time and one half-time—just to keep body and soul together.

"In my high school English class, the teacher asked us to write an essay about our favorite hero. Most of the kids wrote about astronauts or movie stars. I wrote about my mom. The teacher made fun of my paper, and he gave me a bad grade. He said mothers didn't count as heroes. I thought he was wrong then, and I still do."

Joanna bit her lip. Thinking about her own mother and the flawed relationship between them, she felt a twinge of envy. "You like your mother, then?" she asked.

"Why, don't you?" Leann returned.

"Most of the time, no," Joanna answered honestly. "I always got along better with my dad than I did with my mother."

She went on to tell Leann about her own folks, about how Sheriff D. H. "Big Hank" Lathrop had died after being hit by a drunk driver while changing a tire for a stranded motorist and about the high school years when she and her mother had been locked in day-to-day guerrilla warfare. Joanna finished by telling Leann Jessup how, that very afternoon and from two hundred miles away, Eleanor Lathrop had been able to use Jenny's hair to push Joanna's buttons.

From there—from discussing mothers and fathers—the two women went on to talk about what had brought them into the field of law enforcement. For Joanna it had been an accident of fate. For Leann Jessup it was the culmination of a lifelong ambition.

Over coffee, Joanna got around to telling Leann about Andy's death. Recounting the story always brought a new stab of pain. Telling Butch Dixon the night before, Joanna had managed to corral the tears. With Leann, she let them flow, but she was starting to feel ridiculous. How long would it take before she stopped losing it and bawling at the drop of a hat?

"What about you, Leann?" Joanna asked, mopping at her eyes with a tissue when she finished. "Do you have anyone special in your life?"

For a moment, the faraway look in Leann Jessup's eyes mirrored Joanna's own. "I did once," she said, "but not anymore." With that, Leann glanced at her watch and then signaled for the waitress to bring the check. "We'd better go," she added, cutting short any further confidences. "It's getting late."

Joanna took the hint. Whatever it was that had happened to Leann Jessup's relationship, the hurt was still too raw and new to tolerate discussion.

They paid their bill and left the restaurant right after that. Riding in Joanna's county-owned Blazer, they arrived at the capitol mall well after dark and bare minutes before the vigil was scheduled to begin. Folding chairs had been set out on the lawn. A subdued crowd of two or three hundred people, augmented by news reporters, had gathered and were gradually taking their seats. After some searching, Joanna and Leann located a pair of vacant chairs near the far end of the second row.

The organizers from MAVEN had set the make-shift stage with an eye to drama. In the center of the capitol's portico sat a table draped in black on which burned a single candle. Because of the enveloping darkness, that lone candle seemed to float suspended in space. Next to the table stood a spotlit lectern with a portable microphone attached.

A woman who introduced herself as Matilda Hirales-Steinowitz, the executive director of MAVEN, spoke first. After introducing herself, she gave a brief overview of the Maricopa Anti-Violence Empowerment Network, a group Joanna had never heard of before reading the newspaper article earlier that morning.

"The people of MAVEN, women and men alike, deplore all violence," Ms. Hirales-Steinowitz declared, "but we are most concerned with the war against women that is being conducted behind the closed doors of family homes here in the Valley. So far this year sixteen women have died in the Phoenix metropolitan area of murders police consider to be cases of domestic partner violence.

"We are gathered tonight to remember those women. We have asked representatives of each of the families to come here to speak to you about the loved ones they have lost and to light a memorial candle in their honor. We're hoping that the light from those candles will help focus both public and legislative attention on this terrible and growing problem."

Matilda Hirales-Steinowitz paused for a moment; then she said, "The first to die, at three o'clock on the afternoon of January third, was Anna Maria Dominguez, age twenty-six."

With that, the spokeswoman sat down. Under the glare of both stage and television lights, a dowdy, middle-aged Hispanic woman walked slowly across the stage. Once she reached the podium, she gripped the sides of it as if to keep from falling.

"My name is Renata Sanchez," she said in a nervously quavering voice. "Anna Maria was my daughter."

As her listeners strained forward to hear her, Renata told about being summoned to St. Luke's Hospital. Her daughter had come home from her first day at a new job at a convenience store. She had been met at the door by her unemployed husband. He had shot her in the face at point-blank range and then had turned the gun on himself.

"They're both dead," Renata concluded, dabbing at her eyes with a hanky. "I have had some time to get used to it, but it's still very painful. I hope you will forgive me if I cry."

Joanna bit her own lip. The woman's pain was almost palpable, and far too much like Joanna's own.

From that moment on, the evening only got worse. One by one the deadly roll was called, and one by one the survivors came haltingly forward to make their impassioned pleas for an end to the senseless killing that had cost them the life of a mother, sister, daughter, or friend.

Renata Sanchez was right. Because the names were announced chronologically in the order in which the victims perished, the survivors who had lost loved ones earlier in the year were somewhat more self-possessed than those of the women who had died later. That was hardly surprising. The first survivors had had more time—a few months anyway—to adjust to the pain of loss. After speaking, each person took a candle from a stack on the table and lit it from the burning candle. After placing their newly lit candles on the table with the others, the speakers crossed the stage and sat in the chairs that had been provided for them.

Some of the grieving relatives addressed the listeners extemporaneously, while others read their statements hesitantly, the words barely audible through the loudspeakers. Several of the latter were so desperately nervous that their notes crackled in the microphone, rustling like dead leaves in the wind. Their lit candles trembled visibly in their hands.

Joanna could imagine how reluctantly most of those poor folks had been drawn into the fray, yet here they stood—or sat—united both in their grief and in their determination to put a stop to the killing. Listening to the speeches, Joanna was jolted by a shock of self-recognition. These people were just like her. The survivors were all ordinary folk who had been thrust unwillingly into the spotlight and into roles they had never asked for or wanted, compelled by circumstance into doing something about the central tragedy of their lives. And the men and women of MAVEN—the people who cared enough to start and run the Maricopa Anti-Violence Empowerment Network—had given those bereaved people a public forum from which to air their hurt, grief, and rage.

By the time Matilda Hirales-Steinowitz read the fifteenth name, that of Serena Duffy Grijalva, Joanna's pain was so much in tune with that of the people sitting on the stage that she could barely stand to listen. Had she come to the vigil by herself, she might have left right then, without hearing any more. But Joanna had come with Leann Jessup, whose major interest in being there was the last of the sixteen victims—Rhonda Weaver Norton.

And so, instead of walking out, Joanna waited along with the silent crowd while a gaunt old man and a young child—a girl—took the stage. At first Joanna thought the man must be terribly elderly. He walked slowly, with frail, babylike steps. It was only when they turned at the podium to face the audience that Joanna could see he wasn't nearly as old as she had thought. He was ill. While he stood still, gasping for breath, the girl parked a small, portable oxygen cart next to him on the stage.

"My name's Jefferson Davis Duffy," he wheezed finally, in a voice that was barely audible. "My friends call me Joe. Serena was my daughter—the purtiest li'l thing growin' up you ever did see. Not always the best child, mind you. Not always the smartest or the best behaved, but the purtiest by far. When Miz Steinowitz over there asked us here tonight, when they asked us to speak and say somethin' about our daughter, the wife and I didn't know what to do or say. Neither one of us ever done nothin' like this before."

He paused long enough to take a series of gasping breaths. "The missus and I was about to say no, when our granddaughter here—Serena's daughter, Cecelia—speaks up. Ceci said she'd do it, that she had somethin' she wanted to tell people about what happened to her mama."

With a series of loud clicks and pops, he managed to pull the microphone loose from its mooring. Bending over, he held the mike to his granddaughter's lips. "You ready, Ceci, honey?" he asked.

Cecelia Grijalva nodded, her eyes wide open like those of a frightened horse, her knees knocking together under her skirt. Joanna closed her own eyes. How could the people from MAVEN justify exploiting a child that way, using her personal tragedy to make what was ultimately a political statement? On the other hand, Joanna had to admit no one seemed to be forcing the frightened little girl to appear on the stage.

"I have a little brother," Cecelia whispered, while people in the audience held their breath in an effort to hear her. "Pablo's only six—a baby really. Pepe keeps asking me how come our mom went away to wash clothes and didn't come back. At night sometimes, when it's time for him to go to sleep, he cries because he's afraid I'll go away, too. I tell him I won't, that I'll be there in the morning when he wakes up, but he cries anyway, and I can't make him stop. That's all."

Ceci's simple eloquence, her careful concentration as she lit her candle, wrung Joanna's heart right along with everyone else's. When will this be over? she wondered. How much more can the people in this audience take?

While Joe Duffy and his granddaughter limped slowly across the stage to two of the last three unoccupied seats in the row of chairs reserved for family members, Matilda Hirales-Steinowitz stepped to the microphone once again. "The latest victim, number sixteen, is Rhonda Weaver Norton, age thirty, who died sometime last week."

Matilda moved away from the mike. Yet another mourner—a tall, silver-haired woman in an elegant black dress—glided to the podium. "My name is Lael Weaver Gastone," she said. "The man who was my son-in-law murdered my daughter, Rhonda. I'm tired of killers having all the rights. I've been told that Rhonda's killer is innocent until proven guilty. Everyone is all concerned about protecting his rights—the right of the accused. Who will stand up for the rights of my daughter?

"The man who was here a moment ago, Mr. Duffy, is lucky. At least he has two grandchildren to remember his daughter by. I have nothing—nothing but hurt. I've never had a grandchild, and now I never will.

"This afternoon, I went to my former son-in-law's arraignment. Before I was allowed into the courtroom, I had to go through a metal detector. Do you believe it? They checked me for weapons! But now that I think about it, maybe it's a good thing they did."

With the implied threat still lingering in the air, Lael Gastone lit her candle and placed it on the table. Shaking her head, she strode across the stage to the last unoccupied chair. Meanwhile, the mistress of ceremonies returned to the microphone.

"Thank you all for joining us here tonight," she said. "Many of us will be here until morning, until the sun comes up on what we hope will be the dawn of a new day of nonviolence for women in this state and in this country. Some, but not all, of the people who have spoken here tonight will be with us throughout the vigil. I'm sure it means a great deal to all of them that so many of you came here for this observance. Please stay if you can and visit with some of them. It's important. As you have heard tonight, it truly is a matter of life and death."

"Shall we go?" Leann whispered to Joanna.

Joanna shook her head. "Just a minute," she said. "Ceci Grijalva is a friend of my daughter's. I shouldn't leave without at least saying hello."

They made their way through the surging crowd to the makeshift stage where little knots of well-wishers were gathering around each of the speakers. While Leann went to pay her respects to Rhonda Norton's mother, Joanna headed for the spot where she had last seen Joe Duffy and

Cecelia Grijalva. Ceci's grandfather was deep in conversation with Renata Sanchez, one of the other speakers. Meanwhile, unobserved by most of the adults, Ceci had slipped off by herself. In isolated dejection, she sat on the edge of the stage, dangling her legs over the side and kicking at the empty air.

"Ceci?" Joanna asked. "Are you all right?"

Without looking up, the child nodded her head but said nothing.

Joanna tried again. "I know you from Bisbee," she explained. "I'm Joanna Brady, Jenny's mother."

This time Ceci did look up. "Oh," she said.

Joanna winced at the pain in that one-word answer. Ceci Grijalva's voice was weighted down with the same hurt and despair that had taken the laughter out of Jenny's voice, too.

"I'm so sorry about your mother," Joanna said.

"It's okay," Ceci mumbled, staring down at her feet once more.

It is *not* okay, Joanna wanted to scream. It's awful! It's a tragedy! It's horrible. Instead, she hoisted herself up on the stage until she was sitting next to Cecelia.

"Jenny wanted me to come see you," Joanna began. "She wanted me to tell you that she knows how you feel."

Cecelia Grijalva nodded. Joanna continued. "You know, Ceci, Jenny didn't lose her mom the way you did, because I'm still here. But she did lose her daddy. He died down in Bisbee, a few days before your mother died."

Ceci's chin came up slowly. Her dark eyes drilled into Joanna's. "Jenny's daddy is dead, too?"

Joanna nodded. "That's right. Somebody shot him. Jenny thought you'd like to know that you're not the only one going through this and if—"

"Ceci, come on!" a woman's voice ordered from somewhere on the stage behind them. "We've got a long drive home."

Ceci started to scramble to her feet. "But, Grandma," she objected, "this is my friend Jenny's mother. Jenny Brady's mother. From Bisbee."

"I don't care who it is or where she's from. We have to go," Ernestina Duffy said stiffly, not even bothering to nod in Joanna's direction. "It's getting late. You have school tomorrow."

Standing up at the same time Ceci did, Joanna turned to face Ernestina Duffy. She was a middle-aged Hispanic woman whose striking good looks were still partially visible behind an angry, bitter façade.

Ignoring the woman's brusque manner, Joanna held out her hand. "I'm Joanna Brady," she explained. "Ceci and Jenny, my daughter, were in second grade and Brownies together back in Bisbee. I wanted to stop by, to check on Ceci, and to see if there's anything I can do to help."

"You can't bring my daughter back," Ernestina said coldly.

"No. I can't do that. And I *do* know what you're going through, Mrs. Duffy. My husband's dead, too. Jenny's father is dead. He was killed down in Bisbee the same week your daughter died."

"I'm sorry," Ernestina said, "but we've got to drive all the way home. Come on, Ceci."

Joanna wasn't willing to give up. "Jenny's coming up for Thanksgiving tomorrow," Joanna said hurriedly. "I was wondering if maybe the girls could get together on Friday for a visit."

Ernestina shook her head. "I don't think so. We live clear out in Wittmann. It's too far."

"What's this?" Joe Duffy asked, breaking away from the people around him and dragging his oxygen cart over to where Joanna was standing with Ernestina and Cecelia.

"This is the mother of a friend of Ceci's from Bisbee," Ernestina explained. "Her daughter is coming up for a visit on Friday. They wanted us to bring Ceci into town to see her, but I told them—"

"My name's Joanna Brady," Joanna said, stepping forward and taking Jefferson Davis Duffy's bony hand in hers. By then Leann had joined the little group. "And this is my friend Leann Jessup. We'll be happy to drive up to Wittmann to get her," Joanna offered. "And we'll bring her back home that evening."

The offer of a ride made no difference as far as Ceci Grijalva's grandmother was concerned. Ernestina Duffy remained adamant. "I still say it's too far and too much trouble."

"Now wait a minute here," her husband interjected. "It might be good for Ceci to be away for a while, to go off on her own and have some fun with someone her age. What time would it be?" he asked, turning to Joanna.

"Morning maybe?" Joanna asked tentatively. "Say about ten o'clock."

Joe Duffy nodded. "What do you think, Ceci?" he asked, frowning down at the little girl. "Would you like to do that?"

Joanna's heart constricted at the fleeting look of hope that flashed briefly across Ceci Grijalva's troubled face. "Please," she said. "I'd like it a lot."

The old man smiled. "You call us then," he said to Joanna. "We're in information. The only Duffys in Wittmann. My wife manages a little trailer park there. If you call before you come, I can give you directions."

Ernestina Duffy tossed her head and stalked off across the stage. She may not have approved of the arrangement, but she didn't voice any further objections.

"Come on, Ceci," Joe Duffy said, taking Ceci's hand. "Bring Spot along, would you?"

Dutifully Ceci reached out and took the handle of the oxygen cart.

"Spot?" Joanna asked.

Joe Duffy gave her a grin. "The trailer park don't allow no pets. So me an' Ceci an' Pepe decided that my cart here would be our dog, Spot. He don't eat much, and he's never once wet on the carpet. Right, Ceci?"

"Right, Grandpa," Ceci said.

"And we'll see you all on Friday morning," he said to Joanna. "You won't forget now, will you? I don't approve of folks who'd let a little kid down."

"We'll be there," Joanna promised. "Jenny and I both."

"Good."

"Whoa," Leann said, once the Duffys and Cecelia were out of earshot. "That woman is tough as nails. Those kids are lucky they have a guy like him for a grandfather."

"For the time being," Joanna said. "But from the look of things, I doubt he'll be around very long."

There were still people milling in the aisles as they started toward the car. Just beyond the back row of chairs, the lights of a portable television camera sprang to life directly in their path, almost blinding them.

"Sheriff Brady," a disembodied woman's voice said, as a microphone was thrust in front of Joanna's face. "Sheriff Joanna Brady, could you please tell us why you came here tonight?"

FOURTEEN

I **MISSED** the first part of the interview," Leann said later, as they walked from the mall to the car. "Some creepy guy behind us was following so close that when the reporter stopped you, he ran right into me. Stepped on the back of my heel. Did you see him?"

"No," Joanna said. "I missed that completely."

"Then, when I turned around to look at him, he glared at me with these cold, ice-blue eyes as if it was all my fault that he ran into me. Whoever he was, the guy had a real problem. I've always wondered how dirty looks could cause drive-by shootings. Now maybe I know."

The two women walked in silence the rest of the way to the car. "How did that reporter know it was you?" Leann asked, once they were inside Joanna's Blazer.

Still somewhat stunned by her unexpected encounter with a television reporter, it was the same question Joanna had been asking herself all the way to the car.

Since deciding to run for office, Joanna had adjusted to the idea that she was no longer a private person in her own hometown, that down in Bisbee there would be people like Marliss Shackleford poking their noses into Joanna's every move. Until that night, the fact that she was well known on a statewide basis hadn't yet penetrated her consciousness.

"It is a little disconcerting," she admitted at last. "That kind of stuff happens all the time in Bisbee, but Bisbee happens to be a very small pond. Phoenix is a lot bigger than that."

Leann nodded. "By a couple million or so people. Why do you think the reporter singled you out like that?"

"It could be she covered either Andy's death or else the election. The election's more likely."

Leann thought about that for a moment. "Doesn't not having any privacy bother you?"

"It goes with the territory, I guess," Joanna answered.

"Well," Leann returned, "it's never happened to me before. If they put the part with me in it on the news, it'll be my first time. As soon as we get home, I'm going to call my mother. Maybe she can tape it." Leann paused. "What about your mother? Won't she want to tape it, too?"

"It's a Phoenix station," Joanna returned. "Their signals don't get as far as Bisbee. With any kind of luck, my mother won't see it."

"Why do you say that? Will it upset her?"

"Are you kidding? The way I look on TV always upsets her."

Leann laughed. "Still, I'll bet she'd like to see it. If Mom tapes it, I'll have her drop the tape by campus tomorrow. Or else I'll be seeing her sometime over the weekend. That way you can show it to your family if you want to."

"Wait a minute," Joanna said. "You said sometime this weekend. You mean you're not going to your mother's for Thanksgiving dinner?"

Leann shook her head.

"Why not?" Joanna continued. "She lives right here in town somewhere, doesn't she?"

"Just off Indian School and Twenty-fourth Street," Leann answered. "But there's this little problem with my brother and sister-in-law. It's better for all concerned if I don't show up in person for holiday meals. That's all right, though. Mom always saves me a bunch of leftovers."

They drove in silence for the better part of a mile while Joanna considered what Leann had said. "So what *are* you doing for Thanksgiving dinner?"

Leann shrugged. "Who knows? There'll be restaurants open somewhere. I'll have dinner. Maybe I'll go to a movie. As a last resort, I suppose I could always study. I'm sure good ol' Dave Thompson isn't going to let us off for the holiday without a hundred-or-so-page reading assignment."

"Why don't you come to dinner with us?" Joanna asked impulsively. "With Jenny and my in-laws and me. We'll be staying at the Hohokam, right there on Grand Avenue. We have a five o'clock reservation in the hotel dining room. I'm sure we could add one more place if we need to. Where are you going to be for the weekend, then, back in Tempe?"

Leann shook her head. "I'm between apartments right now," she said. "I figured that as long as the APOA was giving me a place to stay for the better part of six weeks, there was no need for me to pay rent at the same time."

"That settles it, then!" Joanna said forcefully. "If you're spending the whole weekend here on campus all by yourself, you have to come to dinner with us."

"I shouldn't," Leann said. "I shouldn't intrude on your family time."

"Believe me, you won't. Besides, you'll love Jim Bob and Eva Lou Brady. Unlike my mother, those two are dyed-in-the-wool SOEs."

"S-O-E?" Leann repeated with a questioning frown. "What's that, some kind of secret fraternal organization?"

Joanna laughed. "Hardly," she said. "It means salt of the earth. They're nice people. Regular people."

After thinking about the invitation for a few seconds, Leann suddenly smiled and nodded. "Why not?" she said. "That's very nice of you. I'll come. It'll give me something to look forward to when I'm locked up in my room doing my homework."

A moment later she added, "I'm glad we went tonight. We both needed to be at the vigil, and dinner was fun. I feel like I made a new friend tonight."

"That's funny," Joanna replied, flashing her own quick smile back in Leann Jessup's direction. "I feel the same way."

By then they had reached the entrance to the APOA campus. The Blazer's headlights slid briefly across Tommy Tompkins's broken-winged angel guarding the entryway. Basking in the glow of a newfound friendship, the angel seemed far less incongruous to Joanna now than it had the first time she saw it.

After parking in the lot, the two women started toward the dorm. "How about going for a jog later?" Leann asked.

"No way," Joanna answered. "Look at me. I can barely hobble along as it is. This afternoon's session of PT almost killed me."

"You know what they say," Leann said. "No pain, no gain."

It wasn't a particularly witty or clever comment. In fact, when Brad Mason had said the exact same thing earlier that afternoon as Joanna came crawling in from running her laps, she had been tempted to punch the PT instructor's lights out. Now, though, for some reason, it struck her funny bone.

She started to laugh. A moment later, so did Leann. They were both still convulsed with giggles and trying to stifle the racket as they struggled to unlock their respective doors.

Joanna managed to open hers first. "Good night," she called, as she stepped inside.

"Night," Leann said.

Closing the door behind her, Joanna leaned against it for a moment. It had been a long, long time since she had laughed like that—until tears ran down her cheeks, until her jaws ached, and her sides hurt. It felt good. She was still basking in the glow of it when her phone began to ring.

Sure the call had something to do with Jenny, she jumped to answer it only to hear Adam York's voice on the line.

"Joanna," he said. "I've been trying to track you down all day. Didn't you get my message?"

"I did, but I haven't had a chance to call. Where are you?"

"The Ritz-Carlton. On Camelback."

"Here in Phoenix?"

"Yes, in Phoenix. There may be streets named Camelback other places, but I don't know of any."

"What are you doing here?"

"I came in from the East Coast this afternoon for a meeting that's scheduled for both tomorrow and Friday. I thought I'd check in and see how things are going for you before you head on down to Bisbee for Thanksgiving."

"I'm not going," Joanna said. "My in-laws are bringing Jenny up here for the weekend." She paused for a moment. "It just seemed like a better idea for us to be here for Thanksgiving rather than at home. What about you?"

"I considered driving back to Tucson, but it would just be for one day. And I've been gone so much that the food in my refrigerator has probably mutated into a new life-form. My best bet is to hang out here where, if I get hungry, I can always call for room service."

"Room service for Thanksgiving dinner? Sounds pretty grim," Joanna said. "If you don't get a better offer, you could always join us. We're all staying at a new place out here in Peoria, the Hohokam. Tomorrow I have to up our dinner reservation by one anyway. I could just as well add two."

"I wouldn't want to barge in . . ." Adam York objected.

"Look," Joanna interrupted, "don't think you'd be barging in on some intimate, quiet family affair. It's not like that. One of my classmates from here at school, Leann Jessup, will be joining us. And Eva Lou's—my mother-in-law's—watchword is that there's always room for one more."

"I'll think about it," Adam said. "Is tomorrow morning too late to let you know?"

"No. Tomorrow will be fine. I plan on checking in to the hotel after class tomorrow afternoon. In fact, you could leave me a message there, one way or the other."

"In the meantime," Adam said, "how about you? How's your training going?"

"All right," Joanna said. "It's hard work, but then I guess you knew that. And some of the instructors strike me as real jerks."

Adam York laughed. "You know what they say. 'Them as can, do. Them as can't—'"

"I know, I know," Joanna interjected. "But still, I expected something better."

"Joanna," Adam York said, no longer laughing, "I know most of the APOA guys, either personally or by reputation. They know the territory. They've been out there on the front lines. They've been there, done that, and got the T-shirt. But for one reason or another, the world is better off with them *out* of doing active police work. They've got the training. They know the stuff backwards and forwards, but they should no longer be out interacting with the public on a regular basis."

"Someone told me the process is called remoting."

"You bet," Adam answered. "I've used it myself on occasion, but that doesn't mean green young cops can't learn from them. Each one of those old crocodile cops has a lifetime's worth of invaluable experience at his disposal. With the crisis in crime that's occurring in this country, those guys are a national resource we can't afford to waste."

"That's easy for you to say," Joanna replied. "You're not stuck in the classes."

"But I've had agents sit through some of the sessions. It sounds to me as though someone's giving you a hard time. Let me take a wild guess. Dave Thompson."

Joanna said nothing. Her silence spoke volumes.

"So it is Thompson. Look, Joanna, I won't try to tell you Dave Thompson's a great guy, because he isn't. But I will say this—if you're up here at school expecting to pick up an education that will stand you in good stead out in the real world, you'll learn a whole lot more from someone who's less than perfect than you will from Mary Poppins."

"Thank you," Joanna said, trying not to sound as sarcastic as she felt. "I'll try to remember that."

"Good," Adam York said. "Thompson does the lecture-type stuff. What about the rest of it?"

"The lab work is great, but I had my first session of PT this afternoon, and I can barely walk."

"Take a hot shower before you go to bed. Doctor's orders."

"I can do better than that," Joanna answered. "I think I'll hop in the hot tub."

"They have a hot tub there on campus? That's a big step up from when the facility used to be downtown. That place was nothing short of grim."

"It's not just a hot tub on campus," Joanna returned. "I happen to have a hot tub right here in my room. It even works."

"Amazing," Adam York said. "I may be staying at the Ritz, but I sure don't have a hot tub in my room."

"I don't know what to tell you," Joanna said with a laugh. "Some people seem to have all the luck."

WHILE CLASSES were in session, Dave Thompson tried to limit his drinking to the confines of his own apartment, but that Tuesday night he sought solace in the comforting din of his favorite neighborhood watering hole, the Roundhouse Bar and Grill.

Holidays were always tough, but Thanksgiving was especially so since that was when the problem with Irene and Frances had come to a head. Even more than Christmas, that was when he missed his kids the most, when he wished that somehow things could have turned out differently. Unfortunately, when it came to living happily ever after, Dave Thompson had ended up on the short end of the stick.

In his mind's eye, he still saw the kids as they had been six years earlier when Irene took them and left town. At least he supposed they had left town. All Dave got to do was send his child support check to the Maricopa County court system on the first of every month. He didn't know where it went from there. He wasn't allowed to know. Irene's lawyer had seen to that. She had been a regular ring-tailed bitch. So was the judge, for that matter. By the time that bunch of hard-nosed women had finished with him, Dave had nothing left—not even visitation rights.

And maybe that was just as well. Truth be known, Dave didn't want to know what kind of squalor Little Davy and Reenie were living in or what they were learning from Irene and that god-damned "friend" of hers. In fact, it was probably far better that he didn't.

For months after that last big blowup—the one that had landed Dave in jail overnight—he had rummaged eagerly through his mail each day, hoping to receive a card or letter. Something to let him know whether or not his kids cared if he was dead or alive. But none ever came. Not one. All these years later, he had pretty much given up hope one ever would. In fact, he doubted he would ever see his children again, especially not if Irene had anything to do with it.

Of course, there was always a chance that eventually they might grow up enough to ignore her. If somebody else ever told the kids their father's side of the story—if they ever got tired of all the lies and bullshit Irene had to be feeding them—they might even come looking for him one day. If and when that happened, Dave was prepared to welcome his children back home with open arms.

But that kind of thing was years away at best. Now the kids were only eleven and twelve. Davy was the older of the two, by sixteen months. Brooding over his beer, Dave wondered how tall the boy was and whether or not he still looked like his father and if, also like his father, Davy was any good at sports. As far as Reenie was concerned, Dave tried not to think about her very much. She had been a sweet-tempered, dark-haired cutey the last time he saw her. But the problem with little girls was that they grew up and turned into women. And then they broke your heart.

Clicker in hand, Butch Dixon was surfing through the local news broadcasts. "Hey, Dave," the bartender said, interrupting the other man's melancholy reverie. "Isn't that one of your students?"

Thompson turned a bleary eye on the huge

television set. Sure enough, there was Joanna
Brady being interviewed about something. Dave
had come in on the story too late to catch what
was going on, but Joanna was there. Next, Leann
Jessup stepped forward and said something about
how the system had to do better.

"What the hell's that all about?" he asked.

"Some kind of big deal down at the capitol,"
Butch Dixon told him. "Something about this
year's domestic violence victims."

"I wonder what those girls were doing there,"
Dave Thompson muttered. "If my students have
time enough to fool around with that shit, I must
not be piling on enough homework. Give me another beer, would you, Butch? It's mighty thirsty
out tonight."

WITHIN MINUTES of hanging up the phone
with Adam York, Joanna was lounging in the tub.
By the time she crawled out and dried off, fatigue
overwhelmed her. There was no point in even pre-
tending to read the assignment in *The Law Enforcement Handbook*. Instead, she set the alarm for 5:00
A.M. and crawled into bed. The evening spent in
Leann Jessup's company and the chat with Adam
York left Joanna feeling less lonely than she had in
a long time. She was starting to forge some new
friendships. She was learning how to go on with
her life. Oddly comforted by that knowledge, she
fell asleep within minutes.

The dream came later—an awful dream that

invaded her slumber and shattered her hard-won sense of well-being. It began with Joanna driving her old AMC Eagle down Highway 80 from Bisbee toward the Double Adobe Road turnoff. A woman—a complete stranger—was riding in the car with her. For some reason Joanna didn't quite understand, she was taking this woman she didn't know home to High Lonesome Ranch.

Behind the Eagle, another vehicle appeared out of nowhere, looming up large and impatient in the rearview mirror. Bright headlights flashed on and off in Joanna's eyes. She tried to move out of the way, but that wasn't possible. She was driving in a no-passing zone through one of the tall, red-rocked cuts that line Highway 80 as it comes down out of the mountain pass into the flat of the Sulphur Springs valley. There was no shoulder on either side of the roadway, only a solid rock wall some thirty feet high.

Ignoring the double line in the middle of the roadway, the vehicle behind Joanna swung out into the left-hand lane. It inched along, slowly overtaking the Eagle, driving on the wrong side of the road, even though there was no way to see around the curve ahead or to check for oncoming traffic.

"My God!" Joanna's unknown passenger yelled. "What's the matter with that guy? Is he crazy or what? He's going to get us killed."

Joanna was too busy driving the car to answer, although she did glance to her left, trying to catch a glimpse of the driver of the other car. But none was visible. All the windows were blacked out. An oncoming pickup came careening around the curve in the other lane. With only inches to spare, the other car ducked back into the lane directly in front of Joanna.

As Joanna clung to the steering wheel and fought to keep her car on the road, an awful sense of foreboding swept over her. Even without glimpsing any of the other vehicle's occupants, Joanna knew instinctively that they were dangerous. Reflexively, Joanna reached for the switch to turn on the flashing lights on the light bar and to activate the siren, but they weren't there. Then she remembered. She wasn't in her county-owned Blazer. This was her own car. Those switches didn't exist in her basic, stripped-down AMC Eagle.

There was a gas pedal, though. As the other car sped up and threatened to outrun her, Joanna plunged the accelerator all the way to the floor. The Eagle leaped forward. Then suddenly, in the peculiar way things happen in dreams, Joanna was no longer in the car. Instead, she was standing outside her own back gate with the idling Eagle parked behind her. While she stood there watching helplessly, a hulking, hooded figure leaped out of the other vehicle, which was now parked directly in front of her back gate. As the frightening specter started up the walk, Joanna yelled at the dogs.

"Sadie. Tigger. Get him."

But the dogs lay panting and unconcerned in the shade of the backyard apricot tree Eva Lou Brady had planted years earlier. Neither dog moved. Meanwhile, the intruder was almost to the door, running full speed. Joanna struggled to loosen her Colt from under her jacket. It seemed to take forever, but at last she was holding it in her hand.

"Stop or I'll shoot," she shouted.

But the hooded figure didn't stop, didn't even slow down. Joanna pulled back on the trigger only to find that instead of holding the deadly Colt 2000, she was aiming a plastic water pistol. The expected explosion of gunpowder never came. Instead, a puny stream of water shot out of the pistol and fell to the ground not three feet in front of her. The intruder, totally undeterred, raced into the house through the back door.

Enraged, Joanna threw down the useless water pistol and then headed toward the house herself just as she heard Jenny start to scream. Jenny! Joanna thought. She's in there with him. I have to get her out!

She started toward the house, running full-out. Even as she ran, she could see a spiral of smoke rising up from the roof of the house, from a part of the roof where there was no chimney, a place where there should have been no smoke.

"Jenny!" Joanna screamed. "Jenny!"

The sound of Joanna's own despairing voice awakened her. Heart pounding, wet with sweat, she lay on the bed and waited for the nighttime terror to dissipate.

When her breathing finally slowed, she glanced at the clock beside her bed. Twelve-fifteen. It wasn't even that late. She turned over, pounded the pillow into a more comfortable configuration, and then tried to go back to sleep.

That's when she realized that although the dream was long gone, the smell of smoke remained. Cigarette smoke—as sharp and pungent as if the person smoking the cigarette were right there in the room with her.

Which is odd, she thought, closing her eyes and drifting off once more. Leann Jessup is my closest neighbor, and she doesn't even smoke.

❀ FIFTEEN

ON WEDNESDAY before Thanksgiving, classes ended at noon. Within minutes, the parking lot was virtually empty. Since the Hohokam Resort Hotel was only a half mile away from campus, Joanna had no reason to pack very much to take with her from dorm to hotel room. If she discovered something missing over the weekend, she could always come back for it later. In fact, the dorm and the hotel were close enough that she and Jenny could easily walk over if they felt like it.

Hauling one of her suitcases down from the shelf in the closet, Joanna tossed in two changes of clothing, her nightgown, and a selection of toiletries. She sighed at the size of the next reading assignment and dropped her copy of *The Law Enforcement Handbook* on top of the heap before she zipped the suitcase. On her way to the parking lot, Joanna stopped by the student lounge

211

long enough to call home and ask Eva Lou to
please bring along Jenny's extra bathing suit just
in case Ceci Grijalva wanted to try swimming in
the hotel pool.

"She's the little girl whose mother died, isn't
she?" Eva Lou asked.

"That's the one."

"How's she doing?"

"Medium," Joanna answered, thinking about
the less than friendly Ernestina Duffy and her
frail, oxygen-dependent husband. "Not as well as
Jenny," Joanna added. "Unfortunately for her,
Ceci Grijalva doesn't have the same kind of support system Jenny does."

"Poor little thing," Eva clucked. "I'll go hunt
down that bathing suit just as soon as I get off the
phone."

For a change there wasn't anyone else waiting
in line to use the phone. Dialing the Sheriff's Department number, Joanna savored the privacy.
Trying to handle both her personal and professional life from an overused pay phone in an
audience-crowded room was aggravating at best.

Once again, Kristin was chilly on the telephone, but she was also relatively efficient. "Chief
Deputy Voland is out to lunch, and Chief Montoya's still over in the jail kitchen."

"What's he doing over there?" Joanna asked.
"Micromanaging the cook?"

"He's been there all morning," Kristin answered. "The last I heard he was supervising the
crew of inmates who are washing all the walls."

"Washing walls? Maybe you'd better try connecting me to the jail kitchen," Joanna said. A few moments later, Frank Montoya came on the line.

"What's my chief of administration doing washing walls?" Joanna asked without preamble.

"Putting out fires," Frank answered, "but I think we've got this little crisis pretty well under control."

"What crisis?" Joanna demanded.

"The cook crisis," Frank Montoya answered. "I wrote you a memo explaining the whole thing. Didn't you get it?"

"Not yet. My father-in-law picked up the packet a little while ago, but I won't get it until later on tonight. What's going on?"

"As soon as the cook figured out I was on his case, he took off, but before he left, he cleaned out the refrigerator."

"Good deal," Joanna said. "He cleaned the refrigerator, and now you've got a crew washing the walls. Sounds like the place is getting a thorough and much-needed housecleaning."

"Not really," Frank Montoya returned wryly. "When I said cleaned out the refrigerator, I meant as in emptying it rather than making it germ-free. When I came in to work this morning, we almost had a riot on our hands. The cook didn't show and the inmates were starving. I thought maybe he'd just overslept, but when I tried calling him, his landlady said he left."

"Left. You mean he moved out? Quit without giving notice?"

"That's right. Not only that, when I went home

last night, there were a dozen frozen turkeys in the walk-in cooler waiting to be cooked for Thanksgiving dinner tomorrow. Today they're gone, every last one of them."

"Gone? He took them?" Joanna asked in disbelief. "All of them?"

"That's right, the turkey. He left town under the dark of night without leaving so much as a forwarding address. *Nada*."

This was just the kind of crisis someone like Marliss Shackleford could turn into a major incident. "Somebody should have called me," Joanna said. "That settles it. I'll call Eva Lou and tell her not to come up. I can cancel the hotel reservations and be home in just over four hours."

"No need to do that," Frank reassured her. "I already told you. It's pretty well handled."

"What did you do, cook breakfast yourself?"

"Are you kidding? I don't have a valid food handler's permit. Besides, I'm a lousy cook. No, Ruby did the whole thing."

"Who the hell is Ruby?" Joanna demanded crossly. "Did you already hire another cook?"

Frank paused momentarily before he answered. "Not exactly," he said.

"What exactly does 'not exactly' mean?" Joanna asked.

"Ruby is Ruby Starr. I think I told you about her. She and her husband are the people who leased the Sunset Inn. She's the one who did the actual cooking."

"In other words, the lady who took after her husband's windshield with a sledgehammer and deadly intent is the one who cooked breakfast in my jail this morning?"

"That's right. When she went before Judge Moore, he set her bail at only five hundred dollars. I think everybody—including Burton Kimball, her lawyer—expected her to get bailed out, but she refused to go. She said if she left on bail that her husband would expect her to go to work and keep the restaurant open while he sits on his tail in his mother's home over in Silver City. She said she'd rather stay in jail.

"So this morning, when I heard the cook had skipped, I drafted Ruby. Right out of the cell and into the kitchen. Seemed like the only sensible thing to do. Breakfast may have been a few hours late, but it drew rave reviews from the inmates. Great biscuits. After that, I asked Ruby if she'd consider cooking Thanksgiving dinner. She turned me down cold. Said she wouldn't set foot in that filthy kitchen again until *after* it got cleaned up. That's when the most amazing thing happened. Once word got out that their Turkey Day dinner hung in the balance, I had inmates lining up and begging for me to let them help clean and cook.

"Believe me, Ruby Starr's a hell of a tough taskmaster. She's been working everybody's butts off all morning long, mine included."

"So you've got an almost clean kitchen and a cook," Joanna said. "But you're missing the fixings."

"I told you, Joanna, everything is under control."

"So what's on the revised menu?"

"Turkey, dressing, and all the trimmings," Frank answered, sounding enormously pleased with himself.

"Wait a minute," Joanna objected. "Where are you going to find a dozen unsold, thawed turkeys in Bisbee the day before Thanksgiving, and how are you going to pay for them twice without cutting into next month's food budget?"

"That's the slick thing. Ruby's lawyer is taking care of all that."

"Burton Kimball?"

"That's right. He and his wife donated the whole dinner," Frank answered smugly. "All of it."

"How come?"

"He says with all the defense work he does, most of the inmates in the jail are clients of his, one way or the other, anyway. He said it was about time he and Linda did something for the undeserving poor for a change. As soon as Burton heard Ruby was willing to cook, he sent Linda to the store to buy up replacement turkeys. They both seemed to be getting a real kick out of it."

Good-hearted people like Linda and Burton Kimball were part of what made Bisbee a good place to live. Part of what made it home.

"That's amazing," Joanna said, "especially considering all they've been through in the past few weeks."

Two weeks earlier, Burton Kimball's adoptive father and sister had both been killed. He had also been divested of whatever positive memories he might have cherished concerning his own biological father. In the face of that kind of personal tragedy, Burton Kimball's selfless generosity was all the more remarkable.

"All I can say is good work, Frank. That was an ingenious solution to a tough problem."

Frank laughed. "That's what you hired me for, isn't it?"

"I guess it is."

Just as Joanna was signing off, the door to the student lounge popped open, and Leann Jessup walked inside carrying a video. "There you are," she said. "There wasn't any answer in your room, but your Blazer was still in the parking lot so I figured I'd find you here somewhere. My mom just dropped off her tape of the news from last night. She says we're both on it. She dropped it by in hopes your family could get a look at it over the weekend because she'd really like to have it back in time to take it to work next week."

"That shouldn't be a problem," Joanna said. "We're booked into the Hohokam on a special holiday package that offers kids under sixteen the use of two free videos a day during their stay. That must mean there are VCRs available. If push comes to shove, we could always come back here and ask Dave Thompson to let us use the one in his classroom."

"Fat chance of that." Leann laughed. She sobered a moment later. "How soon does your company show up?" she asked.

"Not until eight or later. They can't even leave Bisbee until after Jenny gets out of school. It's a four-hour drive."

"How about some lunch, then?" Leann suggested. "I'm hungry."

"So am I, now that you mention it," Joanna said. "What do you want to eat?"

"I wish I knew somewhere around here to get a decent hamburger," Leann moaned.

Joanna laughed. "Boy, do I have a deal for you," she said. "Come with me."

By then Joanna wasn't particularly worried about going back to the Roundhouse Bar and Grill with Leann Jessup in tow. Of all the people Joanna knew, Leann was the one most likely to be sympathetic and understanding of Joanna's more than passing interest in a case that was, on the face of it, none of her business. Besides, what were the odds that they would actually encounter Butch Dixon? Since he was evidently the nighttime bartender, he probably wouldn't be anywhere near his nighttime place of employment at one o'clock in the afternoon.

At least that was Joanna's line of reasoning as she and Leann Jessup walked out to the Blazer and then drove north to Old Peoria. She was wrong, of course. Butch Dixon was the first person she saw once her eyes adjusted to the dimness of the darkened room. He was hunkered over the bar, eating a sandwich. A yellow legal pad with a pen on top of it lay beside an almost empty plate.

"Why if it isn't the sheriff of Cochise, star of *News at Ten*." He grinned in greeting when he saw Joanna. "And this must be your sidekick. You both looked great on TV."

"You saw us?" Leann asked.

"That's right. So what will Madam Sheriff have today, the regular?"

Joanna smiled as she sat down next to him. "You make me sound like a real barfly."

"Aren't you?" he returned. "Is your friend here a heavy drinker, same as you?"

Leann glanced questioningly in Joanna's direction. "Not at one o'clock in the afternoon," she protested. "I'll have a Coke."

"Pepsi's all we have. Diet or regular?"

"Diet."

"Hey, Phil," Butch Dixon called to a bartender who was only then emerging from the door that evidently led to the kitchen. "How about bringing a pair of Diet Pepsis for the ladies." He focused once more on Joanna. "You looked fine on the tube, but I think you're a lot better looking in person."

She laughed. "Flattery will get you nowhere," she said.

"Rats," he returned.

Joanna laughed again. "Besides, not everybody liked our performances nearly as much as you did. Dave Thompson, the morning lecturer, climbed all over us about it this morning."

"That's right," Leann put in on her own. "He seems to think he's running a convent instead of a police academy. He wants his students to live cloistered lives with no outside distractions."

"That would be a genuine shame." Butch Dixon grinned, looking at Joanna as he spoke. "Not only is this lady good-looking, she's a real mind reader, too. I was just about to finish my opus here and was wondering how to get it to her. The next thing I know, she shows up on my doorstep."

"This is Butch Dixon," Joanna explained to Leann Jessup. "I asked him to write me a brief summary of what he could remember from the night Serena Grijalva died. Mr. Dixon here was one of the last people to see her alive."

"When you say it that way, you make me sound like a prime suspect," Butch Dixon returned darkly. "I hope I've remembered all the important stuff, although I don't see what good it's going to do. I gave the exact same information to that first homicide detective when she came around asking questions right after it happened. As far as I can tell, it didn't make a bit of difference."

"You didn't tell me you were conducting your own independent investigation," Leann said accusingly to Joanna.

Joanna shrugged and tried to laugh it off. "I can't afford to advertise it, now can I? And God knows I shouldn't be doing it, especially since there's more than enough going on in my own little bailiwick. One case in particular could be called the Case of the Missing Cook."

"Are we talking about a real cook?" Leann asked. "It sounds like one of those Agatha Christie mysteries."

"That's 'The Adventure of the Clapham Cook,'" Butch Dixon said in a casual aside without bothering to look up from his pen and paper.

"You read Agatha Christie?" Joanna asked.

"Among other things," he replied.

"I'm talking about the jail cook, down in Bisbee," Joanna continued, turning back to Leann. "He quit sometime between dinner last night and breakfast this morning. He took off without giving notice and without making any arrangements for breakfast this morning, either. Not only that, he stole all the Thanksgiving turkeys in the process."

"I've been stung like that a time or two," Butch Dixon put in sympathetically. "Fly-by-night cooks. Don't you just hate it when that happens? It sounds to me like being a sheriff is almost as bad as running a bar and restaurant. What are you going to do about it?"

Phil arrived with the drinks. After Joanna and Leann gave him their lunch order, Joanna went on to explain about the Ruby Starr/Burton Kimball solution to the Cochise County Jail Thanksgiving dinner dilemma.

"Isn't the term 'undeserving poor' from *My Fair Lady*?" Butch asked. "I think that's what Liza Doolittle's father calls himself."

Joanna and Jenny sometimes watched tapes of musicals on the VCR. Since *My Fair Lady* was one of Jenny's all-time favorites—right after *The Sound of Music*—Joanna knew most of the dialogue verbatim. Undeserving was exactly what Liza's father had called himself.

Joanna looked at Butch Dixon with some surprise. Most of the men around Bisbee—Andy Brady included—didn't sit around dropping either Agatha Christie titles or lines from plays into casual conversation, especially not lines from musicals.

"Agatha Christie? Lerner and Lowe? That's pretty literary for a bartender, isn't it? My mother always claimed that you guys were only marginally civilized."

Dixon grinned. "Mine told me exactly the same thing. No wonder I'm such a disappointment to her."

Once again Joanna returned to her story. "The upshot of all this is that one of the jail inmates—a lady who allegedly took after her husband with a sledgehammer on Monday—is currently serving as interim cook in the Cochise County Jail. Just wait until the media gets wind of that. There's one particular local reporter, a lady of the press, who'll have a heyday with it."

Butch chuckled. "You might give her a friendly warning, just for her own protection. It sounds to me as though anybody who gets on the wrong side of your pinch-hitting cook does so at his or her own risk."

Joanna and Leann both ended up laughing at that. They couldn't help it. When their food came, Butch Dixon stood up. Tearing several sheets out of the yellow pad, he folded them and handed them over to Joanna, who tossed them into her purse. Then Dixon excused himself, leaving the two women to enjoy their meals.

When lunch was over, Joanna dropped Leann back at the APOA campus. Joanna felt a moment of guilt as Leann climbed out of the car. "This place looks really lonely. Are you sure you wouldn't like to come over to the hotel and spend the afternoon there?"

Leann shook her head. "Thanks for the offer, but I'll be fine," she said. "I've got plenty of home-work to do. After the way Dave Thompson climbed all over us this morning, I want to be prepared for Monday morning. Thanks for suggesting the Roundhouse for lunch. That hamburger was great."

Two was still an hour too early to show up at the hotel, but Joanna went there anyway.

The afternoon was perfect. With blue skies overhead and with the temperature hovering somewhere in the eighties, it was hard to come to terms with the idea that this was the day before Thanksgiving. Bisbee's mountainous climate lent itself to more seasonal changes. November in Bis-bee usually felt like autumn. This felt more like summer.

Outside the automatic doors, huge free-standing pots and flower beds were ablaze with the riotous colors of newly planted bedding plants—marigolds, petunias, and snapdragons. Inside the lobby, a to-tally unnecessary gas-log fire burned in a massive, copperfaced fireplace. Scattered stacks of pump-kins and huge bouquets of brightly colored mums and dahlias spilled out of equally huge Chinese pots. Looking around the festive lobby, Joanna al-lowed a little holiday spirit to leak into her veins. This wasn't at all like High Lonesome Ranch at Thanksgiving, and that was just as well.

Surprisingly enough, when Joanna approached the desk, she discovered that her room was ready after all. Joanna checked in. Refusing the services of a bellman for her single suitcase, she took a mirror-lined elevator up to the eighth-floor room she and Jenny would share for the next three days. She put down her suitcase and walked over to the picture window overlooking Grand Avenue. Across a wide expanse of busy roadway and railroad track, Joanna had a clear view of the APOA campus.

Turning away from the window, Joanna surveyed the room. Although her dormitory accommodations and the main room at the Hohokam were similar in size, shape, and layout, there were definite differences. The hotel room had two queen-sized beds instead of a single narrow one. In place of a narrow student desk, there was a small round table with two relatively comfortable chairs on either side of it. The uniformly plastered walls of the hotel room were dotted with inexpensively framed prints. Except for the one mirrored wall in the dorm room, the walls there were totally bare.

It was in the bathroom, however, where the difference between hotel and dorm was most striking and where, surprisingly, the Hohokam Resort Hotel came up decidedly short. The hotel bathroom contained a combination bathtub/shower rather than both shower and tub. Not only that, there were no Jacuzzi jets in the tub, although a guest brochure on the table did say there was a hot tub located in the ground-floor recreation area.

After unpacking what little needed unpacking, Joanna sat down at the table and completed the letter she had started writing to Jenny two days earlier. When that was finished, Joanna tore it out of her notebook, folded the pages together, and placed them into an official Hohokam Resort Hotel envelope. Writing Jenny's name on the outside, Joanna left it on top of the pillows on one of the two beds. Then she lay down on the other and tried reading.

Her assignment in *The Law Enforcement Handbook* brought her fully awake only when the book slipped from her grasp and landed squarely on her face. That's it, she told herself firmly. No more homework. Time to go downstairs and have some coffee.

✿ SIXTEEN

IT WAS almost sunset when Joanna ventured downstairs, where cocktails were being served in the posh, leather-furnished lobby. Even though she wasn't particularly cold, she dropped into a comfortably oversized chair within warming range of the glass-enclosed fireplace. For a while she simply sat there, alternately mesmerized by the flaming gas-log or watching holiday travelers come and go. Eventually, though, she flagged down a passing cocktail waitress who graciously agreed to bring her coffee.

Then, with coffee in hand, Joanna settled in to wait for Jenny and the Gs to arrive. She smiled, remembering Butch Dixon's wry comment that Jenny and the Gs sounded like some kind of rock band. What an interesting man he was. With a peculiar sense of humor.

Guiltily, Joanna reached into her purse and extracted the folded pages she had stowed there and forgotten after he handed them to her. Unfolding them, she found pages that were covered with small, carefully written lines that told the story of Serena Grijalva's last visit to the Roundhouse Bar and Grill.

Jorge showed up here first that evening. I didn't know his name then, although I had seen him a couple of times before and I knew he was Serena's former husband. I couldn't help feeling sorry for the guy. He'd show up now and then and hand over money—child support presumably—and she'd give him all kinds of crap. That night she went off the charts about some truck he'd just bought.

With a circular bar, the Roundhouse doesn't offer much privacy. I remembered Serena talking to one of the guys in the bar a few weeks earlier about getting a restraining order against her soon-to-be-ex. I didn't want any trouble, so I kept a pretty close watch on them that night. All Jorge kept talking about was whether or not she'd let him take the kids home to his mother's over Thanksgiving weekend. He offered to come pick them up, drive them to Douglas, and bring them back home again on Sunday, but she just kept shaking her head, saying no, no, no.

Things were fairly calm for a while, then she found out about the truck and all hell broke loose. She was screaming at him, calling him all kinds of names, and he just sat there and took it. Serena was the one causing the disturbance, so I finally eighty-sixed her and told her she'd have to leave.

He had already given her the money. She took it out of her purse, counted it, took some out—twenty bucks maybe—and threw it back down on the bar. "I'm worth a hell of a lot more than that," she said, and stomped out.

He must have sat there for ten minutes just staring at the money on the bar. Finally he picked it up and put it back in his shirt pocket. That's the time a lot of guys will settle in and get shit-faced drunk. I wouldn't have blamed him if he had. In fact, I offered to buy him a drink, and he asked for coffee. It was fairly quiet with only a few of the regulars around, so Jorge and I talked some.

He told me about his kids, asked me if I knew them. I didn't have the heart to tell him how much those poor kids were left to their own devices. Serena would leave them alone in the laundry while she came over here and spent the afternoon cadging drinks. On more than one occasion, when she was in here partying, I took sandwiches and soft drinks out to the kids because I knew they had to be hungry. I didn't tell him that, either. After all, what good would it do for the poor guy to know about it? There wasn't a damn thing he could do about it, other than maybe calling child protective services and turning her in.

He must have stayed for another hour or so, drinking coffee. And I remember wondering why the hell Serena's attorney had gone to all the trouble of swearing out a restraining order on the poor guy. He struck me as beaten down and heartbroken, both. There wasn't anything violent about him, not that night. And he didn't seem to be in any hurry to leave. In fact, from the way he kept hanging around and watching the door, I think he was hoping Serena would change her mind, come back, and take him up on whatever that twenty was supposed to entail.

She didn't though. He left around eleven-thirty. The next thing I knew, he'd been arrested for murder. When Detective Strong came around asking questions, I tried to tell her about Serena— about what she was like. It was no use. Seemed to me that the detective had already made up her mind, and decided that Jorge was guilty, whether he was or not.

I've thought about him a lot since then, pitied him. Serena played the poor son of a bitch like a violin, giving him a piece of ass or not, depending on her mood at the time and whether or not he forked over.

Reading back over this, it sounds pretty lame. If being a sometime whore and a bad mother were capital offenses, there would be a whole lot more orphans in this world. Bad as she was, Serena didn't deserve to die. However, I for one remain unconvinced that Jorge did it. All I can go by is the fact that he never raised either his hand or his voice under circumstances when a lot of men would have.

Thoughtfully, Joanna folded Butch Dixon's handwritten pages and returned them to her purse. She knew that the way a man behaved toward a woman in a roomful of witnesses wasn't necessarily an indication of how he would behave in private. By his own admission, there was at least one domestic violence charge on Jorge Grijalva's rap sheet.

But in other respects, Butch's observations about Jorge Grijalva came surprisingly close to Joanna's own conclusions. Jorge despised Serena for her whoring and yet he hadn't been able to let her go, hadn't been able to stop caring.

The picture of Serena that emerged in the bartender's story was far different from and more complex than the impression of near sainthood that had been part of the revivallike atmosphere at MAVEN's candlelight vigil. There Serena had been cast as a beautiful, helpless, and blameless martyr to motherhood and apple pie. Butch Dixon's version conceded her beauty, but saw her as a troubled, manipulative young woman, as a chronically unfaithful wife, and as a less than adequate mother.

Butch's essay stopped one step short of holding the dead woman partially responsible for her own murder. His sympathetic portrayal of Jorge was compelling. It played on Joanna's emotions in exactly the same way the testimonies of the various survivors had caught up the feelings of all the attendees at the vigil. Sitting there reflecting, Joanna could see why. Dixon's editorializing on Jorge's behalf would be of no more help to a homicide detective than the blatantly emotional blackmail of MAVEN's dog-and-pony show. Both in their own right were convincing pieces of show business—full of sound and fury and not much else.

Joanna shook her head. MAVEN could rail that Jorge Grijalva was evil incarnate and his deceased wife a candidate for sainthood. Butch Dixon could tell the world that Serena Grijalva was a conniving bitch. Depending on your point of view, both were victims.

For Joanna, the real victims were the kids who seemed destined to endure one terrible loss after another. And if the plea bargain . . .

"Mom, we're here!" Jenny crowed from the open doorway.

Lost in thought, Joanna hadn't even noticed when Jim Bob Brady's aging Honda Accord pulled to a stop under the portico. Joanna rose to greet her visitors. Jenny met her halfway across the room, tackling Joanna and latching onto her waist with such force that it almost knocked her down.

"Wait a minute," Joanna said. "You don't have to be that glad to see me."

Bending to kiss the top of Jenny's head, Joanna stopped short. One look at Jenny's hair was enough to take her breath away. The smooth, long blond tresses were gone. In their place stood a fuzzy white Little Orphan Annie halo, a brittle, tow-headed Afro. Jenny's assessment on the telephone had been absolutely right—her hair was awful. Joanna swallowed the urge to say what she was thinking.

"I missed you, sweetie," she said. "How are you doing? How was the trip?"

"The trip was fine, and I missed you, too," Jenny said breathlessly. "But is the pool still open? Is it too late to go swimming?"

So much for missing me, Joanna thought wryly. She glanced at her watch. "The pool doesn't close for almost two hours yet, but don't you want something to eat first?"

"We ate in the car," Jenny answered. "Anyway, I'd rather swim."

"Go help Grandpa with your luggage first," Joanna urged. "Then we'll talk about it. You also need to check with the desk and order your videos."

Jenny's eyes widened. "Videos? Really?"

Joanna nodded. "They have some kind of special deal. Children under sixteen get to order videos from a place just up the street. Two for each day we're here. They even deliver."

Jenny grinned. "This *is* a nice place, isn't it?" She turned and raced back out to the car.

Eva Lou had entered the lobby as well, walking up behind Jenny. She smiled fondly after her granddaughter, then turned to Joanna and gave her daughter-in-law a firm hug. "I can't believe all the flowers out there," the older woman said, glancing back at the entrance. "How can that be when it's almost the end of November?"

Looking after Jenny, Joanna wasn't especially interested in flowers. "What I can't believe is the permanent," she grumbled. "How could my mother do such a thing?"

"Don't be upset," Eva Lou counseled. "Eleanor was just trying to help."

"Help!" Joanna countered. "Don't make excuses for her. She had no right to pull this kind of stunt the minute my back was turned."

"It's only hair," Eva Lou said. "It'll grow out. It was all an honest mistake. I think Helen and your mother got so busy talking that Helen forgot to set the timer for the solution. I know she felt terrible about it afterwards. She sent home three bottles of conditioner. Jenny's gone through the better half of one of those, although I'll admit it doesn't seem to be doing much good."

"Not much," Joanna agreed. "But you're right. The only thing that's going to fix that mess is time."

By then Jim Bob had unloaded an amazing stack of suitcases onto a luggage cart. He and Jenny came into the lobby with the bellman trailing in his wake, aiming for the registration desk. Joanna caught up with him before he got there. She planted a quick kiss on her father-in-law's cheek.

"Registration's already been taken care of," she said, handing two keys over to the bellman. "Mr. and Mrs. Brady are in eight-twenty-seven. The little girl and I are in eight-ten. They're not adjoining rooms, but at least they're on the same floor."

Jim Bob gave her a searching look. "You didn't pay for the room already, did you? It looks to me like this place is probably pretty pricy."

"Are you kidding?" Joanna returned with a laugh. "I'm getting six weeks of free babysitting out of this deal. If you stack that up against a three-night stay at the Hohokam, I'm still way ahead of the game."

"I'm not a baby," Jenny said firmly, frowning. "I'm nine and a half."

"You're right, Jenny. Excuse me," Joanna agreed, then turned back to Jim Bob Brady. "Six weeks of *child care* then, but it's still a bargain. Is anybody hungry?"

"I packed some sandwiches to eat on the way," Eva Lou said. "We're certainly not starving."

Joanna nodded. "All right, then," she said. "We'll let Jenny swim for a while. We'll go out later for dessert."

"As in Baskin-Robbins?" Jenny asked eagerly.

"Probably." At that Jenny clapped her hands in delight.

As the Bradys followed the bellman toward the elevator, Joanna turned to Jenny. "Did Grandma tell you that Ceci Grijalva is coming to town to see us on Friday?"

It was Jenny's turn to nod. "That's why we brought along an extra suit." Jenny's blue eyes filled with concern. "Did you tell her what I said?"

"Yes, but I thought she'd get more out of it if she heard it from you in person. We pick her up at ten o'clock on Friday morning."

They stopped by the concierge desk long enough to make arrangements for Jenny's videos. Joanna also increased the Thanksgiving dinner reservation from four to six.

"Who's coming to dinner?" Jenny asked as they, too, headed for the elevator.

"Leann Jessup," Joanna answered. "She's a new friend, someone I met here at school. And Adam York, the DEA guy from Tucson. You remember him, don't you?"

Jenny nodded. "He's the guy who thought you were a drug dealer."

"Well, he's a friend now, and so is Leann."

"Are you fixing the two of them up?" Jenny asked.

Joanna was stunned. She wasn't quite ready for Jenny's inquiring mind to take on the world of male/female relations.

"What a strange thing to say. No," Joanna declared firmly. "Nobody's fixing anybody up."

"So Mr. York isn't her boyfriend?"

"No. He doesn't even know her."

"Is he your boyfriend, then?"

"Jenny," an exasperated Joanna said. "As far as I know, Adam York isn't anybody's boyfriend. He's a friend of mine and a colleague. What's all this stuff about boyfriends?"

"But why does he want to have Thanksgiving dinner with us?" Jenny asked.

Joanna shrugged. "It's a holiday. Maybe he doesn't want to be alone. Besides, I'll be happy to see him again."

"Why can't he have dinner with his own family?" Jenny asked.

"Look," Joanna said. "Adam York is one of the people who encouraged me to run for office. He's also the one who suggested I come up here and take this course. He probably just wants to see how I'm doing."

"Are you going to marry him?" Jenny asked pointedly.

"Marry him!" Joanna exclaimed. "Jenny, for heaven's sake, what in the world has gotten into

you? Of course I'm not going to marry him. Whatever put that weird idea into your head?"

Jenny frowned. "That's what happened to Sue
Espy. Her parents got a divorce when we were in
second grade. Her mother asked some guy named
Slim Dabovich to come for Thanksgiving dinner
last year. Now they're married. Sue likes him, I
guess. She says he isn't like stepfathers you see on
TV. I mean, he isn't mean or anything."

Joanna almost laughed aloud. "Just because
Sue's mom married the guy she asked to Thanksgiving dinner doesn't mean I will. Now, do you
want to go swimming or not?"

IN ADVANCE of the holiday, Dave Thompson had stocked up on booze. Fighting a hang-
over from the previous night's excess, he went
looking for hair of the dog the moment the last of
the students and instructors left campus. By nine-
thirty that night, he had been drinking steadily
for most of the afternoon and evening. And not
just beer. Booze—the real hard stuff—was the
only thing that could dull the pain on a night
like this. Dave knew that if he drank long enough
and hard enough, eventually he would pass out.
With any kind of luck, by the time he woke up
again, part of Thanksgiving Day would already
be over and done with. He would have succeeded
in dodging part of the holiday bullet, one more
time.

For a real binge like this, he tried to confine his

drinking to inside his apartment, but each time he needed a cigarette, he went outside. That was pretty funny, actually—that he still went outside to smoke. Irene had been a very early and exceptionally militant soldier in the war against secondhand cigarette smoke. She had never allowed him to smoke inside either the house or the car. Her prohibitions had stuck and turned into habit. Despite Irene's betrayal—despite the fact that she had been gone all these years—Dave Thompson continued to smoke outside the house.

It would have surprised Irene Thompson to realize that over time her former husband had found some interesting side benefits to smoking out of doors that had nothing at all to do with lung disease. People didn't expect someone to be standing outside in a yard or patio at night for long stretches of time. Dave Thompson had seen things from that vantage point, learned things about his neighbors and neighborhood that other people never even suspected. As a matter of fact, it was something he had seen through the kitchen window of their old house back in Chandler that had signaled the beginning of the end of Dave's marriage. If it hadn't been for that one fateful cigarette, he might never have found out what was really going on with Irene. He might have gone right on being a chump for the rest of his life.

Dave didn't look at his watch, but it must have been close to ten when he staggered outside for that one last cigarette. He knew he was drunk, but it was a fairly happy drunk for a change. He laughed at himself when he bounced off both sides of the doorway trying to get through it. Since he wasn't driving, though, what the hell?

Dave lurched over to his smoking table—a cheap white resin table and matching chair. His one ashtray—a heavy brass one that had once belonged to his ex-father-in-law—sat there, waiting for him. Pulling the overflowing ashtray closer, he lit up and then leaned back in the groaning chair, gazing up at the sky.

Sitting there, he remembered how, when he was a little kid growing up in Phoenix, it was still possible to see thousands of stars if you went outside in the yard at night. Some of his favorite memories stemmed from that time, standing in the front yard with his folks, staring up in the darkness, trying to catch a glimpse of the newly launched sputnik as it shot across the sky. Now the haze of smog and hundreds of thousands of city lights obscured all but the brightest two or three stars. And if there was space junk up there, as *Discover* magazine said there was, it was invisible to the naked eye from where Dave Thompson was sitting right that moment.

He was still smoking and staring mindlessly up into the milky white sky when a car pulled into the APOA parking lot. Headlights flashed briefly into the private patio that separated Dave's quarters from the building that housed the dormitory.

Shit, Dave thought. Who's that? Most likely one of the students. There was no law against being drunk on the patio of your own home, but finding the APOA's head instructor in that kind of condition wouldn't be great for trainee morale.

He meant to get up and go inside, but as footsteps came toward him across the parking lot, Dave froze in his chair and hoped that not moving would render him invisible.

Within moments, he was sound asleep.

JOANNA PRIED Jenny out of the pool a minute before the ten o'clock closing time. After a quick trip to the nearest 31 Flavors, it was ten-thirty by the time they made it back to their room, where Jenny was delighted to find that the covers on her bed had been turned back. On the pillow was a gold-foil-wrapped mint and a letter addressed to her in her mother's handwriting. She tore open the envelope. Then, munching on the mint, she sat down cross-legged on the bed to read the letter. She looked over at her mother who had settled on her own bed, textbook in hand.

When she finished Joanna's letter, Jenny sighed, refolded the letter, and returned it to the envelope.

"Mom," Jenny said. "Did you ever think your classes here would be this hard?" Jenny asked.

Welcoming the interruption, Joanna closed the book and put it down on the bedside table. "Not really."

"And do they make you do push-ups and run laps, honest?"

Joanna smiled. "Girl Scout's honor," she said.

"That's no fair," Jenny grumbled. "I always thought that when you got to be a grown-up, people couldn't make you do stuff you didn't want to do."

"That's what I thought, too," Joanna agreed.

Suddenly Jenny scrambled off the bed and charged over to her suitcase. "I brought something along that I forgot to show you."

After pawing through her clothing, Jenny came back and sat down on the edge of her mother's bed. She was carrying two pictures. "Look at this," she said, handing them over to Joanna. "See what Grandpa found?"

One was the picture of Joanna taken by her father, the one in her Brownie uniform. The second photo, although much newer and in color, was very similar to the first one. It was a picture of Jennifer Ann Brady, dressed in a much newer version of a Brownie uniform, and standing at attention near the right front bumper of her mother's bronze-colored Eagle. In the black-and-white photo, a nine-year-old Joanna Lathrop posed in front of Eleanor Lathrop's white Maverick. In both pictures the foreground was occupied by the same sturdy, twenty-five-year-old Radio Flyer, and in both pictures the wagon was loaded down with cartons of Girl Scout cookies.

As soon as she saw the two pictures side by side, Joanna burst out laughing. "I guess pictures like that are part of a time-honored tradition," she said, handing them back to Jenny. "Where did you get the second one?"

"Grandpa Brady got it from Grandma Lathrop."

"That figures," Joanna said. "She probably has drawers full of them. I'll bet somebody takes a new picture like that every single Girl Scout cookie season."

Jenny didn't seem to be listening. She was holding the two pictures up to the light, examining them closely. "Grandma Brady thinks I look just like you did when you were a girl," Jenny said. "What do you think?"

Joanna took the pictures back and studied them for herself. It was easy to forget that she, too, had been a towheaded little kid once upon a time. The red hadn't started showing up in her hair until fourth or fifth grade—about the same time as that first traumatic haircut. This picture must have dated from third grade or so since Joanna's hair still hung down over her shoulders in two long braids.

"Grandma Brady's right," Joanna said. "You can tell we're related."

"Yes, you can," Jenny agreed.

"Did I ever tell you about the first time Grandma Lathrop took me out for my first haircut?" Joanna asked.

Jenny frowned and shook her head. "No, I don't think so."

"Well, get back in your bed," Joanna ordered. "It's about time you heard the story of your mother and the pixie."

"I know all about pixies," Jenny said confidently. "They're kind of like fairies, aren't they? So, is this a true story or pretend?"

"This is another kind of pixie," Joanna said. "And it's true, all right. Believe me, it's not the kind of story I'd make up. And who knows, once you hear it, maybe it'll make you feel better about what happened to you when Grandma Lathrop took you to see Helen Barco."

Joanna told her haircut story then. "See there?" she asked as she finished. "It may not make you feel any better, but at least you're not the only kid it's ever happened to."

"I still hate it, though," Jenny said.

"I don't blame you."

Despite Jenny's fervent pleading, Joanna nixed the idea of watching even one video that night. "Tomorrow morning will be plenty of time for *E.T.*," she said, reaching up and turning out the lamp on the bedside table between them. "Right now we'd both better try to get some sleep."

"Good night, Mom," Jenny said. "I love you."

"I love you, too, Jenny. Sleep tight."

And they did. Both of them, until the sounds of police and aid-car sirens brought them both wide awake sometime much later. Joanna checked the time—one o'clock—while Jenny dashed over to the window and looked outside.

"What is it?" Joanna asked. "A car wreck?"

Jenny peered down at the flashing lights and scurrying people far below. "I guess so," she said, "but I can't tell for sure."

Joanna climbed out of bed herself to take a look. In the melee of emergency vehicles and flashing lights, she caught a glimpse of a blanket-covered figure lying on the ground.

"It looks like someone hit a pedestrian," she said, drawing Jenny away from the window. "Come on, let's go back to bed."

But instead of crawling into her own bed, Jenny climbed into her mother's. "I don't like sirens," she said softly. "Whenever I hear them now, I think of Daddy. Don't you?"

"Yes," Joanna answered.

"Do they make you feel like crying?"

"Yes," Joanna said again.

For some time after that, Jenny and her mother lay side by side, saying nothing. At last they heard another siren, that of an ambulance or aid car pulling away from whatever carnage had happened on the street below. As the siren squawked, Jenny gave an involuntary shudder and she began to cry.

Joanna gathered the sobbing child into her arms. When the tears finally subsided and Jenny's breathing steadied and quieted, Joanna didn't bother suggesting that Jenny return to her own bed. By then the mother needed the warmth and comfort of another human presence almost as much as the child did.

Soon Jenny was fast asleep. Joanna lay awake. The fact that Jenny associated sirens with Andy's death jarred her, although it shouldn't have. After all, would she ever be able to see a perfect apricot-colored rosebud or her diamond solitaire engagement ring without thinking of the University Hospital waiting room, without thinking about Andy dying in a room just beyond a pair of awful swinging doors?

Jenny was, after all, a chip off the old block. The resemblance between mother and daughter went far beyond the eerily striking similarity between those two photographs taken twenty years apart.

What was it Jim Bob was always saying? Something about the apple not falling far from the tree.

Remembering that last little proverb should have been reassuring, but it wasn't. Not at all, because if it was true, then there was a fifty-fifty chance Joanna Brady would end up being just like her mother—tinted hair, lacquered nails, lifted face, and all.

SEVENTEEN

IT WAS probably only natural that since Eleanor Lathrop was the last person Joanna thought about before falling asleep, she was also the person who awakened them the next morning. When the phone rang, dragging Joanna out of what had finally turned into a sound sleep, it was a real challenge to find the phone.

The room at the Hohokam was, after all, the third room she had slept in that week. Bearing that in mind, it wasn't surprising that she came on the phone sounding a little disoriented.

"Hello, Mom."

"Happy Thanksgiving," Eleanor said.

"Same to you," Joanna mumbled, stretching sleepily and glancing at the clock. It said 7:15. Jenny was still huddled under a pile of covers that was only then beginning to stir.

"It took so long for you to answer, I was afraid I had missed you altogether," Eleanor Lathrop said. "I was about to try Jim Bob and Eva Lou's room."

"It's late for them. They're probably already down at breakfast."

"I'm glad I caught you, then. You're the one I wanted to talk to. I've changed my mind."

"About what?"

"About coming up to Phoenix for Thanksgiving," Eleanor announced. "Just for tonight, of course. I couldn't stay any longer than that. What time are you planning on eating?"

"Five. Right here in the hotel dining room."

"Good. If you'll add two more places to your reservation, that'll be fine. And we'll need two rooms there as well. I'd prefer to be in the same hotel, but if they don't have rooms, someplace nearby will be just fine."

"Wait a minute," Joanna interjected. "Two dinner reservations. Two rooms. Who are you bringing along, Mother?"

"I can't tell you that. It's a surprise."

"Mother," Joanna objected, "you know I don't like surprises."

"A surprise?" Jenny said, sitting bolt-upright in bed. "Grandma Lathrop's coming and bringing a surprise? What kind of surprise, something to eat?"

"Jenny, hush. I can't hear what Grandma is saying."

Jenny dove out of bed and began pulling on her clothes. "Of course, I'll reserve the rooms, Mother. It's just that . . . No, the dining room is plenty large. I'm sure it won't be any trouble to add two more places to the dinner reservation."

Fully if hurriedly dressed, Jenny was already making for the door. "Wait a minute. No, Mother, not you. I was talking to Jenny." Joanna held the mouthpiece at arm's length. "Just where do you think you're going?"

"Down to have breakfast with the Gs. The sooner I eat, the sooner I can go swimming."

"Wait for me," Joanna said. "We can go down together."

"Do I have to?"

"Yes, you have to."

Sulking, Jenny switched on the television set, flipped through the channels with the remote, then settled on the floor in front of an old Road-runner cartoon.

"Sorry, Mother," Joanna said, returning to her phone conversation. "What were you saying? Yes, I'll get on the room situation right away. But I'll need a name, for the reservation. Hotels require names, you know. . . . All right. Fine. I'll put both rooms under your name."

In the interest of holiday spirit, Joanna tried to keep the irritation out of her voice. For weeks her mother had refused every suggestion that she come along on this Thanksgiving weekend outing. Now she was going to show up after all, at the very last minute, at a time when making room and dinner reservations was likely to be reasonably complicated.

Not only was Eleanor coming herself, she was

bringing along an undisclosed guest. Read boyfriend, Joanna thought.

"What time do you think you'll get here? Around three? We'll try to be down in the lobby right around then. You shouldn't have any trouble finding us. If we're not in the lobby, try the pool. See you then."

Joanna put down the phone and turned to her daughter. "The surprise is whoever Grandma is bringing along to dinner."

"Who's that?" Jenny asked, her eyes on the television set.

"She didn't tell me. If she did, it wouldn't be a surprise. But my guess is it's a man."

"You mean like a man who's a friend, or a man who's a boyfriend?"

"I don't have any idea, but I do have a word of warning for you, young lady."

"What's that?"

"Just because this guy, whoever he is, is showing up for Thanksgiving dinner doesn't mean Grandma Lathrop is going to marry him. In other words, you are not to mention the M word. Do you understand?"

Jenny nodded. "Okay," she said. "Now can we go eat breakfast? I'm starved."

The Bradys were already at a table when Joanna and Jenny wended their way through the tables.

"Well, look here," Jim Bob said. "We've already read the paper and had two cups of coffee. It's about time you two slugabeds showed up. Where've you been?"

"Talking to Grandma Lathrop," Jenny said, slipping into the chair next to her grandfather. "She's coming here for Thanksgiving dinner after all, and she's bringing somebody with her."

"Really, who?" Eva Lou asked.

Jenny shook her head. "She wouldn't tell us, not even Mom. She says it's a surprise, but Mom thinks it's a man." Jenny added, rolling her eyes, "She's afraid I'll use the M word and embarrass everybody."

"M word?" Jim Bob asked. "What's an M word?"

"Never mind, Jimmy," Eva Lou said. "I'll tell you later. Will there be enough room for everybody, Joanna? You already said those two friends of yours would be joining us."

"Remind me. After breakfast I need to stop by the concierge desk and add two more places to the dinner reservation."

Just then a harried waitress stopped by the table, slapping an insulated coffee carafe down on the table next to Joanna. Pulling out her pencil and ticket pad, she focused on Jenny. "What'll you have this morning, young lady?" she asked.

Once the waitress left with their orders, Joanna poured herself a cup of coffee and turned to her mother-in-law. "How'd you sleep?" she asked.

Eva Lou shook her head. "Fine, up until one o'clock or so. Then all those sirens woke me up." The busboy appeared, bearing a pitcher of ice water. "What was that all about, anyway?" Eva Lou asked, turning a questioning eye on him. "All those sirens in the middle of the night?"

The busboy shrugged. "Some lady fell out of a truck right in front of another car. At least that's what I heard. There were still cops outside when I came on shift this morning."

"More than likely it's a fatality accident, then," Joanna put in. "They take a lot longer to investigate than nonfatal ones."

The pained look on Jenny's face at the mention of the accident caused Joanna to drop the subject. After breakfast and with both room and dinner reservations safely in hand, Joanna and Jenny set off on a walking excursion to the APOA campus.

From the sidewalk outside the hotel lobby, Joanna pointed directly across Grand Avenue. "See there?" she said. "That's the running track right there on the other side of the railroad. And the first building you see on the other side—the long one—is the dorm."

Jenny immediately headed for the street, but Joanna stopped her. "We can't cross here. We'll have to walk down to Olive and cross there."

"How come?" Jenny asked, looking up and down the street. "There's not that much traffic. We could make it."

"Maybe we could, but we're not going to. This must be right about where that accident happened last night. Let's don't tempt fate."

They started up Seventy-fifth along the APOA's outside wall. Jenny looked longingly back at the few strands of barbed wire that separated the back of the APOA campus from the railroad tracks. "Couldn't we go that way?" she asked, pointing.

"Why not?" Joanna returned, with a shrug. "It looks like a shortcut to me."

Mother and daughter were both old hands at negotiating barbed wire. Moments later they were striding across the running track heading for the back of the dorm. Joanna had known there was a patio of some kind between the dorm building and Dave Thompson's unit on the end of the classroom building. What she hadn't realized was that it was a walled fort. The only way to reach Joanna's room was to go around the far end of the dorm.

Lulled into a sense of well-being, they ambled around the corner of the building. Once they could see the parking lot, Joanna was startled by the number of cars parked haphazardly just outside the student lounge at the dorm's opposite end.

Joanna and Jenny had barely started down the breezeway when a woman, a stranger, erupted out of Leann's room and marched toward them, tripping along on three-inch-high heels. She was tiny—five foot nothing, even counting the heels. Her small frame was burdened by a voluptuous figure that easily rivaled Dolly Parton's, although a well-cut wool blazer provided some artful camouflage. Also like Dolly, this woman believed in big hair. A glossy froth of coal-black hair blossomed out around her head like a cloud of licorice-flavored cotton candy.

"I'm sorry," she said, still moving forward. "No one's allowed in here at the moment. You'll have to leave."

"Why?" Joanna asked. "I'm a student here. I know the campus is pretty well shut down for the holiday weekend. All I wanted to do was show the place to my daughter."

The other woman was wearing a name tag of some kind fastened to her lapel. Only then did the distance between them close enough that Joanna could read what was printed there. DETECTIVE CAROL STRONG, CITY OF PEORIA POLICE DEPARTMENT.

A chill that had nothing to do with the weather passed through Joanna's body. "What's wrong?" Joanna asked. "Has something happened?"

"A woman was hurt earlier this morning in an automobile accident," Carol Strong answered. "She was hit by a car."

"Leann?" Joanna asked, feeling almost sick to her stomach. "Leann Jessup?"

Carol Strong frowned. "Do you know her well?"

"We're friends," Joanna began raggedly. "At least we're starting to be friends. She was supposed to come to the Hohokam this afternoon to have Thanksgiving dinner with my family. Is she all right?"

"At the moment she's still alive," Carol answered. "She's been airlifted to St. Joseph's Hospital and admitted to the Barrow Neurological Institute. She should be out of surgery by now."

As if not wanting to hear any more, Jenny slipped her hand out of Joanna's and walked away. She stood on the grassy patch in the middle of the jogging track, watching a long freight train head south along the railroad tracks. Shaking her head,

Joanna stumbled over to the edge of the breeze-way and sank down on the cold cement.

"I warned her not to go jogging so late at night," Joanna said miserably. "I tried to tell her it was dangerous."

"What's your name?" Detective Carol Strong asked, sitting down on the sidewalk's edge close to Joanna but without crowding her.

"Joanna Brady. I'm the newly elected sheriff down in Cochise County."

"And you're a student here?"

Joanna nodded, giving the detective a sidelong glance. "Leann and I are here attending the APOA basic training course. Classes for this session started last Monday."

Carol Strong seemed to consider that statement for a moment. "And you're also staying in the dorm?"

"My room's just beyond Leann's, between hers and the student lounge."

A slight, involuntary twitch crossed Carol Strong's jawline before she spoke again. "I see," she said. "I suppose that figures."

Then, after a pause and a brief look in Jenny's direction, she added, "Is there anyone over at the hotel right now who could look after your little girl for a while?" she asked. "If so, I'll be happy to give you a lift long enough to drop her off. Then we can go by my office to talk. I'm going to need some information from you. The sooner, the better."

"Jenny's grandparents are there, but I don't understand why . . ."

"Sheriff Brady," Detective Strong began, and her voice was grave. "It's only fair for you to know that we're not investigating a simple traffic accident. Your friend Leann wasn't injured while she was out jogging. She was hit by a car after falling out of a moving pickup. She was naked at the time. Both hands were tied behind her back with a pair of pantyhose."

That shocking news washed over Joanna with the same wintry impact as if she'd been splashed with a bucketful of ice-cold water. "You're saying it's attempted murder then?"

"At least."

As the last train car rumbled past, Jenny turned back and waved at her mother. There was something trusting and wistful and heart-breaking in that wave, something that brought Joanna Brady face-to-face with her responsibilities, not only to her child, but also to her newfound friend.

She stood up. "Come on, Jenny," she called. "We have to go now."

Jenny came trotting toward them. "So I can go swimming?" she asked.

Joanna nodded. "Most likely, and so I can go to work."

"But it's Thanksgiving," Jenny objected. "You never work on Thanksgiving."

"I do today," Joanna said.

But the plan to leave Jenny at the hotel with her grandparents fell apart back at the hotel, where Eva Lou and Jim Bob Brady were nowhere to be found. "You'll have to come with me, then," Joanna told her disappointed daughter.

"Couldn't I just stay here by myself? I promise, I wouldn't go swimming until they get back, and I wouldn't get into any trouble. I could watch my tapes on the VCR and—"

"Why not bring the tapes along?" Carol Strong suggested. "There's a VCR in the training room. You can watch a movie in there while your mother and I talk in my office. It'll make it easier for her to concentrate."

"Should I go up to the room and get one?" Jenny asked.

Joanna nodded. As Jenny skipped off toward the elevator, Joanna shot Carol Strong a wan smile. "It won't just make it *easier* for me to concentrate," she corrected. "It'll make it *possible*."

They left the hotel minutes later and followed Carol Strong to her office. The Peoria Police Department was located in a modern, well-landscaped complex that included several buildings that seemed to have grown up out of recently harvested cotton fields.

"Why's that statue giving God the finger?" Jenny asked, as Joanna guided the Blazer into the parking lot. Turning to look, Joanna almost creamed a lumbering VW bus that was the only other vehicle in the city parking lot that holiday morning.

"What are you talking about?" Joanna demanded.

Looking where Jenny was pointing, Joanna saw a towering piece of metal artwork—a male nude figure with upraised arm fully extended—that dominated a central courtyard and fountain.

Viewed from where the Blazer was situated in the parking lot, the statue did indeed appear to be making an obscene gesture.

"I'm sure he's really reaching for the sky," Joanna said. "And wherever did you learn about giving somebody the finger?"

"Second grade," Jenny answered.

Pulling into a parking place, Joanna shook her head, sighed, and turned off the ignition. "Get your tape and come on."

When Joanna opened her purse to toss the Blazer keys into it, she caught sight of the video Leann Jessup had given her the day before. That carefree exchange in the student lounge and their light-hearted lunch at the Roundhouse afterward seemed to have happened forever ago. Yesterday, Leann Jessup had been a vital young police officer and a dedicated if foolhardy midnight jogger. Today, she was a crime victim, a surgical patient at the Barrow Neurological Institute, fighting for life itself.

Swallowing the lump in her throat, Joanna pulled the tape out of her purse and handed it over to Jenny. "This was on the news the other night. You may want to see it. Leann said I was on it. We both were."

Jenny stopped in mid-stride and looked her mother full in the face. "Do you think your friend is going to be all right?" she asked.

Joanna gave her daughter a rueful smile. "I hope so." After a pause she added, "You're a spooky kid sometimes, Jennifer Ann Brady. Every once in a while, it feels like you can read my mind."

"You do it to me," Jenny said.

"Do I?"

Jenny nodded. "All the time."

"Well, I guess it's all right, then," Joanna said. "Let's go."

EIGHTEEN

CUTE KID," Carol Strong said, leading the way down a long, narrow hallway. They had left Jenny in the Peoria PD training room, happily ensconced in front of the opening credits of *E.T.*

"Thanks," Joanna replied.

"Your husband was the deputy who was killed a few months back, wasn't he?"

Joanna nodded.

Carol turned into a small office cluttered with four desks. On entering, she immediately kicked off her shoes. Shrugging off her tweed blazer, she turned to hang it on a wooden peg behind her chair. Only then did Joanna note both the slight bulge of the soft body armor Carol wore under her cream-colored silk blouse as well as the Glock 19 resting discreetly in its small-of-back holster in the middle of the detective's slender waist. Joanna had considered purchasing an SOB holster for herself but had nixed the idea because she thought it would be too uncomfortable. The gun and holster didn't seem to bother Carol Strong, however. Crossing one shapely leg over the other, she massaged the ball of first one foot and then the other.

"Pardon me," she said apologetically to Joanna. "In this business somebody my size needs all the help she can get, but these damn shoes are killing my feet."

For several moments, neither woman said anything while Joanna studied Carol Strong. Her age was difficult to determine. Her skin was generally smooth and clear, although dark circles under her eyes hinted at a world-weariness that went far beyond a simple lack of sleep. Here and there a few strands of gray misted through the feathery cloud of black hair that surrounded her face. Her sharply tapered nails were lacquered several layers deep with a brilliant scarlet polish. Everything about the way she looked and dressed seemed to celebrate being female, but there was an underlying toughness about her as well. Joanna sensed that anyone who mistook Carol Strong for just another pretty face was in for a rude awakening.

"Dick Voland told me you had great legs," Joanna said.

"Who the hell is Dick Voland?" Carol Strong asked in return. "And why was he talking about me?"

"He's one of my chief deputies," Joanna explained. "He was the one who helped you when you came down to Paul Spur to pick up Jorge Grijalva. I had planned to come talk to you about that . . ."

Carol Strong's easygoing manner changed abruptly. "About what?" she demanded.

"About Serena and Jorge Grijalva. I know Juanita Grijalva, you see. Jorge's mother. She asked me to look into things."

A curtain of wariness dropped over Carol Strong's face. "And have you?" she asked. "Looked into things, that is?"

There was no sense in being coy about it. "I've done some informal nosing around," Joanna admitted. "I went to see Jorge Monday night down at the Maricopa County Jail. And I picked this up from Butch Dixon, the bartender at the Roundhouse Bar and Grill."

Taking the yellow pages of Butch's essay out of her purse, Joanna handed them over to Carol and then waited quietly while the other woman scanned through them. "And?" Carol said finally when she finished reading and pushed the pages back across the desk to Joanna.

"And what?"

"Did you reach any conclusions?"

"Look," Joanna said. "I'm leaning toward the opinion that Jorge didn't do it. That's based on nothing more scientific than intuition, but my conclusions don't matter one way or the other. I'm not here to hassle you about Jorge. Let's drop it for the time being. I want to know about Leann Jessup. I'm assuming I'm here because you think I could be of some help."

Carol Strong closed her eyes briefly. When she opened them again, she focused directly on

Joanna's face. "We *are* discussing Leann Jessup," she said wearily. "We have been all along."

"But I . . ." Joanna began.

Carol passed a weary hand across her forehead. "You're a newly elected sheriff, but you've never been a police officer before, right?"

"Yes, but . . ."

"Do you know what holdbacks are?"

"Sure. They're the minute details about a case that never get released to the media—the things that are known only to the detectives and the killer. They're helpful in gaining convictions, and they also help separate out the fruitcakes who habitually call in just to confess to something they didn't do."

"Right." Carol Strong nodded. She leaned forward across the desk, her smoky gray eyes crackling with intensity. "Sheriff Brady, what I'm about to tell you is in the strictest confidence. We had plenty of physical evidence in the Grijalva case. Jorge had a new secondhand truck, one he claimed his wife had never ridden in. But when the crime lab went over it, we found trace evidence that Serena had been in the car, including fibers that appear to match the clothing Serena Grijalva was wearing the last time she was seen alive. We also found dirt particles that tested out to be similar to soil from near where Serena's body was found. The murder weapon was a tire iron. With paint particles and wear marks, we've managed to verify that the tire iron that was missing from Jorge's truck at the time we arrested him was the same one we found at the murder scene. Sounds like a pretty open-and-shut case, doesn't it?"

This was the first inkling Joanna had of how extensive the case was against Jorge Grijalva. "I didn't know about any of that," Joanna admitted. "Certainly not the physical evidence part of it."

"No, I don't suppose you did," Carol Strong agreed. "And there's no reason you should. It wasn't a big-name case, and Joe Blow domestic violence is old hat these days. The public is so inured to it that most of the time it doesn't merit much play in the media. In this particular case, though, I did keep some holdbacks—one in particular was more to spare the children's feelings than it was for any other reason."

Carol Strong paused. "Serena Grijalva was naked when we found her. And she was bound with her own pantyhose, trussed with her arms and legs tied behind her in exactly the same way Leann Jessup was found this morning. I may be wrong, but the knots looked identical."

The crowded little office was silent for some time after that. "How could that be?" Joanna asked finally. "Jorge Grijalva's still being held in the county jail, isn't he?"

Carol nodded. "Actually, it could mean any number of things. One of which is that Jorge had an accomplice. The most obvious possibility, however, is that we've arrested the wrong man."

"But what about all the trace evidence?" Joanna asked. "Where did that come from?"

Detective Strong shrugged. "Either the evidence is real or it isn't. Either we found it there because Serena was in the truck at some time or else the evidence is phony, and it was planted there to mislead us, to frame Jorge Grijalva—an innocent man—for the murder of his wife."

"Planted," Joanna echoed. "Who would plant evidence? How would they know how to go about it?"

"A trained police officer would know," Carol Strong answered. "Here's the recipe. You stir in some planted evidence, add in a plausible suspect, and sprinkle it liberally with public-dictated urgency for closing cases in a hurry." She shrugged. "Add to that an ex-husband who's willing to cop a plea, and there you go."

"Jorge is willing to plead because he doesn't want to go to court," Joanna said quietly.

"If he didn't kill her, why would he do that?" Carol returned.

"Because he was afraid the prosecution would bring up Serena's whoring around. He wanted to protect his kids from hearing about it."

Carol shook her head. "The defense would have brought that up, not the prosecution. It's a hell of a lot harder to convict someone of killing a known prostitute than it is to convict them of killing a nun."

There was a momentary lull in the conversation. "If, as you say, the evidence was planted by a cop, do you have any idea what cop?" Joanna asked. "One of yours?"

"Tell me what you know about Dave Thompson?" Carol said.

"From the APOA?" Joanna winced, aware her question made her sound like some kind of dunce.

Carol nodded. "One and the same."

Joanna thought for a moment before answering. "He was a cop somewhere around Phoenix. . . ."

"Chandler," Carol supplied.

"I heard a rumor that he got into some kind of hot water. That the Chandler city fathers dumped him by putting him on permanent loan to the APOA."

"That's pretty much right. I talked to the new chief in Chandler just this morning, right before you showed up on campus. The case against Thompson was a domestic. Never came to trial because Thompson's ex refused to testify. She simply took the kids and left town. This was back in the good old days when there was still a certain tolerance for cops who beat up their wives, but there was enough of a stink that they had to get rid of him."

"You're saying Dave Thompson did this?"

"Did you ever hear of Tommy Tompkins?" Carol Strong asked.

Joanna nodded her head impatiently. Talking to Carol Strong was like being led through a maze of riddles. "I've heard of him," she said. "Tommy Tompkins International. He's the ex-TV evangelist who used to own the property the APOA now occupies, isn't he? I heard he went to prison on some kind of tax evasion charge."

"Right, but what most people don't know is that the person who brought Tommy to the at-

tention of the IRS was a woman, one of his semi-
nary students, who claimed Tommy had broken
into her room in the middle of the night and
raped her. No charges were ever filed. TTI bought
her off for a lot of money, and that was what
raised all the red flags. Randy revivalists are so
prevalent these days that it's become a cliché.
These guys paid off so much, so fast, that the IRS
auditor figured they must be hiding something.
Turns out there was a whole lot more to it than
just cooking the books, but I didn't figure some
of it out until tonight."

Joanna waited without comment while Carol
Strong drew a long breath. "Did you ever wonder
about the mirrored tiles on that one whole side of
your room?"

"Not particularly," Joanna answered. "As part
of a decorating scheme, I thought they were odd—
a little cold."

"They're odd, all right," Carol said. "What I
discovered tonight is that some of them are two-
way mirrors. Mirrors on your side, windows on
the other. Someone could see in, but you couldn't
see out. If you go into that little private courtyard
between Dave Thompson's apartment and the
dormitory, you'll see what looks like the door to
a storage shed of some kind built into the back of
the building. It's not a storage shed at all. There's
a long, narrow passageway back there that runs
the whole length of the building and dead-ends
on the far side. It's only about twenty inches
wide, so it's not recommended for claustropho-
bics. It's not big on comfort, and the ventilation

stinks. But from the number of cigarette butts we found in there, I'd say Dave Thompson or someone else spent a good deal of his off-hours time in there."

The sudden realization sickened Joanna. Of course, the cigarette smoke. Every time she had turned on the exhaust fan in her bathroom, there had been that sudden burst of smoke in the air, and now she knew why. Dave Thompson had been right there, almost in the same room, watching her.

"That son of a bitch!" Joanna murmured. "That dirty, low-down son of a bitch."

"And that's evidently how he gained entry to Leann Jessup's room as well. There's a hidden, half-sized access door into the closet of each of the rooms on the bottom floor. The crack at the top of the door is concealed right under the shelf. The only way to see it would be if you were down on your hands and knees on the floor.

"An alternate light source examination revealed dirty footprints leading from Leann's closet to the bathroom. It looks as though he came in and surprised her while she was relaxing in the hot tub. She evidently put up quite a fight. He may have hit her over the head with her hair dryer. We found pieces of shattered hair dryer all over the bathroom, including in the tub. My theory is that he knocked her senseless. He tied her up while she was out cold, and carried her out to his pickup. Do you know his truck?"

"No."

"It's a white Toyota SR Five, one of those small

four-by-fours with a canopy. He tossed her into the back of it, probably planning on taking her elsewhere to finish the job. He left the campus with her in the back and ended up turning off Olive onto Grand. My guess is he didn't see the northbound car coming around the curve at the underpass south of Olive. He turned right on a red light and pulled out in front of a car driven by a bunch of high-school-aged kids coming home from a party.

"In the meantime, Leann must have come to. I believe she was trying to get out of the vehicle while it was stopped for the light. She somehow managed to open the canopy, but when the Toyota accelerated, the sudden movement pitched her out of the truck. With her hands tied behind her, there was nothing to break her fall. She landed on her head and somersaulted at least twice. Her skin looks like it was run through a cheese grater."

"That's appalling!" Joanna murmured.

Carol nodded and continued. "She came to rest directly in the front of that carload of kids. The other driver's only seventeen. He left skid marks all over the road, but through some miracle, he managed to avoid hitting her. If he had clobbered her traveling at forty-five or so, she'd have been dead for sure. The kids stopped long enough for some of them to pile out of the backseat. Three of them stayed behind to do what they could for Leann while the driver and one of his buddies took off after the Toyota. I have to give them credit for guts if not for brains. They followed the pickup and got close enough to get a partial license before they lost him somewhere out in Sun City. The kids came back to the scene and turned the number over to the officers on the scene. They called me."

"Was she conscious?" Joanna asked. "Could she talk?"

"No."

"If she was naked, how did you know it was Leann?" Joanna asked quietly.

"Bee stings,"

"Bee stings?"

"She's allergic to them, so allergic that she wears an I.D. bracelet that warns medics that in case of a bee sting they should administer epinephrine to prevent her from going into anaphylactic shock. There were two phone numbers on it. One was evidently the apartment where Leann used to live. That one's been disconnected. The other one belongs to Lorelie Jessup, Leann's mother. The ambulance transported Leann to Arrowhead Community Hospital. From there, she was airlifted to St. Joseph's. I picked Mrs. Jessup up at home and brought her to the hospital. She's the one who gave us the positive I.D. and told us Leann was attending the APOA."

"And how did you come up with the Dave Thompson connection?"

"We found the truck. About three o'clock, one of our patrol cars found a white Toyota pickup parked in front of a flooring warehouse a few blocks north of where we found Leann and within walking distance of the APOA. I think he abandoned it there and walked back to his place."

"Where is he now?"

Carol Strong shook her head. "That's anybody's guess. He's not in his apartment. We got a search warrant and went through that, and we've also put out an APB. No luck so far."

"What can I do to help?"

"When was the last time you saw Leann Jessup?"

"Lunchtime. We went up to the Roundhouse and had a hamburger. That's when I picked up that stuff from Butch Dixon."

"What was she wearing?"

"A sweatshirt. An ASU Sun Devil sweatshirt. Yellow and black. Jeans. Tennis shoes. Nikes, I think, and white socks."

There was a pause while Carol Strong scribbled a note in a notebook. "Panties?" she asked.

"Panties. How would I know if she was wearing panties?"

"Did you ever see her undressed?"

"Once, in the women's locker room after PT on Tuesday afternoon, when we were both changing."

"Was she wearing panties then?"

"Yes, but . . ."

"That was the other holdback," Carol Strong said gravely. "We found the clothing Serena Grijalva was wearing when she left the bar that night—everything but a pair of panties. I talked to Cecelia, her daughter. She told me that her mother always wore panties."

"I don't see—" Joanna began, but Carol Strong cut her off in mid-sentence.

"We found the clothes you mentioned in the

bathroom. A sweatshirt, jeans, bra, tennies, socks. Everything was there *except* panties. There was a dirty clothes bag spilled on the floor of her closet. We found three sets of clothing in there, including three pairs of panties. If she wore a clean set of underwear every day, that means one pair is missing."

"What does that mean?"

Carol shook her head. "If Dave Thompson is the one who did it, what happened to Leann Jessup is my fault."

"How can that be?"

"Thompson was one of the people at the Roundhouse the night Serena Grijalva was murdered."

"He was?"

Carol nodded. "His name turned up when we questioned the bartender there. I don't know Thompson personally. When I transferred back here from California, I did my probation duty, and that was it. I didn't have to sit through any classes. But half the Peoria force came through Dave Thompson's program at the APOA. When his name turned up, I didn't see any connection or any reason to consider him a suspect. Now I can see that I should have. It looks as though Dave Thompson is a very troubled and dangerous man. How did he strike you?"

"As an unreconstituted male chauvinist pig," Joanna replied. "Leann and I were the only women in the class. He didn't like having us there, and he made sure we knew it."

"You mean he was hostile? He picked on you?"

"That's how it seemed."

"Did he focus on Leann in particular?"

Joanna thought about that for a moment; then she shook her head. "No. It felt to me as though he was on my case far more than he was on hers, but that could have been an erroneous perception on my part. Leann was a lot more scared of him than I was. If she failed the course, her job was on the line. I'm an elected official. If I flunk, it might make for bad PR, but passing or failing the APOA class doesn't make that much difference to me."

"Did he make any off-color suggestions to either one of you?"

"As in sex for grades? No, none of that. Certainly not to me. If he made that kind of an offer to Leann, she never mentioned it to me."

"Did he threaten either one of you in any way?"

"No, but I know Leann was worried about keeping up. After we attended the vigil on Tuesday, she was worried about falling behind in her reading. That was one of the reasons she didn't come along with me to the hotel on Wednesday afternoon."

"Vigil?" Carol Strong asked. "What vigil?"

"The one sponsored by MAVEN down by the capitol. The one for the domestic violence victims. I went because of Serena Grijalva."

"And Leann went along with you?"

"Not exactly. We went together. She had her own reasons for going. She was the officer who took the missing persons report on the ASU professor's wife—ex-wife. I can't remember her name, but they found her body up by Carefree on Monday."

Carol Strong nodded. "I know which one you mean."

"It hit Leann hard for some reason. Maybe it was too close to what happened to her own mother. Evidently, there was some problem with domestic violence in Leann's family as well. Anyway, we went, and then we both ended up on TV. A female reporter was there. She spotted me and did an on-the-spot interview. When the reporter discovered Leann was a cop, too, she interviewed her as well. Leann's mother taped the news broadcast. I have a copy if you'd like to see it."

"Eventually," Carol said.

The question-and-answer process continued for some time after that. Finally, Carol Strong sighed and looked at her watch.

"No wonder I'm tired. It's eleven o'clock—six hours after my usual bedtime, and I'm due in at six tonight. Will you be at the Hohokam all weekend if I need to get back to you?"

"Until Sunday."

"I'll call you there if I need to ask you anything else. Do you mind if I make a copy of what Butch Dixon wrote for you? It's not that different from what he told me to begin with, but considering what's happened, I'd better take a look at everything related to Serena Grijalva's case and try to see what, if anything, I missed the first time through."

"Go ahead. I'll go disconnect Jenny from the VCR."

Joanna had lost all track of time and was surprised by how much time had passed. When she went into the training room, she was surprised to hear her own voice coming from the VCR. Jenny was watching the tape.

"I just saw Ceci on TV," Jenny said. "She looked real sad."

"She was sad, but why are you watching that? I thought you were going to watch *E.T.*"

"I did. It's over already. You were gone a long time."

"I'm sorry, but we're done now. Come on."

Jenny expertly ejected the tape from the machine and put it back into the box. "Do you think Ceci got to see herself?"

"I don't know," Joanna answered. "You can ask her tomorrow. If not, maybe you can show her the tape."

Carol Strong met them in the hallway, handed Joanna back her papers, and then showed them out of the building. "That lady isn't very big to be a detective, is she?" Jenny asked. "With her shoes off, she's not much bigger than me."

"Than I," Joanna corrected. "Am tall is understood. You wouldn't say me am tall. But detectives use their brains a whole lot more than their muscles."

"Well, she seems nice," Jenny said, as they walked down the sidewalk toward the Blazer.

"She does to me, too," Joanna replied.

But if Jorge Grijalva was innocent of killing Serena, Joanna could see why, tiny or not, he might think of Detective Carol Strong as a witch.

As they left the city parking lot, something was bothering Joanna. She couldn't remember seeing Leann Jessup's Ford Fiesta in the parking lot. It was possible that it had been there, parked invisibly among the collection of police vehicles. Just to make sure, Joanna took a detour past the APOA campus. Except for a single patrol car stationed near the gate, the parking lot was completely deserted. Joanna got out of her car long enough to speak to the uniformed officer.

"I'm Sheriff Joanna Brady," Joanna introduced herself, flipping out both her badge and I.D. "I'm working with Detective Strong on this case. Can you tell me if there was a bright red Ford Fiesta here this morning when officers first arrived? I'm wondering if it's missing or if maybe someone ordered it impounded."

The patrol officer spent several minutes checking back and forth by radio before he finally came up negative.

"You might have Detective Strong add that to her APB on Dave Thompson. The vehicle is probably registered in Leann Jessup's name. If he's missing and the car is, too, chances are pretty good that they'll turn up together."

Again the officer returned to his radio. "Dispatch says Detective Strong's gone home to get some sleep. Do you want them to wake her up to give her the message, or should they let her sleep?"

"Tell them they can give it to her after she wakes up."

Joanna returned to her Blazer. "What are we going to do now?" Jenny asked. "I still haven't been swimming."

"We have one more stop," Joanna said. "I want to drop by the hospital just long enough to say hello and to find out how Leann is."

"Do we *have* to?" Jenny whined.

"Yes," Joanna answered.

Something in her mother's voice warned Jenny not to argue. The child sat back in the passenger seat and crossed her arms. "All right," she said grudgingly. "But I hope it doesn't take too long."

🌵 NINETEEN

SHADOWED BY Jenny, Joanna wandered around the corridors of St. Joseph's Hospital for some time before she finally located the proper waiting room. There were only two other people in the room when they entered. A woman sat on a couch, weeping quietly into a hanky. A grim-faced man in his late twenties stood nearby. Both people looked up anxiously when the door opened. Seeing a woman and a child, they both looked away.

"Mrs. Jessup?" Joanna asked tentatively.

The woman pulled the hanky away from her face and stood up. "Yes," she said. "I'm Lorelie Jessup, and this is my son, Rick. Is there any news?"

Lorelie didn't at all resemble her tall, red-haired daughter. Anything but beautiful, she was short, squat, and nearsighted. Her thinning, dishwater-blond hair was disheveled, as though she had climbed out of bed and come straight to the hospital without pausing long enough to comb it.

Joanna remembered Leann saying that her mother was only in her late forties, but with her face blotchy and distorted by weeping, with her faded blue eyes red from crying, she looked much older than that. Wrinkles lined her facial skin, perhaps as much from sun as age. The corners of her mouth turned down in a perpetual grimace, and there was a general air of hopelessness about her. She looked like someone Jim Bob Brady would have said had been "rode hard and put up wet."

And most likely that was true. Joanna tried to recall how many years Leann Jessup had said her mother had worked two jobs in order to single-handedly support her two children. Years of unremitting labor had taken their toll.

"I'm sorry," Joanna said, "I don't know any news. I'm not with the hospital. My name's Joanna. I'm a friend of Leann's."

"Not another one!" Rick Jessup groaned.

"Another what?" Joanna asked. Instead of answering, Rick Jessup rolled his eyes, stuffed both hands in his pockets, and then stalked off across the room. There wasn't much physical resemblance between Leann and her brother, either; in terms of temperament, they were worlds apart.

"Rick, please," his mother admonished. "Don't be rude. This is Sheriff Brady from down in Bisbee. She and Leann were on that news program together the other night, the one I taped. You and Sherry haven't had a chance to see it yet."

"I'm sure it's no great loss," Rick said.

What's the matter with this guy? Joanna

wondered, but she turned back to Lorelie. "How is Leann?"

"They keep telling me it's too soon to tell. She's heavily sedated right now. They've installed a shunt to drain off fluid to reduce pressure on her brain. She may be all right, but then again, she may . . ." Lorelie broke off, overcome by emotion and unable to continue.

"She brought it all on herself," Rick Jessup groused from across the room. "God is punishing her. If you think about it, her whole life is an abomination."

Lorelie Jessup rounded on her son. "God had nothing to do with the attack on Leann. If that's the way you feel about it, why don't you just leave? I don't need you here spouting that kind of garbage, and neither does Leann."

"What's an abomina—?" Jenny began. Joanna squeezed her hand, silencing the child.

Lorelie crossed the room until she and her son were bare inches apart. For a moment, Joanna worried the war of words would escalate into a physical confrontation.

"Why would you say such awful things about your own sister?" Lorelie demanded. "How could you? I want you to apologize, both to her and to me."

"There's nothing to apologize for," Rick Jessup returned coldly. "After all, it's true. Face it. Leann Jessup is nothing but a godless dyke who doesn't just sin, she wallows in it. This is the Lord's way of giving her a wake-up call. I'm sick and tired of making excuses for her, of even being related."

"Whatever happened to the part of the Bible that says 'Judge not . . .'?" Lorelie asked calmly, her voice turning to ice. "If being related to Leann is a problem for you, Rick, don't worry about it. There's an easy solution to that—stop being related. But if you decide to write Leann out of your life, remember one thing. If you don't have a sister, you don't have a mother, either. Get out of here. By the time I come home from the hospital, I want all of you out of my house."

"Just like that? All of us? You're throwing me out over her?" Rick's face was tight with fury.

"Just like that!" Lorelie returned.

"But what about Junior?" Rick objected. "What about your grandson?"

"I guess I'll just have to learn to take the bad with the good," she said.

For a moment, Rick seemed bent on staring his mother down. When she didn't look away, he backed toward the door. "I brought you over," he said. "If I leave, who'll drive you home?"

"I'll walk if I have to," Lorelie said determinedly. "The company will be better. Now go!"

Rick Jessup went, taking much of the tension from the room with him, while Lorelie turned back to Joanna. "I'm sorry," she said. "There's nothing like bringing your family feud right out in the open."

"You have nothing to apologize for," Joanna said.

"What Rick said is partially true, although there's no call for him to be so mean about it," Lorelie continued. "Leann is a lesbian, but so what?

That doesn't make her some kind of freak. She's also good-hearted and caring. And, no matter what, she's still my daughter."

Joanna hadn't guessed Leann's secret, but Lorelie's matter-of-fact treatment made the whole topic seem less shocking, even with Jenny standing right there beside her. And that's why you're still Leann's hero, Joanna thought.

Glancing at her watch, Joanna knew it was time to take Jenny and head back. "Is there someone you could call to come stay with you here at the hospital?" she asked. "I hate for you to be here alone."

"I suppose I could always call Kim," Lorelie said.

"Who's Kim?"

"Kimberly George. Leann's friend." Lorelie paused, then added, "Her former friend, that is. Lover, really. The two of them had been together for five years at least. They only split up a month ago. They got in a big fight over Leann's new job."

"Why's that?"

"Kim was afraid something might happen to Leann. That she'd get hurt at work . . ." Lorelie sighed. "Anyway, they broke up, and it's just like someone getting a divorce. But still, I am going to call her. I know Kim would want to know what's going on, and she'll be happy to give me a ride home if I need one."

A nurse bustled into the waiting room. "The doctor says you can go in for five minutes, Mrs. Jessup. But only one person at a time, and only immediate family." She shot a meaningful look in Joanna's direction. If the nurse was expecting an argument, it didn't materialize.

"Right. We were just leaving," Joanna said to the nurse, then turned to Lorelie. "If you can't get in touch with Kim, or if you need anything else, please call me. I'm staying at the Hohokam in Peoria. I'll be there all weekend."

"Thank you," Lorelie Jessup said. "And thank you for coming. I appreciate it far more than you'll ever know."

"What's an abomination?" Jenny asked, once they were back in the corridor.

"Something that's evil or obscene," Joanna answered.

"Is your friend evil?"

"I don't think so."

"And neither does her mother."

"Evidently not," Joanna agreed.

"But her brother does."

"It certainly sounds that way."

Jenny and Joanna walked along in silence for several seconds. "I always used to want a little brother," Jenny said. "But now that I've met that Rick guy, I think I'm glad I don't have one."

Joanna shook her head. "Maybe a brother of yours wouldn't have turned into someone like Rick Jessup."

Back at the hotel, Joanna was relieved to find a voice-mail message from Eva Lou Brady waiting on the phone in their room. "We're back," Eva Lou's cheerful voice announced. "Call us."

While Jenny headed for the bathroom to change into her swimming suit, Joanna called the Bradys' room. "Where were you?" she asked.

"I saw an announcement in the paper this morning saying that the Salvation Army needed volunteers to come help serve their holiday meal. You and Jenny were gone, and I couldn't see Jim Bob and me just sitting around all day with him doing nothing but watching football. We decided to go help out for a little while. Now I'm going to take a little nap and let Jimmy watch one football game before dinner. What are you and Jenny up to?"

Briefly, Joanna brought Eva Lou up to date on what had happened to them. "I'd better get off the phone. Jenny has her suit on, finally. She's champing at the bit to get in the pool. I'm going to go down and watch her, but I'm taking along that packet of mail you brought me. I'll use the time to work on my correspondence."

Once Jenny was happily paddling back and forth in the pool, Joanna emptied the contents of a large manila envelope onto a nearby patio table. The item that landed on top of the pile was a second envelope, much smaller than the first. That one, with a Sheriff's Department return address, was hand-addressed to Joanna. Inside she found a handwritten memo from Frank Montoya detailing the problem with the cook. Nothing to do about that one, she thought as she tossed it aside. As Frank had said, that one was handled.

An hour later, she had plowed through the whole collection. There wasn't anything particularly exciting. A whole lot about being sheriff wasn't any more interesting than tracking a life insurance application or reading the proposed agenda for the next Board of Supervisors meeting, which was dutifully enclosed. It dawned on Joanna that she had signed up to do the nuts-and-bolts part of the job—the administrative part—as well as the more exciting ones. When she finished reading through the mail and jotting off answers to whatever required a reply, she felt better.

She wasn't neglecting her duty by leaving home to learn what she needed to know to do the job better. Things at the department were going along just fine without her. She had delegated responsibilities in a way that was getting things done without allowing her absence to undermine her new position.

At ten to three she dredged a protesting Jenny out of the pool. "We need to be back in the room to answer the phone in case Grandma Lathrop calls. Do you want to shower first or should I?"

"You go first," Jenny said.

Joanna was showered, had her makeup on, and was half through drying her hair when Jenny pushed open the bathroom door to say Joanna had a phone call.

"Who is it?" Joanna asked.

Jenny shrugged. "I dunno," she said. "Some guy."

"Hello," Joanna answered.

"Sheriff Brady?"

The voice sounded vaguely familiar. "Yes," she said warily.

"My name's Bob Brundage. I'm down here in the lobby. I was wondering if you'd care to join me for a drink."

"I'm sorry, Mr. . . . What did you say your name is?"

"Brundage," he replied.

"I'm not in the habit of meeting strangers for drinks. Besides, I'm expecting company. . . ."

"We have a mutual acquaintance," Bob Brundage insisted. "I'm sure she'd be very disappointed if we didn't take advantage of this little window of opportunity to get together."

"This isn't about Amway, is it?" Joanna asked.

Bob Brundage laughed so heartily at that question that Joanna found herself laughing as well. "I promise you," he gasped at last. "This has absolutely nothing to do with Amway or with life insurance or with making a donation to your college alumni building fund, either."

The clock on the bedside table said 3:30. There was a whole hour between then and the time Adam York was supposed to show up for dinner. If Eleanor called, Jenny would be right there in the room to answer the phone.

"All right," Joanna agreed finally. "I'll come down for a few minutes, although I can't stay long because we're due in the dining room for dinner at five. How will I know who you are?"

"I'll recognize you," he said. "I've seen your picture."

"Who was that?" Jenny asked, as Joanna put down the phone.

"A man. His name is Bob Brundage. He wants

me to meet him downstairs in the lobby to have a drink."

"Are you going to go?"

"Yes, but if Grandma Lathrop calls while I'm gone, tell her that I'm away from the phone and that I'll call her back just as soon as I can."

Joanna returned to the bathroom. As she finished drying her hair, she began reconsidering her decision. The call had been vaguely unsettling, especially the part about Bob Brundage knowing so much about her while she knew nothing at all about him. Staring at her reflection in the mirror, Joanna shivered, remembering the bathroom of her dormitory room on campus, the one with the two-way mirrors. Carol Strong's assumption was that Dave Thompson was most likely the only person who had availed himself of those two-way mirrors to spy on the female inhabitants of the dormitory's lower-floor rooms.

But standing in the brightly lit bathroom of her room at the Hohokam, Joanna wondered about that. Dave Thompson might have shared the wealth with someone else—maybe even with several people. Some of the other instructors, perhaps, or maybe even some of Joanna's fellow students. As the thought of a whole group of peeping toms crossed her mind, Joanna's cheeks burned hot with indignation.

Who was to say Dave Thompson would limit the invitees to people involved with the APOA? For all Joanna knew, he might have dragged people in off the street and charged admission. In fact, what if Bob Brundage turned out to be as much of a pervert as Dave Thompson was? Brundage claimed he had seen Joanna's picture, but that might not be true. What if he had actually seen her stark-naked in the presumed privacy of her own bathroom? That would explain his knowing her without her knowing him. And what if he was dangerous as well? There was no reason to assume that Dave Thompson had acted alone in the attack on Leann Jessup. If Bob Brundage turned out to be Dave Thompson's partner in crime . . .

There was only one answer to all those questions, and it came straight out of *The Girl Scout Handbook*: Be prepared.

Joanna emerged from the bathroom wearing only her underwear and found Jenny totally engrossed in watching *Beauty and the Beast*. Taking advantage of the video diversion, Joanna dressed quickly and carefully, concealing from Jenny the Kevlar vest she put on under her best white blouse and the shoulder-holstered Colt 2000 she strapped on under her new boiled-wool blazer.

Downstairs, the lobby outside the elevator was crowded with a combination of hotel guests and holiday diners. Efforts to market the Hohokam's Thanksgiving dinner had evidently been wildly successful. Formal seatings in the Gila Dining Room had started as early as one o'clock in the afternoon.

Coming through the lobby, Joanna had planned on stopping by the dining room to let someone know the Brady party with reservations at five would be reduced from eight diners to seven. After glancing at the crowded dining room door and at the harried hostess trying to seat parties, Joanna decided against it.

Instead, threading her way through the crush of people, she headed for the lobby cocktail bar. On the way, she walked past the gas-log fireplace where she had sat for such a long time the previous evening. Was that only yesterday? she wondered. It seemed much longer ago than that.

"Joanna," a man's voice called. "Over here."

Without the subtle distortions of the telephone, Bob Brundage's voice stopped her cold. The timbre was so familiar, she hardly dared turn her head to look. At the far end of the massive fireplace, a man in a military uniform rose from one of a pair of wing chairs and gestured for her to join him. Unable to move, Joanna stood as if frozen in the middle of the room.

D. H. "Big Hank" Lathrop himself could have been standing there. Her father was standing there. And yet he wasn't. He couldn't be. Big Hank had been dead for years. Besides, this man was far younger than Joanna's father had been when he died. But the resemblance was eerie. It was as though the ghost of her father had stepped out of one of those old black-and-white photos and turned into a living, breathing human being.

When Joanna didn't move forward, the man did, coming toward her with his hand outstretched and with a broad smile on his tanned face.

"Bob Brundage," he said, introducing himself.

He took Joanna by the elbow and guided her back toward the two empty chairs. "Colonel Brundage, actually. I told you it wasn't Amway."

"Who are you?" she asked, finally finding her voice.

"I'm the surprise," he said. "Eleanor had her heart set on introducing us at dinner, but it seemed to me that might be too much of a shock for you. Judging by your reaction, I believe I'm right about that. What would you like to drink?"

Joanna watched him in utter fascination. When Bob Brundage's mouth moved, it was Joanna's father's mouth. He had the same narrow lips that turned up at the corners, the same odd space between his two front teeth.

"I don't care," she answered. "I'll have whatever you're having."

Bob Brundage signaled the cocktail waitress. "Two Glenfiddich on the rocks," he said. "So your folks never told you about me, did they?"

"No. I knew there were a series of miscarriages before they ever had me, but . . ."

Bob Brundage laughed again. The laughter, too, was hauntingly familiar. "I've been called a lot of things in my time, but never a miscarriage," he said. "Your mother—my birth mother, as we say in the world of adoptees—was only fifteen when she got pregnant with me.

"According to Eleanor—you don't mind if I call her that, do you?"

Joanna shook her head.

"According to Eleanor," Bob continued, "Hank had just come back from the Korean War and got stationed at Fort Huachuca when they first re-opened it. They met on a picnic on the San Pedro River. Eleanor wandered away from the church picnic and met up with a group of soldiers. She told me it was love at first sight. Of course, those were pre-birth control days. Her folks shipped her out of town when she turned up pregnant, forced her to give me up for adoption. But she told me that she and Hank secretly stayed in touch by letter the whole time she was gone, and that they took up again as soon as she came back to town. By then he was out of the army and working in the mines. After Eleanor graduated from high school, her folks finally consented to their getting married.

"It's a very romantic story, don't you think?"

The waitress brought the drinks. Romantic? Joanna thought, No, the story didn't sound the least bit romantic to her. It sounded absolutely hypocritical. Do as I say, not as I do. Do as I say, not as I've done.

Bob Brundage's torrent of words washed over her, but she couldn't quite come to grips with them. Her parents—her mother and her father—had another child, a baby born out of wedlock? Was that possible? For almost thirty years, Joanna had thought of herself as an only child. Now it turned out she wasn't.

"Those were the days of closed adoptions," Bob Brundage continued. "My adoptive parents were wonderful people, but they're both gone now. My father died of a stroke ten years ago, and my mother passed away just this last spring. And once I knew it wouldn't hurt them—once they could no longer feel betrayed by my actions—I decided to start looking into my roots.

"I've actually known Eleanor's and your names and where you live for several months now. Congratulations on your election, by the way. I saw a blurb about that in *USA Today*. I always check the Arizona listings, just for the hell of it, and one day, there you were. Then, when I found out a month ago that I would be coming to Fort Huachuca to do an inspection this month, it just seemed like the right thing to do. You're not upset, are you?"

"Upset?" Joanna echoed, plastering an insincere smile on her face. "Why on earth would I be upset?"

But she was upset. Bob kept on talking, but Joanna stopped listening to him. Her ears and heart were tuned to the past, where she was rehashing Eleanor's hysterical outbursts and the ugly things she had said once she had discovered Joanna was pregnant with Jenny. How could Joanna do such a stupid thing? Eleanor had raged. How could she do that to her own mother? How could she?

For over ten years, Joanna Brady had tolerated her mother's barbed comments, her constant sniping. Eleanor had run down Andy Brady and their shotgun wedding at every opportunity. She had claimed Andy was never good enough for Joanna, that he had ruined her life, stolen her potential. And all the while . . .

After all those years of criticism—both stated and implied—a decade's worth of suppressed anger rose to the surface of Joanna Brady's heart.

"Why exactly did you come here?" Joanna asked.

"I already told you," Bob Brundage answered. "I wanted to find my roots. I wanted to find out if my interest in the army was genetically linked."

After that small quip, he stopped for a moment and examined Joanna's face. "You *are* upset," he said. "I was afraid of that, but Eleanor said she thought you'd be fine."

"How long have you known"—Joanna couldn't bring herself to say the word *Mother* right then—"Eleanor?" she added lamely.

"I called her for the first time three and a half weeks ago. I didn't know what her reaction would be—"

"And she doesn't know mine," Joanna interrupted. "In fact, she probably understands you better than she does me."

Bob held up a calming hand. "I'm sorry. I can see this is all very disturbing to you. I certainly didn't want that to happen. If you'd like, I'll just go back to D.C. and disappear. . . ."

Joanna shook her head emphatically. "Oh, no you don't. Don't you dare do that. She'd hold me responsible for it the rest of my life. If you leave now, she'll never forgive me. It would mean she'd been cheated out of her son twice. I don't want that responsibility. Not on your life."

Up to that point, Joanna had taken only a

single sip of her Scotch. Now she downed the rest of the drink in one long unladylike swallow, letting the icy liquor slide down her throat.

She took a deep breath. "I guess I sound like a real spoilsport, don't I. A brat. I'm angry with Eleanor. . . ."

"Why are you angry with her? It wasn't her fault. . . ."

"Why am I angry? Because I've been betrayed, that's why. Eleanor Mathews Lathrop always set herself up on a pedestal as some kind of Madam Perfect. And according to her, I never once measured up. When all the while . . ."

Joanna paused. "That's not fair of me, of course, to just blame my mother. She wasn't the only one who lied to me. After all, it takes two to tango," she added bitterly. "Obviously, Big Hank Lathrop was in on it from the beginning, too. The whole time I was growing up, I damn near broke my neck a dozen times trying to be the son my father claimed he'd never had. Well, guess what? It turns out he did have that son after all, one he somehow neglected to tell me anything about. In fact, now that I think about it, I probably have you to thank for him turning me into a hopeless tomboy and for the fact that I'm sheriff right now. . . ."

"Joanna, I—"

"Mom, there you are," Jenny exclaimed, skidding to a stop on the polished stone floor behind them.

"Jenny, what are you doing down here?"

"I came looking for you. Detective Strong just

called. She said for you to call her back right away. She said it's urgent!"

Jenny came around the arm of Joanna's chair. Seeing Bob Brundage, she ducked back out of sight.

The interruption had allowed Joanna to get a partial grip on her roiling emotions. She took a deep breath. "Jenny," she said, forcing her voice to be even. "I want you to meet Mr. Brundage here. Colonel Brundage. He's your uncle. He'll be joining us for dinner tonight."

With a purposeful shove from her mother, Jenny stepped out from behind the chair and held out her hand. "I'm glad to meet you," she said politely. Then she turned back to Joanna, frowning. "But you always told me I didn't have any aunts or uncles."

"That's because I didn't think you did."

Joanna stood up. "You'll have to excuse us, Colonel Brundage. Thanks for the drink. I hope you'll forgive my outburst. As you can see, this has been something of a shock."

Bob Brundage nodded sympathetically. "Better here with just the two of us than at dinner in a whole crowd, wouldn't you say?"

"I suppose so," Joanna allowed grudgingly. It was the best she could do. She turned to her daughter. "Come on, Jenny. Let's go." As they headed back toward the elevator, Joanna asked, "Did Detective Strong say what was wrong?"

"No. But she made me write down her number. Here it is." Jenny handed over a piece of paper with a phone number scribbled on it. Instead of bothering with going all the way back upstairs, Joanna stopped by a pay phone in the elevator lobby and dialed.

"Thanks for getting back to me so fast," Carol Strong said. "I'm almost dressed and ready to leave. Meet me at the APOA campus as soon as you can, would you?"

"Why? What's wrong?"

"I think we've found Dave Thompson."

"You *think*?"

"Yes. You know him. I need someone to identify him."

"Where is he?"

"In a red Ford Fiesta registered to someone named Kimberly George. One of the patrol officers looked through the window of one of the APOA outbuildings. It turned out to be a garage with a red car inside it. He broke in as soon as he realized there was someone sitting slumped over in the front seat. The ignition was on, but the engine wasn't running. It was out of gas."

"He's dead, then?"

"Yes."

Joanna closed her eyes, feeling an odd combination of both sadness and relief. "I'll meet you there," she said. "I'll be on my way as soon as I drop Jenny off with one grandmother or the other."

TWENTY

CAROL STRONG had obviously cleared the way. When Joanna arrived at the APOA campus, there was no question about whether or not she was to be allowed through the barriers and given access to the crime scene. A young patrol officer named Reiner walked up to the Blazer as she was switching off the ignition.

"This way, Sheriff Brady," he said. "Detective Strong is expecting you."

Officer Reiner led Joanna into a two-car garage, where, even though the roll-up doors were wide open, the smell of auto exhaust still lingered in the air. As she approached the car, Joanna recognized another smell as well—the ugly odor of death. In a matter of weeks, Joanna had learned the unpleasant truth—that investigating death scenes was anything but antiseptic.

She bent over and peered inside the car. A slack-jawed Dave Thompson slumped over the steering wheel. Wrinkling her nose in distaste, Joanna straightened back up. "It's him," she said.

"I thought so," Carol said. "We're trying to find the car's registered owner. No luck so far."

"Have you checked with the hospital?" Joanna asked.

"What hospital?"

"St. Joseph's. My guess is she's in the waiting room keeping Lorelie Jessup company."

"You know her?"

"Not exactly. I've never met her, but I was told Kimberly George is Leann Jessup's former lover."

"Lover?" Carol Strong repeated sharply. "Are you telling me Leann Jessup is a lesbian?" Joanna nodded.

"I didn't know that."

"Neither did I," Joanna admitted. "Not until this afternoon."

"How did you find out?"

Joanna shrugged. "After we left your office, Jenny and I went down to the hospital to check on Leann. We talked to her mother and to her brother. What a jerk!"

"Well, that certainly explains a lot," Carol Strong mused, almost to herself.

"Explains what?" Joanna asked.

"What happened here. Was there some hanky-panky going on between them?"

"Between Dave and Leann? No. I'm certain nothing like that was going on."

"Look," Carol said, shaking her head. "You can't be sure, not unless you were with her twenty-four hours out of every day. Let's say, for argument's sake, that they were fooling around a little. One way or another Thompson learns about Leann's sexual preference, and he freaks. He flips out completely and decides to kill her. After all, it's the second time this has happened to him. And then, when it falls apart and she gets away, he comes to his senses, realizes that he's about to be caught, and doesn't want to face the consequences. So he bolsters his courage with a little more booze and does himself in. You did see the empty vodka bottle on the seat beside him, didn't you?"

Joanna shook her head. "No, I didn't. And I don't understand what you're saying. What do you mean the second time this happened?"

"It's the second time Dave Thompson fell for a lesbian," Carol answered. "His wife left him for a woman, not for another man. I thought you knew that."

"No," Joanna said. "I didn't know. But what about the other women, Serena and Rhonda? What about them?"

"We're working on it," Carol answered. "Anyway, thanks for coming and helping us I.D. him." The detective looked at her watch. "I guess you'd better be getting back to the hotel. It's almost four-thirty. Aren't you supposed to be having dinner with your family?"

"That's at five," Joanna said. "I have plenty of time."

Just then two men came pushing a body-bag-laden gurney into the garage. One of them waved at Carol Strong. "What've you got?"

"Suicide," she answered. "We've already identified him for you."

"Good," the other replied. "That'll save time. If I'm not home for dinner by six, my wife will kill me."

Despite Carol's urging, Joanna wasn't ready to leave. "Doesn't it all seem just a little too pat?" she asked.

"What?"

"Dave tries to kill Leann in a fit of rage and then takes his own life."

"It happens. As soon as Leann Jessup is well enough to talk to us about it, we'll get the whole thing cleared up. So let's leave it at that for the time being."

With that, Carol turned as though to follow the medical examiner techs back toward the car.

"Did you find Leann's panties, then?" Joanna asked.

"Not yet," Carol answered. "They weren't in Thompson's apartment or we would have found them by now. Maybe they're still on him—in a pocket or something. Or maybe he hid them in the car."

"What if you don't find them?" Joanna prodded.

Carol shook her head emphatically. "Then maybe they never existed in the first place," she said.

For a moment, the two women stood looking at each other. Homicide detectives are judged by a very public scoreboard—by cases opened and by cases promptly closed. Here was a classic twofer.

The attempted homicide/successful suicide theory cleared two of Carol Strong's cases at once and in less than twenty-four hours. With that kind of payoff waiting in the wings, the mysterious disappearance of a pair of panties diminished in importance. And two pairs of missing panties linked the deaths of Leann Jessup and Serena Grijalva.

"If you don't mind, I'll hang around for a while," Joanna said. "I want to see if they turn up in the car."

"Suit yourself," Carol said, and returned to the group of investigators gathered around the car. "All right, you guys. Let's get him out of here, then."

Removing the body took time. Joanna stayed in the background waiting, watching, and thinking. What if the panties didn't show up at all? If that happened, it was likely that the possible connection between Dave Thompson and Serena Grijalva would be ignored. Jorge would go to prison on the negotiated plea agreement, and no one would ever come close to knowing the truth. Other than Juanita Grijalva, Joanna Brady, and a literary-leaning bartender, nobody else seemed to care.

UP TO then, relations between Detective Carol Strong and Sheriff Joanna Brady had been entirely congenial if a little unorthodox. During the hours of questioning earlier in the day, Carol had treated Joanna with a good deal of respect,

handling her like a colleague and treating her with
the deference one police officer usually accords
another. But Joanna was smart enough to realize
that if she once questioned Detective Strong's professional judgment or challenged her authority,
that cordiality would evaporate. After that, any
further investigation Joanna did on Jorge Grijalva's behalf would be strictly on her own. She
would be starting over from square one with only
the few scraps of information she herself had managed to accumulate.

Those didn't amount to much. She still had
Juanita's collection of clippings. Then there was
the essay from Butch Dixon, but that didn't seem
likely to be of much help. After all, in his "opus,"
as Butch had called it, he had failed to mention
the very important fact that Dave Thompson had
been in the bar the night Serena was killed.

"So far no luck," Carol said, pulling off her la-
tex gloves and walking over to where Joanna
was standing. "I personally checked his pockets.
Nothing. The crime scene guys will be going over
the car, but it doesn't look promising. You could
just as well go. You're late now as it is."

Joanna nodded. "I guess you're right. But do
you mind if I stop by my room to pick something
up before I go back to the hotel?"

"No problem," Carol said.

Joanna walked back across the parking lot
feeling uneasy. This would be the first time she
had ventured back inside the room since learning about the two-way mirrors. Still, she could
just as well get it over with. She'd have to do it

sooner or later, if for no other reason than to pack up her stuff to go back home.

After unlocking and opening the door, she paused for a moment on the threshold of the darkened room, feeling like a child afraid of some adult-inspired bogeyman. Don't be silly, she chided herself, and switched on the light. She walked purposefully to the desk and opened the drawer. The envelope wasn't there.

Frowning, she stared down into the empty drawer. That was odd. Wasn't the drawer where she had last seen it? Puzzled, she went through the stack of papers she had left on top of the desk. The envelope wasn't there, either.

For several seconds, she stood in the middle of the room looking around. She had been in the room for only a matter of a few days. The place was still far too neat for something as large as a manila envelope to simply disappear. With a growing sense of apprehension, Joanna walked over to the closet. Nothing seemed to be out of place. The two suitcases she hadn't taken along to the Hohokam were still right where she had left them.

Dropping to her hands and knees, Joanna examined the wall underneath the single shelf. With effort, she succeeded in finding the secret access door Carol Strong had told her about. Even knowing it was there, finding it in the gloom of the closet took careful examination. The cracks surrounding it were artfully concealed. A professional job. The door was there because it was supposed to be there. It was something that had been there from the beginning, not something that had been remodeled in as an afterthought.

Joanna stood up and took a deep breath. Had Leann Jessup's attacker let himself into Joanna's room as well? Someone had been here. After all, the envelope was gone. Was anything else missing? Using a pencil, she pried open the other drawers in the room—the ones in the nightstand and in the pressboard dresser. Nothing seemed to be out of order.

She went into the bathroom. Again, at first glance, nothing seemed to be amiss. The shampoo and conditioner, the large container of hand lotion—things she hadn't needed to take along to the hotel—all stood exactly where she had left them. Turning to leave the room, she caught sight of the dirty-clothes bag hanging on the hook on the back of the bathroom door.

Dragging the bag down from the hook, Joanna shook the contents out on the floor. There should have been three days' worth of laundry in that scattered heap. Joanna sorted through it, almost the way she would have if she had been doing the laundry—separating things by colors. When she first noticed the missing pair of panties, she thought that maybe they were still caught in the legs of a pair of jeans. But that wasn't the case. Three sweatshirts, three bras, two sets of jeans, one pair of pantyhose, and two pairs of panties. Only two pairs. The third one had disappeared.

With her pulse pounding in her throat, Joanna turned and fled from the room. Out in the breezeway, she could see Carol Strong and several of her investigators gathered outside the still-open door of the garage.

"Hey," she shouted, waving. "Over here."

Carol obviously heard her, because she waved back, but she didn't understand what Joanna wanted. When Carol made no move in her direction, Joanna loped off across the parking lot. Her PT shin splints yelped in protest. At one point, she slipped on loose gravel and almost fell. No matter what they show on those television commercials, she said to herself, running in high heels isn't easy.

"What's the matter?" Carol asked, as Joanna made it to within hearing distance.

"Do these guys have an alternate light source with them?" she asked.

"Sure. Why?"

"Because someone's been in my room," Joanna answered.

"Is anything missing?"

"Yes. An envelope full of press clippings on the Serena Grijalva case. And a pair of panties from my laundry bag."

"Panties?" Carol repeated. "You're sure?"

"Believe me. I'm sure."

"Bring the ALS and come on," Carol said over her shoulder to the technicians as she and Joanna started back across the parking lot. "Can you describe the missing pair?" she asked.

Fighting back an overwhelming sense of violation, at first all Joanna could do was nod.

"What's wrong?" Carol asked, frowning worriedly in the face of Joanna's obvious distress. "Is there something more that you haven't told me?"

Joanna swallowed hard. "I can describe the panties exactly," she said. "They're apricot-colored nylon with a cotton crotch and with a column of cutout lace flowers appliquéd down the right-hand side."

After saying that, Joanna gave up trying to fight back her tears.

"I'm not sure I could describe any of my own underwear with that much detail," Carol said, more to fill up the silence and to offer some comfort than because the words made sense.

Joanna nodded, sniffling. "I'm sure I shouldn't be so upset. They are only panties, after all, but they were a present from Andy last Christmas, the last Christmas present he ever gave me. They're part of a matching set—bra, full slip, and panties. You can't buy fancy underwear like that anywhere in Bisbee these days. Andy ordered them from a Victoria's Secret catalog and had them shipped to the office so I'd be surprised. He's been dead for months now, but they're still sending him catalogs. They show up on my desk in the mail."

"I'm sorry," Carol said.

Joanna nodded. "Thanks," she said, sniffing and wiping the tears from her face.

By then they had reached the breezeway. Carol waited while Joanna unlocked the door to the room. "Where were they again?"

"The panties? In the laundry bag hanging on the back of the bathroom door."

"And the envelope?"

"I'm not absolutely sure, but I think I left it in the desk drawer."

By then the technician was bringing the ALS into the room. "Where do you want it?" he asked. Carol looked questioningly at Joanna, and she was the one who answered.

"Over there by the closet."

Once plugged in, it took a few moments for the equipment to reach operating temperature. Then, with the lights off, the technician, crawling on his hands and knees, aimed the wand toward the floor.

"There you go," he breathed as a ghostlike footprint appeared on the carpeting. "There's one, and here's another. Looks to me like it's the same as in the other room," he added. "The guy came into the room through the door in the closet. Some of these prints have been disturbed, though. Could be he left the same way."

"No, that was me," Joanna said. "I was crawling around trying to get a look at the access door in the closet. I wanted to see it for myself."

Carol nodded. "All right, guys. I want photos of the footprints, and I want the entire room searched for fingerprints as well."

"Will do," the technician replied.

Carol took Joanna by the arm. "Come on outside," she said. "We'll go out there to talk and leave the techs to do their jobs."

Once they were standing in the breezeway, Joanna realized the sun was going down. That meant it was long past five o'clock. The shock of knowing someone had broken into her room left her in no condition to face the emotional mine-field of that Thanksgiving dinner right then. Her guests would simply have to go on without her.

"What does it all mean?" Joanna asked.

"I don't honestly know," Carol replied.

"Do you think he planned on killing me, too?"

"That's possible. Actually, now that you men-tion it, it's probably even likely."

"But why?" Joanna asked.

For a while both women were silent. Carol was the first to speak. "Supposing Dave Thompson did kill Serena Grijalva," she suggested grudgingly. "Since the envelope with the press clippings in it is the only thing missing from your room, we have to look at that possibility. And let's suppose further that he killed her with the intention of blaming the murder on someone else."

"Jorge," Joanna supplied.

"Right. Fair enough," Carol continued, "but why try to kill Leann? Getting rid of you I can understand. After all, Dave had committed the perfect murder. Jorge was about to take the rap for it. Then you show up from Bisbee and start asking questions—the kinds of troublesome questions that could mess up his whole neat little game plan. So if I were Dave, I'd go after you for sure. But why Leann?"

"And where are the panties and the envelope?" Joanna added. "Why did he take them in the first place, and why can't we find them now?"

Carol nodded thoughtfully. "There's no way to

tell what the timing is exactly, but it doesn't seem like he had a lot of time to get rid of them between the time Leann fell out of the truck and the time officers found it abandoned a few blocks away. So maybe that's where we should look— around the lot where we found the Toyota. Maybe he tossed them in a Dumpster somewhere over there. You're welcome to come along if you like. And we should also see if we can find out how he got back to the campus from there. He must have walked."

With her mind made up, Carol headed off toward her Taurus, striding purposefully along on her usual three-inch heels. A few steps into the parking lot, she stopped cold. "Wait a minute. You're supposed to be eating dinner with your family right now. And you're not exactly dressed to go rummaging through garbage cans."

"Neither are you," Joanna retorted. "If you can go Dumpster dipping the way you're dressed, so can I. Not only that, for some strange reason, I'm not the least bit hungry right now. Maybe you could get someone from the department to call the hotel and let people know that I'm not going to make it."

"Sure thing," Carol said.

They started at the flooring warehouse, which was located in a small industrial complex along with five or six other businesses—all of them shut down for the holiday. Using flashlights from Carol's glove compartment, they searched all the Dumpsters in the area. All of them had trash in them, which meant there had been no pickup that day. But there were no panties anywhere to be found. In one Dumpster, they came across several manila envelopes, but none of them were Juanita Grijalva's.

In the next hour and a half, they went south and searched through three more industrial neighborhoods with similar results.

"I give up," Carol said finally as she banged shut the heavy metal lid on the last Dumpster. "The running track's right here, so if we were going to find them, it seems to me we would have by now. What say we clean up and see about having some dinner."

Joanna looked bedraggled, but she was feeling better. The activity had done her a world of good. The idea that Dave Thompson might have tried to kill her had rocked her, but at least she wasn't sitting around doing nothing. "God helps those who help themselves." That was something else Jim Bob was always saying. Tracking through dusty back parking lots and wrestling with Dumpsters meant Joanna Brady was helping herself.

"Now that you mention it, I'm hungry too, but I still don't want to go back to the hotel while there's a chance everyone will still be down in the dining room," Joanna said. "Not with a run in my pantyhose and smelling like this. My mother would pitch a fit."

"Who said anything about a hotel?" Carol Strong responded. "Besides, if you're game, we still have some work to do."

She drove straight to the Roundhouse Bar and

Grill, where the parking lot was jammed full of cars.

"What are we going to do?" Joanna asked. "Talk to Butch Dixon?"

"I don't know about you," Carol Strong replied, "but my first order of business is to wash my hands. Second is get something to eat. I'm starved. I've only been here a couple of times, but some of the guys down at the department were saying this place puts on a real Thanksgiving spread."

At seven o'clock, the bar wasn't very full, but the entryway alcove that led into the dining room was packed full of people, most of them with kids, waiting for seating in the restaurant. "Name please," a young woman asked.

Joanna looked at the hostess, looked away, and then did a double take. The young woman was dressed in a Puritan costume, complete with a long skirt and a ruffled white apron.

"It'll be about forty-five minutes for a table in the dining room, or you can seat yourself in the bar."

"My aching feet say the bar will be fine," Carol Strong said. "But first I need to use the RR."

When they walked into the bar a few minutes later, Butch Dixon was standing behind the bar, gazing up at an overhead TV monitor with rapt attention. Only when they got closer did Joanna realize that he, too, was dressed in a Puritan costume, complete with breeches, socks, and buckled shoes.

As they came toward him, he glanced away from the set. "Oh, oh," he said. "My two favorite female gendarmes. You haven't come to arrest me, have you?"

"Arrest you?" Carol Strong returned. "What for?"

"Video piracy," he answered with a grin. "I know it says for home use only, but it turns out this is my home. I live upstairs, so that makes this my living room. We have a few important customs around here. One is that on Thanksgiving, the wait staff, me included, dresses up. They can choose between Puritan or Indian, it's up to them. And in the bar we have continuous screenings of my favorite Thanksgiving movie—*Planes, Trains, and Automobiles*. It's just coming up on the best part, where John Candy sets the car on fire. What'll you have to drink, Diet Pepsi?" he asked, looking at Joanna.

She nodded.

"I'll have one of those, too," Carol Strong said. "Wait a minute. She didn't give us menus. I'd better go get one."

"No need. Everybody gets the same thing today," Butch Dixon said. "Turkey, dressing, and all the rest." He went down the bar and returned with the two soft drinks.

"How much does it cost?" Carol asked.

Butch shrugged. "Whatever," he said.

"Whatever?"

Butch waved toward the crowded dining room. "Some of these people won't be able to pay anything at all. No problem. That's the way it is around here. If you can pay, fine. If you can't pay, that's fine, too. Let your conscience be your guide."

He looked up at the television set. "You've got to watch this. The part with the jacket always cracks me up."

The food was delicious. The movie was a scream. Joanna laughed so hard she was almost sick. But during the last few frames when Steve Martin drags a hapless John Candy—his unwanted and yet welcome guest—home for dinner, Joanna found herself with tears in her eyes.

And not just because of John Candy, either. It had something to do with family and with reconciliation and with forgiveness. Something to do with Eleanor Lathrop and Bob Brundage.

"Great dinner," Joanna said to Butch when he came to take their empty dessert plates. She turned to Carol. "I think I'd better go back to the hotel now," Joanna said. "After missing dinner, I probably have a little fence-mending to do."

Carol nodded. "That's probably a good idea. We'll both think about this overnight and then put our heads together tomorrow morning. What do you say?"

"What time?"

"Not before noon," Carol said. "I'm going to need my beauty sleep."

They were headed for the door when Butch called after Joanna. "You haven't seen Dave

Thompson around today, have you? I would have thought he'd be in for dinner by now."

Carol and Joanna exchanged looks. "We'd better tell him," Carol said, turning back.

And so they did.

 **TWENTY-ONE**

IN THE backseat of the Blazer the next morning, Jenny was babbling to Ceci Grijalva. "And so this man comes to see us. It turns out he's my uncle. Grandma Lathrop wants me to call him Uncle Bob, but I'd rather call him Colonel Brundage. Uncles should be someone you know, don't you think?"

"I guess," Ceci mumbled.

Joanna and Jenny had picked Ceci up from her grandparents' no-frills trailer park in Wittmann at ten o'clock on the dot. They were now in the process of driving her back to the Hohokam, where Bob Brundage and Eleanor Lathrop were supposed to join them for an early lunch in the coffee shop before Bob caught a plane back to Washington, D.C.

With Bob running interference, Joanna had almost managed to work her way back into her mother's good graces. Still, she wasn't looking forward to the ordeal of a mandatory lunch. Requiring Joanna's attendance was Eleanor's method of exacting restitution from her daughter for being AWOL from the previous evening's Thanksgiving festivities.

Joanna found it ironic that, with the notable exception of Eleanor, no one else seemed to have missed her at all. Adam York had come to the Hohokam, stayed for dinner, and left again without Joanna ever laying eyes on him, although she had talked to him late that night after they both had returned to their respective hotels. It sounded as though Adam had made the best of the situation. He had spent most of the dinner chatting with Bob Brundage. The two of them had hit it off so well that they had agreed to try to get together for lunch the next time Adam traveled to D.C.

"The company gets to choose what we do," Jenny was earnestly explaining to Cecelia. "Do you want to watch movies or swim?"

"What movies?" Ceci responded. "I can't go swimming because I don't have a suit."

"Yes, you do," Jenny told her. "Grandma Brady brought one along for you. I think it'll fit. And when we get to the hotel, we can choose the movies. What do you like?"

"I don't care," Ceci said. "Anything will be all right."

Driving along, Joanna only half listened to the chattering girls. More than what was being said, she focused on Ceci Grijalva's tone of voice. The lethargic hopelessness of it was heartbreaking. It seemed as though the little girl's childhood had been stretched to the breaking point. At nine years of age, all the playfulness had been ripped out of her.

"Oh, I almost forgot," Jenny continued. "Did you know you were on TV?"

"Me?" Ceci asked. "Really?" For the first time, there was a hint of interest in her voice.

"Yeah, really. You were on the news. Mom has a tape of it. I saw it last night after dinner. We can watch that, too, if you want."

"I've never been on the news before."

"I have a couple of times," Jenny said. "It's kinda neat. At first it is, anyway."

Cecelia Grijalva's eyes were wide as they walked into the lobby. "I've seen this place, but I've never been inside it before."

"Come on," Jenny said. "I'll show you the pool first, and then I'll take you up to the room."

While the girls wandered off for a quick tour of the hotel, Joanna headed back to the room. She felt tired. She'd been awake much of the night, worrying about whether or not Dave Thompson had acted alone. Up in the room, she found the telephone message light blinking. On the voice-mail recording, she heard Lorelie Jessup.

"I just now came home from the hospital," Lorelie said. "Kim brought me here so I could sleep in a bed for a while. From your call this morning, I thought you'd want to know that Leann's doing better, but she's still not able to talk. They've upgraded her condition to serious. I did speak with her doctor. He says that with the kinds of injuries she received, it's unlikely she'll have any recollection of events leading up to what happened. He says short-term memory is usually the first casualty, so I doubt she'll be able to help you. If you need to talk to me, here's my number, but don't call right away. It's ten o'clock. I'm going to bed as soon as I get off the phone."

Relieved that Leann was better, Joanna erased the message and replaced the receiver. But, she knew that the doctor was most likely right. The critical hours both immediately before and after a severe trauma or a skull-fracturing accident can often be wiped out of a victim's memory banks. That meant Leann Jessup would probably be of little or no help in establishing the identity of her attacker.

Jenny's electronic key clicked in the door lock and the girls bustled into the room. Jenny gave Ceci a quick tour of the room and then dragged her back to the television set. "We'll watch the news tape before we go to lunch and *Snow White* after," Jenny said, expertly shoving a tape into the VCR. Clearly, she was enjoying the opportunity to boss the listless Cecelia around. "And we'll go swimming right after lunch."

"You'd better get with it, then," Joanna said. "It's only a few minutes before we're supposed to meet Grandma Lathrop and Colonel Brundage."

As Jenny fooled with the tape, running it backward and forward to find the right spot, Joanna watched Ceci Grijalva closely, worrying about the child's possible reaction to the emotionally wrenching material she was about to see.

"In our lead story tonight," the television anchor said smoothly into the camera, "longtime ASU economics professor Dean R. Norton was arraigned this afternoon, charged with first-degree murder in the slaying of his estranged wife, Rhonda Weaver Norton. Her partially clad body was found near a power-line construction project southwest of Carefree late last week.

"Here's reporter Jill January with the first of two related stories on tonight's newscast. Later on this half hour, Jill will be back with another story concerning a local group determined to do something about the increasing numbers of Valley homicide cases resulting from domestic violence."

The picture on the screen switched to the figure of a young woman standing posed, microphone in hand, on the steps of a building Joanna instantly recognized as the Maricopa County Courthouse. Only when the camera zoomed in for a close-up did she realize the reporter was the same young woman who had thrust a microphone in Joanna's face as she and Leann Jessup were filing out of the MAVEN-sponsored vigil.

The photographed face of a good-looking young woman flashed across the screen. "A month ago, Rhonda Weaver Norton moved out of the upscale home she shared with ASU economics professor Dean Norton," Jill January said. "She moved into a furnished studio apartment in Tempe. At the time, Rhonda told her mother that she feared for her life. She claimed that her husband had threatened to kill her if she went through with plans to leave him."

While what looked like a yearbook head-shot of a balding and smiling middle-aged man filled the screen, the reporter continued talking. "This afternoon, Professor Norton was arraigned in Maricopa County Superior Court, charged with first-degree murder in the bludgeon slaying of his estranged wife. Rhonda Norton had been missing for three days when her badly beaten body was found by a Salt River Project utilities installation crew working on a power line south of Carefree.

"Judge Roseann Blacksmith, citing the gravity of the case, ordered Professor Norton held without bond. Trial was set for February eighteenth.

"Rhonda Norton's mother, well-known Sedona-area pastel artist Lael Weaver Gastone, was in the courtroom today to witness her former son-in-law's arraignment. She expressed the hope that the prosecutor's office would seek either the death penalty or life in prison without possibility of parole.

"At the Maricopa County Courthouse, I'm Jill January reporting."

When the reporter signed off, the picture returned to the studio anchor. "In the past eleven months, sixteen cases of alleged domestic violence have resulted in death. Because the accused is a well-known and widely respected college professor, the Norton homicide case is the most high-profile of all those cases. Later in this newscast, Jill January will take us to a candlelight vigil that is being held on the steps of the capitol building this evening to focus attention on this increasingly difficult issue. In other news tonight . . ."

With lightning fingers running the remote control, Jenny fast-forwarded the video through weather and sports, stopping only when Jill January's smiling face reappeared on the screen.

"The crime of domestic violence is spiraling in Phoenix just as it is in other parts of the country. Domestic violence was once thought to be limited to lower-class households. Increasingly, however, authorities are finding that domestic violence is a crime that crosses all racial and economic lines. Victims and perpetrators alike come from all walks of life and from all educational levels. Often, the violence escalates to the point of serious injury or even death. So far this year, sixteen area women have died as a result of homicidal violence in which the prime suspects have all turned out to be either current or former spouses or domestic partners.

"Tonight a group called MAVEN—Maricopa Anti-Violence Empowerment Network—is doing something to address that problem. At a chilly nighttime rally on the capitol steps in downtown Phoenix this evening, domestic violence activist Matilda Hirales-Steinowitz read the deadly roll."

The tape switched to the podium onstage at the candlelight vigil, where the spokeswoman from MAVEN stepped forward to intone the names of the victims. "The first to die, at three o'clock on the afternoon of January third, was Anna Maria Dominguez, age twenty-six."

Again, the reporter's face appeared on-screen. "Anna Maria Dominguez was childless when she died as a result of a shotgun blast to the face. Her unemployed husband then turned the gun on himself. He died at the scene. She died a short time later after undergoing surgery at a local hospital.

"Often, however, when domestic violence ends in murder, children of the dead women become victims as well."

"Get ready," Jenny warned Cecelia. "Here you come."

Ceci Grijalva's wide-eyed face filled the screen. Her voice, trembling audibly, whispered through the television set's speakers. "I have a little brother . . ." she began.

Joanna turned away from the televised Cecelia to watch the live one. When tears spilled over on the little girl's cheeks, Joanna moved to the couch and placed a comforting arm around Ceci's narrow shoulders.

". . . he cries anyway, and I can't make him stop. That's all," Cecelia finished saying on-screen while the child on the couch sobbed quietly, her whole body quaking under the gentle pressure of Joanna's protective arm.

"They wanted me to say something nice about my mom," Ceci said, her voice choking. "But when I got there, all I could think about was Pepe."

"You did fine," Joanna said.

"Nana Duffy says it's my daddy's fault, that he did it, but I don't think so. Do you?" Ceci looked questioningly up at Joanna through tear-dewed eyelashes. Joanna wanted to comfort the grieving child, but what could she tell her?

Torn between what she knew and what she

could say, "I don't know" was Joanna's only possible answer.

"And now here's my mom," Jenny said.

The camera focused on Joanna and Leann making their way through the crowd.

". . . police officers in attendance," Jill January was saying. "Cochise County Sheriff Joanna Brady."

"Cecelia Grijalva is a friend of my daughter's . . ." Joanna heard herself saying when suddenly Ceci scrambled out from under her arm.

"I know him, too," she said, pointing to a spot on the screen where a man's face had momentarily materialized directly over Leann's shoulder. He was leading a crowd of people filing down the aisle toward the exit.

When first Joanna and then Leann stopped, so did he, but not soon enough. He blundered into Leann, bumping her from behind with such force that he almost knocked her down.

The camera was focused on Joanna in the foreground. Her words were the ones being spoken on tape. Still, the jostling in the crowd behind her was visible as well. As she watched the televised Leann turn around to see what had hit her, Joanna remembered Leann telling her about the incident on their way back to the car after the vigil.

And the glare Leann had mentioned—the one she had said might have been enough to spark a drive-by shooting—was there, captured in the glow of the television lights. Even thirdhand—filtered through camera, videotape, and TV screen—the man's ugly, accusing stare was nothing short of chilling. He and Leann stood eye to eye for only a moment. Then he glanced up and into the camera as though seeing it for the first time. A fraction of a second later, he ducked to one side behind Leann and disappeared into the crowd.

"You know him?" Joanna asked.

Ceci nodded.

"Who is he?"

Ceci shrugged. "One of my mom's friends."

"What's his name?"

"I don't know. She didn't tell me her friends' names."

"Jenny," Joanna said, "would you please run the tape back to that spot and stop it there? I want to look at that sequence again."

Jenny's agile fingers darted knowledgeably over the remote control. Moments later, the man's face reappeared. With his features frozen in place on the television screen, the glower on his face was even more ominous than it had seemed in passing.

"Did you know he was there that night?" Joanna asked.

Ceci shook her head. "No. I didn't see him until just now."

"Were there other people there that you knew?"

"Some," Ceci answered. "There were two teachers from my old school, Mrs. Baker and Mrs. Sandoval. And a man named Mr. Gray from the place where Mom used to work, but he talked to Grandpa, not to me."

"Didn't this friend of your mother's come talk to you?" Joanna asked. "Or to your grandparents?"

Ceci shook her head. "If he did, I didn't see him."

"Okay, Jenny. Let it play again."

As Cecelia's words played back one more time, Joanna closed her eyes momentarily, remembering the vigil, recalling how people had poured up onto the stage after the speeches, how they had gathered in clumps around the various speakers, offering condolences and words of support. Everyone there had come to the vigil with some cause to be angry, but it was only on the face of that one man that the anger had registered full force. Still, if he had felt that strongly about what had happened to Serena, why hadn't he come forward to visit with the dead woman's family?

"Did he come to your house while your mother was alive?"

"A couple of times."

"What kind of car did he drive?"

"Not a car. A truck. A green truck with a camper on it. He brought us an old chair once. He said someone in Sun City was throwing it away because nobody bought it at a garage sale. He said he knew we needed furniture. And sometimes he'd help my mom bring the clothes home from the laundry."

The phone rang just then, and Jenny pounced on it. "It's Grandma," she mouthed silently to Joanna, holding her hand over the mouthpiece as she handed the receiver over to her mother.

"Well," Eleanor Lathrop said huffily to Joanna, "are you coming down to lunch or not? We're already down in the coffee shop. Bob's plane is at two, so he doesn't have all day. Surely you aren't going to stand us up two days in a row, are you?"

"Sorry, Mother," Joanna said. "We were watching something on the VCR. The girls and I will be right there." Joanna put down the phone. "Turn it off, Jenny. We'll have to finish this later. Come on."

Jenny switched off both the TV and VCR. "Have you ever met Grandma Lathrop?" Jenny asked Ceci as they started down the hallway.

"I don't think so," Ceci answered.

"She's a little weird," Jenny warned. "She sounds mad sometimes, even when she isn't."

"Nana Duffy's like that, too," Ceci said.

Walking behind them, Joanna realized that having a thorny grandmother was something else the two little girls had in common.

TWENTY-TWO

HALFWAY ACROSS the Hohokam's coffee shop, Joanna could hear Eleanor. Already in fine form and haranguing as usual, she was reeling off one of her unending litanies to Bob Brundage, who sat, head politely inclined in her direction, providing an attentive and apparently sympathetic audience.

"From the time that man was elected sheriff," Eleanor was saying, "I don't believe we ever again ate on time, not as a family. He was perpetually late. It was always something. I kept roasts warm in the oven until they turned to stone. And now that Joanna's sheriff, it's happening all over."

Hearing Eleanor's familiar whine of complaint, Joanna found herself wondering what had happened to her mother. What had divested her of what must have been freethinking teenage rebelliousness and turned her into an unbending prig? What had happened to that youthful, romantic love between her parents—the forbidden Romeo-and-Juliet affair her long-lost brother had found so captivating? By the time Joanna had any recollection of D. H. and Eleanor Lathrop, they had settled into a state of constant warfare, perpetually wrangling over everything and nothing.

As Joanna and the two girls crossed the room, Bob Brundage stood up to greet them in a gentlemanly fashion. To Joanna's surprise, however, when he came around the table to hold her chair for her, he winked, but only after making sure the gesture was safely concealed from Eleanor's view.

"And you must be Cecelia," he said gravely, helping Ceci into her chair as well. "Jenny was telling me about you last night at dinner. I'm sorry to hear about your mother."

"Thank you," Ceci murmured.

"Marliss Shackleford wants you to call her," Eleanor said sourly to Joanna, sidestepping Bob's polite attention to social niceties. "She wants to talk to you. Something about a picture."

"Oh, no," Joanna said. "I forgot all about that."

"All about what?"

"She asked me for a picture—an eleven-by-fourteen glossy of me. She asked for it just before I left town. She's on the facilities committee at the Women's Club. They need the picture to frame and put up in the department. It's supposed to go in that glass display case at the far end of the lobby along with pictures of all my predecessors."

"But, Mom," Jenny objected, "you don't have a picture like that. All those other guys are standing there wearing their cowboy hats and their guns. And they all look sort of . . . well, mean, even Grandpa Lathrop."

Eleanor shook her head disparagingly. Jenny's observant objection might not have met with Eleanor Lathrop's approval, but to Joanna's way of thinking, it was on the money. The display in question, located at the back of the department's public lobby, featured a rogues' gallery of all the previous sheriffs of Cochise County, who did all happen to be guys.

The photos in question were primarily of the formally posed variety. In most the subject wore western attire complimented by obligatory Stetsons. All of them wore guns, while only one was pictured with his horse. Most of them frowned into the camera, their grim faces looking for all the world as though they were battling terrible cases of indigestion.

Ignoring Eleanor's disapproval, Joanna couldn't resist smiling at Jenny. "The mean look shouldn't be any trouble. I can handle that," Joanna said. "And I've already got a gun. My big problem is finding a suitable horse and a hat."

"You're not taking this seriously enough, Joanna," Eleanor scolded. "You're an important public official now. Your picture ought to be properly displayed right along with all the others. That doesn't mean it has to *be* exactly like all the others. Maybe you could use the same picture that was on your campaign literature. That one's very dignified and also very ladylike. If I were you, I'd give Marliss one of those. And don't let it slide, either. People appreciate it when public servants handle those kinds of details promptly."

With Bob Brundage looking on, Joanna couldn't help smarting under Eleanor's semipublic rebuke. "Marliss only asked me about it in church this last Sunday, Mother," Joanna replied. "I wasn't exactly in a position where I could haul a picture out of my purse and hand it over on the spot. And I've been a little busy ever since then. Besides, I don't know why there's such a rush. They don't make the presentation until the annual Women's Club luncheon at the end of January."

"That's not the point," Eleanor said. "Marliss still needs to talk to you about it, and probably about everything else as well."

"What everything else?" Joanna asked. "The food at the jail?"

"Hardly," Eleanor sniffed. "Obviously, you haven't read today's paper. Your name's splashed all over it as usual. It makes you sound like—"

"Like what?" Joanna asked.

Eleanor frowned. "Never mind," she said.

A folded newspaper lay beside Eleanor's place mat. Jenny reached for it.

"That's great. First Mom's on TV, and now she's in the paper," Jenny gloated. "Can I read it? Please?"

Eleanor covered the paper with her hand, adroitly keeping Jenny from touching it. "Certainly not. You shouldn't be exposed to this kind of thing. It's all about that Jessup woman. It's bad enough for your mother to be mixed up in all this murder business, but then for them to publish things about people's personal bad habits right there in a family newspaper. . . ."

"Oh," Jenny said. "Is that why you don't want me to read it? Because it talks about lesbians? I already knew about that from going to see Mom's friend at the hospital yesterday. Her brother called her a dyke, so I sort of figured it out."

"Jenny!" Eleanor exclaimed, her face going pale. "What language!"

"Well, that's what he said, didn't he, Mom?" Jenny returned defiantly.

"So you know about lesbians then, do you, Jenny?" Bob Brundage asked, gently nudging himself into what had been only a three-way conversation.

" 'Course," Jenny answered offhandedly.

"Did you learn about that from your mom or from school?" he asked, carefully avoiding the icy disapproval stamped on Eleanor Lathrop's face. "Or do the schools in Bisbee have classes in the birds and the bees?"

Knowing Eleanor's attitude toward mealtime discussions of anything remotely off-color, Joanna observed this abrupt turn of conversation in stunned silence. What in the world was Bob Brundage thinking? she wondered. Was he deliberately baiting Eleanor by encouraging such a discussion? But of course, since Bob didn't know Eleanor well, it was possible he had no idea of her zero-tolerance attitude toward nonparlor conversation, as she called it.

On the other hand, maybe he did. As he gazed expectantly at Jenny, awaiting her answer with rapt attention, Joanna caught what seemed to be a twinkle of amusement glinting in his eyes. I'll be, Joanna thought. He's doing it on purpose.

At that precise moment, she made the mistake of taking a tiny sip of water.

"Mom told me some of it," Jenny said seriously. "But we mostly learn about it in school, along with AIDS and all that other icky stuff. Except we don't call it the birds and the bees."

Bob Brundage raised a questioning eyebrow. "You don't? What do you call it, then?"

Jenny sighed. "When it's about men and women, we call it the birds and the bees. But when it's about men and men or women and women, we call it the birds and the birds."

"I see," Bob Brundage said, nodding and smiling.

"Jennifer Ann!" Eleanor gasped, while Joanna choked on the water, sending a very undignified and unladylike spray out of her mouth and nose into a hastily grabbed napkin. When she looked up at last, Bob Brundage winked at her again.

"Such goings-on!" Eleanor said, shaking her head. "And in front of company, too. Jenny, you should be ashamed of yourself." Eleanor picked up the newspaper and handed it over to a still-coughing Joanna. "If you're willing to let your daughter see this kind of filth at her tender age, then you're going to have to be the one to give it to her. I certainly won't be a party to it."

Joanna took the paper and stuffed it into her purse.

"And you'd better decide what you want to order," Eleanor continued. "Bob and I have already made up our minds. We had plenty of time to study the menus before you got here."

Obligingly, Joanna picked up her menu and began looking at it. She held it high enough that it concealed her mouth where the corners of her lips kept curving up into an irrepressible smile.

Bob Brundage may have been a colonel in the United States Army, but he was also an inveterate tease. Even now, while Joanna studied the menu, he managed to elicit another tiny giggle of laughter from Eleanor Lathrop, although the previous flap had barely ended.

To Joanna's surprise, instead of still being angry, Eleanor was smiling and gazing fondly at Bob Brundage. Her doting eyes seemed to caress him, lingering on him as if trying to memorize every feature of his face, every detail of the way he held his coffee cup or moved his hand.

And while Eleanor studied Bob Brundage, Joanna studied her mother. That adoring look seemed to come from someone totally different from the woman Joanna had always known her mother to be. Gazing at her long-lost son, Eleanor seemed softer somehow, more relaxed. With a shock, Joanna realized that Eva Lou Brady had been right all along. Eleanor was different because there *was* a new man in her life. In all their lives.

"What can I get you?" a waitress asked.

How about a little baked crow? Joanna wondered. "I'll have the tuna sandwich on white and a cup of soup," she said. "What kind of soup is it?"

"Turkey noodle," the waitress said. "What else would it be? After all, it is the day after Thanksgiving, isn't it?"

"Yes," Joanna said. "It certainly is."

The remainder of the meal passed uneventfully. When it was over, Joanna said her goodbyes to both Bob Brundage and to her mother while standing in the Hohokam's spacious lobby. "You're sure you don't want to stay another night, Mother?"

"Heavens no. I have to get back home."

Joanna turned to Bob Brundage. They stood looking at one another awkwardly. Neither of them seemed to know what to do or say. Finally, Joanna held out her hand. "It's been nice meeting you," she said.

The words seemed wooden and hopelessly inadequate, but with Eleanor looking on anxiously, it was the best Joanna could do.

"Same here," he returned.

Jenny, unaffected by grown-up awkwardness, suffered no such restraint. When Bob Brundage bent down to her level, she grabbed him around the neck and planted a hearty kiss on his tanned cheek. "I hope you come back to visit again," she said. "I want you to meet Tigger and Sadie."

"We'll see," Bob Brundage said, smiling and ruffling her frizzy hair. "We'll have to see about that."

Back in the room, Ceci and Jenny disappeared into the bathroom to change into bathing suits, while Joanna extracted Eleanor's folded newspaper from her purse. She wasted no time in searching out the article Eleanor Lathrop had forbidden her granddaughter to read:

A Tempe police officer was seriously injured early Thanksgiving morning and a former long-time Chandler area police officer is dead in the aftermath of what investigators are calling a bizarre kidnapping/suicide plot.

After being kidnapped from her dormitory room at the Arizona Police Officers Academy in Peoria, Officer Leann Jessup jumped from a moving vehicle at the intersection of Olive and Grand avenues while attempting to escape from her assailant. A carload of passing teenagers, coming home from a party, narrowly avoided hitting the gravely injured woman when her partially clad body tumbled from a moving pickup and landed on the pavement directly in front of them.

Two of the youths followed the speeding pickup and managed to provide information that led investigators back to the APOA campus itself and to David Willis Thompson, a former Chandler police officer who has been the on-site director of the statewide law enforcement training facility for the past several years.

Thompson's body was discovered on the campus later on yesterday afternoon. He was found in a vehicle inside a closed garage, where he is thought to have committed suicide. Investigation into cause of death is continuing, and an autopsy has been scheduled.

Meantime, Leann Jessup is listed in serious but stable condition at St. Joseph's Hospital, where she underwent surgery yesterday for a skull fracture and where she is being treated for numerous cuts and abrasions.

Thompson, a longtime Chandler police officer, left the force there under a cloud in the aftermath of a serious altercation with his estranged wife in which both she and a female friend were injured.

In this latest incident, the injured woman and Cochise County Sheriff, Joanna Brady, were the only two women enrolled in a class of twenty-five attending this session of the Arizona Police Officers Academy, an interdepartmental training facility that attracts newly hired police officers from jurisdictions all over the state. Sources close to the case say there is some reason to believe that Ms. Brady was also in danger.

Melody Daviddottir, local spokeswoman for the National Lesbian Legal Defense Organization, the group that was instrumental in forcing Thompson's ouster from the Chandler Department of Public Safety, said that it was unfortunate that a man with so many problems could be placed in a position of responsibility where he was likely to encounter lesbian women or women of any kind.

"Dave Thompson left Chandler because, as a danger to women, he was an embarrassment to his chain of command. He could not have gone from disgrace there to directing the APOA program without the full knowledge and complicity of his former superiors," Daviddottir said.

With Thompson now dead, Daviddottir said, her organization is considering filing suit to see to it that those people, whoever they are, should be held accountable for injuries Leann Jessup suffered in the incident with Thompson.

Lorelie Jessup, mother of the injured woman, expressed dismay that her daughter, a lesbian, had been singled out for attack due to her sexual persuasion. "That won't stop her," Mrs. Jessup said. "It might slow her down for a little while, but all Leann ever wanted was to be a police officer. She won't give up."

"How do we look?" Jenny asked, as she and Ceci paraded out of the bathroom in their suits.

"You look fine."

"Grandpa said for us to call when we were ready. He says he'll watch us."

"Good. Go ahead then."

As soon as the girls left the room, Joanna returned to the newspaper. Or at least she intended to, but her eyes stopped on two words in the article's third paragraph: "partially clad." Carol Strong had said that, except for the pair of pantyhose that had been used to bind her hands and feet, Leann Jessup had been nude. Since when did hand and foot restraints qualify as being partially clad? But the words sounded familiar—strangely familiar— and that bothered her.

Putting down the newspaper, Joanna picked the television remote control off the coffee table where Jenny had left it and switched on the VCR. Joanna wasn't nearly as handy with the remote as her daughter was, but after a few minutes of fumbling and running the tape back and forth, she managed to turn the VCR to the very beginning of the taped newscast.

Once again the anchor was saying, ". . . long-time ASU economics professor Dean R. Norton was arraigned this afternoon, charged with first-degree murder in the slaying of his estranged wife, Rhonda Weaver Norton. Her partially clad body was found near a power-line construction project southwest of Carefree late last week."

Thoughtfully, Joanna switched off the tape and rewound it. Then, for several long seconds, she sat staring at the screen with the fuzzy figure of the news anchor poised once more to begin the ten o'clock news broadcast. Even though she no longer had Juanita Grijalva's envelope of clippings, Joanna had studied the articles so thoroughly that she had nearly committed them to memory.

She was almost positive one of the early articles dealing with finding Serena Grijalva's body had made reference to her being "partially clad." Of course, in that case, that particular media euphemism had spared Serena's children from having to endure embarrassing publicity about their dead mother's nakedness. And the words used no doubt reflected the information disseminated to reporters on that case since, according to Detec-

tive Strong, the exact condition of the body—
including the pantyhose restraints—had been one
of her official holdbacks.

Once again Joanna switched on the tape. The
anchor smiled and came back to life. ". . . Rhonda
Weaver Norton. Her partially clad body was found
near a power-line construction project southwest
of Carefree late last week."

Joanna turned off the machine. What did the
words partially clad mean when they were applied
to Rhonda Weaver? Was it possible they meant
the same thing? If Carol Strong had resisted embarrassing two orphaned Hispanic children, what
was the likelihood that another investigator might
do the same thing in order to spare a grieving
mother who was also a well-known, nationally
acclaimed artist?

It was only a vague hunch. Certainly there
was nothing definitive enough about the nig-
gling question in Joanna's head to justify dragging Carol Strong into the discussion. At this
point, the possible connection between this new
case and the others was dubious at best. But if
Joanna could come up with a solid link between
them . . .

Purposefully, Joanna hurried across the room
and retrieved the telephone book from the nightstand drawer. Her experience at the jail on Monday, where she had fought her way up through
the chain of command, had convinced her there
was no point in starting at the bottom. She called
the Maricopa County Sheriff's Department and
asked to speak with the sheriff himself.

"Sheriff Austin is on the other line," the receptionist said. "Can I take a message?"

"This is Sheriff Joanna Brady," Joanna answered. "From Cochise County. If you don't mind, I'll hold."

Wilbur Austin came on the line a few moments later. "Well, hello, Sheriff Brady. Don't believe I've had the pleasure, but I'm sure we'll run into one another at the association meeting in Lake Havasu in February. I hear you've been having all kinds of problems with this session at the APOA. Someone mentioned it today at lunch. I just heard about it this afternoon. It's a damn shame, too. Dave Thompson was a helluva nice guy once upon a time. Went a little haywire, I guess, from the sound of things."

A little *haywire*? Joanna thought. I'll say! But she made no verbal comment. Wilbur Austin's stream-of-consciousness talk button required very little input from anyone else.

"I heard, too, that you visited my jail here the other night. Hope my people gave you whatever assistance you needed. Always glad to oblige a fellow officer of the law. Had a few dealings with poor old Walter McFadden from time to time. . . ."

Austin's voice trailed off into nothing. Joanna waited, letting the awkward silence linger for some time without making any effort to fill it. Her father had taught her that trick.

"If you run into a nonstop talker and you need something from that person," Big Hank Lathrop had advised her once, "just let 'em go ahead and talk until they run out of steam. People like that gab away all the time because they're afraid of the silence that happens if they ever shut the hell up. If you're quiet long enough before you ask somebody like that for something, they'll break their damn necks saying yes."

The heavy silence in the telephone receiver settled in until it was almost thick enough to slice. "What can I do for you, Sheriff Brady?" Wilbur Austin asked finally.

"I'd like to speak to the lead investigator on the Rhonda Weaver Norton homicide," Joanna said.

It worked just the way Big Hank had told his daughter it would, although Austin was cagey. "This wouldn't happen to have any connection with your visit to my jail the other night, would it?" he asked.

"It's too soon to tell," Joanna admitted. "But it might."

"Well, that'll be Detective Sutton," Wilbur Austin said. "Neil Sutton. Hang on for a minute, I'll give you his direct number."

"Thanks," Joanna said.

Moments later, after she dialed the other number, Detective Sutton came on the line.

"Neil Sutton here," he said.

"This is Joanna Brady," she returned. "I'm the new sheriff down in Cochise County. Sheriff Austin told me to give you a call."

"Oh, yeah," Neil Sutton said. "Now that you mention it, I guess I have heard your name. Or maybe I've read it in the newspaper. What can I do for you, Sheriff Brady?"

"I need some information on the Rhonda Weaver Norton murder."

"You might try reading the papers," he suggested, attempting to ditch her in the time-honored fashion of homicide cops everywhere. Longtime detectives usually have a very low regard for meddlesome outsiders who show up asking too many questions about a current pet case.

"Most of what we've got has already turned up there," he added blandly. "There's really not much more I can tell you. Why do you want to know?"

"There may be a connection between that case and another one," Joanna returned, playing coy herself, not wanting to give away too much.

As soon as Joanna shut up, Sutton's tone of casual nonchalance changed to on-point interest. Recognizing Sutton's irritating lack of candor when it surfaced in herself, she wondered if the malady wasn't possibly catching. Maybe she'd picked it up from the other detective over the phone lines.

"What other case?" Sutton asked.

Joanna became even less open. "It's one Carol Strong and I are working on together."

"Carol Strong?" he asked. "You mean that little bitty detective from Peoria?"

Little bitty? Joanna wondered. If Carol Strong had that kind of interdepartmental reputation, things could go one of two ways. Either Sutton held Carol Strong in high enough mutual esteem that he could afford to joke about his pint-sized counterpart, or else he held her in absolute contempt. There would be no middle ground. And based on that, Sutton would either tell Joanna what she needed to know right away, or else he would force her to fight her way through a morass of conflicting interdepartmental channels.

"Yes, that's the one," Joanna agreed reluctantly.

Neil Sutton audibly relaxed on the phone. "Well, sure," he said. "Why didn't you say so in the first place? What is it you two ladies need?"

Joanna took a deep breath. Here she was, a novice and an outsider, about to send up her first little meager hunch in front of a seasoned detective, one whose official turf she was unofficially invading. What if he simply squashed her idea flat, the way Joanna might smash an unsuspecting spider that ventured into her kitchen?

"What was she wearing?" Joanna asked.

"Wearing? Nothing," Sutton answered at once. "Not a stitch."

"Nothing at all?" Joanna asked, dismayed that the answer wasn't what she had hoped it would be. "But I just watched the television report. I'm sure it said 'partially clad.'"

"Oh, that," Sutton replied. "That was just for the papers and for the television cameras. She was wearing a pair of pantyhose all right, but they weren't covering anything useful, if you know what I mean."

Joanna felt her heartbeat quicken in her throat. Maybe her hunch wasn't so far off the mark after all. She tried not to let her voice betray her growing excitement.

"Maybe you'd better tell me exactly what the pantyhose *were* covering," Joanna said.

"Oh, sorry," Neil Sutton responded. "No offense intended. Her husband used her own pantyhose to tie her up. Did a hell of a job of it, too, for a college professor. Must have studied knots back when he was a Boy Scout. He had her bent over backwards with her hands and feet together. Must have left her that way for a long damn time before he killed her. Autopsy showed that at the time of death there was hardly any circulation left in any of her extremities."

Sutton paused for a moment. When Joanna said nothing, he added, "Sorry. I suppose I could have spared you some of the gory details. Any of this sound familiar?"

"It's possible," Joanna said evasively. "We'll have to check it out. Where will you be if I need to get back to you?"

"Right here at my desk," he answered. "I'm way behind on my paper. I won't get out of here any before six or seven."

It was a struggle, but Joanna managed to keep her tone suitably light and casual. "Good," she said. "If any of this checks out, I'll be in touch."

TWENTY-THREE

HEART POUNDING with excitement, Joanna dialed Carol Strong's numbers—both home and office—and ended up reaching voice mail at home and a receptionist at the office.

"What time is she expected?" Joanna asked.

"Detective Strong is scheduled from four to midnight today," the receptionist said. "May I take a message?"

What Joanna had to say wasn't something she wanted to leave in message form, electronic or otherwise. "No," she answered. "I'll call back then."

Disappointed, Joanna put down the phone. It was barely twelve-thirty. That meant it could be as long as three and a half hours before she could reach Carol Strong. If that was the case, what was the most profitable use she could make of the intervening time?

Reaching for pencil and paper, Joanna drew a

series of boxes, to each of which she assigned a name that showed the people involved. Serena and Jorge Grijalva. Rhonda and Dean Norton. Leann Jessup and Dave Thompson. She drew arrows between each of the couples and then studied the paper trying to search for patterns, to see what, if anything, they all had in common.

The use of pantyhose for restraints was the most obvious. In the upper-right-hand corner of the page, she wrote the word "pantyhose."

What else? Both Serena and Rhonda had been bludgeoned to death. No stab wounds. No gunshot wounds. Bludgeoned. Leann Jessup hadn't died, but there were no wounds to indicate the presence of either a knife or a gun. In the corner, she wrote: "Bludgeon (2) ? (1)."

In each case, there had been a plausible suspect who became the immediate focus of the investigation. Both Jorge Grijalva and Professor Dean Norton had a history of domestic violence. So did Dave Thompson, for that matter. That became the third notation: "Domestic violence."

She sat for a long time, studying the notes. And then it came to her, like the second picture emerging from the visual confusion of an optical illusion. With a physical batterer there to serve as the investigative lightning rod in each of the three separate cases, the real killer could possibly blend into the background and disappear while someone else was convicted of committing his murders. Her hand was shaking as she wrote the fourth note: "Handy fall guy."

For the first time, the words *serial murderer*

edged their way into her head. Was that possible? Would a killer be smart enough to target his victims based on the availability of someone else to take the blame?

Lost in thought, Joanna jumped when the phone at her elbow jangled her out of her concentration.

"Joanna," a reproving Marliss Shackleford said crossly into the phone, "your mother told me you'd call me back right away."

Irritated by the interruption, it was all Joanna could do to remain reasonably polite. "I've been a little too busy to worry about that picture, if that's what you're calling about, Marliss. I'll try to take care of it next week, but I'm not making any promises."

"Too busy with the Leann Jessup case?" Marliss asked innocently.

For a guilty moment, Joanna felt as though Marliss, like Jenny, was some kind of mind reader. "You know about that?"

"Certainly. It's in all the papers. And with you up at the APOA during all these goings-on, I was hoping for a comment on the story from you— one with a local connection, of course."

Before Marliss finished making her pitch, Joanna was already shaking her head. "I don't have anything at all to say about that," she answered. "It's not my case."

"But you are involved in it, aren't you? Eleanor told me that you missed Thanksgiving dinner because—"

"It's not my mother's case, either," Joanna said

tersely. "I can't see how anything she would have to say would have any bearing at all on what's been happening."

"Well," Marliss said. "I just wondered about that woman who was injured. Is Leann Jessup a particular friend of yours?"

"Leann and I are classmates," Joanna answered. "We're the only women in that APOA session, so naturally we've become friends."

"But she's, well, you know. . . ."

"She's what?" Joanna asked.

Marliss didn't answer right away. In the long silence that followed Marliss Shackleford's snide but unfinished question, Joanna finally figured out what the reporter was after, what she was implying but didn't have nerve enough to say outright.

Of course, the lesbian issue. Since Leann Jessup was a lesbian and since she and Joanna were friends, did that mean Joanna was a lesbian, too?

Knowing an angry denial would only add fuel to the gossip-mill fire, Joanna struggled momentarily to find a suitable response. She was saved by a timely knock on the door.

"Look, Marliss, someone's here. I've got to go."

Joanna hung up the phone and hurried to the door, where she checked the peephole. Bob Brundage, suitcase in hand, stood outside her door.

"I came by to tell you good-bye in private," he said, when she opened the door and let him in. "Good-bye and thanks. I couldn't very well do that with Eleanor hanging on our every word."

"Thanks?" Joanna repeated. "For what?"

He shrugged. "I can see now that showing up like this was very selfish of me. I was only interested in what I wanted, and I didn't give a whole lot of thought as to how my arrival would impact anyone else—you in particular."

"After all those years of being an only child, I confess finding out about you was a bit of a shock," Joanna admitted. "But it's all right. I don't mind, not really. Was Eleanor what you expected?"

Bob shook his head. "Over the years, I had conjured up a very romantic image of the young woman who gave me away—a cross between Cinderella and Snow White. In a way, I'm sorry to give her up. It's a little like finding out the truth about Santa Claus."

"What do you mean?" Joanna asked.

"I mean the woman I spent a lifetime imagining is very different from the reality. I'd say Eleanor Lathrop was a lot easier to live with as a figment of my imagination than she is as a real live woman who can't seem to resist telling you what to do."

"Oh, that." Joanna laughed. "You noticed?"

He nodded. "How could I help but?"

"She's done it for years," Joanna said. "I'm used to a certain amount of nagging."

Bob Brundage grinned with that impish smile that made him look for all the world like a much younger Big Hank Lathrop. "So am I," Bob said, "but I usually get it from higher-ups and then only at work. You get it all the time. You're very patient with her," he added. "That's why I wanted to thank you—for handling my share of Eleanor Lathrop's nagging all these years—mine and yours as well."

"You're welcome," Joanna said.

This time Bob Brundage was the one who held out his hand. "See you again," he said.

"When?"

He shrugged. "I don't know. The next time I'm out this way on business, I suppose," he said a little wistfully.

"You and your wife could come for Christmas, if you wanted to," Joanna offered. "It'll be our first Christmas without Andy, so I can't make any guarantees of what it'll be like, but I'm sure it'll be okay. I've been told I cook a mean turkey."

Bob looked both hopeful and dubious. "You're sure you wouldn't mind?"

"No," Joanna said. "I wouldn't mind. Besides, we could pull a fast one on Eleanor and not tell her you were coming until you showed up. She loves to pull surprises on everyone else, but she hates it when someone puts one over on her."

"That's worth some thought then, isn't it?" Bob's eyes twinkled. "Marcie and I will talk it over and let you know, but right now I'd better go. Eleanor's waiting downstairs to take me to the plane."

Joanna escorted him as far as the door and then watched as he walked down the hall. "Hey, Bob," she called to him, when he reached the elevator lobby.

He turned and looked back. "What?"

"For a brother," she said, "you're not too bad."

He grinned and waved and disappeared into the elevator. Joanna turned back into the room. Making her way back to the desk, she expected it would be difficult to return to her train of thought after all the interruptions. Instead, the moment she picked up the paper, she was back inside the case as though she had never left it.

Marliss had called in the midst of the words *serial killer.* Coming back to her notes, Joanna knew she was right. It wasn't a matter of guessing. She *knew.* Proving it was something else.

Joanna still wanted to reach Carol, but it was too soon to try again, so she picked up the paper and resumed studying it once more. Assuming her theory was correct—assuming there was only one killer in all this—where was the connection? How did all those people tie together? What was the common link?

Joanna started a new list in the upper-left-hand corner of the paper: "Cops (2)." Divorced? First she wrote down: "3." Then, reconsidering what Lorelie Jessup had said about Leann's breakup with her long-term friend, Joanna Xed out the three and wrote in: "4 of 4."

What else? Joanna stared at the paper for a long time without being able to think of anything more to add. Finally, it hit her: The Roundhouse Bar and Grill. According to Butch Dixon, Serena, Jorge, and Dave Thompson had all been in the Roundhouse the night Serena died. And Joanna herself had taken Leann there. That meant only two people on the list, Rhonda and

Dean Norton, hadn't been there, although they might have.

Dean Norton had been a professor at the ASU West campus, which was just a few miles away on Thunderbird. Maybe he and Rhonda had turned up in the Roundhouse on occasion, along with everybody else. After a moment, Joanna realized that there was one way to find out for sure.

Ejecting Lorelie's tape from the VCR, Joanna dropped it into her purse. She made it as far as the door before she stopped short. She wasn't on duty, but she was working.

One of the lessons Dave Thompson had harped on over and over again in those first few days of instruction was the importance of officer safety. It would have been easy to dismiss the advice of a likely Peeping Tom who was also suspected of attacking Leann Jessup. But now Joanna was living with the growing suspicion that somehow Dave Thompson was also a victim. If that turned out to be the case, maybe his advice merited some attention.

Putting down the purse and unbuttoning her shirt, she slipped the Kevlar vest on over her bra. She had ordered her own custom-made set of soft body armor, but until it arrived, she was stuck wearing Andy's ill-fitting and uncomfortable cast-off vest. By the time she put on a jacket that was roomy enough to cover both the vest and her shoulder-holstered Colt, she felt like a hulking, uniformed football player. In comparison, Carol

Strong's small-of-back holster had disappeared completely, even on her thin, slender frame.

Joanna stopped by the pool long enough to tell Jim Bob and Jenny she was going out for a while; then she drove straight to the Roundhouse. As expected, Butch Dixon was on duty. He brought her a drink without any of his accustomed camaraderie. Only when he set it in front of her did she realize she had screwed up.

If the Roundhouse was a common denominator, that meant so was Butch Dixon. What if he . . .

Joanna took a sip of her drink. "This tastes more like diet Coke than Diet Pepsi."

He grinned and nodded. "Good taste buds. Got some in special, just for you. Ask for it by name. Joanna Brady Private Reserve Diet Coke. If I'm not here, tell Phil it's in the fridge next to my A and W root beer."

It was hard to persist in believing that someone that thoughtful would also be a serial killer. Joanna raised her glass in salute. "Thanks," she said.

"You bet," he said. But then the grin disappeared and Butch shook his head. "I just can't seem to get Dave Thompson out of my head today. He came in here all the time, you know."

Joanna studied Butch's face. "As a matter of fact, I didn't," she said. "Not until last night. Remember the first time I came in here asking about the night Serena Grijalva died? Why didn't you tell me then that Dave Thompson was a regular?"

"I don't recall your asking me that question straight out," Butch returned easily. "Besides, if you had asked, I probably wouldn't have told you. I don't even tell wives and girlfriends who comes and goes around here. Why would I tell anyone else?"

"You don't tell? Why not?"

Dixon smiled. "Client/counselor privilege."

"You're no lawyer, are you?"

Dixon shook his head.

"Since when do bartenders have the protection of client privilege?"

"You're right," he said. "It probably wouldn't hold up in court, but I do try to protect the privacy of my clientele, for business reasons if nothing else. Dave was one of my broken birds. I was hoping that eventually he'd get his head screwed on straight. And he was working on it. That's why this so-called suicide crap doesn't wash. Ol' Dave maybe imbibed a bit more than was good for him . . ."

"A bit?" Joanna questioned, raising an eyebrow.

Butch shrugged. "So okay, maybe a lot more than was good for him. It's bad business for me to run down the drinking habits of some of my very best customers. It doesn't pay. But still, mentally, I'd say Dave was in much better shape in the last few months than he was when he first started coming here. And if he drank too much, at least he was responsible about it. If he was planning to tie one on, he always had me keep his car keys. If

I asked for them, he always handed them over without any argument. Whenever he ended up too smashed to drive, I'd keep his car here overnight and get someone else to drive him back home."

"Did he talk about his wife much?" Joanna asked. "About his ex-wife?"

A curtain seemed to fall over Butch's face. He didn't answer right away. "The man's dead," Butch said finally. "It doesn't seem right for us to be picking him apart when he isn't even buried yet."

"Don't go invoking client/bartender privilege on me again," Joanna said. "Dave Thompson is dead all right, and I'm trying to find out who killed him."

"Hey, barkeep." Three stools down the bar, a grizzled old man raised his glass. "Medic," he said.

Butch hurried away to fill his thirsty customer's drink order. He returned to where Joanna was sitting with a thoughtful expression on his face.

"As in murder?" he asked.

"That's right."

Butch shook his head. "What the hell's going on? First Serena Grijalva and now Dave Thompson. Does someone have a grudge against my customers, or what?"

Joanna reached in her purse and pulled out the videotape. "That's what I was hoping you could tell me. Would you take a look at this and see if there are any other familiar faces on it?"

"You think someone's knocked off more of my customers? If that's the case, before long, I'll be out of business completely," Butch said. But he took the video and slipped the tape into the VCR that sat on the counter behind the bar. "What is it?" he asked as the television set blinked over from an afternoon talk show to the tape.

"The news," Joanna answered. "From Tuesday night."

"Oh, that," he said. "I think I already saw it."

Moments later, the now-familiar face of the studio anchor came on the screen introducing the equally familiar reporter, Jill January. As the taped newscast ran its course, Joanna watched Butch Dixon's face for any sign of recognition. There wasn't any in the first segment. Both Rhonda and Dean Norton's flashed across the screen without any noticeable response from Butch. That changed when Ceci Grijalva's face appeared in the second segment.

"Damn!" he said. "That poor little kid. What's going to happen to her?" Then later, when Joanna's name was mentioned, he looked and nodded. "I'll bet this is the part I saw already."

The taped Joanna Brady was just beginning to answer Jill January's question when Butch Dixon clicked the remote.

"Wait a minute. Let me play that back. I don't want to miss anything."

The action on the screen slipped into reverse. Joanna Brady and Leann Jessup were walking backward up the aisle at the end of the vigil rather than down it.

"Hey, looky there," the old man down the bar exclaimed, squinting up at the television set. "Isn't that there Larry Dysart?"

"Where?" Butch asked.

The old man pointed. "Right there, over that one broad's shoulder. Nope, now he's gone."

Butch grabbed the remote and stopped the action once again. "Where?" he said.

"Right there," the old man said. "Wait'll they get almost up to the camera. See there?"

"I'll be damned," Butch said. "It is him. And he looks like he's all bent out of shape. That sly old devil. He never once said anything about going to the damn vigil. If he had, I would have made arrangements to go along with him."

Joanna felt a sudden clutch in her throat. "What did you say his name was?"

"Larry. Larry Dysart."

"He's a regular here, too? Did he know Serena?"

"Sure." Butch nodded.

"Was he here the night Serena died?"

"I'm pretty sure he was," Butch answered.

"If Larry's a regular, then he knows Dave Thompson as well?"

"As a matter of fact, Larry drove Dave home several times. Larry doesn't drink booze anymore, so I could always ask him to drive somebody home without having to worry about it. He never seemed to mind."

"And what exactly does Larry Dysart do for a living?" Joanna asked. There was a tremble of excitement in her voice, but Butch Dixon didn't seem to notice.

"As little as possible. He's a legal process server. It was a big comedown from what he might have expected, but he never seemed to carry a grudge about it."

Joanna fought to keep her face impassive, the way her poker-playing father had taught her to do. This was important, and she didn't want to blow it. "Carry a grudge about what?" she asked.

"About his mother giving away the family farm," Butch answered. "And I mean that literally. In the old days, his grandfather's farm—the old Hackberry place—was just outside town here, outside Peoria. It was a big place—a whole section of cotton fields. If Larry had been able to talk his mother into selling it back when he wanted her to, he would have made a fortune. Or else she could have held on to it. By now it would be worth that much more. Instead, she and Larry got in some kind of big beef. She ended up giving most of it away."

"Who to?" Joanna asked.

"TTI," Butch answered. "Tommy Tompkins International. Tommy was one of those latter-day Armageddonists who believed that the world was going to end on a certain day at a certain hour. Before that happened, however, his financial world collapsed. He and his two top guys ended up in the slammer for income tax evasion.

"Now that I get thinking about it, I believe the

APOA dormitory is right on the spot where the house used to be. That's where Larry lived with his mother and stepfather back when he was a kid. The stepfather died young, and Larry and his mother went to war with each other. They patched it up for a while after she got sick. Since she was the one who'd donated the land to TTI, she was able to wangle her son a job running security for Tommy back in the high-roller eighties, when he had the whole world on a string. Then everything fell apart. When the dust cleared, the world didn't end as scheduled, Tommy was gone, and the property went into foreclosure. All Larry was left with was a bad taste in his mouth and what he had inherited directly from his grandfather."

"What was that?"

"The old Hackberry house on Monroe."

"Where's that?" Joanna asked. "In downtown Phoenix?"

Butch chuckled. "A different Monroe," he said. "This one's right here in Peoria, only a few blocks from here. Listen," Butch added. "If you want to talk to Larry, it wouldn't be any trouble for me to find him. He was in for lunch a little while ago, so I don't think he's working today. Want me to give him a call and let him know you're looking for him?"

Joanna stood up, dropping two dollars on the bar to pay for her drink and to leave a tip. "No," she said, trying to sound casual. "Don't bother. Could I have that video back, please? I've got some errands to run right now. I'll get in touch with Larry later if I need to."

Butch handed over the tape. "Here you go. Sure I can't talk you into having another?"

Joanna shook her head. "No, thanks, but I'll be back."

"Sure you will," Butch Dixon said, looking disappointed. "You and Arnold Schwarzenegger."

TWENTY-FOUR

ONCE IN the Blazer, Joanna couldn't decide what to do. For one thing, even though she had learned something important, it was all purely circumstantial. And although she might not be entirely clear on what it all meant, she recognized that the connections she had made were a good starting place.

She knew Larry Dysart's name, the color of his eyes, and where he lived—the location at least, if not the exact address. She had established a definite link between the guy who had almost knocked Leann Jessup down at the candlelight vigil and Serena Grijalva. She had also learned that there was a link between Dysart and Dave Thompson—a man who might possibly turn out to be as much victim as he was perpetrator.

Even though Joanna's quick trip to the Roundhouse had garnered a good deal of information, she had failed to accomplish her original purpose—to establish a link between the Round-house and the Nortons. Had she been able to find a connection from them to the Roundhouse, she would have automatically ended up with a con-nection to Dysart as well. Unfortunately, after watching the video, neither Butch Dixon nor his grizzled, permanent-fixture customer had been able to verify such a link with either Rhonda or her husband.

So there are a few holes in my thinking, Jo-anna thought, leaning forward to turn the key in the ignition. But that's why there were real hom-icide cops in the world; why there were detec-tives like Carol Strong who would know exactly what to do with the vague patchwork quilt of in-formation Joanna had managed to assemble. And as soon as it was humanly possible, she would hand what she had over to Carol and let the detective go after it.

At one-thirty, however, it was still too early for that. Four o'clock would be plenty of time to talk to her.

In the meantime, Joanna returned to the hotel to wait and think and to relieve Jim Bob Brady of his baby-sitting responsibilities. She stopped by the pool and was happy to find that the girls were finally out of the water. If they were spending the afternoon up in the room watching videos, it would give Ceci's waterlogged braids time enough to dry out before she had to go back home to Witt-mann.

But when Joanna stopped outside the door to room 810, there was no sound at all coming from inside. And when she opened the door, the room wasn't exactly as she'd left it. There were two wet towels on the bathroom floor in place of the girls' clothing, which was gone. Obviously, Jenny and Ceci had come back to the room long enough to change, but where were they now?

Joanna picked up the phone intending to dial the Bradys' room, but the staccato sound of the dial tone told her she had voice-mail messages—three in all.

The first was from Jim Bob Brady.

"I don't know where you two girls have gone off to," he said. "I thought I told you to stay put. Maybe you're in the bathroom with the shower on or a hair dryer goin'. Anyway, Grandma and I are gonna run across the street to Wal-Mart and do a little Christmas shopping. You girls stick around the room until your mom gets back, Jenny. I haven't had a chance to talk to her today, so I don't know what the plan is for dinner."

A half-formed knot of worry began to grow in the pit of Joanna's stomach. She replayed the message and listened again to Jim Bob saying, "You girls stay around the room . . ." No, there was no mistake. Jim Bob had left the girls in the room and expected them to stay there. So where were they?

The second and third messages were from Carol Strong. Both of those had come in within the last ten minutes and both said Carol would call back later.

Once again, Joanna searched the bathroom,

pulling the shower curtain all the way aside. She expected to find two wringing-wet bathing suits on the floor of the tub, but the tub was dry and empty. So was the sink. The drain plugs were still closed in the exact same way the housekeeper had left them earlier that morning.

Joanna stood in the bathroom, staring at her reflection in the mirror, trying to ward off a rising sense of panic, trying to think what to do. Don't overreact, Joanna told herself firmly. They probably just went back downstairs. Strangely enough, the thought of possible disobedience made Joanna feel better.

Resolutely, she headed downstairs herself. In addition to the pool, the hotel's recreation area boasted a hot tub as well as a sauna. Posted rules indicated that the last two were off limits to unaccompanied children, but that didn't mean Jenny would necessarily regard that as the final word. In her daughter's egocentric, nine-year-old view of the world, what she regarded as unreasonable rules were made to be badly bent if not outright broken.

Jim Bob probably got tired of hanging out at the pool and now Jenny's trying to pull a fast one, Joanna reasoned grimly. Stalking through the recreation facilities, at first Joanna was more angry than worried. As she searched the hot tub and sauna, she rehearsed a carefully phrased dressing down. She couldn't be all that hard on Ceci Grijalva because she was a guest. Most likely she didn't fully understand the rules, but for Jennifer Ann Brady, there could be no such excuse.

Except it turned out the girls weren't anywhere to be found. Not in the hot tub or in the sauna or in the pool itself. Joanna asked everyone she met if they had seen two little girls, one with short curly blond hair and the other with long dark braids. No one had seen them, not for at least an hour. What had started out as a tiny knot of worry in the pit of her stomach turned into a cement block.

Maybe they got hungry, she told herself hopefully, fighting down a rising sense of panic. Maybe Jenny had realized that armed with a room key she might be allowed to sign for food in the coffee shop. Joanna hurried in that direction, rushing along on tiptoe, trying to scan the few busy tables as she approached in hopes of spotting them. But none of the tables was occupied by the two AWOL little girls.

"Mrs. Brady," a man's voice said quietly at her elbow. "Maybe you'd like to come with me."

Joanna looked up, expecting the speaker to be some hotel official who had nabbed Ceci and Jenny in the act of doing something they weren't supposed to be doing. Instead, she found herself staring into the astonishingly impenetrable blue eyes of Larry Dysart.

"What are you doing here?" she demanded.

"Not who are you?" he returned lightly. "That figures. It means you know who I am. Let's go sit down and have a drink—a drink and a little talk."

He took her by the arm and guided her across the lobby. Joanna allowed herself to be led toward the massive fireplace. Larry Dysart directed her to the same chair where she had sat the previous afternoon while she visited with Bob Brundage.

"What about?" she asked.

"About what you want and what I want."

"The only thing I want right now is my daughter."

"I know," Larry Dysart said soothingly. "Of course, you do. Maybe you and I can do a little horse-trading."

A half-drunk cup of coffee was already sitting on the coffee table. Larry signaled a passing cocktail waitress. "The lady will have a diet Coke," he said without bothering to ask.

Joanna's world spun out of control. If Larry Dysart knew all about Joanna's drink of choice, that meant his information could have come from only one source. Butch Dixon, the nice man! Butch Dixon, the feeder of starving multitudes! Butch Dixon, that blabbermouthed son of a bitch!

"What have you done with Jenny and Ceci?" Joanna demanded angrily.

"Shhhhhh," Larry said, casually waving his coffee cup to encompass the rest of the lobby. "You wouldn't want the whole world to hear our little discussion now, would you? It should be public enough so no one can pull anything off the wall, but private enough so no one else hears, don't you think?"

"I don't care if the whole world hears. Where are the girls?" Joanna asked, not bothering to lower her voice. "If you have them, I want you to tell me where they are."

"I won't tell you where they are, not right now. They're safe, at least for the moment. But they won't be forever, not if you insist on being stupid. Lower your damn voice!"

Gripping the end of the armrests, Joanna forced her breath out slowly. When she spoke again, her voice was a bare whisper. "What is it you want?"

"That's more like it," Larry said.

Joanna stared back at him. Years of battling with Eleanor had taught her the futility of raised voices. What Larry most likely misread as terrified compliance was, on her part, nothing more or less than self-contained fury.

"I want you and Carol Strong off my back," he said easily. "I want to leave town. I want things to go the way they would have gone if you hadn't come around sticking your nose into things that were none of your concern."

"What things?" Joanna asked, willing her face to remain impassive.

Larry looked at her and didn't answer. His lips smiled; his eyes didn't. There was no relationship between his eyes and mouth. It was easy to imagine that the two curving lips and the implacable eyes belonged to two entirely separate faces. The effect was disconcerting, but Joanna didn't look away.

"You mean like letting Jorge Grijalva's plea bargain go through?" she asked. "You mean like letting Dean Norton go to prison for a crime he didn't commit? And as for Dave Thompson . . ."

In answer, Larry let his glance shift briefly

from her to his watch. "I want you to call Carol Strong."

"It's too early. She isn't due into the office until four."

"Call her anyway. Have them find her. And when you reach her, tell her we need to talk. Tell her I have the girls."

Hearing him say the words aloud, Joanna's heart skipped a beat. "How do I know that you—"

Before Joanna could finish framing the sentence, Dysart reached down beside his chair, picked up one of the Hohokam's plastic laundry bags. He tossed it into her lap. There was something wet and heavy in the bottom of the bag. The weight of it sickened her. Afraid of what warped trophy might be inside, Joanna didn't want to look. And yet, she had to.

Stomach heaving, she finally peered inside. Jenny's still-wet bathing suit lay in a soggy pink wad at the bottom of the bag. Larry Dysart had told Joanna that he had the girls, but visible confirmation more than words brought the horrifying reality of it home to her.

Larry Dysart really *did* have Jenny. And Ceci, too. The awful realization rocked Joanna to her very core. The lunchtime bowl of turkey noodle soup curdled in her stomach.

"Where *are* they?" she asked, fighting to keep her voice steady.

"Like I said, they're safe enough for right now," Larry told her. "Where they are doesn't really matter. What does matter is whether or not you're going to do as you're told. Go call Carol Strong. Now. Use the pay phone over there by the elevators so I can see you the whole time. Don't try anything funny. And remember, if anything happens to me, the girls die. You do have her number, don't you?"

Nodding woodenly, Joanna stood up. She walked across the room feeling like she was balancing on a tightrope hundreds of feet above the ground—a tightrope with no safety net. A monster chess-master held Jenny's life in his hands and he was using her as a sacrificial pawn. Carol Strong would never agree to a deal. She couldn't possibly. But with Jenny's and Cecelia's very survival hanging in the balance . . .

It took forever for Joanna to fumble a quarter out of her purse. Then, when she tried to put it in the coin slot, her hand trembled so badly, it was all she could do to make it work. And even after she finally heard the buzz of the dial tone, she could hardly force her fingers to do the dialing.

"Detective Strong, please," Joanna said. At least her throat and voice still worked. That in itself seemed amazing.

Expecting to be told Carol wouldn't be in until after four, Joanna was surprised when the clerk said, "Who's calling, please?"

"Joanna Brady," she answered. "Sheriff Joanna Brady."

Carol Strong came on the line a moment later. "Thank God it's you," she said breathlessly. "I've been calling your room every five minutes. I didn't want to leave a message on the voice mail for fear Jenny, not you, might pick it up. I think we've got him, Joanna. I should have figured it out lots sooner than this. I mean it was right there in front of me all along, but until I talked to Serena's attorney just now—"

"Larry Dysart has Jenny," Joanna interrupted. "Jenny and Ceci Grijalva both. He told me to call you and tell you he wants a deal."

Carol stopped abruptly. "You know about Larry Dysart?" she asked. "You say he has Jenny?"

"Yes."

"Damn! What kind of a deal is he looking for?"

"He says he wants to leave town with no repercussions. He wants us to let him go."

"Where are you?" Carol asked.

"At the hotel. In the lobby. We're sitting right in front of the fireplace."

"I can be there in five minutes. I'll call in the Special Ops boys—"

"A SWAT team?" Joanna almost screeched into the phone. "No way! Are you crazy? The hotel is full of people. Someone would get hurt. Not only that, he says that if anything happens to him, the girls will die."

"He's bluffing." Carol Strong's answer was firm and brisk, but that was easy for her. It wasn't Carol Strong's daughter who was missing.

"Carol," Joanna insisted. "Listen to me. He's got the girls. This isn't a bluff!"

There was a long pause. "Get a grip, Joanna," Carol ordered.

"Get a grip?" Joanna echoed. "What the hell do you mean, 'get a grip'?"

"I mean stop thinking like a mother and start thinking like a cop. What if it's already too late? What if he *is* bluffing and the girls are already dead?"

The stark words hit Joanna with the force of a smashing fist to the gut. The sheer pain of it almost doubled her over. Nausea rose in her throat. She fought it down, but somehow the terrible shock of hearing those words vaporized her rising sense of panic.

"What do you want me to do?" she asked finally.

"Tell Dysart I'll deal," Carol continued. "While I'm arranging backup, you open negotiations. Ask him what he wants. Try to keep him talking."

Leaving the phone dangling off hook, Joanna walked back across the room. It was only then that she realized that the Thanksgiving pumpkins were all gone. She saw the poinsettia- and Christmas-tree-decorated lobby for the first time. And, although the spacious lobby wasn't crowded, there were still far more people there than she had noticed earlier.

Near the desk, a harried young couple tried to check in while riding herd on two active toddlers and a cartful of luggage. A silver-haired, knickers-clad golf foursome stood just inside the lobby door, noisily rehashing the day's golf game. On the other side of the bank of elevators, teenage organizers from a church youth group were setting up registration tables for a weekend conference. All of the people in the room—hotel employees and guests alike—were going about their business with no idea of the life-and-death drama playing itself out in their midst. And of all of them, only Joanna Brady was wearing a Kevlar vest.

She straightened her shoulders as she approached the fireplace. "Detective Strong says she'll deal. She wants to know what you want."

Larry nodded and once again smiled his chilly, humorless smile. "That's more like it. Tell her—"

"Yoohoo, Joanna," Jim Bob Brady's hearty voice boomed from across the room near the hotel entrance. "We're back."

With sinking heart, Joanna watched as the Bradys, arms laden with bags of merchandise, marched purposefully across the lobby.

"Get rid of them," Larry Dysart whispered urgently. "I don't want them here."

"Did you have a good time shopping?" Joanna asked, turning a phony smile on her in-laws.

The phoniness of her smile didn't seem to faze Eva Lou, who sank gratefully into a nearby chair and kicked off her shoes. "My feet hurt like mad," she announced. "That place was crazy. I didn't think we'd ever get checked out."

"This is Larry Dysart," Joanna said lightly, while briskly rubbing her earlobe with the thumb and forefinger of her right hand. "He's an old navy friend of Andy's. These are Andy's folks, Jim Bob and Eva Lou Brady."

During the election, Joanna and Jim Bob had gone out doorbelling together. On a quiet street in Willcox, while Jim Bob went to the house next door, Joanna had rung the bell of a modest bungalow. The man who answered the door had seemed fine at first, but when he discovered Joanna was a candidate for the office of sheriff, he had started telling her a long, complicated story about how his neighbors on either side were really Russian spies who were planning to kill the President and overthrow the government.

Realizing the man was somewhat disturbed, Joanna had tried to drop off her literature and leave. At the prospect of her walking away, however, the man had become highly agitated. Jim Bob had gone on to two more houses before he realized Joanna was still stuck at the first one. He had come back to retrieve her. Between the two of them, Jim Bob and Joanna had effected a reasonably graceful exit.

From then on, however, a rubbed earlobe had meant that whoever Joanna was involved with at the time was trouble in one way or another. In addition to the tugged earlobe, both the Bradys and Joanna knew that Andy had served a two-year hitch in the army—not the navy.

"Is that so?" Jim Bob put down his packages and then offered a hand to Larry Dysart in greeting. "Did you say navy? Glad to meet you, Larry," Jim Bob said, then the old man turned and focused his eyes on Joanna's face.

A dismayed Eva Lou looked back and forth between them, but she was familiar enough with the Willcox story to say nothing and follow her husband's lead.

"And what did you do in the navy?" Jim Bob

asked cordially, sitting down and leaning back as if settling in for a genial chat. "Andy was involved in communications."

"Me, too," Larry said. "That's how Andy and I met."

The lie seemed to come easily. He played along, all the while looking daggers at Joanna with the same hard-edged stare he had used on Leann Jessup at the end of the candlelight vigil.

"Anyone care for a drink?" a cocktail waitress asked.

"Sure," Jim Bob said. "If you don't mind, the wife and I will join you. We'll both have coffee, black."

"You'd better get back to your friend on the phone," Larry said. "She'll think you've forgotten all about her. Tell her to come here and we'll talk."

Joanna walked back to the phone. "What took you so long?" Carol demanded.

"My in-laws showed up. They're sitting there chatting with us. They've ordered coffee."

"Get rid of them," Carol said, repeating verbatim the same thing Larry had said. "I've called for backup. The SWAT team is gearing up, but it'll take a little while to get everybody in place. They'll take up strategic positions outside the hotel. Cars should be on the scene within two minutes. I told them no lights, no sirens. Nobody's to try going inside until I give the word, and I'm leaving my office now. Can you tell if he's armed?"

"I don't know. I can't tell for sure, but most likely."

"That's my guess, too. Are you?"

"Yes."

"Good girl. Hang in there, Joanna. Believe me, everybody here's on top of this thing. We're getting a search warrant for both his house and vehicle. And don't worry. No matter what happens, we'll find those girls."

"You'd better," Joanna said, but it was a hollow threat, fueled by desperation and hopelessness and nothing else.

TWENTY-FIVE

JOANNA HUNG up the phone and started back toward the congenial-looking group gathered in front of the poinsettia-banked fireplace. As she walked, the physical weight of the Colt under her jacket was almost as heavy as the terrible weight of responsibility pressing against her heart.

This time it was no dream. Wide awake now, she was back in her worst shoot/don't shoot nightmare—with Jenny in danger and with people she loved sitting directly in the line of fire. Carol Strong and her backup officers were riding to the rescue, but none of them knew this lobby layout as well as Joanna did. And if Dysart caught a glimpse of cops taking up positions outside, he might turn a gaily decorated hotel lobby into a killing zone.

While Joanna had been on the phone, a school bus had pulled up outside the hotel entrance. Now with whoops of laughter, a crowd of thirty or so teenagers, all of them carrying luggage, swarmed into the lobby. At the sight of all those kids, something came together in Joanna's heart—an urgency and a determination that hadn't been there before. As a police officer and as a parent, she had a moral obligation to do something to prevent a gun battle from erupting in a room packed with other people's innocent children. Ready or not, the way to do that was to stop the battle before it ever had a chance to start.

Joanna was almost back at her chair when the cocktail waitress arrived carrying cups, saucers, and a pot of coffee on a tray. Seeing an opening, Joanna paused, letting the waitress step in front of her.

"Carol's coming," she said to Larry, carefully establishing and maintaining eye contact with him as she continued forward. "She'll be here in just a few minutes."

As Joanna stepped around the waitress, she reached out and snagged the coffeepot's handle. With one smooth movement, Joanna shoved the waitress out of the way and sent the glass coffeepot and its steaming contents hurtling past Jim Bob's startled face. It landed, upside down, in Larry Dysart's lap.

He screamed and lurched to his feet, shattering the pot as well as his cup and saucer into a thousand pieces on the brass-and-glass coffee table in front of him. While Joanna fought the Colt out of its holster, Jim Bob sprang to his feet as well. The older man made a flying tackle, grabbing for Larry's knees. Leaping almost three feet straight up in the air, Larry managed to dodge out of the way.

"Stop or I'll shoot," Joanna ordered.

Instead of stopping, Larry sidestepped both Jim Bob and the chair. As the waitress scrambled to her knees, he grabbed her arm and yanked her toward him. With his forearm angled across her throat, he pinned the struggling woman to his chest, using her as a living shield between his body and Joanna's deadly Colt.

Behind them in the lobby, horrified hotel customers started to scream. "Oh, my God," someone wailed. "She's got a gun. Somebody call the cops."

"I am a cop," Joanna shouted over her shoulder, but without taking her eyes off Larry. "Everybody down." To Larry Dysart, she said, "Let her go!"

"You bitch," he snarled back, his face distorted with unreasoning rage. "You goddamned, interfering bitch!"

Pressing his forearm against the terrified waitress's throat, he held her captive against his chest while his other hand sought to retrieve something from his jacket pocket.

"Watch it, Joanna," Jim Bob warned. "He's going for a gun."

Then, disregarding any possible danger to himself from Joanna's drawn Colt, Jim Bob rose to his knees and lunged at Dysart a second time. Because the second tackle was launched from below waist level, Dysart never saw it coming. Jim Bob's unexpected weight pounded into the waitress's wildly flailing knees. In what seemed like slow motion, Dysart toppled over backward toward the fireplace, pulling the struggling waitress and Jim Bob with him.

All three of them hit the floor in a writhing heap of arms and legs. Before the tackle, Dysart must have managed to pull his handgun—a small-caliber pistol—loose from his pocket. The force of Jim Bob's blow knocked it from his grip. The revolver clattered to the floor and then came skidding past Joanna's feet, spinning across the polished surface like a deadly Christmas top. Joanna turned and knelt to retrieve it. By the time she regained her feet, Larry Dysart had rolled behind Eva Lou's chair. When she saw him again, he was on his feet and halfway across the room, sprinting toward the door to the pool area.

The lobby erupted in a chorus of yells and shouts. A woman's high-pitched scream rent the air. Joanna barely heard it. She paused only long enough to press Larry Dysart's .22 into Jim Bob's hand, then she raced after the fleeing man. By the time she threw open the gate to the wrought-iron fence to the pool, Dysart was already beyond the deep end, pushing his way past a startled gardener and scrambling over the six-foot stucco wall that separated the pool from the hotel's back parking lot.

With the gardener standing right there, Joanna couldn't risk a shot. She was enough of a marksman that she probably could have hit Dysart, even from that distance, but what if the terrified gardener dodged into the bullet rather than away from it?

The sore muscles she had strained during physical training earlier in the week screamed in protest as she pounded down the pool deck after him. When she reached the wall, she found it was too high for her to pull herself up.

Holstering the semiautomatic, she turned to the gardener for help. "I need a boost."

Without a word, the man knelt down in his freshly planted petunias and folded his hands together, turning them into a stirrup. His strong-armed assist raised Joanna high enough to pull herself up onto the wall. She dropped heavily onto the other side, hitting the ground rolling, the way she'd been taught. Even so, the graceless landing knocked the breath out of her. Gasping for air, she scrambled to her feet just as Larry Dysart disappeared behind a huge commercial garbage bin.

Hoping for help, Joanna looked around. There were no cop cars anywhere in sight. If Carol Strong's reinforcements were on the scene, where the hell were they? But Joanna knew the answer to that. Based on what she had told Carol about where they were, the cops were focused on the front of the building—on the lobby not on the loading dock.

Fueled by adrenaline, Joanna took off after Dysart. She stopped at the corner of the building long enough to reconnoiter. Peering carefully around the stuccoed wall, she caught sight of him and knew that his back was toward her before she stepped into the clear. Instead of waiting for her in ambush, Larry Dysart was still running.

Joanna ran, too. Past the back of the kitchen

where a cook and a dishwasher stood having a companionable smoke; past the open door of the overheated laundry with its heavy, damp air warmed with the homey smell of freshly drying linens. Halfway down that side of the building, Dysart veered sharply to the left and headed for Grand Avenue. Half a second later, Joanna saw why. An empty cop car, doors ajar, sat parked at the front corner of the building. The reinforcements had arrived, all right, but they had been sucked into the lobby by the panicked uproar there.

Realizing she was on her own, Joanna despaired. Dysart was headed for the street. She was running flat out behind him. Even so, she was still losing ground.

This way, Joanna wanted to shout to the invisible cops in the lobby. Come out and look this way.

But there wasn't yet enough air in her tortured lungs to permit yelling and running at the same time. And there was no one to hear her if she had. Instead, straining every muscle, she raced after him.

Dysart burst through a small landscaped area that bordered on Grand Avenue and then paused uncertainly on the shoulder of the road. A moment later, he darted out into traffic. Horns honked. Brakes squealed. Somehow he dodged several lanes of oncoming traffic. Making it safely to the other side, he disappeared down an embankment.

Joanna, too, paused at the side of the road. She

looked both ways, across six lanes of traffic. Then, taking advantage of a momentary lull in vehicles, she too plunged across Grand. Halfway to the other side, she heard the unmistakable rumble of an approaching train.

Her heart sank. By then, Dysart had gained so much ground that if he managed to cross the tracks just ahead of the train, he might be able to disappear behind the seventy-five or so freight cars in the train before Joanna or anyone else would be able to come after him.

When she finally reached the far shoulder of Grand Avenue, Joanna looked down in time to see Larry Dysart climbing over the barbed-wire-topped chain-link fence that separated railroad right-of-way from highway right-of-way.

"Stop or I'll shoot." She screamed the warning over the roar of the approaching train. And he must have heard her, because he turned to look. But he kept on climbing. And when he hit the ground, he kept on running, straight toward the tracks, less than fifty yards ahead of the rumbling southbound train.

He was out in the open now, with nothing but open air between him and Joanna's Colt 2000. She dropped to her knees and held the semiautomatic with both hands. A body shot would have been far easier. His broad back would have offered a far larger target, but she didn't want to risk a body shot. That might kill him. Instead, she aimed for his legs, for the pumping knees that were carrying him closer and closer to the track.

Joanna's first shot exploded in a cloud of dirt

just ahead of him. It had no visible effect on Dysart other than making him run even faster. Gritting her teeth, Joanna squeezed off a second round and then a third. The fourth shot found its mark. Larry Dysart rose slightly in the air, like a runner clearing a curb. When he came back down, his shattered leg crumpled under him. He pitched forward on his face.

Giddy with relief and triumph, Joanna stumbled down the rocky incline from the roadway. By then the train was bearing down on the injured man. She had him. All she had to do now was wait for help. With a broken leg, he'd never be able to cross the tracks before the train reached him. And even if he did, the leg would slow him down enough that someone would be able to catch up with him.

"Hold it!" she yelled, running toward the fence with her Colt still raised. "Hold it right there!"

He must have heard that, too. He raised up on both elbows long enough to look back at her, then he started crawling toward the track, dragging the damaged leg behind him. By the time Joanna realized his intentions, there was nothing she could do.

"Stop!" she screamed. "Please! Don't do it."

But without a backward glance, Larry Dysart threw himself under the iron wheels of the moving train. He disappeared from sight while behind him a single severed foot and shoe flew high in the air. Spewing blood, it landed in the dirt thirty feet from the tracks.

Joanna stopped and stared in utter horror and

disbelief at the place where he had disappeared. The train rumbled on and on, not even slowing. By then the lead engine had almost reached the next crossing. Totally unaware of the terrible carnage behind him, the engineer sounded his whistle.

To Joanna's ear, that terrible screech sounded like the gates of hell swinging open to swallow her alive. She dropped to her knees. "Please, God," she prayed. "Don't let him be dead."

But of course, he was.

Moments later, before the last car clattered by, Joanna felt a steadying hand on her shoulder. "Are you all right?" Carol Strong asked.

Joanna nodded. "But . . ."

"I know," Carol said. "I saw it happen. Let me have your weapon. You'll get it back after the investigation."

Without a word Joanna handed over the Colt. Carol helped her up. "Stay here," she ordered. Joanna nodded numbly and made no effort to follow when Carol walked away.

Standing there alone, Joanna dusted off the knees of her pants. She didn't look at the track. Whatever was left of Larry Dysart, she didn't need to see it. Behind her, she heard sirens as emergency vehicles left the hotel and screamed across the intersection to reach the northbound lanes of Grand Avenue. They pulled up on the shoulder, lights flashing, feet thumping on the dirt as a group of uniformed officers followed by an intent aid crew jogged down the embankment. They came to an abrupt stop when they reached the spot by the fence where Joanna was standing.

While the emergency crew milled around her, Joanna was only vaguely aware of them. Larry Dysart was dead. By his own hand. Crushed to pieces beneath the iron wheels of an onrushing train.

All Joanna Brady could hear right then, in both her head and her heart, was his voice—his chilling, humorless voice—saying the awful words over and over, repeating them again and again like a horrific broken record.

"If anything happens to me, the girls will die . . . the girls will die . . . the girls will die."

A uniformed man appeared at Joanna's side. "Are you all right?" he asked.

She neither heard nor comprehended the question until the second time he asked. Only then did she realize that he was a medic worried about her condition.

"I'm fine," she said, brushing him aside. "I'm okay. I'm okay."

"No, you're not," Carol said, coming back to Joanna. "Come on. I'll get you a ride back to the hotel. We'll have officers there for the next several hours taking statements, yours included. And I'll—"

"What are you going to do?" Joanna asked.

"As soon as I get you back to the hotel, I'm going to go search Dysart's house on Monroe," Carol Strong answered. "Somebody should have the search warrant in hand by now. I told Detective Hansen I'd meet him there. And I've already called for Search and Rescue. They'll be bringing dogs. When I go, I'll need to take along something that belongs to Jenny, and to Ceci, too, if you have anything available."

Barely aware of her legs moving, Joanna allowed herself to be led to a patrol car and driven back to the hotel. Blindly, she made her way through the lobby without even pausing long enough to talk to Jim Bob and Eva Lou. In the room on the eighth floor, it was easy for Joanna to find something of Jenny's—her well-worn denim jacket. But once the piece of faded but precious material was in Joanna's hand, it was almost impossible for her to hand it over to Carol Strong. After that, a careful search of the room revealed absolutely nothing that belonged to Ceci Grijalva.

"That's all right," Carol said. "We'll make do with the jacket for right now. I'll send someone out to Wittmann to pick up something of Ceci's from her grandparents' house."

"I should do that," Joanna said. "If anyone goes to talk to the Duffys, it should be me. After all, I'm the one who picked her up this morning. They entrusted her to my care."

"You're not going anywhere," Carol Strong returned. "I'll send an officer out to notify them. You're going to go back down to the lobby and give your statement to the sergeant I've left in charge. That way you'll be right here so I can find you at a moment's notice once we locate the girls."

Joanna could see there was no sense in arguing. "All right," she agreed reluctantly. "All right."

At Carol's insistence, Joanna returned to the lobby. She had no idea how many officers worked for the Peoria Police Department, but the place was alive with cops, both in and out of uniform. A young uniformed officer was huddled with Jim Bob and Eva Lou Brady. A plainclothes detective was questioning the waitress.

While Carol consulted with her sergeant, Joanna went over to the lobby bar and sat down. "What can I get you?" the bartender asked solicitously.

"A glass of water, please," Joanna said. "That's all I want."

Carol came back. "I've told the sergeant where you are," she said. "As soon as someone is ready to talk to you, he'll send them here."

Joanna nodded. "Thanks," she said.

"Can you tell me anything Dysart said that might help us know where to look?"

Joanna shook her head. "Just that if anything happened to him, the girls would die. As though he had rigged some kind of timer or maybe left them with someone else."

"Okay." Carol nodded. "We'll go to work."

She left then. Desolate, Joanna sat at the bar. Jim Bob stopped by when the officer finished questioning him. "Are you all right?" he asked.

Joanna nodded. "How about you?"

"I'm all right. Eva Lou went up to lay down. She was feelin' a trifle light-headed. As for me,

I'm just all bent out of shape that I'm not as young as I used to be," he said disconsolately. "If I'da been ten years younger, he wouldn't of made it past me."

"It was a good try," Joanna said. "It was a very good try."

"We'll be up in the room," Jim Bob said. "You let us know if you need anything."

"Right," Joanna said.

An hour and a half later, Joanna had finished giving her statement to both a Peoria police officer named Sergeant Rodriquez and a female FBI agent named LaDonna Bright. She was still sitting at the bar and still sipping her water when Butch Dixon sauntered into the room. Uninvited, he hoisted himself up on the stool beside her.

"I heard," he said. "When it comes to bad news, Peoria's still a very small town."

"What the hell are you doing here?" Joanna asked. "Go away. Leave me alone."

"Wait a minute," Butch said. "The last thing I knew, you and I were pals. You came into my place and had a drink. Now you're treating me like I have a communicable disease."

"You *are* a communicable disease," Joanna returned pointedly. "I don't know what you had to do with all this, but—"

"Me?" he asked. "What makes you think I had anything at all to do with anything?"

"Larry Dysart walks in here, he takes my daughter God knows where, and then the next thing I know, he's buying me a drink. 'Diet Coke,' he says. 'The lady will have a diet Coke.' Where would he have picked that up, if not from you?"

"Sure he got it from me," Butch Dixon said. "So what?"

"Why were you talking to him about me?"

"Damn Larry Dysart anyway. Why shouldn't I talk about you?" Butch returned. "Pretty girl walks into my bar and walks right back out again with my heart on her sleeve. I've been doing what any red-blooded American male would do— bragging like crazy. Telling everybody who'll hold still long enough to listen all about her. You think I put in private reserve drinks for everybody?" He sounded highly offended.

Joanna looked at him as though she couldn't quite decipher what he was saying. "You mean you were talking about me to him because you like me?"

"What else?" Butch exploded. "What's not to like? Now, are you going to tell me what's happening with Jenny, or not?"

And so she told him. In the middle of telling the story, the phone at the end of the bar rang. Joanna held her breath when the bartender said the call was for her.

"Yes?" she said hopefully, when she heard Carol Strong's voice.

"Nothing so far," Carol answered. "We've gone over the whole house. The dogs are out searching the yard right now. We haven't found his car yet, but we're looking."

Joanna took a deep breath and let the words

soak in. "I've got to know, Carol. You told me on the phone that you had him. What did you mean?"

"I talked to Serena's attorney. I was reading over that thing Butch Dixon wrote for you, the part about Serena's attorney swearing out a restraining order. Madeline Bellerman is a junior attorney for a very big-time firm here in Peoria—Howard, Howard and Rock. For the first time, I found myself asking how Serena Grijalva came to have such a gold-plated attorney representing her in the no-contact-order department. It's Thanksgiving weekend, and I had to track Madeline down at a ski lodge in Lake Tahoe. Larry Dysart was a process server. He did some work for Madeline. He talked her into doing Serena's restraining order on a *pro bono* basis. Turns out he also served divorce papers on Dean Norton."

Carol paused for breath. "I finally figured it out. He only targeted women for murder when he thought he could get away with it because—"

"Because there was someone else to blame," Joanna finished.

"I'm sorry to say," Carol Strong added, "he sucked me right in."

When Joanna put down the phone, Butch Dixon was anxiously watching her face. "Anything?" he asked.

"Not yet," she returned.

Joanna resumed her seat on the stool. By then Butch had ordered her a diet Coke, which she accepted with good grace. With Jenny in danger, Joanna was surprised she could drink a soda or sit still or even talk. It was as though she existed—living and breathing—in a little vacuum of normalcy, one that Butch Dixon somehow helped make possible.

When she came back from the telephone, he didn't say anything for a long time. He seemed to be lost in thought. "While you were gone," he said, "I was sitting here thinking. I just remembered something. Larry Dysart didn't stop drinking booze until just a few months ago. And sometimes, when he used to be on the sauce, he'd get off on a big nonstop talking kick. One time he was telling me about what a crazy bastard old Tommy Tompkins was. I always figured that was the pot calling the kettle black.

"But anyway, he was talking about this bomb shelter Tommy used to have. It was supposed to be a big secret, because when Armageddon came, Tommy didn't want too many people knowing about it. I'll bet it's still there. You don't suppose . . ."

Joanna was already on her way to track down Sergeant Rodriquez. "Get hold of Detective Strong," Joanna told him. "Tell her they're looking in the wrong place."

Moments later, the phone rang at the end of the bar. Joanna answered it herself.

"Where?" was Carol Strong's one-word question.

"Somewhere on the APOA campus," Joanna answered. "My best guess is you're looking for a bomb shelter."

TWENTY-SIX

IT WAS almost 8 P.M. when the Search and Rescue dogs picked up a trail that led to a manhole just off the railroad right-of-way. The manhole was labeled UTILITIES, with no specification as to what kind of utilities might be involved. Inside were conduit runs and circuit-breaker boxes—all of which proved to be dummies.

The girls' trail led down the ladder and through a concrete tunnel to what was, ostensibly, a dead end. Carol Strong had Butch Dixon and Joanna brought to the scene while a lock technician tried to solve the problem of how the trail the dogs had followed down the tunnel could pass through what appeared to be a solid concrete wall.

"They're in there," Carol told an anxious Joanna once she was standing near the head of the line of people at the far end of the tunnel. "I don't know if they're both there, and I don't know if they're all right," Carol continued. "All I do know for sure is that when we tap on the wall, some-body taps back."

Joanna felt her knees go weak with relief, but it was another half hour before the locksmith discovered the release mechanism. With a creak-ing groan, the seemingly massive wall slid aside, moving smoothly on well-oiled rollers. At once, seven separate flashlights probed the darkness beyond the opening.

Jennifer Brady, wearing the same clothes she had worn that morning, stood illumined in the glow of lights, both hands on her hips. Blinking in the sudden glare, she tumbled out of the dark-ness with Ceci Grijalva right on her heels. Tears of joy coursed down Joanna's face as she gath-ered both girls into her arms.

After enduring her mother's fierce hug for as long as she was willing, Jenny pushed away. "Mommy," she said accusingly. "It was dark in there. What took you so long?"

A jubilant Butch Dixon let out a yip that was a cross between a rodeo rider's triumphant *Yippee* and a fairly respectable imitation of a coyote's yip.

"Who's that?" Jenny asked, peering up at him. "And what happened to his hair?"

"That's Butch Dixon," Joanna said. "He's a friend of mine. It's because of him that we found you as soon as we did. And as far as his hair is concerned, it all fell out because his grandmother gave him a permanent when he was a little boy."

Jenny's eyes widened. "No! Is that true?"

Butch Dixon grinned. "If your mother says so," he told her, "then it must be."

EPILOGUE

BUTCH DIXON hosted the celebration dinner that night. All the cops and FBI agents who could be corralled into doing so came to the Roundhouse Bar and Grill for freebie dinners, which included Caboose dishes of ice cream, peanuts, and chocolate syrup all the way around.

The party lasted until well after midnight. The Duffys had long since taken Pablo and Ceci and headed for home. Joanna and the Bradys were about to do the same with Jenny when a drained Carol Strong limped into the restaurant carrying her signature high heels, one of which was sheared off under the sole. The lighting in the bar wasn't the best, but even in its dim glow, Joanna was surprised by the haggard expression on the detective's face.

"What's wrong?" Joanna asked when Carol sat down beside her. "You look awful."

"You would, too, if you'd just been through what I've been through."

"What?"

"We discovered Larry Dysart had closed off all the air ducts to the bomb shelter," Carol answered. "I don't know exactly how long the girls would have lasted before they ran out of air, but it wouldn't have been forever. It's a good thing we found them when we did."

"Oh," Joanna said. It was all she could manage.

"And we found a jewelry box," Carol continued. "A jewelry box that he evidently used as a trophy case. It had nine pairs of panties in it. Eight officially, because I didn't catalog this one."

Reaching into her pocket, she pulled out a pair of nylon panties and placed them in Joanna's hands. "Mine?" Joanna asked without looking.

Carol nodded. "You said it was part of a set your husband gave you. If I had listed them in the official evidence inventory, you never would have seen them again. Put them away fast before anybody else sees them," Carol ordered. "That FBI agent, LaDonna Bright, and I are the only ones who know about them so far. I want to keep it that way."

Guiltily, Joanna shoved the panties into her blazer pocket. "Thank you," she murmured.

"You're welcome," Carol Strong replied.

They sat in silence for a moment watching and listening while Butch Dixon charmed a weary Jenny with an old shaggy-dog story that was nonetheless brand-new to her. She laughed delightedly at the punch line.

"You said eight other pairs?" Joanna asked eventually.

Carol nodded. "There's an index of sorts taped to the bottom of the box," she said quietly. "It contains names and dates. Matching codes have been inked into the labels of each pair of panties. I guess he must have been afraid the toll might one day go so high that he'd forget which panties belonged to which victim."

Joanna swallowed hard. "Eight. How could there be so many?"

"Scary, isn't it," Carol said. "Number six was Serena Grijalva. Seven was Rhonda Weaver Norton. Leann Jessup is listed as number eight, except she didn't die. Once we finish examining all the trace evidence, I'm pretty sure we'll find that Dave Thompson didn't commit suicide."

"Larry killed him, too? Why?"

"I think so. This morning, before I went looking for Madeline Bellerman, I went by the hospital to see Leann Jessup. I ended up talking to her friend, Kimberly George."

"Her ex-lover, you mean."

"Current, not ex," Carol returned. "Kimberly told me that after she saw you on the news with Leann, she realized she was wrong, that she wanted to get back together."

"When she saw the two of us?" Joanna echoed. "But I'm not—"

"I know," Carol said. "Don't worry about it. I told Kimberly that this morning. But on Wednesday evening, Kim evidently stopped by Leann's room on the APOA campus to see if they could patch things up. I don't know how explicit their reconciliation was, but I think Larry Dysart saw what was happening. He saw one more chance to add to his collection, this time with a deceased Dave Thompson holding the bag.

"I'd like to think that it wouldn't have worked, that we would have been smarter than that. And I think Larry was beginning to fall apart. That's what happens to guys like that. They convince themselves that they're all-powerful and that the cops are too stupid to figure it out. They kill at shorter and shorter intervals until finally their fuses blow."

Another long silence fell between the two women. "Who were the others?" Joanna asked finally. "Were they all from around here?"

Carol shook her head. "I believe we'll find they're from other parts of the country and that the murders took place over a number of years. Larry Dysart knocked around some, working pickup jobs here and there. We're currently checking with other jurisdictions where he either lived or traveled. Only one other case—number five—for sure happened anywhere around here. When that victim died, her death was listed as natural causes. You'll never guess who that one was."

"Who?" Joanna asked, wanting to know and yet feeling a sense of dread as she waited for Carol's answer.

"Emily Dysart Morgan," she said. "Larry's

mother. She was an Alzheimer's patient right here in Peoria. She disappeared from a nursing home during a rainstorm in the dead of summer four years ago. Everyone assumed she had died of natural causes and had been washed down the Agua Fria. Her body was never found. Until today."

"Today?"

Carol Strong nodded, her mouth grim. "Today wasn't the first time Larry used Tommy Tompkins's vapor-barrier-wrapped bomb shelter. With Jenny and Ceci, it didn't work, thank God, but with Larry's mother, I'd say it did."

Butch Dixon came around the bar. "Are you off duty now?" he asked Carol Strong.

"Yes."

"What can I get you to drink, then? It's on the house."

"Whiskey," Carol Strong said. "Jack Daniel's straight up."

By Sunday afternoon, as the Bradys were packing up to go back to Bisbee, Joanna already knew that the remainder of her APOA session would be postponed until after the first of the year. "So why can't you come home today?" Jenny insisted.

"Because I need to pick up my stuff from the dorm," Joanna answered. "And that won't be available until tomorrow morning. Not only that, Dave Thompson's funeral is scheduled for tomorrow afternoon. I should go to that."

"All right," Jenny said. "But I wish you were coming with us today."

"So do I," Joanna said.

The next morning, Joanna had to pack twice—first to check out of the hotel and next to leave the dorm. Even so, the process didn't take long. After closing up her own APOA room, Joanna helped Lorelie Jessup pack up Leann's things.

"Will Leann be coming to the funeral this afternoon?" Joanna asked.

Lorelie shook her head. "She wanted to, but the doctor says no. It's still too early for her to leave the hospital."

"That's probably just as well."

At noon, Joanna stood on the steps of the Maricopa County Courthouse, watching from among the crowd while a newly released Jorge Grijalva emerged with his children. As the television cameras rolled, Joanna tried to slip away, but Ceci had spotted her. She dragged the man she knew as her father over to where Joanna was standing.

"Thank you," Jorge said.

"You're welcome," Joanna answered. "Will the kids be going back to Bisbee with you?"

Jorge shook his head. "Not right now. They're in school. They'll stay with their other grandparents, at least until the end of the year. It'll all work out."

"Yes," Joanna said. "I'm sure it will."

Four hours later, Joanna was part of a large contingent of police officers, both in and out of uniform, who gathered respectfully in Glendale Memorial Park for Dave Thompson's graveside

funeral service. Listening to the minister's lauda-
tory eulogy, Joanna found herself wondering what
the truth was about Dave Thompson. On the one
hand, some of the cigarette stubs from the tunnel
behind the mirrored walls were the same brand
Dave Thompson smoked. But no one—Butch
Dixon included—had ever seen Dave smoking inside.

Had he been the one in the tunnel or not? If
Larry Dysart had been smart enough to plant evidence in Jorge's pickup, he might also have planted
the incriminating cigarette stubs. But there was
no way to know for sure. Not ever.

Toward the end of the service, Joanna watched
the mourners. There was an elderly couple—
probably Dave's parents—and then two children—
a boy and a girl—who were evidently Dave's kids.

The program provided by the mortuary listed
among Dave's survivors his children, Irene Dan-
ielle and David James Thompson. The girl looked
to be a year or so older than Jenny, while the boy
was maybe a year or so older than that.

The funeral was over and Joanna was almost
ready to leave when she saw the boy standing
off by himself. Despite the warm afternoon sunshine, he stood with his shoulders hunched as if
to ward off the cold. He looked so lost and miserable that Joanna couldn't walk past without
speaking to him.

"David?" she asked tentatively.

He turned toward her, his face screwed up with
anguish. "Yes?" he said, and then quickly looked
away.

Studying him, Joanna found that David James Thompson resembled his father. He couldn't have been more than twelve, but he was almost as tall as Joanna. His sport coat, although relatively new, seemed to be several months too small. His tie was uneven and poorly knotted. Searching for something comforting to say, Joanna felt the lump grow in her throat. Tying ties properly is something boys usually learn from their fathers.

"I'm Joanna Brady," she said, holding out her hand. "I was one of your father's students at the APOA."

David Thompson looked at Joanna. "Was he a good teacher?" he asked. "At home we never heard any good stuff about him, only bad."

"Your father wasn't an easy teacher," Joanna answered. "But sometimes hard ones are the best kind. He was teaching us things that will help us save lives."

"I wish I'd had a chance to get to know him," David Thompson said. "Know what I mean?"

"Yes," Joanna said. "I certainly do."

ON THE third of January, Joanna returned to Peoria to complete her interrupted session at the APOA. When she checked into her dormitory room—the same one she'd been assigned to before—she was relieved to discover that, under the auspices of an interim director, the mirrored walls had all been replaced with plaster-coated wallboard. The door leading into the tunnel along the back of the dorm no longer existed. The opening had been stuccoed shut.

After unpacking, Joanna climbed back in her Blazer and drove to the Roundhouse Bar and Grill. Carrying a bag full of Christmas goodies, she walked into the bar.

Butch Dixon grinned when he saw her. "The usual?"

"Why not?" she asked, slipping onto a stool. "How are the hamburgers today?"

Butch waggled his hands. "So-so," he answered. "I'm breaking in a new cook, so things are a little iffy."

"I'll try the Roundhouse Special, only no Caboose this time. I've had enough sweets for the time being."

Butch wrote down her order. "How's your new jail cook working out?" he asked.

"Ruby's fine so far," Joanna answered. "She got out of jail on the assault charge one day, and we hired her as full-time cook the next. The inmates were ecstatic."

"I only hope mine works out that well," Butch returned.

Joanna pushed the bag across the bar. "Merry Christmas."

"For me?"

Joanna nodded. "Better late than never," she said.

One at a time, Butch Dixon hauled things out of the bag. "Homemade flour tortillas. Who made these?" he asked.

"Juanita Grijalva," Joanna answered. "She says she'll send you some green corn tamales the next time she makes them."

"Good deal," Butch said, digging deeper into the bag. There were four kinds of cookies, a loaf of homemade bread, and an apple pie.

"Those are all from Eva Lou," Joanna explained. "I tried to tell her that since you own a restaurant, you didn't need all this food. She said that a restaurant's the worst place to get anything homemade."

Butch grinned. "She's right about that."

From the very bottom of the bag, Butch pulled out the only wrapped and ribboned package. Tearing off the paper, Butch Dixon found himself holding a framed five-by-seven picture of a little blond-haired girl in a Brownie uniform standing behind a Radio Flyer wagon that was stacked high with cartons of Girl Scout cookies.

"Hey," he said. "A picture of Jenny. Thanks."

"That's not Jenny," Joanna corrected. "That's a picture of me."

"You're kidding! I love it."

"Marliss Shackleford doesn't care for it much," Joanna murmured.

"Who's Marliss Shackleford?"

"The lady who received the other copy of this picture, only hers is much bigger. Eleven by fourteen. I gave it to her to use in a display at the Sheriff's Department. It's going up in a glass case along with pictures of all the other sheriffs of Cochise County. If you ever get a chance to see it, you'll recognize me right away. I'm the only one wearing a Brownie uniform."

"I'll bet it's the cutest picture in the bunch," Butch said.

"Maybe you're prejudiced," Joanna observed with a smile. "My mother doesn't think it's the least bit cute. She says the other pictures are serious, and mine should be, too."

"Speaking of your mother," Butch said. "How did your brother's visit go? You sounded worried about it when I talked to you on the phone."

"It was fine. He and his wife came in from Washington, D.C. It's the first time I've ever met my sister-in-law."

"What are they, newlyweds?" Butch asked.

"Not exactly," Joanna answered. "It's a long story."

Other customers came in and occupied the bartender's attention. Joanna sat there, looking at her surroundings, realizing with a start that she felt safe and comfortable sitting there under Butch Dixon's watchful eye. No doubt Serena Grijalva had felt safe there as well. But Larry Dysart would have been dangerous no matter where someone met him.

Butch dropped off Joanna's Roundhouse Special and then stood there watching as she started to eat it. She caught the quick, questioning glance at her ring finger as she raised the sandwich to her lips.

Her rings were still there. Both of them. Andy had been gone since September, but Joanna wasn't yet ready to take off the rings and put them away.

"It's still too soon," she said.

Butch nodded. "I know," he answered quietly. "But you can't blame a guy for checking, can you?"

"No."

She put down her sandwich and held her hand in the air, examining the rings. The diamond engagement ring—Andy's last gift to her—sparkled back at her, even in the dim, interior gloom of the Roundhouse Bar and Grill.

"If you and Andy had ever met, I think you would have liked each other," she said at last.

"Why's that?" Butch Dixon asked.

"You're a nice guy," Joanna said. "So was Andy."

Shaking his head and frowning, Butch began polishing the top of the bar. "People are always telling me there's no demand for nice guys."

"You'd be surprised about that," Joanna Brady said. "You just might be surprised."

Here's a sneak preview of
J. A. Jance's novel

Available now
wherever books are sold

March

I AM NOT a wimp. Maybe that sounds too much like Richard Nixon's "I am not a crook," but it's true. I'm not. With twenty plus years at Seattle P.D., most of it on the Homicide Squad, and with several more years of laboring in the Washington State attorney general's Special Homicide Investigation Team, I think I can make that statement with some confidence. Usually. Most of the time. Right up until I got on the Mad Hatter's Tea Party ride at Disneyland with my six-year-old granddaughter, Karen Louise, aka Kayla.

She had been in charge of the spinning. She loved it. I did not. When the ride ended, she went skipping away as happy as can be toward her waiting parents while I staggered along after her. Over her shoulder I heard her say, "Can we go again?" Then, stopping to look at me she added, "Gramps, how come your face is so green?"

Good question.

When Kayla was younger, she used to call me Gumpa, which I liked. Now I've been demoted or promoted, I'm not sure which, to Gramps, which I don't like. It's better, however, than what she calls Dave Livingston, my first wife's second husband and official widower. (Karen, Kayla's biological grandmother, has been dead for a long time now, but Dave is still a permanent part of all our lives.) Kayla stuck him with the handle of Poppa. As far as I'm concerned, that's a lot worse than Gramps.

But back to my face. It really was green. I was having a tough time standing upright, and believe me, I hadn't had a drop to drink, either. By then, though, Mel figured out that I was in trouble.

Melissa Majors Soames is my third wife. That seems like a bit of a misnomer since my second wife, Anne Corley, was married to me for less than twenty-four hours. Our time together was, as they say, short but brief, ending in what is often referred to as "suicide by cop." It bothered me that Anne preferred being dead to being married to me, and it gave me something of a complex—I believe shrinks call it a fear of commitment—that made it difficult for me to move on. Mel Soames was the one who finally changed all that.

She and I met while working for the S.H.I.T. squad. (Yes, I agree, it's an unfortunate name but we're stuck with it.) Originally we just worked together, then it evolved into something else. Mel is someone who is absolutely cool in the face of trouble, and she's watched my back on more than one occasion. And since this whole idea of having a "three-day family bonding vacation at Disneyland" had been her bright idea, it was only fair that she should watch my back now.

She didn't come racing up to see if I was all right because she could see perfectly well that I wasn't. Instead, she went looking for help in the guise of a uniformed park employee who dropped the broom he was wielding and led me to the First Aid Station. It seems to me that it would have made sense to have a branch office a lot closer to the damned Tea Cups.

So I went to the infirmary. Mel stayed long enough to be sure I was in good hands, then she bustled off to "let everyone know what's happening." I stayed where I was, spending a good part of day three of our Three Day Ticket Pass flat on my back on an ER-style cot with a very officious nurse taking my pulse and asking me questions.

"Ever been seasick?" she wanted to know.

"Several times," I told her. I could have added everytime I get near a boat, but I didn't.

"Do you have any Antivert with you?" she asked.

"I beg your pardon?"

"Antivert. Meclizine. If you're prone to seasickness, you should probably carry some with you. Without it, I can't imagine what you were thinking? Why did you get on that ride?"

"My granddaughter wanted me to."

She gave me a bemused look and shook her head. "That's what they all say. You'd think grown men would have better sense."

She was right about that. I should have had better sense, but of course I didn't say so.

"We don't hand out medication here," she said. "Why don't you just lie there for a while with your eyes closed. That may help."

When she finally left me alone, I must have fallen asleep. I woke up when my phone rang.

"Beau," Ross Alan Connors said. "Where are you?"

Connors has been the Washington State Attorney General for quite some time now, and he was the one who had plucked me from my post-retirement doldrums from leaving Seattle P.D. and installed me in his then relatively new Special Homicide Investigation Team. The previous fall's election cycle had seen him fend off hotly contested attacks in both primary and general elections. With campaigning out of the way for now, he seemed to be focusing on the job, enough so that he was calling me on Sunday afternoon when I was supposedly on vacation.

"California," I told him. "Disneyland actually."

I didn't mention the infirmary part. That was none of his business.

"Harry tells me you're due back tomorrow."

Harry was my boss, Harry Ignatius Ball, known to friend and foe alike as Harry I. Ball. People who hear his name and think that gives them a license to write him off as some kind of joke are making a big mistake. He's like a crocodile lurking in the water with just his eyes showing. The teeth are there, just under the surface, ready and waiting to nail the unwary.

"Yes," I told him. "Our plane leaves here bright and early. We should be at our desks by one."

When Mel had broached the Disneyland idea, she had wanted us to pull off this major family-style event while, at the same time, having as little impact as possible—one and a half days' worth—on our accumulated vacation time. We had flown down on Thursday after work and were due back Monday at noon.

On my own, I've never been big on vacations of any kind. Unused vacation days have slipped through my fingers time and again without my really noticing or caring, but Mel Soames is another kind of person altogether. She has her heart set on our taking a road trip this summer. She wants to cross over into BC, head east over the Canadian Rockies and then come back to Seattle by way of Yellowstone and Glacier. This sounds like way too much scenery for me, but she's the woman in my life and I want to keep her happy, so a-driving we will go.

"Mel can go to the office," Ross said, "but not you. I want you in Ellensburg at the earliest possible moment."

If you leave the Seattle area driving east on I-90, Ellensburg is the second stopping-off place after you cross the Cascades. First there's Cle Elum and next Ellensburg. Neither of them strikes me as much of a garden spot.

"Why would I want to go to Ellensburg?" I asked.

"To be there when the Kittitas ME does an autopsy. Friday afternoon some heavy-equipment operator was out snow-plowing a national forest road over by Lake Kachess where he ended up digging up more than he bargained for. This is number six."

I didn't have to ask number six what—I already knew. For the past two months S.H.I.T. had been working on the murders of several young Hispanic women whose charred remains had been found at various dump sites scattered all over western Washington. So far none of them had been identified. As far as we could tell, none of our victims had been reported missing. We'd pretty well decided that our dead girls were probably involved in prostitution, but until we managed to identify one of them and could start making connections, it was going to be damnably difficult to figure out who had killed them.

These days it's routine for the dental records of missing persons to be entered into a national missing persons database. That wasn't possible with our current set of victims. None of them had teeth. None of them! And the teeth in question hadn't been lost to poor dental hygiene, either. They had been forcibly removed. As in yanked out by the roots!

"Same MO?" I asked.

"Pretty much except for the fact that this one seems to have her teeth," Ross said. "So either we have a different doer or the guy ran out of time. This victim was wrapped in a tarp and set on fire just like the others. The body was found late Friday afternoon. It took until Saturday morning for the Kittitas County Sheriff's Department to

retrieve the remains. Unfortunately, their ME
has been out of town at a conference, so that has
slowed down the process. They put the remains
on ice until she returns and expect the autopsy
to happen sometime tomorrow afternoon. That's
where you come in. I want you there when it
happens in case there's some detail that we know
about that the locals might miss."

"Our plane's due in at ten-twenty," I told him.

"That'll be cutting it close then," Ross said.
"God only knows how long it'll take for you to
get your luggage once you get there."

Thanks to a legacy from Anne Corley, Mel and I
had flown down to California on a private jet. All
we'd have to do is step off the plane and wait for
the luggage to be loaded into our waiting car before we drove it off the tarmac, but rubbing my
boss's nose in that seemed like a bad idea.

"I'll make it," I said. "I'll drop Mel off at the
condo to pick up the other car and then I'll head
out."

"All right," Ross said. "Be there as soon as you
can."

"Do you have a number for the Kittitas ME's
office?" I asked.

"Sure. Can you take it down?"

I had no intention of telling him that I was flat
on my back in the first aid station and I wasn't
about to ask the nurse to lend me a pen or pencil.

"Can you text it to me?" I asked.

This was something coming from someone
who had come to twenty-first-century technol-
ogy kicking and screaming all the way. I'm

surprised I wasn't struck by lightning on the spot, but that's what comes of having Generation X progeny. I had learned about text messaging the hard way—because my kids, Kelly and Scott, had insisted on it.

"Sure," Ross said. "I'll have Katie send it over to you."

Katie Dunn was Ross's Gen X secretary. Knowing Ross is even more of a wireless troglodyte than I am made me feel better—more with it, as we used to say back in the day.

I had just stuffed the phone back into my pocket when the nurse led Kelly into the room.

"How are you?" she asked, concern written on her face. "Mel told us what happened and that you needed to take it easy for a while. Are you feeling any better?"

I swung my feet off the side of the bed and sat up slowly.

"Take it easy," the nurse advised.

But the nap had done the trick. I was definitely feeling better. "I'm fine," I said. "One hundred percent."

"Mel went with Jeremy. He's taking the kids back to the hotel," Kelly explained. "She'll help get them fed and make sure the babysitter arrangements hold up. If you're still feeling up to having that dinner, that is."

That was what Mel said, of course. And that's what she was doing. But the reasons she was doing those things were a whole lot murkier—to Kelly at least if not to me.

Kelly and I haven't always been on the best of

terms. In fact we've usually not been on the best of terms. She had run away from home prior to high school graduation and managed to get herself knocked up. Her shotgun wedding had ended up being unavoidably delayed so Kayla had arrived on the scene before her parents had ever tied the knot. I have always thought most of this Kelly-based uproar is deliberate.

Mel takes the position that it's more complex than that—both conscious and not. She thinks Kelly's ongoing rebellion has been a way for her to get back at her parents—at both Karen and me. Although I didn't know about it at the time, Kelly was mad as hell at her mother for coming down with cancer and dying while Kelly was still in her teens, and she was mad as hell at me for having been drunk most of the time while she was growing up. And now she's apparently mad at me for not being drunk. When it comes to kids, sometimes you just can't win.

So Mel had designed this whole Disneyland adventure, complete with inviting my son and daughter-in-law, Scott and Cherisse, along for the ride, for no other reason than to see if she could help smooth out some of the emotional wrinkles between Kelly and me. So far so good. As far as I could tell everyone seemed to be having a good time. There had been no cross words, at least none I had heard. And I suspected that was also why Mel had sent Kelly to drag me out of the infirmary.

"I should have gone on the Tea Cups with her," Kelly said as we walked toward the monorail.

"Jeremy won't set foot on one of those on a bet, but rides like that don't bother me. They never have. And Kayla loves them so much. She rode the Tea Cups three more times after you left. She didn't want to ride on anything else."

I stopped cold. Kelly turned back to look at me. "Are you all right?" she asked.

It took me a minute to figure out what to say. I now knew something about Kelly and her mother and her daughter, and it was something she didn't know about me. As I said already, I was mostly AWOL when Kelly and Scott were little—drinking and/or working. Karen was the one who took them to soccer and T-ball and movies. She was also the one who "did the Puyallup" with them each fall. When it's time for the Western Washington State Fair each September, that's what they used to call it—"Doing the Puyallup." It was Karen instead of me who walked them through the displays of farm animals and baked goods; who taught them to love eating cotton candy and elephant ears; and who took them for rides on the midway.

"You're just like your mother," I said, over the lump that rose suddenly in my throat and made it difficult to speak. "And Kayla's just like you."

"What's that supposed to mean?" Kelly asked. She sounded angry and defensive. It was so like her to take offense and to assume that whatever I said was somehow an underhanded criticism.

"Did your mother ever tell you about the first time I took her to the Puyallup?"

"No," Kelly said. "She never did. Why?"

"She wanted to ride the Tilt-a-Whirl, and I knew if I did that, I'd be sick. Rides like that always make me sick. So I bought the tickets. Your mother and I stood in line, but when it came time to get on, I couldn't do it. She ended up having to go on the ride with the people who were standing in line behind us. Here I was, supposedly this hotshot young guy with the beautiful girl on his arm, and all I could do was stand there like an idiot and wait for the ride to end and for her to get off. It was one of the most humiliating moments of my life. We never talked about it again afterwards, but she never asked me to get on one of those rides again, either."

Kelly was staring up into my face. She looked so much like her mother right then—was so much like her mother—that it was downright spooky. It turns out DNA is pretty amazing stuff.

"So why did you do it?" she asked.

Now I was lost. Yes, I had been telling Kelly the story, but her question caught me off guard. I didn't know what "it" she was asking about.

"Do what?" I asked.

"If you already knew it would make you sick, why on earth did you get on the Mad Hatter's Tea Party with Kayla?"

"I thought maybe I'd grown out of it?" I asked lamely.

Kelly shook her head as if to say I hadn't yet stumbled on the right answer. "And?" she prompted.

"Because my granddaughter wanted me to?" I added.

The storm clouds that had washed across Kelly's face vanished. She reached up, grabbed me around the neck, and kissed my cheek.

"Oh, Daddy," she said with a laugh. "You're such a dope, but I love you."

See what I mean about Mel Soames? The woman is a genius.

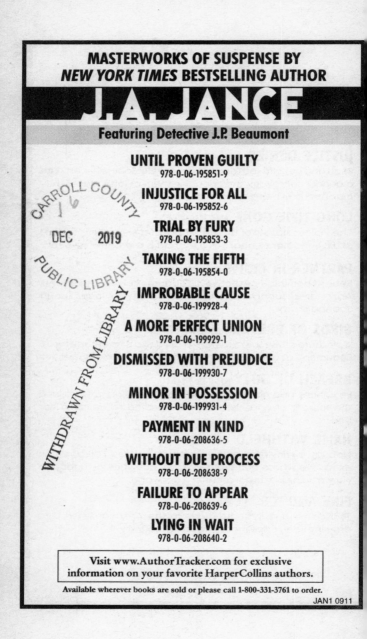